PRAISE FOR *T*

Wow, oh, WOW. WHAT an emotional roller coaster ride! I loved, loved, LOVED it! This is some of the best reading I've done in years. The writing is fast paced, riveting, and WONDERFULLY descriptive.

—Debbie, *from WriteOn by Kindle*

"The Adoption" is a stunner! I was hooked from the first page and could not put the book down. Greg Meritt is a master storyteller, up there with the best of them! A psychological thriller of thoughtful and creative proportions. Not one boring page in the entire book. A definite A+ from me!

—Valerie Byron, author of *No Ordinary Woman, The Man Who Lost His Genius,* and *The Man on the Train*

I enjoyed reading "The Adoption" so much!! Everything about this work is 5 out of 5 stars. Greg Meritt is on my authors "to watch for" list.

—Paris, *from WriteOn by Kindle*

"The Adoption" is a great book. Well-written, very descriptive, A+ writing for sure. I hope they do it justice when they make the movie!

—Richard Kennett, author of *Medium Dead*

"The Adoption" is an awesome book that keeps the reader on the edge of your seat and constantly wondering what will happen next.

—Teresa Skaggs, *from WriteOn by Kindle*

THE ADOPTION

A Psychological Thriller

by Greg Meritt

Cover design: Canva.com
Editor: Valerie Byron

Meritt, Greg M.
The Adoption

gregmeritt.com

10 9 8 7 6 5 4 3 2 1

For Susan

ACKNOWLEDGEMENTS

A special thank you to my three wonderful adopted children: Curtis, Coara, and Cannon. If not for them, this book may never have existed. After a few years of trying to conceive, my wife and I decided to adopt. And then, not long after that momentous decision, I was standing naked in the shower (I haven't showered with my clothes on since my drinking days), when this thought came out of nowhere: *What if the impending adoption isn't anything remotely close to what we expect? What if everything we were told was a lie?* From those thoughts, this book was born. Of course, this is fiction and real life turned out much, much different. What a relief.

Thank you to my family and friends for their support and encouragement. They put up with my whining and sniveling through the process and hung around anyway.

And a HUGE shout out to all the beta readers at Writeon by Kindle (an Amazon site for authors and readers), who finally convinced me to publish my work. There are so many, I am forever grateful.

A special thanks to Valerie Byron, my editor, for her tireless efforts and wonderful encouragement.

And most of all, to Michelle Kidd, a fantastic writer and friend, who read this story in its infancy and offered invaluable insight and suggestions, most of which I heeded. You are the best!

ONE

At eight-fifteen on Sunday morning, November 8th, Claire Keller walked slowly up the concrete path leading to 2012 Black Hills Drive in the City of Black Ridge, a suburb forty-five minutes southeast of Seattle. She had a hollow, nauseous feeling in the pit of her stomach.

It was chilly; it always was this time of year. The custom-built home in the quiet upscale neighborhood of Wyndham Heights was meticulously maintained: weed-free gardens, neatly manicured hedges and a perfectly cut lawn.

Claire stepped onto the white wraparound porch. She looked at the engraved wooden sign suspended from the roof and, in spite of her nervousness, chuckled softly:

THELMA GRISHAM, MEDIUM & PSYCHIC - BY APPOINTMENT ONLY.

Claire opened the screen door, knocked, and stepped back. A few seconds later the door opened, and an elderly woman appeared.

"Claire! What a lovely surprise! Come in, come in," Thelma Grisham said, holding the door open for her guest.

Stepping over the threshold and into the luxurious home, Claire said, "Thanks, Thelma. Sorry to bother you so early, but I was wondering … do you have a few minutes?"

"Of course, dear, gives me a break from dealing with those boring spirits. Sometimes they can get downright irritating with all their problems and boohooing and carrying on." She laughed. "How 'bout I make us some tea – or do you prefer coffee?"

Claire smiled at the eccentric old woman. "Tea would be fine, thank you."

"Why don't we go into the kitchen to chat? We can talk while I'm preparing the tea."

Following her through the house, Claire glanced to her left, towards the parlor, noticing the Tarot Cards and Ouija Board sitting on the Queen Anne coffee table. In addition to incense burners and oil warmers, candles of all shapes and scents were carefully placed throughout the cozy room.

Claire sat at the little wooden table in the kitchen. She studied Thelma as she heated water, sorted through an assortment of exotic tea bags and retrieved two teacups from the cupboard.

"So what's on that pretty little mind of yours?" Thelma asked, sitting across from Claire. "And does Logan know you're here?"

"No, Logan doesn't know I'm here. You know how he feels about psychic stuff - that people like John Edwards, Sylvia Brown, and James Van Praagh are just scammers capitalizing on the misfortunes of others." Thelma leaned forward, placing her bony, liver-spotted hands over Claire's. "But you don't believe that, do you, Claire?"

"Oh, you know I don't. I do find it sad, though, that naysayers try and hurt the reputations of people who really are trying to help – people like you."

"Hon, most people are afraid of what they don't understand, so they think if they can discount it in some way, make the world believe it's a joke – a hoax – then they won't have to acknowledge it, won't have to deal with what frightens them most."

"Yeah, I guess…."

"Claire, honey, you haven't answered my question. What do you really need to talk about? Something is on your mind."

Claire looked at the old woman sitting across the small table - the woman she had come to adore - and noticed how frail she appeared. *She still has vigor, though, her spunk*, Claire thought. *Nobody will ever take that from her.*

"It's about tomorrow," Claire replied. "You know that Logan and I are trying to adopt."

"Yes, yes ... you told me. Can I play grandma? Please ... Please, Claire?" Thelma grinned.

"Of course! I can't imagine a better grandma in the whole world! Just think, our little girl will be able to tell her schoolmates that grandma plays funny games, looks into crystal balls and has parties with dead people!"

Thelma and Claire looked at each other for a moment, then burst out laughing.

"Wait," Thelma said, catching her breath, "Did you say little girl?"

"Yes, we found out last week. Logan is thrilled – he's always wanted a daughter. But you know him. Even though he's excited about the prospect of a daughter, he has to take his time and analyze everything. Oh, and the agency even gave us a name: Samantha ... Samantha Jennings. Isn't that great?" The teakettle whistled, startling Claire.

Thelma got to her feet slowly, her right hand bracing her lower back. As she made her way across the kitchen to silence the teakettle, her wrinkled face revealed the physical pain of seventy-years. "What a perfect name Claire. And what about you – you thrilled?"

"Well ... I don't know, Thelma, I'm scared. Scared I won't be a good mother, or that the child won't like us, or ..." Claire sighed.

"Or what?"

"Or that I'm making the biggest mistake of my life. It's not like we can just give the child back if we find out it isn't what we think it will be.

I'm just scared – probably because it's no longer just an idea, but something that's real." Claire looked down at her hands.

"Claire, darling, look at me," Thelma said, returning with two teacups steeping with raspberry-flavored tea.

Claire raised her head. Tears shimmered in her eyes.

"We all wonder at times if we're making the right decision and sometimes we just have to go on faith. Call it "intuition," call it "gut feeling," but whatever you call it – follow it."

Claire smiled but said nothing.

"Is it Logan?" Thelma asked.

"God no," Claire said. "I just have a bad feeling. I don't know why. And I'm thirty-seven now, which is a little old to be trying to get pregnant. The doctors said we can continue to try fertility drugs, perhaps go the surrogate route, but Logan says adoption is the best way to go and much, much cheaper."

Thelma nodded and handed her a box of tissues. "So what's tomorrow all about?"

"We have an appointment with the adoption agency at two-thirty. I don't know what to expect," Claire said, blowing her nose.

"I'd go with you for support, dear, but I think your husband might not be all that enthralled with the idea. Ever since Harold's death, ever since I did a one-eighty and joined the ranks of the crackpots, I don't think Logan likes me all that much," Thelma said, looking hurt.

"That's just not true!" Claire replied, shocked.

"Claire, I'm no different from anyone else, I'm only trying to make sense of the night when Harold came to me. I know now that things in this world are not always what they appear to be and—"

"Thelma ... Thelma," Claire said, trying to calm her, "you don't have to explain to me. I understand, I really do ... I love you like a mother; you know that, and I don't judge your life – ever. Logan loves you too. It's just that ... he loved Harold like a father. His death affected him, too – it really did. Logan and I think of you as a mother."

"Really?" Thelma seemed relieved and touched at the same time.

"Really. And I think Logan just hides behind his pain by ignoring what scares him, that's all. It's easier to turn his back than to explore the unknown. He really is a good man. He'll come around."

"Yeah, he probably will, after I'm dead. Maybe he'll show up at my funeral." Thelma laughed. "What adoption agency are you working with?"

"It's called Children's World Adoption Services. It's on Queen Anne. Ever hear of it?"

"No, can't say that I have. Where did you hear about them?"

"From Peter Ellison, Logan's business partner. You met him a long time ago, not long after we moved to the neighborhood."

"Yes, I remember Peter. Amazing that my brain still works after all these years, huh? So did Peter adopt too? Is that how he heard about Children's World?"

"No, Peter and MaryAnn have two children of their own. Come to think of it, I don't know how Peter knew about the agency. Maybe he knows someone who works there or he did the company's books at one time. I can't remember. It doesn't matter."

"No, it doesn't."

"So I got on the computer and checked out the website. They've been doing adoptions and children's services for over seventy years, starting out as an orphanage back in the twenties. But with the development of foster care over the succeeding years, they closed down the orphanage, changed their name, and started licensing foster homes and providing adoption related services. They really seem to care about the kids."

"Sounds like you found the perfect agency to help you in your quest, Claire."

"Yeah, I think so. I called and spoke with a Sylvia Tran. We chatted for a while and then she told me about a girl named Samantha. And now we have an appointment."

"That sounds great! I'll ask the good spirits to watch over you. You know - Harold's people." She chuckled, and her eyes twinkled.

Claire looked at her watch. "I really should be getting home, I still have a lot to do. Thanks for letting me come over and talk about this. I love you."

As she made her way to the front door, Claire turned and said, "I'll let you know how it goes tomorrow, okay?" She opened the door and stepped outside. God it was cold.

"Okay," Thelma said, poking her head outside. "It was great seeing you. And tell that bum of a husband that I think about him often; tell him to come see me, okay?"

Claire nodded. "Okay."

Thinking about tomorrow, she walked down the porch steps, turned left and headed home.

It was the last time she saw her friend alive.

*

Thelma closed the door and went back to the kitchen. As she rinsed out the teacups, her mind drifted back to that day thirteen years ago when Claire and Logan had purchased the home two doors down. At that time, Thelma didn't believe in psychic nonsense. Back then, if you had asked her about astrology, séances, crystal balls, reading tea leaves or contacting the dead, she would have tactfully replied that your next appointment should be with a shrink – and it had better be a good one.

But when Harold, Thelma's husband of forty-two years, passed away last year, that all changed.

Harold had put on his work clothes, pecked his wife on the cheek and whispered in her ear: "Just wait 'till I get home. Boy, do I have a surprise for you!"

Around three that afternoon, Thelma received a phone call from the plant foreman. Harold had collapsed at about two-thirty, and when the medics arrived, they were unable to revive him. He was pronounced dead at the hospital.

As it turned out, a blood vessel in his brain had burst like an over-inflated inner tube, flooding the area between the arachnoid membrane and the pia mater with blood. The official cause of death was listed as *subarachnoid hemorrhage*.

Thelma never found out what "surprise" Harold was planning to bestow on her that evening. But three nights later, the evening after the funeral, Thelma saw him again.

Wearing his corduroy work shirt, blue jeans and steel-toed boots, wearing that, "I've got a surprise!" smile, Harold looked exactly as he had that morning three days before when he set off for work. At first, Thelma was sure she was dreaming, but it seemed so *real*. Although he didn't speak, she could *feel* him. She sat up and switched on the bedside lamp. The glow from the lamplight didn't make the hallucination vanish, however – it seemed to solidify it. Hugging her arms to her chest as if she were cold, she stared at the foot of her bed.

"Harold?"

No reply.

"Harold, am I dreaming?" she asked. The question was directed more to herself than the apparition standing at the foot of her bed.

"Oh Harold, I'm so sorry – God, I miss you." She started to cry.

Harold raised a finger to his lips: *shhhhh*. He blew Thelma a kiss and slowly faded away like steam evaporating in air. Then he was gone.

"Harold!"

Leaping out of bed, Thelma rushed to where he...*it*...had stood. Strands of her shoulder-length gray hair rose as if she had rubbed her head on a balloon. *Something* had been here. Although she never saw Harold again, Thelma never gave up hope, never stopped searching. The experience in her bedroom that night changed her, rearranged her belief system, and now she tried to help others find lost loved ones through séances and psychic readings. It seemed that Harold had imparted a gift that night: the gift of an open mind.

Now, still thinking about her dead husband, Thelma made her way to the parlor. The room was warm: a comfy fireplace on the north wall, pictures of Harold and Thelma (in their younger days) on the mantle, hurricane candles on each end. Van Gogh's "The Starry Night" hung on the wall above the fireplace. A large Persian area rug covered most of the stained hardwood floor, and two Victorian-style rocking chairs flanked an antique settee. The walls were tastefully done in green and yellow flowered wallpaper.

"Oh Harold," Thelma whispered to the empty room, "What's a seventy-year-old woman doing playing games with the afterlife? What do I think I'm doing?" As she had a hundred times over the past year – perhaps thousands - Thelma waited for a response.

Nothing.

And then: *Ouija board!*

Those two words slammed into her head with hurricane-like force.

"Harold?" she cried.

Grabbing the Ouija board from the coffee table, Thelma headed to the kitchen. With trembling hands, she set the board on the little table. Sitting down, she drew in a deep breath and lightly placed her fingertips on the planchette.

"Okay Harold, here we go, what—"

Before she could finish, her fingers were *flying* across the board.

Girl.

"Girl? What girl – do you mean Claire?" Suddenly, her fingers were on the move again, as if they were full of electricity.

No.

"Then what girl, Harold, what girl are you talking about?"

Samantha.

"The girl Logan and Claire are thinking of adopting?"

Yes.

"What about her? Harold, what do I need to know - what do you need to tell me?"

The board was still; the room was silent.

"Harold, it is you, isn't it?"

Yes.

"Oh, thank God, I knew it! I just knew it!" Thelma jumped up and down (as much as she could with those hips), clapping her hands, giggling like a high school girl.

And then, out of the corner of her eye, she noticed movement.

Thelma stopped and stared.

Incredibly, the planchette began to move on its own, spelling out another word, one word that made her legs go weak and her heart start racing.

Thelma Grisham collapsed, unconscious.

T W O

Claire and Logan Keller arrived at Children's World Adoption Services on Queen Anne shortly before two o'clock, thirty minutes prior to their two-thirty appointment. They parked in the underground garage and walked silently hand-in-hand to the bank of elevators.

Although Children's World's home was on the fifth floor, Claire and Logan departed the elevator when it reached the main lobby. They still had plenty of time, and Claire needed to collect herself. She was nervous, and she didn't know why.

Sitting on the comfortable leather sofa, Logan took Claire's hand. "It'll all work out. All we're doing today is meeting with the adoption specialist and finding out what the next step is. So really this is just a preliminary meeting, Claire, and it's all going to be fine. Just fine. Really."

"Yeah, I know you're right, but I just have this feeling, and I'm not even sure what it is. A mix of anxiety, fear, and excitement, which I'm sure is normal in cases like this, but I also have - oh, I don't know - a feeling that something bad is going to happen. That's just weird, right?"

"No, no not weird at all. It's just your emotions running to extremes – probably just stress. And I'm sure that you're not the first person who has felt this way when they are going to adopt a child. I mean, nobody knows what they're getting into when they take a step like this, do they?" Logan said, looking at his watch.

"No, I guess not."

"We should head up."

"Okay."

They rode up to the fifth floor in silence. Stepping out of the elevator, Logan read the directory. "This way," he said, taking Claire by the hand and leading her down the long, polished hallway, stopping in front of suite five-twelve. "This is it," Logan said. The sign on the door read: CHILDREN'S WORLD ADOPTION SERVICES. EVERY CHILD DESERVES A HOME.

Taking a deep breath, Claire entered the office, Logan on her heels. Sitting behind the reception desk was a young woman filing her nails. She looked as if she belonged on the local high-school cheerleading squad. A half-finished J.D. Robb Paperback lay face down on the desk. When she heard the door open, she looked up and smiled. "Hi, may I help you?" She sounded like a twelve-year-old.

"Yes," Claire said. "We have a two-thirty appointment with Sylvia Tran. Mr. & Mrs. Keller."

"Who?"

"Keller, two-thirty appointment," Logan said. This woman – this *girl* – seemed out-of-place behind the desk.

"Oh, yeah… right. Let me tell Sylvia you're here. Be right back." She disappeared down the hall.

"God, I hope that's not the regular receptionist. She doesn't seem to have a clue. Why didn't she just buzz the woman?" Logan said.

"Probably doesn't know how to work anything but a cell phone or iPod. Can't text from the reception desk phone," Claire said, shaking her head.

The young receptionist-cheerleader returned with an attractive Asian woman who was wearing a simple black dress belted around the middle. Her neatly cropped shoulder-length hair was similar to an Asian bob, parted on the left and colored in a sassy copper-red tone, giving her an almost mysterious look.

The woman approached Logan and Claire with her arm extended. "Hi, I'm Sylvia Tran."

Smiling, Claire took her hand, excitedly pumping her arm up and down. "It's a pleasure meeting you Miss Tran. Logan and I are so excited … so happy … that we have this opportunity to help a child and add something more to our lives in the process." She knew she sounded giddy and strange, but she couldn't stop herself. "I'm Claire … Claire Keller."

Laughing, Sylvia said, "Mrs. Keller—"

"Please, call me Claire."

"Claire, it's a pleasure meeting you." She turned to Logan and shook his hand. "And may I call you Logan? Or do you prefer Mr. Keller?"

"No, no Logan's fine."

"Let's go back to my office and we can talk," Sylvia said. "May I get you some coffee or water?"

"No, I'm fine, thank you," said Claire.

"Logan?"

"No thank you."

"Follow me, please." She led them to a tastefully decorated office. To the right of the large desk was a leather sofa. Adjacent to the sofa was a matching loveseat. An aerial view of Seattle and Lake Washington hung on the wood-paneled north wall. On the opposite wall, in direct contrast, was a still life of red and yellow roses, painted in superb detail.

Sitting down, Sylvia gestured to a couple of comfortable-looking overstuffed chairs across from her desk. "Please, have a seat."

After they had been seated, Sylvia said, "Logan … Claire, I want to give you a clear picture of what to expect over the next few days. Here at Children's World, we believe that the interests of the children are paramount; with that being said, I want you to be prepared for a quick decision because Samantha needs to be placed in a permanent home as quickly as possible."

"Oh, why is that?" Claire asked, glancing at Logan with a puzzled look.

"The place she is in now won't keep her but a few more days, and we don't want to keep moving her around. The emotional impact is just too great."

"Now wait just a minute," Logan said, nervously fidgeting in his seat, "are you telling us that she might be coming home with us in just a few days? Isn't that a little sudden? This is all happening so fast. And don't you guys have to do a bunch of legal stuff first, like home studies, and court filings?"

"I understand your apprehension in taking on something of this magnitude on such short notice Logan, I really do, but in my experience it is sometimes better to just do it... just jump right in - you can never really prepare yourself for something like this, anyway. As for the legal stuff, we can rush it through the system – God knows we've done it before - so don't worry about any of the details, let me take care of that."

"Honey, this is a little fast, don't you think?" Logan said. "I mean—"

"I have a surprise for you," Sylvia interrupted. "Samantha's here; she's across the hall in the playroom. I'll be right back." Without waiting for a reply, she got up and left the office.

When Sylvia was gone, Logan turned to his wife. "I think she had this all planned out, Claire. Almost sounds like a setup."

"She probably did have it all planned. She said it herself: the child's welfare is paramount. But I don't know about being setup Logan, setup how—?"

Sylvia returned with a little girl who was tightly clutching a well-worn doll. The child walked with her head down, eyes on the floor, as if she were looking for something. Her steps were careful, calculated. When she reached Logan and Claire, she continued to stare at the floor.

"Logan ... Claire ... I would like to introduce you to Samantha Jennings," Sylvia said, "but she goes by Sam or Sammy."

Claire immediately hunkered down to the little girls' level. Placing a finger under her chin, she gently lifted little Sam's head so she could look in her eyes. Before her was a sullen, frightened little child. Claire's heart went out to her. In that instant, Claire knew that this was meant to be and all the fear and paranoia of making a mistake, of the adoption not working out, evaporated as soon as she looked in Sam's eyes. At that moment, she knew her purpose: being a mother.

Logan stood directly behind his wife, watching. Sylvia Tran let go of the child's hand. "Why don't you guys talk a little? I'll go out to the lobby and see what trouble our young help has gotten into. Be back in a bit."

Samantha started to follow, but Claire gently pulled her back. "Honey, it's okay, really it is ... why don't you come sit with Logan and me for a minute?"

The girl didn't resist. She let Claire lead her to the couch. Sitting down, Logan looked at his wife, smiled and nodded: She's perfect.

"Hi Sam, I'm Claire, and this is my husband, Logan."

"Hi beautiful," Logan said.

Sam looked at Logan and Claire, studying the couple. Finally, she said, "Hi." Although she didn't smile, she no longer seemed so frightened. And then she whispered quietly, "Please, please take me with you."

Claire and Logan exchanged glances.

"Honey, how old are you?" Claire asked.

"I'm five ... almost six!" she proudly exclaimed.

"Wow! That's old!" Claire said. Sam giggled.

"And I bet you're smart too."

"Oh, yeah, I'm smart. Thelma says so," Sam said.

Claire looked at Logan: What the hell?

Logan shrugged.

"Who's ... Who's Thelma Sam?" Claire asked. "Is that a foster sister?"

"No, no, no, no ... this is Thelma," Sam said, holding up the doll. "She's smart too. Thelma knows things."

Claire was relieved to find out that Thelma was Sam's doll, but she couldn't shake the feeling that something was strange here, that this wasn't mere coincidence. How many Thelma's were there? What were the odds?

"We would love for you to come home with us," Claire said. "You—"

"Wait a minute Claire," Logan said in a whisper, "Shouldn't we discuss this first?"

Ignoring him, she continued, "You will have your own room, with lots of toys. And a dog, Axle, and there are plenty of other kids in the neighborhood to play with. How does that sound?"

Sam slowly lifted her head and this time she did smile. "You have a dog? What a funny name. Axle?" She giggled, her brownish-blonde pigtails bouncing up and down.

Claire grinned. "Yup, his name is Axle, just like on a car. So what do you say, Sam? – Want to give it a try?"

She studied them both for a moment, clutching her doll tightly to her chest, rocking her. "I'll ask Miss Sylvia if it's okay. I hope she says yes."

"Oh, honey I'm sure she will. And if Miss Sylvia says okay, you're sure that you want to come with us? I mean ... we just met and ... well ..." Claire stopped, afraid that she might say too much and change the little girl's mind.

Before Claire could collect her thoughts, Sylvia returned. "You just can't find competent help these days, it seems, especially with the younger crowd. You know what Amanda – she's the temp help – was doing? She was texting her boyfriend and listening to heavy metal on her iPod. How could she possibly hear the phone while listening to that crap? Oh well ..." she sighed, "Did you three get acquainted while I was gone?"

"A little, yeah," Logan said. He cleared his throat. "Um, can we talk privately?" He glanced at Sam, who was mumbling to her doll. Oblivious of her surroundings, she was concentrating on the make-believe dialogue between herself and Thelma, smiling and nodding, sometimes giggling.

Claire knelt in front of the girl. "Hey Sammy, it's Claire honey. Thelma sure is a great friend, isn't she? And I bet she is super-duper smart, huh? May I speak with her too?" Claire spoke in an assuaging, soothing tone, while gently rubbing Sam's back.

Sam regarded the doll a moment longer, and then shifted her attention to Claire. She smiled, "Yes, Thelma's super smart. What do you want to talk to her about?"

"Oh, you know, girl stuff: what she likes to wear, her favorite makeup, what boys she likes, that kind of stuff."

Sam giggled. "Boys! Yuuuuuck…"

"Yeah, I know what you mean," Claire said, giving Logan a perfunctory smile.

"Sam, let's go back across the hall to the playroom. We need to give Claire and Logan a little time to themselves, okay?" Sylvia said.

"No!" Sam protested, "I wanna stay with Claire and Logan. Please. *Pleeeease.*"

"Honey, we'll be together soon, I promise you that…"

"Claire," Logan whispered, "stop it now."

"Just give us a little time, okay, Sam?" Claire finished.

Samantha sighed and hung her head. "Okay … you promise?"

"Yes."

Sam slowly shuffled towards the door. Sylvia followed. "You two take all the time you need and come get me when you're ready. We'll be just across the hall in the playroom."

When they were gone, Logan turned to his wife. "Claire, what the hell are you doing getting that little girl's hopes up? We haven't discussed this, and there are some things that bother me."

"What do you mean, we haven't discussed this?" Claire said, angry now. "We have tried to have a child for years, and when that didn't work we both agreed on adoption, didn't we? Or am I missing something? I thought we discussed this at length, Logan."

"Well, yes … but we haven't discussed this particular little girl, Claire. I thought that we would have more time, go home and sleep on it once we met a few kids … you know, weigh the pros and cons of each child and then make a rational decision together. This is like jumping out of an airplane at thirty thousand feet without a parachute. And what happened to that feeling you had downstairs in the lobby?"

"You said it yourself; it was just emotional nervousness … stress, and now that I've met Samantha, I feel much better about the whole thing. And are we ever going to be sure we chose the right kid? I think that we need just to do it, and I also know - don't ask me how I know – that Samantha Jennings is the perfect child for us."

"Yeah … well, where is everybody? That girl up front trying to play receptionist doesn't seem as if she's ever held a job in her life. And Sylvia is the only other person in this office. Don't you find that odd? Shouldn't there be other staff members?"

"I think you're reading too much into this. Maybe other staff members are doing home studies, or meeting with lawyers or other kids. I think you're just paranoid. Sylvia seems very nice. If you're so worried, why don't you talk to her?"

"I will, believe me."

"Fine, I'll go get her," Claire said, getting up.

When Claire returned with Sylvia, Logan was slowly pacing the room, deep in thought.

"Hello, Logan!" Claire snickered, "Whatcha thinking about?"

"Oh … just about Samantha and how cute she is," Logan lied.

"Samantha will be okay playing by herself for a while. That's one of the great things about that child – she can entertain herself for hours." Sylvia said.

"Yeah, I saw that. She sure gets engrossed with that doll, doesn't she?" Logan said, quietly studying Sylvia. "I'd – we – would like to ask a few questions."

"Of course."

"Where is the rest of your staff? It isn't just you in this office, is it?"

"No, no of course not. Two staff members are performing home studies; one is on vacation, and my boss is down in Olympia testifying before the Washington State Legislature regarding Not-For-Profit Adoption Agencies. Why do you ask?"

"I just find it odd that there are only two people in this office. Just seems strange, that's all."

"I see," Sylvia said, "what other questions do you have?"

"We don't know anything about Samantha's past. Don't you think that—"

"What my husband is trying to say, Sylvia," Claire interrupted, "is that we would like some information about Sam that we can go over together while you and your agency take care of the details." Claire gave Logan a casual smile. He glared back at her.

"Of course. I will send you home with the file on Sam's background. But I ask two things in return."

"Oh, and what would that be?" Logan asked sharply. He felt like a defenseless mouse being played by a couple of mischievous cats.

"You open your house for a visit tomorrow and give us permission to set an appointment with Dick Lambert, the attorney, to do the paper-work. If you decide against this, we can always cancel the appointments. But please understand I … we need to place this child now. I do not want her getting lost in the system, shuffled around like cattle going to the slaughterhouse."

"Okay. Sounds fair to me," Claire said.

Logan sighed and slumped back on the couch. "Fine, but if we decide not to go through with this, we cancel the appointments, understood?" He looked at the two women. They both smiled and nodded.

Handing Claire a manila file, Sylvia turned to Logan and said, "Logan, this child is a good little girl … she's just had a few bad breaks in her young life. She certainly didn't ask to be orphaned. With a good family support system, Samantha will thrive. I'm sure of it."

"Uh-huh."

"Set that appointment with the attorney. What time do you want to come visit our home?" Claire asked.

Sylvia retrieved an appointment calendar from the desk drawer. She studied it for a moment and then said, "How about ten o'clock tomorrow morning for the home visit and two o'clock tomorrow afternoon with Mr. Lambert?"

"That would be great!" Claire said. "Logan, you can take a little more time off from work, can't you? Maybe work just half a day tomorrow so we can meet with the attorney. He doesn't have to be there for this home thing, does he?"

"No," Sylvia said, "we can go over things with Logan at a more convenient time."

"Alright … alright … I'll go into the office in the morning, and we can see the attorney at two if we decide to move on this."

"I'll call you later and confirm the appointments," Sylvia said.

"Thank you," Claire said, standing up. She held out her hand. Taking it in both of hers, Sylvia Tran smiled. "Claire, this is going to work out – I just know it will." She patted her hand.

"Me too. May we say goodbye to Sam?"

"Of course, I'd be disappointed – and so would she – if you didn't."

"Goodbye, Logan. And thank you for helping a young child who otherwise wouldn't have much of a chance in this world."

This woman doesn't quit. "Goodbye, Miss Tran."

Logan followed Claire across the hall to the playroom. They said goodbye to Sam, assuring her that they would see her soon.

THREE

At home later that evening, Logan sat on the king-size bed, wearing nothing but an old pair of boxers, thumbing through the file on Samantha Jennings. Claire was in the master bath washing her face, performing her nightly routine. Instead of her usual bedtime attire, though, she wore the purple teddy that Logan had bought her for Christmas three years earlier. Looking at herself in the full-length mirror, Claire was pleased to see that she still looked as good as someone half her age. Although she was thirty-seven, she could easily pass for someone in their late twenties or early thirties: Her breasts did not sag, her tummy was hard and flat and, at five-ten, her long legs were still shapely.

Switching off the bathroom light, Claire stood in the doorway, leaning seductively on the frame like a downtown streetwalker leaning on a lamppost. She cleared her throat; Logan looked up from the file on his lap.

"Claire, what are you doing? Don't you think we need to talk about that little girl?"

"Her name is Samantha, and we will have plenty of time to talk after." She smiled seductively and strutted barefoot across the room to where Logan lay. Climbing on top of him, she grabbed the file and set it on the headboard.

"Hey! I was looking at that!"

"Later ... you can look at it later." Breathing hard now, she began nuzzling his neck. Placing her left hand on Logan's crotch while continuing to nuzzle his neck, she gently rubbed him through the worn material of his boxers. "Make love to me," she whispered.

"Claire, what's gotten into you?"

"Hopefully you," she said with a grin.

Afterward, lying naked in the large, four-poster bed, Logan rolled onto his side, propping his head up on his arm. Looking at his wife of thirteen years, Logan said, "Don't think I don't know what you're up to Claire. If you think you can seduce me into taking on this little girl ... um ... Samantha, well ... you're wrong. We need to be clear-headed about this, think this through."

"Sure, you bet."

"You oughta read what's in this file. I can hardly believe what this girl's gone through in her short life."

Intrigued, Claire sat up. "What? What's in the file?"

Logan retrieved the manila folder from the headboard, handing it to her. "Read it for yourself."

Claire took the file and began reading. Logan lay back down, clasping his hands behind his head and closing his eyes. Every few minutes Claire would whisper "my goodness" or "poor girl" or "unbelievable."

"Logan, did you read this? I mean...her parents were killed in a tragic car accident when she was only two. Is this for real? And then she was sent to a foster home that was later found guilty of abusing the kids? That poor child!"

"Yeah Claire, I read it. Still thinking about taking on this kid?"

"Now more than ever."

"What?" he said, sitting up. He couldn't believe what he'd just heard.

"Logan, she needs us. Probably more than she's ever needed any-one. And I think Sylvia Tran knows that too, and that's why she's rushing this through. She doesn't want Samantha to have any more unnecessary trauma in her life."

"Think about what you're saying here...you have no idea what those events could have done to the kids mental state at this young age and—"

"Stop analyzing everything for once in your life and follow your heart. Today, when Samantha first came into the room, your eyes lit up. Admit it. You would be a great father to Sam, and she needs you. And you would have the daughter I know you've always wanted."

Lying back down, he sighed. "Fine. But first, I'm going to check out this adoption agency, see if they've had any problems or complaints in the past. If they're clean, then we move forward."

Ecstatic, Claire hugged him and whispered, "I love you."

Logan got out of bed, put on a bathrobe and switched on the computer. The first website he went to was the BBB. He typed "Children's World Adoption Services" in the box and clicked search. Nothing. Then he tried just "Children's World." The screen filled with businesses - mostly daycares - but no adoption services. Then he typed "Adoption Services." The screen filled with local adoption agencies, however, Children's World was not among them.

Logan sat back, rubbing his chin. "Hey Claire, it seems this agency of yours isn't listed with the Better Business Bureau."

"That's good, right? Means they haven't had any trouble or been reported for violations, doesn't it?"

"Yeah, I guess so. But I would think an agency that has been around for as long as they have would be a member of the BBB. And even if a company wasn't a member, wouldn't they come up? I thought all companies show up."

"There ya go, analyzing everything again. Come on Logan, let's start a family! You just said we would move forward if nothing came up and nothing came up!"

"Yes, I did. I guess you're right, but I just want to make sure we're making—"

"Stop, honey, please."

"Okay." Not wanting to fight, he thought it better to drop the whole thing. Besides, if they did fight, she would win. She always did.

Turning back to the computer, he went to the Children's World website. According to the site, Children's World had a staff of eleven and had been in their current location for the past seven years. But when they had visited the office earlier that day, Logan had only noticed three offices and a playroom. And didn't Sylvia herself only mention a few other employees? Where did they house the rest of the staff? Maybe there was another area of suite five-twelve he hadn't seen today. Or maybe some of the staff worked from home. They do that a lot nowadays. Claire's right, he thought, I scrutinize everything... just let it go.

He switched off the computer, climbed into bed, and pulled the covers up to his chest. He turned to his wife and said, "Let's start that family."

FOUR

Dr. Ben Carlson sat behind his desk in the large office deep underground in Western Utah, studying the test results of their latest subject, seven-year-old Scott Riley. Ben Carlson was head of the project, which some of his colleagues had dubbed, "The Experiment." To him, that sounded as if they were madmen, running around stealing corpses, then trying to bring them back to life, like some deranged scientists who had lost their minds and, quite possibly, their souls.

No, he was a biologist, a scientist striving to eradicate disease, eliminate sickness and improve mankind's existence on the planet.

Many found his work to be immoral and unethical; he had no use for such cynics.

Centered under the semi-arid desert, one mile underground, the complex structure boasted state-of-the-art laboratories with the finest equipment available. A staff of experts in the fields of pharmacology, biology, mathematics, chemistry and physics was on hand at all times and a sophisticated computer system controlled everything from the climate to the security system to what you watched on TV.

Prior to completion of the underground facility, staff members of the Larenx Corporation, the company behind the project, had approached Dr. Carlson with a proposition.

Seven years ago, three men had appeared on Ben Carlson's doorstep conveying a set of documents outlining the purpose of the massive undertaking. The largest of the three informed Dr. Carlson that because of his recent work he had been chosen to oversee the project, which would require his complete dedication. He would be forced to vacate his current position at the University, sell his home and live in the underground facility. They assured him that he would have all the comforts of home.

"Flat screen TV, exercise room, pool, large living quarters and your own chef, all the amenities of life Dr. Carlson," the big man said. "My employer has followed your work for quite some time and is convinced that you are the only man for this position." The big man smiled at him, revealing his crooked, yellow-stained teeth. *You should see a dentist and go on a diet*, Ben thought. The man was at least six-five and tipped the scales at three-fifty or more.

Carlson was given the night to sleep on it, but that wasn't necessary. Ben had made his decision an hour earlier when he was reading the scope of the project. It had been a long time since he was this excited about anything and the promise of the ensuing years gripped him like an iron fist.

His life was his work; he had never married. "And what is your name?" Ben asked the big man. There was a hint of impatience and sarcasm in his voice.

"Call me Charlie, okay? If you are going to be a part of our little family, it might do you good to make friends," Charlie said, showing him those ugly, stained teeth.

"Okay, Charlie. And who are your buddies?"

"This is Mike," Charlie said, nodding to the man on his left, "and Ralph."

Both men gave him a slight nod. They told him they would return in the morning to pick him up. Then the four of them would take the company Lear to the facility, or New Life as it was now known.

And not to worry, the corporation would take care of the details: putting his house on the market and informing his current employer of his resignation.

Now, seven years later, Ben Carlson was sitting at his desk studying Scott Riley's test results. He felt uneasy. The electroencephalogram showed extremely heightened brain activity, almost approaching 100 hertz, signifying an almost off-the-chart electrical impulse associated with paranormal occurrences. Scott had already exhibited extreme intelligence, adaptability and the capacity for learning that stunned the staff at New Life.

But yesterday the boy had displayed a frighteningly new talent; he had read the mind of one of the staff. And when he wasn't given the toy he demanded, he willed it into his possession. One minute the toy truck sat in a corner across the room, and the next moment it was in Scott's hands. It didn't roll across the floor; it didn't jump up and fly through the air – it *dematerialized* and then *rematerialized* exactly where Scott wanted it.

As Carlson was pondering this, trying to make sense of it, someone knocked on his office door.

"It's open!" he yelled, irritated by the interruption.

In walked a short, balding man wearing a white medical overcoat. He had a stethoscope hanging around his neck and a pocket protector crammed full of pens like some school-aged science geek. His glasses were so thick that they magnified his eyes to a hideous size, making him look like a sideshow freak.

"Dr. Carlson, we have Scott sedated now. He should sleep through the night with no more episodes," Tom Whiting said, nervously licking his lips.

"Sedated? Why? What do you mean 'no more episodes'?" Carlson said, standing now.

"Well ... about an hour ago Scott somehow got into Dr. Hammond's head. But unlike yesterday, Ben, this time it's bad – really bad," Whiting said quietly.

Tom Whiting was the leading pharmacologist, and Carlson knew that he was indispensable to the project and New Life. But Carlson didn't like the man. He was a martyr and a wimp.

"What do you mean 'really bad,' in what way? And get to the fucking point, would you? I have things to do," Carlson said.

"Well, his nose started bleeding, just a little at first, and then it just ... um ... sorta gushed. His shirt was soaked in blood when we got to him. And then I noticed that he wasn't just bleeding from the nose, he was bleeding from his ears and his ocular cavities. Dr. Carlson ... Ben ... Mark Hammond instantly fell unconscious, and now he is comatose. I'm talking about something unlike anything we've ever seen. That kid can crawl into your brain, get what he wants and destroy you in the process." Tom Whiting ran his hand over his barren scalp; his tongue shot out over his dry lips like a snake.

"When you say sedated, do you mean Scott is completely out? Or is he semi-conscious?"

"He's completely out."

"Okay. Good. Here is what I want you to do: When he starts coming around, I want you to sedate him just to the point where his brain function is in the normal range. While in that condition, he won't be able to cause harm. But under no circumstances do I want him all the way out, you understand?"

"But—"

"But nothing, just do it."

"This is getting a little out of hand, don't you think? The consensus among the staff is that we should shut down the project – temporarily, of course – until we can figure out what is going on, how to properly deal with this."

"We are NOT shutting anything down!" Carlson's cheeks turned purplish-red, and his jaw began to hurt. "I gave you simple instructions a four-year-old could follow. Now follow them please!" Carlson said, his temples throbbing.

"I hope you know what you're doing," Whiting muttered under his breath.

"What?" Carlson asked.

"Um ... I'll inform the others that we will keep the boy – Scott – under control until you decide what you're going to do with him. And just what are you going to do?"

"Don't you worry about that, Tom, just keep him under our control and make sure his brain waves stay in the normal range. I'll take care of the rest." Carlson had settled down some, the redness in his cheeks had receded to a more normal pinkish-tan.

"You're the boss," Whiting said. He left the office, quietly closing the door behind him.

"What a mess," Ben Carlson mumbled as he headed back to his desk. Taking a deep breath and closing his eyes, he tried to calm himself so he could think clearly, get a handle on the situation. This project was his baby, and he wasn't about to let a couple of incompetent fools jeopardize everything he had worked towards the last seven years. Project 29 – Scott – had been cultivated from scratch, created in a tube and nurtured by his own hands. The intelligence the young boy exhibited was phenomenal for anyone so young. These new abilities manifested over the past few days had Carlson excited beyond words. Even now his mind was teeming with the possibilities of harnessing and using this newfound power to his advantage.

Rubbing his chin thoughtfully, he picked up Scott's file from his desk, searching for any hint – any clue – as to what might be the cause of the boy's sudden power. It has to be the medication, the experimental drugs, he thought.

There was another knock on his door. *What's happened now?*

31

Greg Meritt

"It's still open!" Carlson said, rubbing his temples.
It was Sylvia Tran.

FIVE

On Tuesday morning, Logan, dressed in his favorite charcoal gray suit, climbed behind the wheel of his Chevy Suburban and headed west on Lawson Street. He took a right on Highway 169 and followed it for eleven miles.

Unlike most commuters, Logan enjoyed the scenic forty-minute drive to the office. At five-thirty in the morning traffic was practically non-existent, giving him the freedom to ponder the activities of the day ahead or just sit back and take in the tall evergreens that surrounded both sides of the two-lane road. To his right was the well-used jogging and bike path that, even at this hour, had a few health-nuts giving their cardiovascular systems a workout. On the eastern side of the trail, the chilly Cedar River flowed peacefully to its Lake Washington destination.

Today, though, Logan had no interest in the pristine view as he drove to work. His mind was on one thing: Samantha. Last night Claire had received a call from Sylvia Tran confirming today's appointments. At ten, two people from the adoption agency were visiting their home, checking to make sure it was safe for a child. And later today, at two, they had an appointment with the lawyer, Dick Lambert, to go over the necessary adoption paperwork.

He switched on the radio. Logan sang along with Don Henley to *Take It to the Limit*. By the time he turned onto I-405, headed towards Bellevue, he was lost in the music.

It was six-thirty in the morning when he pulled into the underground parking garage at the corner of NE Fourth Street and Bellevue Way. When he parked the Suburban in the space marked RESERVED: ELLISON & KELLER, he noticed a white cargo van a few stalls down in the near-empty garage. Probably just making an early delivery, he thought.

*

Seventeen years ago, at the age of twenty-eight, Logan had co-founded the Ellison & Keller Accounting Firm with his good friend, Peter. Peter and Logan had met in high school and became best friends, both of them sharing a love of mathematics and numbers. After graduation from high school, they both attended the University of Washington. Logan, unlike most other college students, spent more time studying than partying. Peter, however, loved to party and put as much effort into rolling joints, scoring pills and tapping kegs as he did crunching numbers. He also had an eye for the opposite sex, making a game of how many bras he could collect from drunk girls and joyfully trying to break the I-slept-with-more-girls-than-anybody college record.

But then Peter met MaryAnn. She blatantly informed him that if he wanted to be with her, he had better finish his college studies, stop smoking all that dope and sleeping with all those girls. To Logan's amazement, Peter settled down the last few years of college, cut way down on his boozing, and devoted the necessary time to his studies. Not long after graduation, with his accounting degree in hand and a bright future, Peter asked MaryAnn to be his wife. Nine months later, they were married.

The first six years out of college, both Logan and Peter took shitty jobs with separate financial firms, learning the ropes. And then, one drunken October night in 1997, in Peter's apartment, they talked and laughed about how much better they could do with their own company, and how much smarter they were than most of the jerks in the industry.

"No, no, no ... I'm fucking serious Logaaan," Peter said, slurring his words and trying to keep on his feet. "Just think, we could keep all that moolaaaa for ourselves and not be giving it to them assholes." He burped and sat down on the floor hard; he had completely missed the couch.

"I think you're a little tipsy there, big guy ... better keep it down or you'll wake MaryAnn."

"Who?"

"Your wife, numbnuts."

"I have a wife? Is she cuuute? Please, *pleeease* tell me she's cuuute," Peter said, laughing.

"She's gorgeous Peter. Hey, I like the idea of starting our own company, but it takes money and just where would we get that kind of capital? I don't have a ton of money. Do you?" Logan asked.

"Uhhh...me? No, not me. MaryAnn spends as fast as I can make it." Peter looked as if he were going to puke at any moment. Stepping back a bit, Logan made sure he was out of range. "My dad ... the greatest one ... my dad, Mr. Gregory Ellison, purveyor of high-rise buildings and seedy hotels. He's rich! He'll give us the money!"

In the Western United States, Gregory Ellison was known to many as The Man with the Midas Touch – everything he did turned out right, somehow. He would purchase, for pennies on the dollar, dilapidated and poorly managed high-rise commercial properties, or hotels, giving them a facelift and new management, then attracting new tenants with special incentives. His real key to success, though, was his salesmanship, his charisma. The man had a knack for getting others to do what he wanted.

Peter tipped up the bottle of Jack, taking a huge swallow.

"I think you've had enough," Logan said, taking the bottle from his friend. Peter didn't resist, he was either too weak or too drunk. Perhaps both. "Let's talk about this when we're both sober. But now I think we need to get some sleep; it's getting late."

"Party pooper," Peter said, staggering to his feet. "Oh … I don't feel so good."

"Yeah, well you'll be better in the morning. Get some sleep," Logan said. "Goodnight Peter." He opened the door to leave, then stopped and turned around. "Don't throw up on your wife, okay? Throw up in the bathroom first, before you go to bed. I don't want that wife of yours blaming me for being covered in her drunken husband's vomit. See you tomorrow." Logan stepped outside into the chilly fall night, pulling his coat tightly around him. He yawned and checked his watch. It was after eleven. He needed to get some sleep.

The next day Logan and Peter met for lunch and discussed the trials and pitfalls and rewards of going into business independently. Earlier that morning, Peter had talked with his father about what he and Logan would like to do, convincing the Senior Ellison that they could be successful in their own business if given the opportunity.

Agreeing to finance their new venture, Gregory Ellison made it clear that he expected – *demanded* – success, and that every penny would be paid back, with interest, within ten years' time, regardless of what happened. No matter that Peter was his son; when it came to business, everyone was treated as equals.

Although it was tough going the first couple of years, Ellison & Keller thrived. Through hard work, long hours, dedication and some lucky breaks, the company turned a profit in the third year and, after that, grew into one of the top accounting firms in the state with twenty-five full-time employees, high-profile customers, and wealthy owners. With an I-told-you-so attitude, Peter and Logan repaid the borrowed funds, with interest, at the end of their fourth fiscal year, six years earlier than required. The day they wrote the check for the final installment, Peter, MaryAnn and Logan went out on the town in celebration.

That was the night Logan met Claire. The trio was having dinner at the Space Needle when Logan was captivated by their waitress. The woman was tall, with shoulder-length black hair, long legs, and a hearty laugh. Her face, even without makeup, could challenge the beauties of the past hundred years. The physical attributes of this person, although very nice, were not the actual reason for his attraction. The woman carried herself confidently, without any hint of arrogance or pride; she radiated more of a humbleness reserved for those few humans who knew who they were and where they belonged in the world. And those twinkling greenish-brown eyes illuminated an intelligence and sense of humor that made Logan want her even more.

During dinner and after a few glasses of wine, Logan asked for her number. He was dumbfounded when she gave it to him. He had expected her to refuse politely, stating her boyfriend probably wouldn't like the idea. She informed him that she didn't have a boyfriend, and she wasn't married, which confused him even more.

After dating for a few months, Logan asked Claire why she still waited tables and why she wasn't married.

"Well Mr. Need-To-Know-Everything, I still wait tables for the money, honey. I made over six figures last year … not bad for a waitress. A good server, in the right restaurant – and we're talking high-priced, high-end here - can make five or six hundred bucks a night in tips alone."

"Wow – I had no idea, Claire," Logan said, shaking his head.

"And the reason I'm not married and don't have a boyfriend? See answer to question number one." She laughed. "Oh, I've dated some, and my girlfriends try to fix me up, but I just haven't met the right guy yet, haven't felt that weak-kneed, heart gone all-a-flutter, can't-live-without you feeling, at least not until now," she said with a wink.

"I can never tell if you're serious or not, Claire. Don't tease me like that, you know I'm vulnerable…fragile," Logan shot back.

Six months later they were married.

*

L ogan arrived at the office at six-thirty. Employees would start drifting in and rushing the coffee pot around seven-thirty or seven-forty-five. And that is why Logan came in early: peace and quiet.

At the north end of the hall was his office. Hanging from the door in block letters, etched in bronze, was a tasteful, professionally crafted sign that read: LOGAN KELLER CO-FOUNDER. Peter had insisted on this gaudy display of pomp. Every time Logan looked at it, it seemed surreal, as if this office belonged to someone other than himself.

In the kitchen, he started a pot of coffee and sat down at the large table. He retrieved the morning newspaper from his briefcase, sat back and waited for the coffee to brew.

When the coffee was done, he poured himself a cup and went back to his office to finish reading the paper and go over his calendar for the day, making a list of any afternoon appointments so Jill, his secretary, could reschedule them. He had paperwork to complete and a child to adopt, after all.

Logan was reading the sports page when his cell rang, startling him.

"Hello?"

"Hey there sexy," Claire said.

"Good morning beautiful," Logan replied.

"Sylvia Tran called, and the appointment with the attorney has been moved up to one o' clock. And I was thinking—"

"Boy, that's gotta hurt," Logan interrupted, taking a sip of coffee.

"Ha ha, funny man. Anyway, why don't you tell Peter you want some time off, like maybe a month or two."

"A month or two? What for Claire?" He already knew where she was going with this, but he wasn't going to make it easy for her.

"To get to know your daughter, that's what for. Some quality bonding time - Daddy's little girl time."

"Ah … now you're going to appeal to my agreeable emotional side, huh?" Logan sighed and sat back in his chair, taking another drink of coffee. Maybe he should have something stronger than coffee today. Yeah, that will go over great with the attorney. The smell of alcohol on the potential adoptive father's breath at one in the afternoon. Good. Real good. "We don't know yet if we are going to get the little girl—"

"Her name is Samantha!" Claire said. The words came out clipped, rough. "Sorry, Logan … but her name is Samantha," she said, quieter now. Claire decided against telling him about the rest of the conversation she'd had with Sylvia a few minutes ago. This wasn't the time, when he still showed signs of doubt, to tell him the paperwork and home visit were only formalities. During their conversation, Sylvia informed Claire that they could expect Samantha to be living with them by Friday, which was only three days away.

"Samantha then. We don't even know if Samantha will be ours, Claire. I mean … anything can still happen."

"The odds are in our favor, though, honey. Just ask Peter about some time off, if we get to adopt, okay?"

"Yeah … yeah. I don't have a lot of choices now, do I?" he asked, not expecting an answer. "I'll see you at one, gotta get some work done," he lied.

"Okay, you have the address? Of the attorney?"

"Yes Claire, I do. See you at one," Logan repeated, terminating the call.

"That woman can be a pain in the butt sometimes," Logan mumbled quietly, as his thoughts turned to Samantha. The more he thought about her, the better he felt. Remembering that cherubic smiling face, the cute pigtails and her infatuation with her doll, Logan couldn't help but smile. His irritation and doubt were slowly replaced by a hint of anticipation – of quiet intoxication – at the adventure and promise of a new life. The truth, if he was honest with himself, was his life had become boring. Yes, he loved Claire deeply, and they had a great life, but he intuitively knew there was more for them to experience. Much more. Logan didn't want to end up like a lot of people: the regrets of not chasing a dream, of not taking a chance, of not trying something new even if it seemed scary. And one of Logan's dreams was raising a daughter.

He jumped at the knock on his door, almost spilling his coffee. Before he could reply, the door opened, and Peter poked his head in.

"Hey, Logan! How are you this morning?" Peter asked in that everything-is-always-wonderful tone.

"I'm fine Peter – you?"

"Great! I just wanted to say good morning."

"Hey, I need to talk to you when you have some time."

Peter's smile wavered. "Everything okay buddy?"

"Yes, everything's fine; I just have something to run by you. Don't go all crazy worried on me now."

"My office, ten minutes," Peter said. He turned and headed down the hall.

As the years had passed, and now that they were both married, Peter and Logan spent less time together. Logan tired quickly of his partner's childish antics, his devil-may-care-attitude. Like Logan, Peter was forty-seven now, but he was still the same boy who drank and fucked his way through the first half of college. Work was a different matter, though; when it came to his company, Peter was professional: smart, tactful and a great salesperson. He treated his clients with respect, admiration, and dignity.

For the next five minutes, Logan tried to read the newspaper, but he couldn't seem to retain what he had just read. His mind kept drifting, so finally he gave up and tossed the paper back in his briefcase. He left his office and headed down the long hallway.

Arriving at Peter's office, Logan smiled at the nameplate on the door. Unlike Logan's, it did not say co-founder. Peter's gold-plated plaque, which had cost three times as much, screamed the title: FOUNDER & CEO.

Logan knocked.

"Come in, Logan," Peter hollered from the other side of the door.

"How did you know it was me?"

"Who else is here this early? Besides, you're right on time, as usual. Have a seat," Peter said, motioning to the chair across from his desk. Pictures of Peter's father, Greg Ellison, graced the walls. There was a photo of the older Ellison standing in front of a sixty-story high-rise, his arm around his son, looking like Donald Trump of the West Coast. Another one showed him shaking hands with Steve Largent - the former Seahawk wide receiver turned politician. On Peter's desk was an autographed Ken Griffey, Jr. baseball; it wasn't made out to Greg Ellison, however, but to Peter.

Sitting down, Logan said, "We've done well, haven't we? I mean, the company is thriving, we make a great living, have lucked out in the wife department ... who woulda thought back in our high school and college days that we would end up here?"

"Yes, we've done well, but we can always do better. What are you getting at Logan? What did you need to talk about – is it a client problem?" Peter asked.

"Oh no, not at all." Logan hesitated, not sure how to proceed.

"Spit it out, man. What's on your mind Logan? Just get to the point – I've found that's always easiest."

Yeah, easy for you to say, Logan thought. "Claire and I have a meeting this afternoon with the adoption attorney at one, so I am going to leave early."

"No big deal, ole buddy. Is that all you're worried about? ... That's it?" He sounded relieved and a little confused, as if he expected Logan

41

to tell him that Claire was diagnosed with a rare form of cancer and had two weeks to live.

"Actually, no, there's more. If - and I do mean if - we adopt, Claire wants me to take a couple of months off to bond with the kid. I think she's been reading those parenting magazines and probably some child psychology magazines to boot and—"

"No sweat," Peter said.

"What?" Logan said, surprised. "I thought you'd be pissed with me just up and taking off like that."

"Logan, this place practically runs itself. The company doesn't need us here every day; that's why we have staff. And you know what a great staff we've cultivated over the years. Don't you have confidence in your people? Why don't you take off now, spend some time with Claire before your appointment?"

After all these years, it was hard to hear that he was no longer required, but it also meant that he had done a great job. Maybe he should head out and spend some time with his wife. If they did adopt, he knew his life would change, and he wouldn't often have the opportunity to be alone with his wife.

"I think I will leave now. I'll call you later Peter. I won't need to take a leave of absence for a while yet, I guess. But taking today off is starting to sound pretty good," Logan said. "Thanks for understanding."

"Sure. Call me later and drive safe out there. A bunch of nuts on the road." Logan and Peter shook hands as if they had just consummated a business deal, instead of being longtime friends and partners. *Our relationship sure has changed*, Logan thought as he stood up to leave.

"Bye Peter."

"Bye Logan," Peter said with a slight nod of his head.

When Logan entered the elevator, the anticipation and excitement he felt earlier slipped into melancholy. He climbed behind the wheel of the Suburban and sat there staring at the concrete wall, his mind blank. After a few minutes, Logan sat up and started the vehicle. He waited a few seconds for it to warm up and then he drove out of the garage, heading home.

He didn't notice the white van that pulled out behind him.

SIX

The room was equipped with everything a seven-year-old boy could want: motorized train sets, toy guns, dump trucks, police cars, army men. On the west side of the room was a thirty-two inch HD TV. To the left of the TV was a large mahogany bookshelf; movies occupied the first two shelves, the remaining space held children's books. The full-size bed was on the opposite side of the room; footballs, basketballs, and baseballs decorated the coverlet. It was the perfect boys' room.

Scott Riley enjoyed it at first, but after a few months, he grew tired of the toys and the movies. The books, however, were different; they were intriguing, stimulating. At the age of three Scott began to read proficiently. He dove headlong into every book, devouring each impetuously, never seeming to tire. In a short time, he had read everything and demanded more. Supplied with dozens of books of a more advanced nature, he tore through those, clamoring for still more. Now, at the age of seven, Scott was reading at college level.

His talent wasn't just reading - it extended to mathematics, composition, memory function and science. It seemed there was nothing this young man couldn't accomplish. His learning capacity was unlike any-thing witnessed in this century, and Dr. Carlson was excited and pleased, yet cautious. Scott Riley had never been outside these walls, never had much social contact except for the staff at New Life. And the girl, of course.

Samantha Jennings - named by the lead of the bio-tech research team, Sara Davidson - never exhibited the skills, abilities or the aptitude for learning that the perspicacious Scott Riley did. In fact, as far as any-one could tell, Samantha Jennings was a normal, well-adjusted five-year-old content to play with dolls and stuffed animals and watch Dora the Explorer.

Because Samantha exhibited none of the extraordinary capabilities of her predecessor, Dr. Carlson had made the decision to remove her from the project so he and the staff at New Life could concentrate their efforts and attention on Scott, their true success.

Carlson had noticed that Scott was different before he was one. By the time he was five - Samantha's age - Scott's mental development had reached that of a twenty-year-old. And now ... well ... Carlson could only say that the boy had exceeded his wildest expectations, and he was-n't quite sure what might happen next. Whatever did, though, would be unprecedented - he was certain of that.

*

The boy slowly opened his eyes. His lids were heavy with sleep, and he felt sluggish, as if he had been drugged. When he tried to sit up, he noticed the straps that bound his arms and legs. His room looked as it always had, except for one thing: the door was now bolted with a spe-cial pneumatic lock, controlled by the master computer system. Before the incident with Mark Hammond, Scott was allowed to come and go whenever he wanted. He could walk the halls, visit with staff and play with Samantha.

When playing with Samantha, Scott felt more like a child, more content and at ease than when he was being tested and poked by the staff. He had grown to despise this place and the people who ran it, especially the man Carlson. Scott knew they were deep underground, and that above him lay a vast world to be explored where normal kids roamed and played. Scott longed to be like these children, the ones he read about in the world of books; he wanted to be like Samantha. She didn't have special powers or unique gifts; she was just a kid, and she was happy. And then he learned that Samantha was going away. She was going to leave New Life; she was going to leave him. Stricken with a deep sadness, Scott had become despondent.

After a few days, though, his despondency turned to anger. He was angry at being stuck here, angry that Sam was gone and angrier still that these monsters were hiding him from the world as if he were a leper.

And then a week ago, one of the staff, Dr. Greg Hammond, spoke to Scott. But Hammond's lips didn't move, and he made no sound.

I can read his mind, Scott realized. *This is my way out!*

For the next few days, Scott gained control over his newfound talent, edging into Hammond's brain, and then retreating before being discovered. He could sense when Hammond became uneasy, and would then back off slightly until the man relaxed. Then, he would go back into his mind, being careful to stay on the outer edges, waiting for the right opportunity to burrow deep like a mole directly into his cerebral cortex.

Scott had now cultivated such superior mastery over this extraordinary manifestation that he was ready and determined to go deep inside Dr. Hammond's brain. And that is exactly what he did.

Scott was searching the gray matter for escape routes, elevator shafts, emergency exits – anything - when he felt something snap like an overstretched rubber band. And then came the blood - pouring from Hammond's nose, coming out his ears and dripping from his eyes.

Hammond screaming.

People running.

From behind him, arms encircled his chest, restricting his movement. And before he could react he felt a small, sharp pain in his left arm. That was the last thing he had remembered before he woke up strapped down in his bed.

Lying here now, Scott concentrated on sending his mind out to meld with Dr. Hammond's.

Nothing. Just blackness.

He tried Dr. Carlson. Nothing.

They didn't understand and never would. I'm not a seven-year-old boy. I'm much more than that, more than they're capable of comprehending, and some drugs, a few tie-down straps, and a cheesy lock won't hold me.

Nothing can hold me.

SEVEN

When Logan pulled into the driveway, it was nine thirty in the morning. The sky was cloudless and the morning was crisp, the air fresh. The mercury was all the way up to thirty-nine degrees and, according to the Seattle meteorologists and their fancy Doppler radar, by two that afternoon it would reach a scorching fifty-two degrees.

Two blocks away and out of sight, a white panel van pulled to the curb and the driver shut off the engine. He turned to his passenger and said, "So now what?"

"We wait, that's what," the bearded man replied, typing something on the computer balanced on his lap.

"For what?"

"Instructions."

"Well, I don't like this, not at all. We're out in the open like a couple sitting ducks, and if we keep following this guy, he'll figure out we're tailing him." The driver nervously licked his lips and ran a hand through his greasy hair. "What if he comes driving back down the road?"

"Don't be stupid," the passenger said, "I'll let you know when Mr. Keller is on his way before he even gets close. Then you can move this piece of junk without him ever catching sight of us." Mumbling something incomprehensible, he returned his gaze to the computer screen.

After typing a few commands, his cell phone rang. Grabbing the Samsung off the dashboard, he flipped it open. "McFadden here," he said.

"Are you in position?" asked the voice on the other end.

"We're just a few blocks away," McFadden replied.

"Good. I have the other team on the way. Do you have your ID?"

"Yes."

"Everything in working order?"

"Yes," McFadden said, though he hadn't checked the surveillance equipment since last week when they had taken it out of the corporation's inventory.

"Alright then. Watch for the other team and once they're inside the house, make your move. They will keep the Keller's occupied while you take care of business. Got it?" the man said.

"Yeah, got it," McFadden muttered, terminating the call.

Before entering the house, Logan stood on the steps and surveyed the quiet neighborhood, thinking about what it would be like to have a child – his child - out riding her bike, playing with friends, or walking the dog. The idea excited him.

And then he thought of Thelma, two houses up, and was ashamed that he had not visited her for so long. She would adore having a child around. Logan's parents were both deceased, as were Claire's, and it would be good for the girl to have a grandmotherly figure in her life.

Taking off his tie and unbuttoning the top button of his hand-tailored shirt, Logan entered the house. He stood in the entryway for a moment, listening. It was eerily quiet. Usually, after hearing the Suburban pull in, Axle would be at the front door, waiting for him to come up the walkway and into the house, his tail wagging furiously in anticipation.

This morning, though, there was no dog to greet him, nor any sound. Not even the incessant *beep, beep, beep* of the home alarm system begging to be silenced, which meant that, if Claire had gone out, she'd forgot to set it.

"Claire? I took the day off so I could be here when the adoption people arrive."

Baffled, Logan turned to his left and headed up the carpeted stairs, his tie dangling from his right hand. When he reached the top landing, he stopped and listened. The house was as quiet as if it had been abandoned years ago.

To his left was the master bedroom. To his right was Claire's office, where she worked on her interior design projects. Adjacent to that, was the "media room," complete with a 60" HD TV, home theater system with surround sound, and sound-proofed walls to stave off complaints from the neighbors when Logan decided to crank up the volume on some action movie.

He went into the bedroom and retrieved a pair of blue jeans from the dresser. Then he went to the walk-in closet in search of an appropriate shirt. Wanting to make a good impression on his future visitors, Logan applied fresh deodorant, splashed on a little Old Spice and ran a comb through his still-thick hair.

As soon as he stepped from the bathroom into the master bedroom, Logan was hit. He went scrambling backward, arms flailing like an epileptic suffering a seizure. He landed on his rear, but before he could get to his feet, he was pinned to the floor by two hairy legs. A grotesquely wet and rough tongue slopped kisses on his cheeks and lips. "Axle, get off! Enough!" Logan gasped, holding the animal at bay.

Claire stood in the doorway with her arms clasped across her chest, laughing. "What a great picture that would make. Sure wish I had a camera right now. You guys make a great couple."

"Very funny Claire," Logan said, getting to his feet. He wiped his face with a grimace. "Dog slobber – yuck! Why didn't we teach him to attack intruders instead of the owners of the house? And just where have the two of you been?"

"I took our furry companion for a walk. Unlike you my dear, Axle likes to exercise, don't ya boy," she said, rubbing him behind the ears. The dog's tail wagged furiously, and he nuzzled Claire's crotch.

"Why does he always get to do that and I don't?" Logan said, trying to sound mischievous and failing miserably.

"Because you're not as sexy as my boy here, that's why. And, my needy husband, what are you doing home? I thought we were going to meet with the lawyers later this afternoon."

"Thanks to my superior salesmanship, I convinced Peter that I should be here for my wife and show support for the whole adoption thing," Logan said.

"Logan, you are the worst liar I have ever met. It was Peter that told you to go home, wasn't it? And did you talk to him about taking some time off?" Claire was now standing with her hands on her hips, staring at him with a smirk on her face.

"Yes, I did tell him that you wanted me to take a month or so off if we end up adopting."

"If? What do you mean if? Logan, this is pretty much done, just some formalities to go through, but I'd say we're at about ninety percent go here. Now, why don't you go make some coffee while I change, and then we can talk before they arrive; we still have thirty minutes or so."

"Anything for you, Claire. See you downstairs. Come on you face-licking ball of fur. I'll get you a doggy treat." As soon as Axle heard the word *treat*, he went nuts, running halfway down the stairs and, when he realized Logan wasn't on his heels, he stopped, turned and ran back up. Whining, he ran back down the stairs, stopped, turned back, waited, whined once more and then bolted for the kitchen.

Ten minutes later, dressed in black pants and a frilly white blouse, Claire joined her husband. She poured herself a fresh cup of coffee, added some half-n-half, and sat down next to Logan at the marble-black kitchen bar.

"Wow, you sure look beautiful," Logan said.

"Thank you. I usually lounge around the house all day dressed like this. Seems to be good for my self-esteem. Plus my boyfriend really likes it," she said, winking at him.

"I'll bet he does." Logan replied, "It probably frustrates the poor guy thinking of you out of those clothes, knowing that he can't touch you because your psycho husband would feed his body, piece by severed piece, through the nearest wood chipper."

"What a lovely thought."

"Hey, I thought about Thelma today - how much I miss her, and how good she would be for Samantha," Logan said quietly. His cheeks felt warm and flushed, as if he was embarrassed to admit, even to his wife, that he missed the old woman.

"I saw her a few days ago," Claire said. "I went over to her house and had a short visit. She misses you, too, honey, and I think you should go see her after we get through this adoption stuff. She would really, really like that."

The doorbell rang. Barking with excitement, Axle ran to the front door to see who had come to visit.

"Axle, stop that! Come here boy," Logan said, knowing that his commands were futile. He grabbed the dog by the collar, holding him back, while Claire answered the door.

Two women stood on the stoop: one Korean, one Caucasian. The Korean woman was young; she couldn't have been more than thirty, while her companion looked to be at least fifty.

"Please, come in. You must be from Children's World," Claire said. Logan was straining every muscle to keep Axle from jumping on their two guests and licking them to death.

"Yes, we are," the Korean woman replied, stepping inside. Her friend followed. "My name is Sun Kim, and this is Janelle Walker." The older woman smiled and nodded. "We're pleased to meet you – I assume you're Claire and the man losing the war with the dog is your husband." Sun Kim spoke in perfect English, without any trace of an accent.

53

Born and raised in the good old USA, Logan thought.

"Yes, my husband Logan always loses to Axle – that's our dog. It really is sad and a little disheartening to watch him try. He seems to believe that, even after many attempts, he'll win. Never happens."

"Very funny," Logan said, still holding Axle in a death grip. His arm was beginning to hurt; slowly he loosened his hold and led the Golden Retriever to the women. "He's really friendly, unless you're an intruder, of course. Then watch out! Axle loves kids, plays with the neighborhood children all the time." Tentatively sniffing his newfound friends, getting their scent, Axle whined, tucked his tail between his legs and padded to the kitchen.

"Shall we go into the living room where we can talk?" Claire asked.

"That would be lovely, thank you," Janelle Walker replied.

"This way," Claire said, motioning for her guests to follow.

"Have a seat, make yourself at home. Can I get you anything to drink? We have coffee, tea, water, soda – it's only diet, though - or fruit juice."

"Coffee's great, Claire, thanks," Sun Kim replied.

"Coffee sounds good," Janelle chimed in.

"I'll be right back. Logan, would you please keep our guests entertained while I'm gone?"

"Of course."

The doorbell rang, but this time Axle didn't come running. "Now who could that be?" Claire said, perplexed.

"I got it, honey," Logan said, "why don't you get the drinks?"

"Yeah…okay."

Logan opened the door to two men wearing white overalls with a *City of Black Ridge* patch sewn just above the left pocket. The large man smiled and held up an ID badge. "Is this the Keller residence?" he asked politely, referring to his clipboard.

"It is. What may I do for you, gentleman?"

"Sorry for the interruption Mr. Keller. The city is testing the back-flow pressure for homes in this area, so we need to run a few tests."

"Oh?" Logan raised an eyebrow. "Well, what do you need from us?"

"Not much really, just access to the pipes. If we could come in and do our thing, we'll be done in under twenty minutes."

"May I see that ID again please?" Logan said, glancing behind him to where Claire was now serving coffee to the two woman from the agency.

"Of course," the man said with a smile. He held up the laminated ID card again, and Logan stared at it for a minute.

"This isn't the best time. We have some people here—"

"I promise we'll be quick, Mr. Keller. In fact, you won't even know we are here.

Logan sighed. "Fine, come on in."

"Thanks. My name is Bryce, and this is Lester," the man said, stepping across the threshold. He was carrying a large red metal toolbox. When he noticed Logan looking at it, he said: "Testing equipment."

Logan nodded. "Right."

"We'll start upstairs if that's okay."

"Well…alright, let me show you."

"No need, we can find our way. You should get back to your company. As I said, we'll be done in a jiffy."

Logan looked over at Claire, who seemed impatient. "Honey, come sit and let them do their job," she said, patting the cushion next to her.

Logan looked back at the men. "Alright, do what you need to do."

The two men headed upstairs, and Logan joined his wife in the living room.

"We have a list of questions for the two of you, and then we will tour the home to make sure it is childproof. If we find something that needs fixing, such as outlets or escape routes, we will let you know."

"Let's get started," Logan said, visibly irritated.

"Of course," Sun said, removing a stack of papers and a pen from a brown briefcase. "Have either of you ever been convicted of a felony?"

"No, never," Claire said. Sun Kim turned to Logan.

"No," Logan said before she could speak.

"Ever been accused of a crime against a child: molestation, rape, abuse – physical or emotional?"

"I don't like this – and no, of course not!" Claire said.

"We have to ask, Mrs. Keller, sorry," Janelle said.

Sun turned her attention to Logan: "You?"

"Just once back in '87, but it was only molestation, not full-blown rape," he joked.

"That is NOT funny, Mr. Keller," Sun Kim said.

"I suppose not. And no, I never have been accused, arrested, tried or convicted of any such thing, thank you very much."

For another twenty minutes, Logan and Claire endured more questions. When finished, Sun Kim put the questionnaire back in her briefcase. "And now if we may tour your home?"

"Of course," Claire said.

Just then the men from the city appeared. "All done upstairs. Just about five more minutes down here and then we'll be gone, it'll be like we were never here. Ain't that right Lester?"

"Yup," the skinny man said.

"Then why don't we start the home tour upstairs, so we are out of the way?" Janelle said. "That way by the time these guys finish, we'll be done upstairs. Works out perfectly."

Claire nodded. "Okay."

Fifteen minutes later they were done and back in the living room. The men from the city had already left.

"Here is a list of what you need," Sun said, handing Claire a handwritten list. "Nothing big, just some electrical outlet covers, another fire extinguisher, a fire escape ladder, and a few other things."

"Thank you," Claire said, taking the list from Sun Kim.

"Yeah thanks," Logan said. "I need to use the bathroom. Goodbye, ladies." With that, he turned and headed out of the room.

Claire watched him thoughtfully, biting her lower lip. Then she turned back to the women, thanked them and walked them to the door.

"Goodbye Claire, we wish you the best of luck with Samantha. She couldn't be in better hands," Sun said.

Janelle nodded in agreement. "Yes, Mrs. Keller, you and your husband seem like you'll make great parents. Good-bye and best of wishes."

"Good-bye," Claire said. She watched as the two women walked down the steps and got in their car. After she had closed the door, she leaned against it for support. It was all so surreal, as if she were going to wake up in her bed at any moment. Looking at her watch, she realized that it was already after eleven; they still had to meet the lawyer at one.

"Logan!"

"What?" He came out of the bathroom. "Are they gone? Those two beautiful, lovely ladies - did they leave?"

"Yes, honey they left. We should grab some lunch soon. We still have the lawyer to see at one."

"Why don't we get something on the way? We could grab a sandwich at Subway. I suddenly have a craving for a Big Philly Cheesesteak and a root beer. And maybe some chips."

"Sure, why not?"

*

Safely back in the van, McFadden flipped open his laptop. After a few clicks, the inside of the Keller's residence appeared on the screen. Eight separate camera images covered all areas of the home. The feed was superior, this was state-of-the-art equipment and software, after all. Everything had gone according to plan. The other team had kept the Kellers occupied giving them the needed time to secure the tiny cameras and load the software.

57

"What if they find the cameras?" Briggs asked, crunching on a bag of Doritos. Yellow-orange flakes of cheese littered his lips and the legs of his pants.

Before he could answer, McFadden's phone rang. "Hello."

"I see you've completed the task admirably. I'm looking at the feed right now. Beautiful picture," the man said, "this technology is unbeatable. Now get back to the office."

"On our way." Bryce McFadden didn't wait for a response. He closed the cell and turned to Briggs. "Get moving. And wipe your face, you have Dorito dust all over it. What were you trying to do, snort the stuff?"

Briggs grunted, started the van and pulled out of the neighborhood.

*

At the lawyers, Claire and Logan completed more paperwork, agreed to background checks and answered more questions. Just when they thought they were finished, Dick Lambert looked up from the file in front of him and addressed the couple: "It looks as if everything is in perfect order. Logan … Claire, you should be taking little Samantha home with you day after tomorrow. I have already spoken with Children's World and the home study is fine, background checks will be rushed through tomorrow, and my good friend, the commissioner, has already agreed to sign this into law on Friday."

Stunned, Logan stared at the pudgy lawyer.

Claire began to cry.

EIGHT

"What the hell are you doing here?" Carlson asked. "I thought you were taking care of Samantha Jennings; we don't need any more mistakes." He sounded tired, exhausted.

"It's all under control Ben, and what do you mean mistakes? Has something happened?" Sylvia Tran asked.

"Our young man has decided to exhibit some phenomenal powers – things like mind reading, teleportation – and now I have a valuable member of my staff in a coma; a fucking coma for Christ sakes!"

"You're kidding! Teleportation? Reading minds? Think of what we can do, what we can accomplish when we harness this power and control it and use it to our advantage. Ben, the possibilities are infinite," Sylvia said. But she looked shocked and more than a little worried. Carlson sighed and laid his head on his desk.

"You haven't answered my question. What is going on with Samantha Jennings?" Carlson asked again.

"You worry too much. The Keller's will be taking possession of the little girl in a couple of days. We had two operatives pose as employees from Children's World, who visited the home, performing the necessary home study. While they kept the couple occupied two other operatives, posing as city employees, placed surveillance equipment in the home. The Kellers also met with Dick Lambert, who had them sign the necessary documents, making everything legal. See? All under control."

"And where is the girl now?"

"She's fine - you don't need to worry about her."

"Where is the girl?" he repeated, the vein in his neck becoming more prominent. He clenched his teeth.

"She is with Sun Kim at her apartment in Bothell. She's probably sleeping right now."

"Has she shown any special abilities?"

"None," Sylvia said.

"Okay good. Now that Samantha is off the meds completely, I am confident we won't be witnessing any paranormal activity. I do, however, want to monitor her for the next month, perhaps two, just in case."

"And just what do you propose if the girl happens to manifest powers like Scott?"

Carlson stood, rubbing his eyes. Then he looked at Sylvia and grinned. "We dispose of her, of course. And anyone that knows her; can't be having a bunch of witnesses, now can we?"

"But why wouldn't you just bring her back here? Study her, keep her under control, like Scott?"

"Because she will never be like Scott." He rubbed his chin and shot her a strange, sly smile. "Scott is one-of-a-kind, Sylvia, don't forget that and don't underestimate him, either. The girl would never be able to harness his type of power if she ever exhibits anything at all."

Out of twenty-nine attempts, there had been only two survivors – Samantha and Scott. When Carlson found out the first survivor was male, he was extremely pleased. The team at New Life had taken great care in mapping the genetic code of the subjects. Through the cloning process, the team assembled recombinant DNA molecules, replicating them within the host organisms. Specifically instructed to produce only male subjects, the New Life team monitored and manipulated the SRY gene on the Y chromosome; however, a small mistake on the part of a tired, overworked staff member helped bring little Samantha into the world.

Carlson had been furious. Females were weak. He thought about killing the child. But then he realized if she had special talents, she might be of use to him. Now, after five years of frustrations, he couldn't just eliminate her. Too many staff members had grown close to the little girl; regarded her as a human being worthy of life. He would be frowned upon, looked upon as a murderer by some staff (though not all) and would lose the respect of the people he needed to bring the project to its successful conclusion.

So he had done the next best thing. He had Samantha removed from the facility. She was gone from this place, out in the world, and away from him. Carlson could now put his full attention on his prize: seven-year-old Scott.

Disconcerted by the doctor's words, Sylvia said, "Don't you think that's a little harsh? You can't just go around killing people when they don't behave the way you want. Not only is that immoral and unethical Ben, but it's also illegal."

"Illegal means nothing unless you get caught."

"Has it ever occurred to you that you might be crazy?"

Ben Carlson only smiled and rubbed his chin.

NINE

S cott Riley lay in his bed laughing. He looked at the pneumatic lock on his door and laughed. Looking down at the straps on his arms, which secured him to the bed frame, he laughed even harder, until tears came out of his eyes. Upon awakening, for a brief moment, he had forgotten what he was capable of, what his powers could do.

Closing his eyes, Scott went to that empty place in his mind, devoid of all things. Once his mind was completely barren, he increased the firing of his neurons, bringing his brain's electrical activity to a whopping 100 Hz within a matter of seconds. He did not know how he did this, nor did he care. It was the result that mattered. In his mind, he saw the two brown leather straps, each one securing his arms. He pictured them disappearing, melting away as if they had never existed. Suddenly they were gone.

Lying harmlessly on the brown carpet like a couple of dead snakes were the two leather restraints, which had held him prisoner seconds earlier.

He sat up and swung his legs over the side of the bed. Sitting there, dangling those young legs, he intuitively knew that he was ancient, that something or someone had infiltrated this tiny body. Something from another time, another place.

This small body, such as it was, might be put to good use. The innocence of a small child could be used to advantage. The downside, though, was the loss of physical strength and agility found in a fully-grown human; he knew, however, that mental prowess far exceeded brute physical strength.

Turning his attention now to the lock on his door, Scott again went to the no-where place and sent the inanimate object to the middle of the room.

He rubbed his temples. His head hurt, directly above his left eye. Two days ago, when he had transported – *teleported* – the toy truck, his head hurt only slightly. Then yesterday, when he entered Hammond's mind, the pain had become more intense. And now, after manipulating the restraints and the lock, his head really hurt, as if clamped between the jaws of a vise. There was a little trickle of blood dripping from his left nostril. Absently, he wiped it away with the back of his hand. He sat on the edge of the bed for a few minutes, waiting for the throbbing in his temples to subside.

When his head was better, he got up, went to the door and quietly turned the knob, wondering if there would be a sentry located on the other side. Pulling the door open a few inches, he peered through the crack, surveying the hallway beyond. No guard.

Scott closed the door and went to the closet and flipped on the light, searching for something to wear. Choosing a pair of soft rubber-soled shoes, which would be quieter on the tile, and a sweatshirt that read: NEW LIFE, NEW HOPE, NEW DREAMS, he dressed quickly. He went back to the door, opened it and looked out. The hall was still deserted.

He stepped out of the room, closing the door behind him. Walking as fast as his short legs would carry him, he headed straight for Dr.

Carlson's office. Scott knew that they were watching him, but hoped he would reach Carlson's office before being stopped.

Utilizing strategically placed cameras, the massive computer system – Phoebus III – had eyes everywhere. Even if he knew the location of every camera, though, he still couldn't hide, for they covered every inch of New Life.

Being the only seven-year-old in the building did not bode well for being invisible in this world of adults. Strangely enough, Scott made the two-minute trek to Carlson's office unnoticed. Although he had passed a few New Life staff members in the hallways, no one seemed to notice him. They left him alone just as they had before the incident that left a highly respected staff member lying down the hall in a coma, fighting for his life.

Reaching Carlson's office, Scott raised his tiny hand to knock when a voice called out: "Come on in Scott, I've been waiting for you."

Tentatively, Scott opened the door and cautiously stepped inside.

"Shut the door please," Carlson said.

Scott did as he was instructed, closing the door behind him, yet he didn't come any closer. Although he had rare and unique talents, Scott still felt a pang of fear whenever he was around this man. There was something strange about him. It was like something deep inside him had snapped a long time ago.

"Come here; I want to talk with you about something, something I think you'll find interesting." Unlike his colleagues, Carlson had no fear of the boy; he knew that what he created he could destroy at any time.

Walking into the room, Scott looked at the man and smiled. "Why didn't you have me stopped? You knew as soon as I got the straps off my arms, didn't you? And you could have stopped me at any time."

"Yes, young man, I could have stopped you from coming here, but that just makes no sense," he said, shaking his head. "No sense at all. Why would I spend all these years cooped up in a place like this, working endless hours to perfect the greatest thing the planet has ever witnessed, just to tie it up, to imprison it? Hmm? No, makes no sense."

"I'm not an *it!*" Scott said furiously. "I am flesh, bone and blood - and a lot more than that!"

"Calm down there, boy," Carlson said, trying to placate him. "I know that. I also know you're not a normal seven-year-old. You may sound like a child, you may look like a child, but you have the intelligence of Hawking and the charisma of a President. But you also have the needs of a Hitler. What a perfect combination! And that is exactly what I want to speak with you about. But not here, not in the office - let's go back to my living quarters, Scott, and talk man to man.

Carlson started across his sumptuous office, motioning for Scott to follow. They went through the door that separated Carlson's private office from the place he had called home for the past seven years.

To Scott's surprise, Carlson's living room was handsomely decorated: a large leather sofa with reclining footrests, a steel and slate coffee table sat atop a large, colorful throw, and a fifty-two inch HD Plasma TV was mounted on the far wall, all signs of wires and cords carefully tucked away within the plasterboard. Black and white aerial photographs in tasteful frames hung on one side of the room; opposite these were oil paintings laid down on expensive canvas.

"Nice place."

"It's home," Ben said. "Not that I spend a lot of time here. It seems most of my time is spent in that damn office or the labs. But, we didn't come here to talk about me and my home life. Want something to drink?"

"How 'bout a bourbon and coke?" Scott said.

"You can't be serious. You're seven!" Ben laughed.

Scott looked at Carlson silently, his face blank.

"Well ... and why ... why not?" he said, trying to catch his breath. "It would be fun to have a few drinks with... um ...such a young man.

Let me just get you that bourbon and coke," he said and began laughing again.

TEN

When they got home from the lawyer's, Claire immediately went to the kitchen, grabbed the bottle of Jack Daniels from the cupboard and poured herself a drink. *I need to calm down. I can hardly breathe.* Axle followed her into the kitchen, looking for some attention. As she was pouring the drink, Axle cocked his head and gave her a quizzical look, as if to say: What the hell are you doing? You don't drink.

Logan had hardly said two words on the drive home. Subdued, he couldn't quite collect his thoughts. Now, as he entered the kitchen, Claire asked: "Want a drink?"

"Yes ... yes, I do. I sure could use a drink. Hey there Axle, how's my good buddy doing?" Logan said, scratching him behind the ears.

Claire finished pouring drinks and motioned to the dining room. "Let's sit down and discuss what just happened, okay?"

"Yes ... I think we should," Logan replied, joining Claire at the dining room table.

Claire took Logan's hand in hers. She looked him in the eye and grinned. "Logan, honey, I have a million things running through my head right now: need to get her room ready, need to buy a bed, what toys should I get? What clothes do I buy? Do I check into preschools? What about a pediatrician?" Claire spoke rapidly, in one long breath, sounding like an auctioneer at Sotheby's.

"Claire, slow down, will ya? We still have a couple a days before Sam will be here, plenty of time to get ready. Plenty of time to figure things out." Claire's excitement was understandable, and Logan was happy for her. He didn't share in her enthusiasm, though. At the moment, he wasn't sure exactly how he felt. The idea of having a daughter was exciting, yes, but he was still tentative about adopting this little girl. Or any child, for that matter.

"Why don't you make a list of everything that needs to be accomplished over the next couple of days, and then we can get started on buying all the stuff we need," Logan said. If he just put his mind to the task at hand, got involved with setting up the house for a child, supported his wife, perhaps that gnawing feeling of uncertainty would transform into the joy of fatherhood.

Wednesday and Thursday, they visited Bed, Bath & Beyond, JC Penney, Sears and Toys R' Us. They came home proud owners of a girl's white panel bed, complete with matching nightstand, dresser, and vanity. They neatly arranged stuffed animals - bears, horses, and teddies - on the pink polka-dot coverlet.

At Toys R' Us, Claire had purchased Bitty Twins Dolls with the belief that Sam would welcome the idea of Thelma having some playmates. Completing the look, Logan installed a six-inch ceiling border of Disney princesses, running it the length of the room. When they were finished renovating the tired, drab spare room into a lively and beautiful haven, fit for a princess, Logan put his arm around his wife, and together they admired their handiwork.

"She'll be here tomorrow, in the morning," Claire said.

"I know," Logan replied. He wasn't as apprehensive as he had been a few days ago. In fact, he was looking forward to welcoming Sam into their family. "Is Sylvia bringing her?"

70

"I think so. I do know that it will be Children's World who will bring Sam and her belongings – could be one of the women who came here for the home study. It doesn't matter. Wow, honey, look at this room – can you believe it? We're going to have a daughter!" Claire exclaimed. She was giddy with excitement.

At nine o'clock Friday morning the doorbell rang and Axle went on his usual tirade, trying his best to make sure that no one in the neighborhood slept in on this important day. Logan was upstairs on the computer, checking his email, and Claire was in the kitchen making another pot of coffee (they already had demolished one). Claire pushed the brew button on the coffee machine and walked to the front door. She hollered, "I got it!" hoping Logan could hear her over Axle's barking.

She drew in a deep breath, held it for a moment, and then let it out. She opened the door. And there was Samantha, standing on the porch in the chilly November sunshine, clutching her doll tightly to her chest. Standing directly behind her, with a hand on each of Sam's shoulders, was Sylvia Tran.

Claire smiled. "Come in … please come in." She motioned them into the house, while holding onto Axle's collar, trying her best to keep him from licking the girl to death. "Hi Samantha, how are you?"

"I'm okay," she said, staring at her feet. As soon as the girl spoke, Axle made his move. Claire had loosened her grip a little on the dog's collar, and Axle sensed it. He pulled quickly, breaking free of Claire's hold, and went directly to the girl. Because Sam was still staring at the floor, Axle rolled over onto his back, so he was looking directly up at her. Sam giggled. "Is it asshole?" she asked Claire. Sylvia clamped a hand over her mouth; Claire didn't know if it was to stifle a laugh or if she was actually shocked by the girl's words.

"No honey, but that's close. Axle is his name." As if this was his cue, Axle got to his feet and licked Sam's face. She giggled again, turning her head and pushing him away.

"Yuck. I like him; he's nice."

71

"Yes, honey, Axle is a great dog, we've had him since he was a puppy. He takes care of us, makes sure that no strangers bother us."

"I have a few things for Sam in the car," Sylvia said, "clothes, some toys—"

"She has other toys?" Claire asked.

"Yes, a few things anyway. But she doesn't play with them much. Her doll seems to be the most important thing to her right now, but I think she'll outgrow that as most girls do."

"I'm sure she will," Claire agreed.

"I'll run out and get her things. I need to make a quick call to the office anyway. Be back in a few minutes, okay?"

"Sure."

Sylvia went down the steps to her Mercedes, which was parked at the curb. She pulled a cell phone out of her purse, pressed and held one, and heard it ring on the other end. After the third ring, a voice came on the line.

"What?"

"It's me. Do you have the laptop in front of you?"

"Yes."

"How's the feed? Do you see the girl and the woman?"

"Picture perfect, sound is great too. Those microphones in the cameras are fantastic; it's as if you're there in the room with them. Come to think of it, the video is as great as the audio. Modern technology – fantastic!"

"Good, thanks, gotta go." Without waiting for a response, Sylvia terminated the call. She retrieved Sam's items from the car and headed back to the house.

When Sylvia returned, Logan had joined Claire and Sam in the living room. Axle was lying contentedly at Sam's feet.

"Hi, Mr. Keller," Sylvia said.

"Hello, Miss Tran. Thank you for bringing Samantha, we do appreciate it."

"Sure, happy to place a child in a good home. Here are her clothes," Sylvia said, setting a large suitcase on the floor. "And here are some more toys for her to play with if she ever gets bored with Thelma." She pointed to the bag she had put next to the suitcase.

"Thelma's my best friend," Sam said quietly, clutching the doll to her chest.

Claire looked at Logan and grinned. Turning her attention back to the girl, Claire said, "Best friends are forever, aren't they honey? You keep playing with Thelma for as long as you want, okay?"

"Yes … yes …"

"Well, I need to get going, I have a full calendar today. Sorry to just rush off like this, but Sam is definitely in good hands," Sylvia said.

"We understand. Thank you again for all your help Sylvia," Claire said.

"You're very welcome. We should be thanking you, Claire, and you, Logan. So thank you. If you ever need anything, please call me directly." She headed for the door but stopped halfway there. "Oh … and use my cell number – not the office – you can always reach me by cell. Bye."

Claire turned to the little girl. "Would you like to see the rest of the house and your new bedroom?"

"Yes!"

"This way young princess," Logan said. He bowed, placing his right arm across his midsection and extending his left towards the back of the house. Samantha giggled. Claire watched them, smiling.

Logan and Claire gave Sam the tour of their elegant home, reserved only for the most beloved of guests: The living room, the formal dining room, the expansive kitchen with marble countertops and island, the nook, the pantry (which was larger than most bedrooms), the bathroom and the den, complete with French doors. The deeper into the house they went, the wider Sam's eyes grew as if she could not believe that she could ever live in such a castle. Throughout the tour, Axle stayed close to her, following her everywhere, not letting her out of his sight. Every once in a while, Axle would nuzzle and lick her hand, and she would giggle, patting his head.

When they finished downstairs, the three of them, with Axle on their heels, climbed the exquisite wooden staircase to the upper floor of the five-bedroom home. Claire was holding Samantha's hand, silent but smiling. As they reached the top of the stairs, Sam let go of Claire's hand and bolted to the right, with Axle following close behind. She stopped in the doorway of her new room, stood for a moment, and then started jumping up and down, clapping her hands. "Is it mine? Is it? Is it?"

"Yes, it's yours. Do you like it?" Claire asked. Logan stuffed his hands in his pockets and leaned against the wall, watching.

"Yes, yes, yes, yes," she said, running into the room. She jumped up on the bed, still clutching Thelma with one little hand and grabbing as many stuffed animals as she could hold in the other.

"Looks like you have a hit on your hands," Logan said. "Why don't you go in and talk with her, bond a little, just the two of you? I have some things I can do around the house that I've been putting off and since I won't be working for a while ... well ... what a better time to catch up on projects, huh?"

"Yeah ... okay. I'll spend some time with her this morning, just girl to girl, and then later you can—"

"Claire, we have our whole lives – remember, she is our daughter. Or will be this afternoon. What time do we have to be in court to sign papers?"

"Three."

"Perfect. Gives me plenty of time; I can start on a one-hour project, which means it'll take me at least three, so I can be ready before it's time to leave for court. Good luck with your daughter there," Logan said, nodding to Sam. She was still on the bed, enjoying her new room and stuffed animals.

"Thanks." Claire walked into the room. "May I sit down?" she asked Sam.

"Yes," Sam replied. "It's your house. Do I get to keep the animals?" She looked at Claire with sad, imploring blue eyes.

"Sam," Claire said, cupping her face in both hands. "This is your home forever; you don't need to leave if you don't want to. And everything in this room is yours; you don't have to give any of this back. Not the dolls, or stuffed animals or games or your bed – nothing."

"Mean it?" Sam asked. Her tone – one of disbelief and fear - almost made Claire cry.

"Yes, honey, mean it. Is it okay if I give you a hug?"

"Okay."

They sat on the bed, just holding each other. Axle was at the foot of the bed, watching them, his head resting on his paws. Claire was astounded at how quickly the girl took to her. She had heard where, in cases like this, the initial reaction was rebellion, defiance. But Sam was different; Sam was special. Rocking her, Claire stroked her hair.

And silently, she wept.

ELEVEN

Richards sat on Ben Carlson's plush sofa, his pudgy fingers wrapped around his expansive belly. "It's been seven years now, Dr. Carlson. We have discussed this at length. We should've already introduced a gifted human being to the outside world, yet here we are still overcoming these obstacles. I'm a patient man, doctor, really I am. But my patience is wearing thin. Do you have any idea how much money my partners and I have poured into this project?"

"No, can't say that I do." Carlson hated these meetings; the man sitting across from him was demanding, egotistical.

"Of course you don't," Richards replied. "So I want a timeline – a timeline you *will* meet – of when you will have this kid stable; when you will have him ready to see the world and for the world to see him. We understand each other?"

Carlson smiled and said, "I can have Scott ready for the outside world in three months. That work for you?" He did his best to put some respect in his tone, although respect was the last thing he felt for this man.

Richards stood up, nodding. "Three months. I will give you three more months. If I don't have results by then, you will be replaced, understand?"

"Yes … yes, I do." In his mind, Carlson saw his hands wrapped around that fat neck, squeezing the ugly life out of this prick, enjoying his cries for mercy until he finally fell silent.

"Good," Richards said, pulling on his charcoal-gray overcoat, protecting his two thousand dollar suit. "I will be in touch when we get closer to that day." Without another word, Richards walked out the door, through Carlson's office and into the empty hallway, where Charlie, his personal bodyguard, was waiting. "Let's get out of this claustrophobic hellhole, shall we?"

"Yeah, the place gives me the creeps," Charlie said. He saw Carlson standing at the open door of his office, watching them. He waved. "See ya later Doc!" he said, laughing.

After they had left, their footsteps echoing down the empty hallway, Carlson muttered, "Good riddance," and went back inside, closing the door. He went to his desk, unlocked the lower right drawer and retrieved a small box. It looked like a small safe. On the face was a combination lock. Ben swung the tumbler left, then right, then left again. He opened the box and retrieved the key from inside.

He walked through his office and into his living quarters. Going to the north wall, carrying the key in his left hand, he thought of the bastard who had left his residence a few minutes earlier. When this is all over, he thought, I will put a bullet in that man's brain or perhaps Scott will have the capacity to crush his gray matter into a gelatinous pile of mushy pulp.

That thought lifted his spirits. As he removed the aerial photograph of the desert from the wall, revealing the safe behind it, he began to calm down.

The wall safe also contained a combination lock. Once opened, the inside of the safe revealed another steel box. This one required the key

Ben held in his hand. Inside was a slip of paper. On the paper, in alphanumeric code, was the password to the computer system that ran New Life.

Brian Ross, the head of computer programming, changed the password three times a week. Besides Ben, Brian was the only staff member with access to the wall safe. Brian would slip in, destroy the old password, replace it with the new one, and then slip back out. This security measure ensured that, if breached, it could only be the fault of one of two men.

Taking the password from the safe, he neatly copied it down and returned it to its original hiding place. He locked the box, placed the picture back on the wall and locked the key in his desk.

As Dr. Carlson headed to the data center, his mind turned toward Scott and yesterday's conversation. For the first time in the seven years since Scott's conception, Ben had gotten to know the young man. He didn't consider him a seven-year-old child anymore, but a vastly intelligent human being. Child prodigies of the past century paled next to him. It didn't bother Ben in the least that Scott had been created in a lab.

Scott shared the same vision, the same dreams as his creator. And nothing would stop them from attaining the world they envisioned. Now that they had agreed to consult with one another, work together as a team, like father and son, Carlson knew he had the greatest weapon: better than money, tanks, drugs, guns, or military forces; he had the ultimate killing machine.

He arrived at the six-inch thick, drill-resistant steel door, which secured the data center and placed his right palm on the reader. When the computer recognized his prints, red lights turned to green, indicating clearance; he then situated his right eye on the retina scanner. A beam of low-energy infrared light rapidly traced the retinal blood vessels, sending the reflection to the computer database to be compared with information on file. Passing the retinal test, he punched in the seven digit code on the lighted panel to his right and stepped back, watching as the impenetrable steel door hissed and clanked. Huge locking mechanisms within the massive structure were released, sounding like a small cannon.

Once opened, Ben stepped inside the data center, marveling at the technology that was in this little twenty-foot-by-twenty-foot room. He walked over to the control center, pulled out a chair and sat down at the keyboard. Retrieving the password from his shirt pocket, Ben typed the thirteen digit alphanumeric code into the system, gaining him access and control over the entire facility.

Whenever Richards visited New Life, certain protocol had to be followed. All personnel were confined to their living quarters, all videos and cameras were shut-down, and all access to secure areas was denied. For some reason, Richards did not want to be observed by any staff, nor did he want to be videotaped. *The man sure is paranoid*, Carlson thought.

Now, at the keyboard to Phoebus III, the advanced computer system, Carlson typed his commands: relinquish control on all private quarters, engage full operation of all video displays and re-activate all security cards.

That done, Carlson decided to visit his protégé, who was in the recreation room solving a myriad of puzzles, Rubik cubes, and various algorithms. When Carlson approached Scott, he was working on the fifteen-puzzle, which required the application of metaheuristics. Fascinating, Carlson thought. This kid is beyond smart; he makes the most intelligent men of science look like third-graders.

"Hey Scott, sorry to interrupt, but I need to speak with you."

"Go ahead," Scott said, fiercely concentrating on the object in front of him.

"Not here, in private. We can go to my office." Carlson said. He paused, and then added, "When you're finished here, of course."

"Okay, I'll be there in a few minutes. I don't think I'll solve this today anyway, but I *will* solve it."

Ben smiled at the young man's determination, his fortitude and adaptability.

"Alright," Ben said. He left Scott to work on his puzzle and headed back to his office. Whistling, he walked down the hallway, listening to the sound echoing off the walls, nodding at staff members as he passed. They nodded back.

After he had settled into his oversized office chair and made himself comfortable, Carlson booted up his laptop. He was excited to see what was happening at the Keller residence; his adrenaline was pumping; he felt a little like a peeping Tom.

But just as he was opening up the webcam, there came a knock on the door.

"Come in Scott," Carlson hollered, not bothering to look up.

The door opened. "Unfortunately, I'm not Scott, Dr. Carlson. I'm here to speak with you about the girl – about Samantha Jennings." It was Dr. Tom Whiting.

"Oh … it's you," Carlson said, not hiding his disappointment, "What about the girl, what now?"

"I'm worried about her, Ben. After doing some more testing, looking at MRI's of the hippocampus and other studies, I'm concerned about her implanted memories of her past life. In some of the tests we have conducted, the drugs the team and I developed for memory implantation and erasure, specifically T39 Triclomamine, have started breaking down in the test animals; what an unfortunate discovery after all this time. I thought the effects were permanent. Now I'm afraid the drugs might break down in Sam, too. Her true memories may slowly return, which could mean disaster for us. She could recall this place and what really happened.

"Dammit, don't you ever have any good news, man? I swear. So what can you and *your team* do about fixing this, Dr. Whiting?" Carlson calmly asked.

The small, balding man looked at Carlson with bafflement. He had come here expecting to be berated, put down, and castigated. Instead, he was responded to in a calm, professional, almost friendly manner. Strange.

"I do know that if I can give her another dose of T39 Triclomamine, we can keep her memory of the past intact for at least another year or two. That will give us time to alter the drug for permanence; I'm sure of it."

"A few years we may not have," Carlson replied, thinking of his recent visit with Richards.

"What do you mean?"

"Never mind, we should just kill the little bitch."

Ah, now there's the man I've come to know and hate, Whiting thought.

TWELVE

At the end of November 2002, Claire and Logan Keller officially became the adoptive parents of Samantha Jennings. The court proceedings went smoothly, and the Commissioner signed the paperwork into law, just as the lawyer, Dick Lambert, had said he would.

The next three weeks were some of the best times Logan and Claire could recall in recent years. They took Samantha to the zoo, ate hot dogs in the park, took Axle on long walks, went to the mall, to the movies - did all the wondrous things normal families did. Claire was amazed at how quickly the little girl had adapted and was even more amazed at how close they had become in such a short time.

Now, on Thursday morning, Logan and Claire were sitting at the kitchen table, hands wrapped around their coffee mugs, lost in thought when Logan suddenly blurted, "I called Thelma yesterday."

Claire looked up from her coffee. "Really?"

"Really."

"I bet she was excited to hear from you. Are you going to see her? Did you tell her all about Samantha?"

Logan smiled. "Of course I did Claire. And that is exactly why I called her. I think it would be good for both of them to meet. Samantha would have a grandmother, and Thelma would have a granddaughter to spoil. And we would have a babysitter when we need some time to ourselves." His smile grew. "I'm going to see her tomorrow afternoon."

"Oh, I'm so happy!" Claire said, beginning to tear up.

The next day, after a busy morning, they had lunch together, and then Claire put Samantha down for a nap. Logan kissed his wife and headed up the street to see Thelma.

After Logan had left, Claire checked on Samantha. She found her breathing heavily and peacefully. She was in a deep sleep. Claire stood in the doorway of her daughter's bedroom for a few minutes more, just watching Samantha sleep, still marveling at the good fortune that had come their way. Then she closed the door softly and went to take a shower.

Twenty minutes later, after Claire had finished her shower and stepped out of the tub to dry off, Samantha was standing in the doorway. The girl had a glazed, vacant look in her eyes. She was holding the headless body of her plastic doll, which was hanging limply in her left hand. The other hand held the severed doll's head by its long yellowish hair. A thin line of blood leaked from Samantha's left nostril.

Not bothering to grab a towel, Claire moved quickly to the little girl, wrapping her arms around her. "Honey, are you okay? What happened?" she asked, looking from Sam to the doll, to the trickle of blood coming from her nose. None of this made any sense.

Before she could think of what to do next, Sam spoke, but it wasn't the sound of a little girl. It was the voice of a grown woman. "Thelma is dead. Scott. Carlson. They did this." She pushed Claire away and crumpled to the linoleum in a fetal position, sound asleep, still clutching the dismembered doll in both hands.

"God help us," Claire whispered, bewildered. Even after the hot shower, she felt cold. Her hands were shaking. She looked down at the little girl, who seemed serene now. Tentatively, Claire reached for the doll's head, trying to release Sam's hold on it without waking her. She was successful at removing the doll's head from Sam's grip. The girl just moaned softly and curled up even tighter.

"This is just sleepwalking; it will pass," Claire mumbled to herself.

But for some reason, she didn't believe that.

Claire scooped Samantha off the floor and carried her back to her bedroom. The girl never stirred as Claire tucked the covers up around her neck. She was in such a deep sleep that nothing could wake her.

Suddenly Claire didn't feel well. *I think I'm gonna puke.* She ran into the bathroom. Then came the bang of the toilet seat, followed by retching, as Claire Keller hung her head over the toilet, purging herself of what she had witnessed.

THIRTEEN

In the darkness, Sylvia Tran picked up the phone and dialed her friend Anna Day. It was three o' clock in the morning. Sylvia couldn't sleep. It wasn't that she hadn't tried. Every time she laid her head on the pillow and closed her eyes, her thoughts turned to the little girl. She needed to talk to someone, and that person should not be associated with the project or New Life; she didn't trust them.

Sylvia paced the small apartment, biting her lower lip, listening to the ringing of the phone on the other end. On the ninth ring, just as Sylvia was about to hang up, a sleepy voice answered.

"This better be an emergency," the woman said, yawning.

"It is Anna, it really is – I need to talk to you. Sorry to bother you so late ... I mean so early ... or whatever. I can't sleep." Sylvia was nervously twisting her short, reddish-golden hair, something she hadn't done since she was a child.

"Sylvia? What's going on, are you okay?"

"Actually, no ... no, I'm not Anna. I'm not okay. I need some help, some guidance here. I would appreciate it if you would come over – I ... I can't talk about this, don't want to talk about this, over the phone."

"Wow Sylvia, why all the mystery?" Anna was fully awake now, intrigued.

"I just told you. I can't talk about this over the phone!"

"Okay, okay, calm down. I'll come over, but you're gonna owe me big time. I'll be a wreck at work later today, you know that, don't you?"

"Sorry Anna," Sylvia said meekly. "How soon can you get here?"

"Give me thirty minutes. Good thing for you that I didn't bring home that hunk of a man I met last night. I wouldn't have answered the phone; in fact, I probably would have turned the ringer off. God, he was gorgeous. Bet he's good in—"

"Anna, please."

"All right, sorry. He was gorgeous, though," Anna mumbled. "I'm on my way, see you in thirty minutes or less, like Dominoes," she said, laughing.

"Don't forget the file," Sylvia added.

There was a long pause. And then quietly: "Yeah…okay."

Sylvia sighed, pressing the END button on her cell.

Sitting down on the couch, in the darkness, Sylvia wondered if sharing details of the project, and her concerns, was such a good idea – involving an outsider like Anna might bring consequences – painful consequences. If she were careful, though, nobody would find out; no one would know. Sylvia trusted Anna more than anyone else; she was like a sister. Although not a religious woman, Sylvia now prayed that she was doing the right thing.

Reaching over, she switched on the table lamp next to the couch, casting shadows around the small living area of her apartment. She let her eyes adjust to their newfound light, then got up and went into her bedroom. Grabbing her robe, she caught a glimpse of herself in the dresser mirror. *I look awful,* she thought.

As she put on the fluffy white robe, there was a knock on the door. She switched off the bedroom light, crossed the living room and opened the door.

"Anna—"

"Hello Miss Tran, how are you this morning? Or is it night? Too early … or late to tell," Briggs said, pushing his way inside, knocking Sylvia to the floor. "One sound bitch and you're dead, got it?"

Looking up at Briggs, Sylvia nodded.

Coming in behind Briggs was that bastard, McFadden. What the hell were they doing here anyway? Why all the rough stuff?

"Well, well, well," McFadden said, rubbing his beard. "I've been waiting for this day, Sylvia. I knew all along you weren't one hundred percent with the program. I sense these things, you know. Now take Briggs here," he said, gesturing at the six-foot-two, hundred seventy pound rail of a man, "we can always count on him, can't we Lester?"

Briggs nodded. "Yessir, ya sure can, always." He smiled, revealing a set of teeth that looked as if they hadn't seen a toothbrush in twenty years.

Still on the carpet, afraid to get up, Sylvia said, "I-I don't understand, what are you two doing here? What did I do?"

"Like most women, you're just a stupid bitch," McFadden said. "You don't get it, do you? We've been keeping a close eye on you, Sylvia, and know everything you've been up to, including calling your friend Anna."

Shocked, she said, "You tapped my phone? You bastard!" She scrambled to her feet, but before she could take two steps, Briggs stepped in, hitting her in the face. Hard. Blood squirted from her broken nose, and she fell back to the carpet, screaming.

Briggs was on her in a second, placing one gloved hand over her mouth, silencing her. "I told you not to scream, didn't I? Huh? Didn't I?" He was inches from her face now, sniffing her blood as if he were sniffing a fine wine.

McFadden watched the festivities with his arms crossed on his massive chest, smiling. "I would suggest that you do what this greasy little man tells you. He packs quite a punch for such a skinny guy, no? Now, let's all just calm down. We can sit and talk while we wait for your friend Anna."

Stumbling to her feet, holding her broken nose, Sylvia said, "Please leave her out of this; she doesn't know a thing."

Briggs laughed. "You sound nasally, like you broke your nose or something."

The white robe Sylvia was wearing was no longer white; the front had now turned a reddish-purple color. "Let me at least get something for my nose, something to plug up the bleeding, please?" Sylvia asked. The skin under and around her eyes was starting to bruise from the blow. She was frightened – not for herself, but for Anna.

"Sure, go ahead," McFadden replied, "we're not animals."

"And is it okay if I use the bathroom?"

"Only if I can watch," Briggs said with excitement.

"Knock it off you pervert," McFadden said, "let the lady do what she needs to do."

"Thank you," Sylvia said, struggling to suck in air through her broken nose. She went into the bathroom, quietly locking the door behind her. Grabbing some cotton balls from under the sink, she crammed them up her nose, stifling the bleeding as best she could. Opening the right sink drawer, she found what she was after: a pair of manicure scissors. She didn't have a clue what she was going to do with them, but she knew one thing: they were sharp. From the first aid kit, she got a roll of medical tape, tearing off three strips. Using these strips of tape, Sylvia attached the small scissors high up and back of the inside of her left thigh, praying that Briggs wouldn't try to cop a feel. She flushed the toilet and came out of the bathroom.

The two men watched her carefully. "Come here," McFadden demanded. "Let me see what you have in your pockets."

Oh shit, they're going to frisk me, she thought. She was nauseous now; she didn't know if it was from her broken nose or pure fright.

Sylvia walked over to the two men and turned out her pockets. They were empty except for some balled up snotty Kleenex.

"Open your robe," McFadden said.

Making certain she was facing both men, she opened her robe while keeping her knees and thighs together. Only wearing a pair of white cotton panties, no bra, Sylvia knew that Briggs was getting his rocks off staring at her breasts. She didn't care, though, she was too worried about keeping the scissors out of sight and preferred for Briggs to keep his eyes on her chest, not on her legs.

Bryce McFadden had no interest in her sexually, and that suited her just fine. He instructed her to belt up after the perfunctory once over. Briggs seemed deeply disappointed when she closed her robe; Sylvia shuddered at the thought of that freak even touching her.

"Sit down Sylvia," McFadden said, pointing to the couch. "We're going to wait for your friend Anna together, but I think we should have a little chat before she gets here."

Sylvia did as she was told, sitting on the leather couch. Briggs was wandering around her apartment, fingering pictures, looking at books, mumbling some inane comments from time to time, looking bored.

"What about him?" she asked, nodding to the thin man walking around her apartment.

"Well you see, Briggs is what we call an imbecile, an idiot. But he is good at some things – like following directions, doing as he's told, unlike some people who want to think for themselves," he said, looking at her.

"You talking about me?"

"Let's just say that you should've done what was asked of you and not stuck your nose where it doesn't belong. Should've let the people higher up on the food chain take care of things and just followed their orders. Isn't that what they pay you that huge amount of money for? Huh?"

"How do you know what I get paid?" she asked.

"I am head of security and I know everything about everyone on staff at New Life, Miss Tran, including Dr. Carlson. Being a former detective has its perks. I know people; I can get any information I need. I—"

There was a knock at the door.

Lester Briggs turned his attention from the painting he was intensely studying, as if he could find the meaning of life within its strokes, and addressed McFadden: "I'll get it, Boss, bet it's that Anna woman."

"Of course it is. Who else would it be at this time of the morning, you dimwit," McFadden replied, shaking his head.

Briggs went to the front door and yanked it open. The Caucasian woman on the other side looked to be about thirty or so. She was dressed in white cotton slacks and a red pullover sweater. Her blonde hair hung loosely around her shoulders; a handbag was draped over her left side. Her lips were painted bright red, in contrast to her blonde hair.

Briggs grabbed the woman by her right arm, yanked her into the room and slammed the door.

As she was stumbling into the apartment from the force of Briggs's violent thrust, trying to keep her balance, Anna turned toward Briggs while simultaneously producing a silencer-equipped Walther P22 from her purse.

Before he could react, she shot Lester Briggs in the face.

Without hesitation, Anna Day turned to McFadden. He was fumbling for his ankle holster and the gun buried within it. Sylvia noticed with smug satisfaction that he was no longer the cool, got-everything-under-control man who had sat here just moments before. He had been reduced to a scared, shaking, nervous wreck. She bolted from the couch to give Anna a clear target.

Anna placed a bullet directly in McFadden's heart, killing him instantly.

Turning back to the screaming man on the floor, who was now lying in a widening circle of blood, Anna noticed that part of his lower jaw was missing. Lester's face was drawn into a permanent, hideous grin, revealing his ugly, stained teeth.

Anna raised the Walther, pointing it at the squirming thing on the floor.

"No. Let me," Sylvia said.

Anna raised her eyebrows and cocked her head. Her straight-lipped expression slowly turned into a grin. "Why, of course, my love. Be my guest," she said, handing the Walther to her friend.

Taking the gun from Anna, Sylvia pointed the barrel directly at Lester Briggs's crotch. "This is for all the little girls you probably fingered – hell, probably raped, you sick bastard!" She empty three rounds in his groin, and put another bullet in his head, silencing the man forever.

That done, she turned back to Anna and handed her the gun, shuddering. "I thought you'd never get here," she said. "You are one of the best agents I've seen. Quick on your feet and excellent at assessing a situation in a hurry."

"Well, you did give me the code you were in trouble. By the way, how did we ever come up with 'Don't forget the file?'"

"I don't remember," Sylvia said, shaking her head. "Doesn't matter now."

"Yeah, doesn't matter. You sure look great with that cotton stuffed up your nose and you sound even better. Is it broke?" Anna asked.

"What do you think?"

"Of course it is. Let me set it for you. I did go to nurse's training a few years back, you know."

Sylvia raised an eyebrow in disbelief. "No, I didn't know. You did?"

"I really did. Wanted to be a nurse before I decided on this lovely career change."

Sylvia smiled. She liked Anna. A lot. "Yeah, go ahead and set it, can't risk the emergency room right now anyway," she said, her voice sounding as if she had a terrible cold.

"Hold still, this is gonna hurt, but only for a second. Try not to scream. It's early, and we do have two dead bodies keeping us company. Wouldn't want the neighbors to get nosy."

Anna walked behind Sylvia, reached around to her nose, planted her feet, got into position and whispered, "Ready?"

"Yessss," Sylvia breathed.

There was an audible *crack!* As Sylvia's crooked nose popped into its natural place. She didn't scream, but tears ran down her face.

Anna went into the bathroom and came back with the first aid kit. As best she could, she bandaged her friend's nose. "That will have to do for now," she said, standing back with her hands on her hips, admiring her work.

"Thanks, Anna."

"You're welcome."

Sylvia unbelted her robe and removed the pair of scissors from the inside of her thigh.

"What the hell did you think you were going to do with those?" Anna asked. "Poke 'em to death?" She was laughing now.

Shaking her head, Sylvia said, "I don't know. I really don't know."

FOURTEEN

Scott Riley sat in the overstuffed chair in Ben Carlson's office, his head down, concentrating on the video game in his lap. Carlson was behind his desk, rubbing his chin thoughtfully as he perused the papers in front of him. He grunted.

Setting the papers down and looking at the boy, Ben said, "Put that stupid thing away, we have things to talk about – we have things to do."

"What do we need to talk about?" Scott asked, switching off the video game.

"First, I want you to give me your word that you won't hurt anyone unless you are instructed to do so. I don't want you drugged anymore, but I need to make sure that you don't use your gifts – like you did with Dr. Hammond – without my consent. Understand?"

"Yes, yes, I understand. I was just playing when that unfortunate thing happened with Dr. Hammond. It was an accident, really it was."

Carlson couldn't shake the feeling that he was conversing with something other than a seven-year-old. The boy sounded like a child and looked like a child, but he didn't act or speak like a child.

Placing his fat forearms on the desk and leaning closer, Carlson said, "It's time you and I went out into the real world, see what you can do in real situations with real people, not some game in a lab. You ready for that young man?"

"Of course I am."

"Excellent, just excellent." Carlson seemed almost giddy with excitement. "Okay, in a few days we will venture out of this place. I have some things to address before we can do that, but they won't take long. Not long at all."

"Leave Samantha alone, let me have her," Scott said. His tone made it clear that this was not a request.

For the first time in years, Carlson was unsure of himself. Rubbing his chin, he looked across his desk at the boy and thought, now I'm taking orders from a kid. That thought was quickly supplanted with: what if he can read my mind? He had no intention of letting his creation tell him what to do. But he was an intelligent man, and he intuitively knew that he had better appease Scott, tell him what he wanted to hear. He could always figure things out later.

"Why of course, Scott, the girl is yours, but what do you want with her?"

"Oh … I don't know yet, but I think we have some things we need to discuss, but it isn't a concern of yours, just leave her alone." He got up and walked to the door. "If you don't have anything else to talk about, I'm going back and work on some of those puzzles. Let me know when you're ready for our adventure into the real world."

"I need to be careful what I'm thinking about when I'm around that little shit," Ben muttered after Scott had gone. Suddenly realizing why Scott wanted Samantha to himself, he smiled. Maybe this could work to his advantage, after all. The uneasiness floated away, and Ben Carlson felt like his old self.

He left his office and went to his private quarters. He went into the kitchen, poured himself a drink, and then settled in on the comfortable leather sofa. On the coffee table in front of him was his personal HP laptop, which contained personal files, documents, and games he loved to play. But he didn't want any of those things now. Carlson wanted to watch the video feeds from the Keller place. He wanted to see how Samantha was fitting in with her new family and how Logan and Claire were adjusting to their adoptive daughter.

He flipped open the laptop and powered up the machine. Sipping his drink, he sat back and waited for the programs to load. When the hourglass turned into a pointer, Carlson sat up and clicked on the secure documents folder. Once opened, he went to the secure video file, clicked on it, typed in the required password and opened the feed.

Each icon on the screen had a date and time stamp. Carlson chose yesterday's video file, turned up the volume and once again sat back on the sofa. In anticipation, he took a long swallow from his drink. He felt flushed, and his heart started racing, excited at the prospect of eavesdropping on someone else's life, perhaps catching them doing personal things and listening to their intimate conversations when they thought they were alone.

At the click of a button, Carlson could view any area of the house. He first watched the bedroom. When there wasn't any activity, he switched to the master bath. Still nothing.

The living room was also empty.

Just as he was switching to the kitchen, a voice came over the intercom.

"Carlson, I need to talk to you – it's important!" There was an urgency in the man's voice.

"Dammit!" Carlson said, frustrated. He got up and walked over to the intercom. He pushed the talk button: "What's so important that it can't wait?"

"Let me in and I'll tell you. It's Mike, Dr. Carlson. Mike Romero, Charlie's friend."

Charlie was Richards's personal bodyguard and head of security for the Larenx Corporation. Mike had been with Charlie and Ralph when they'd approached Carlson about the project over seven years ago. He had seen and spoken with this man only briefly over the years; they had never become friends. Now Ben remembered what Charlie had told him that night so many years ago: If you are going to be a part of our little family, it might do you good to make friends.

"Right, okay," Carlson replied, buzzing him in.

Ben went to the outer office to greet the man. Mike Romero was tall, about six-three and pushing at least two-forty, if not more. But he wasn't fat. He looked like a man who worked out at least twice daily; he could break your neck with one arm tied behind his back. He had one of those thick necks found only on professional football players or professional wrestlers.

"Sit down Mr. Romero; you make me nervous standing there like that," Ben said.

"Thank you," Mike replied. His mellifluous voice in no way gave hint to the man's massive size.

"What's so important, has something happened?"

"Well … yes, actually. The security department has been monitoring the video feeds from the Keller place, and we stumbled across something today that has … well, let's say it has made us a little uneasy."

"Oh?" Carlson raised his eyebrows, perplexed. "I was just starting to go over the videos myself. Samantha has only been at the Keller's for what - a couple of days?"

"Yeah. But we heard the little girl mention Scott and …" He trailed off and looked down at his hands.

"And what? The little bitch mentioned my name, too, didn't she? Didn't she!"

Mike Romero didn't respond. He didn't even look up.

"Answer me man!"

Still not looking up, Mike said, "Yes, she mentioned you. But only once and she looked to be sleepwalking or something. I don't think the Keller woman gave it any weight. She took it as a dream or some problem from the girls' past. Don't think it is an issue."

"I am a problem from her past! And it is an issue! If you didn't think it was an issue, then why did you feel the need to come here and tell me?"

"She mentioned the Keller's next door neighbor, too, and that seemed to upset the woman more than anything. Neighbor has the same name as the kid's doll – Thelma. Weird, huh? Supposed to be some psychic or something, but I hear she's pretty good."

"We know of the Thelma woman. We know of all the Keller's neighbors. Most are average families with ordinary occupations: salesmen, store managers, small business owners, things like that. These are ordinary, everyday people. Except Thelma Grisham – she worries me. She knows all about Samantha and because she's close to the Kellers, I'm worried that she'll stick her nose where it shouldn't be stuck if you know what I mean." And why the hell am I telling you this? Carlson wondered.

"Oh … didn't realize you already knew. So what would you like us to do about it? What should I tell Ralph and Charles?" Mike asked, fidgeting again. He just wanted to get out of this office. Even though Carlson was a short, pudgy man, who probably couldn't run down the hall without having a heart attack, and Mike was in perfect shape, the man made him very uneasy, as if at any moment he might go off like a ruptured tank of propane.

"You tell Ralph and Charlie that we have it under control. If we need your assistance, we will let you know." He paused. "And relay a message to McFadden. Tell him I want Sylvia Tran watched carefully. Something about her bothers me."

"Okay, sure."

"Now please leave, I'm in the middle of something."

Without replying, Mike turned around and left. He was more than happy to leave.

In fact, he would prefer never to see or deal with Dr. Carlson again.

FIFTEEN

While Claire watched Samantha nap, Logan was on his way to Thelma's.

Except for a few white clouds in the west, the sky was a bright shade of blue, and the mercury had pushed past the fifty-degree mark, almost hot for November.

Both Logan and Claire were born in the Pacific Northwest. Although they had visited other places over the years, neither could fathom calling anywhere else home. The clean crispness of the air, the beauty of the trees, oceans, lakes and mountains more than made up for the amount of rainfall they had to endure being residents of Washington State.

Hands stuffed in the pockets of his jeans, Logan walked east along the sidewalk towards Thelma's two-story, white and gray home, feeling a little nervous. After all, he hadn't seen Thelma for almost a year – way too long.

He stepped up onto the porch and before he could ring the bell, the door opened. Thelma Grisham stood there with a huge grin, wearing an apron that read: HE DIDN'T MARRY ME FOR MY COOKING. Her hands were on her hips; her head cocked slightly to one side.

"Well? Whaddaya waiting for? An invite? You don't need an invitation Logan. You're always welcome here – you know that. Please, come in," she said.

"Hi Thelma," Logan said, stepping inside. "I must admit that I was nervous coming here to see you."

"Nervous? You're kidding me, aren't you? Why would you ever be nervous coming to visit me?"

"Because I haven't seen you … well … you know …"

"Since Harold died? Logan, relax a little, will you? After a year, I've come to terms with it – although in a way you might not understand – and it is time you do the same. Come into the parlor and have a seat. Want something to drink?"

"No, thanks," he replied, following her into the parlor. He sat down, wondering why he had made such a big deal of coming here in the first place. No matter his mood, Thelma had always made him feel comfortable as if he had come home. And, in a way, he had.

Thelma sat next to him. "I'm so glad you've finally come back to see me. Just like you were nervous about coming over, hon, I was scared that I might never see you again. I know that when we spoke on the phone, I said we wouldn't talk about … you know … psychic crap, but I just need to say one thing in my defense." She paused and looked at him as if asking permission.

"Go ahead, Thelma."

"When Harold died I was devastated. A few days later, after the funeral, he appeared at the foot of my bed …"

"Thelma—"

"Let me finish please," she said sternly.

"Okay, sorry," Logan said. He shifted in his chair.

"I thought I was dreaming or hallucinating or even going crazy. Don't you remember what I thought of all this psychic mumble jumble? It's all a scam; that's what I thought."

Logan smiled.

"But everything changed that night," Thelma continued, "because it was real. I don't know how to explain that I know it was real, but it was nonetheless. Anyway, as I read and learned, met so-called psychics, clairvoyants, dream interpreters and studied the paranormal, I came to believe. But I don't ask anyone else to believe as I do, I only ask that they leave me alone. Except you – I love you like a son, and I know that you think I've gone off the deep end – maybe Alzheimer's, old-age disease, whatever you want to call it – but I haven't Logan, I haven't gone off the deep end." She had taken his hand in both of hers, patting it softly while looking imploringly in his eyes.

"Thelma, how long have we known you? Twelve, maybe thirteen years? I never have, nor will I ever, think you're crazy – a little eccentric, perhaps, but crazy? Never. I had a tough time when Harold died, too. We became very close. But you know that, don't you?"

"Yes…yes, I do."

"And then when you started doing the psychic thing, well … it was a little much for me. I've come to realize, though, that it's not worth losing our relationship over. Nothing is worth that."

"I'm so glad to hear that," Thelma said, squeezing his hand. "I'd have to come hunt you down, and get my spirit friends to teach you a lesson."

Logan laughed. "Thelma, I need to talk with you about Samantha, the little girl Claire and I adopted. I know that Claire spoke with you a day or so before the adoption and – Thelma, are you alright?"

The old woman had turned pale, almost white, and she looked like she had just drunk a bottle of Liquid Plumber.

"I-I don't know. I really don't know. I feel sick," Thelma said, getting up and stumbling toward the bathroom. Logan jumped up, grabbed her by the arm to steady her, and helped her to the commode, where she promptly threw up. With trembling hands, she pulled off some toilet paper and wiped her mouth, smiling weakly. "Sorry."

"You need me to call the doctor or something?" Logan asked.

"No, no, I'm okay," she said.

They made their way back to the parlor and sat down.

"Logan, I need to tell you something. Something that I'm afraid might cause you to want to run away again, but I have to risk it. Because if something happens that might have been prevented I would never be able to forgive myself."

"Wow, why so serious all of a sudden?"

She smiled. "Because this is serious business, son. Don't think that it ain't. I'm going to talk to you about what I told you we wouldn't talk about if you came over, but I realized with you sitting here that I don't have a choice." She paused and sighed.

Logan could see the weariness now in her face and eyes. She looked not just tired, but exhausted. He wasn't sure if Thelma's exhaustion was a result of her being sick or from the dread of speaking of something she would rather keep to herself.

"Say what you need to say, Thelma," Logan said.

"Promise me one thing first. You promise me that you will listen all the way to the end before you leave - before you go stormin' off, okay?"

"Of course." He was worried. In all the years he had known Thelma, Logan couldn't remember her ever being this secretive or this troubled about anything. His palms were sweating; he absently wiped them on his jeans.

"Something happened after Claire left when she was here last week."

"What?"

"I came in here, sat where you're sitting now when – and I'm sorry about this Logan – a voice, a loud voice came into my head, screaming Ouija board!"

Thelma watched Logan closely as she recounted the story of Harold speaking to her through this medium, her fingers taking on a life of their own, out of her control.

Logan sat back, rubbing his face, but he did not interrupt Thelma's story. He had promised to hear it through to the end.

"And then the planchette began to move on its own. I was standing by the table, I looked down, and it was moving. It then revealed a word supposedly associated with Samantha, and that's when I passed out."

"What was the word, Thelma? What was the word?"

"Death."

"Oh come on Thelma!" Logan said, getting up. "Why are you telling me this? Why?"

"Because I need to warn you, Harold is warning you ... us, that's why. Please ... please calm down."

Running his sweaty hands through his hair, Logan looked at Thelma. He knew this wasn't her fault, but it didn't take away the anger. He drew in a deep breath and waited a moment.

"I'm sorry to have blown up like that ... it's ... she's my daughter for goodness sakes."

"I understand. Logan, I'm not sure what it means, but I do know that there's trouble surrounding this girl. She might not be the cause of the trouble, but I think we need to find out. I know someone who can help. I've helped him find missing people in the past year, and he owes me some favors. He will be glad to help; I'm sure of it."

"Who is he Thelma? Who are you talking about?"

"His name is Aaron Reynolds. He was with the Seattle PD for over twenty years. Worked his way up to detective, then quit to start his own private practice. He has a stellar reputation as an honest, hard-working, and fair businessman with a spotless reputation. Aaron is passionate about the cases he takes, Logan, so he won't take a case unless he believes in it."

"And what kind of case do we have here Thelma? Some eccentric elderly woman with an Ouija board heard some voices in her head about an adopted little girl, who is nothing but trouble? Philip Marlowe or Sam Spade would be fighting to take a case like this," Logan said, shaking his head. "What makes you think this man - this Aaron guy - would even be slightly interested?"

"He believes ..."

"He believes? What's that mean?"

"Aaron has witnessed first-hand the power of the mind and the miracles of faith. He will believe, without any reservation whatsoever, what I share with him. I haven't led him down the wrong path yet. I've helped him solve a few cases, find some people he never would have found."

"I don't know about this Thelma. I'll have to run this by Claire."

"Of course." She paused and smiled. "I'll be right back, want to get you his contact information in case Claire talks some sense into you." Standing slowly, bones popping like sparks in a fire, Thelma groaned. Slightly hunched over, she left the room at a slow walk.

She's getting older; she'll be joining Harold soon, Logan thought.

Smiling, Thelma returned to the room. "Here's a few of Aaron's business cards, one for you and one for your lovely wife; you know, the sensible one," she said, handing them to Logan.

Turning one of the cards over, Logan studied it. He suddenly felt numb, as if he had been transported to another dimension, another world. Everything seemed so surreal now.

At the top of the card was a blue and white circular logo. An image of the United States, in blue, was stamped in the middle with the letters NCISS superimposed in white. Around the outer circle, also in white, were the words: NATIONAL COUNCIL OF INVESTIGATION AND SECURITY SERVICES. And below that: REYNOLDS INVESTIGATIONS. In the lower left corner was a magnifying glass with a cartoonish eye staring through the lens; opposite that, in the lower right corner, was Aaron's contact information and a pair of binoculars.

Cute.

"Thanks … I guess," he said, putting the cards in his wallet.

"You're welcome. Please call Aaron and tell him Thelma sent you, all right? If you want, I'll call him for—"

"I have to speak with Claire first. You know that."

"Yes, yes, I know. But when you do call Aaron," Thelma said, sitting back down, "have him call me so we can discuss what I know of the situation."

"If."

"What?"

"If we call him. *If.* We'll see," Logan said.

"Okay," Thelma replied, sounding resigned. "I'm sure glad you came by, it's been way, way too long. What have you been doing with yourself? Besides adopting, I mean."

"Running a business, keeping Claire in the opulence she has become so accustomed to, cleaning house, taking vacations every three months or so to exotic places, and staying in touch with the mistress. You know, the usual stuff."

"Same old Logan," she said, shaking her head and giggling that cute old lady giggle. She must've been a man-killer back in her day, Logan thought, she's so delightful.

Her smile suddenly faded. It turned into a grimace of pain. She opened her mouth to speak, yet nothing came out but a barely audible gasp.

"Thelma?"

The white of her right eye turned dark red. Logan noticed a small trickle of blood, like a tear, dripping from the corner. Thelma's nose started to bleed. She tried to stand, hanging on to the side of the chair to keep her balance.

Scared now, Logan reached out to her. "Thelma!"

She tried again to talk. Nothing.

With horror, Logan saw blood pooling in her left eye. Blood was also leaking from her ears and nose.

What the hell?

"Thelma! Thelma!" he yelled, grabbing the old woman before she fell. "What's happening? WHAT'S HAPPENING?"

Once more, Thelma opened her mouth. This time, however, Logan was greeted with a gush of blood; Thelma hemorrhaged from the mouth.

Soaked in blood, Logan laid Thelma on the floor. She was unconscious now but still bleeding.

Trembling, Logan fumbled in his pocket for his cell. He pressed and held 1 with a bloody thumb.

"911, what is your emergency?" asked a female voice from the other end of the phone.

"I-I … I need help," Logan panted. He was scared and shaking and couldn't seem to catch his breath. "A woman, Thelma Grisham, is in need of medical attention!" he managed to yell.

"Sir, please calm down so I may help you," said the operator. "What is the nature of her injuries?"

"Jesus lady, send an ambulance!" he screamed.

"An ambulance is on its way, sir. Now, what is the nature of her injuries?" she repeated calmly.

"I don't know. She just started bleeding. From the eyes, the nose, ears … everywhere." Logan was hysterical now.

"Help is on the way, sir. You said she started bleeding from her eyes, nose and ears?"

"Y-yes."

"I will relay that to the paramedics, sir. They should be arriving shortly. Please stay on the line."

How can she be so calm?

"What is your name please?"

"Logan Keller, I live a couple of houses down," he replied quietly.

"How old is Thelma Grisham?" the woman asked.

"Maybe about seventy or so, not sure …"

"And you are located at 2012 Black Hills Drive?"

"That's Thelma's address, yes," Logan replied. He was down on the floor, sitting in a pool of blood, holding Thelma's head.

"They are almost there sir."

In the distance, Logan heard sirens. As they approached the residence, their sirens grew louder. A Fire Department Aid Unit with MOUNTAIN VIEW FIRE AND RESCUE on the side pulled up first. Behind the Aid unit was Black Ridge Fire Engine #98, which pulled across the street.

"Have the medics arrived?" the operator asked.

"Yes."

"Thank you, sir, they will take over now," she said, terminating the call.

They're too late, he thought. How am I going to tell Claire?

Hugging Thelma tightly, Logan Keller did something he hadn't done in years.

He wept.

SIXTEEN

Pronounced dead at the scene by the paramedics, Thelma was subsequently zipped up in a body bag. The next stop would be the County Coroner's office.

After about thirty minutes of questioning from the local authorities regarding the circumstances surrounding her death, Logan was informed that he was free to go, but to be available if they needed to speak to him again.

It was almost five o' clock; the air was turning chilly. He started back home, pulling his coat tighter around his chest. He was a mess: hair awry and dotted with specks of blood, puffy, bruised eyes from his prolonged crying fit, and his white T-shirt turned dark with Thelma's blood.

Head down and shoulders slumped, Logan walked up the steps to his home feeling a mixture of fear and anger. He knew the anger was part of grieving. His fear, though, was the realization that what Thelma told him was true. Danger – and death – surrounded his little girl.

He walked into the house. Relieved that Claire and Sam weren't downstairs to see him in such a shocking state, Logan quickly made his way to the bathroom. He tore off his coat, then his ruined T-shirt and scrubbed the dried blood from his hands and arms until they were raw. Looking into the mirror, he noticed the blood on his face. He also saw a frightened, confused man who barely resembled the happy, joyful person he had been only that morning.

Logan scrubbed the blood from his face. The cold water helped to clear his head. Looking at his reflection, Logan whispered, "Get it together man, you need to be strong for Claire and the child. The best thing to do is tell her the truth; tell her what happened." He shuddered. Turning off the water, he grabbed the bloody clothes and opened the door.

His breath caught in his throat.

Claire was standing there with her arms crossed under her breasts.

Seeing Logan, her eyes widened in disbelief and her arms dropped to her sides. Her jaw went slack. "W-what the hell happened to you? What—?"

"Wait a minute Claire, just wait please," Logan said, coming out of the bathroom, quickly surveying the living room. "Where's Sam?"

"Upstairs in her room playing with Axle. What's happened to you, Logan? Is Thelma okay?"

He looked his wife directly in the eyes. "No ... no, she's not Claire. Thelma passed away about an hour ago." His eyes were filling with tears again. A few drops spilled out of the corners and ran down his cheeks.

Grabbing the counter to steady herself, Claire bent over and took three deep breaths. As soon as she knew she wasn't going to pass out, she straightened up and said, "Oh ... Logan. Oh my God ... no, no."

Logan dropped his clothes to the floor and went to his wife. Without speaking, he put his arms around her and hugged her tight. Claire buried her face in his chest and sobbed. After a few minutes, she pushed off and looked up. "She didn't even get to meet Sam ... she wanted so much to be a grandmother ... w-what ... how'd she die? Heart attack?"

"Yeah, probably," Logan lied, "we'll have to wait for the coroner's report to be sure, though." There wasn't any sense in telling Claire how she died. It didn't change the fact that Thelma was dead. And he didn't see the point in recounting the bizarre circumstances surrounding her demise.

"Something...something happened while you were gone," Claire said. Her voice was barely audible. Even though she was looking at her husband, she wasn't seeing him. Logan knew that she was crawling into herself. It was her escape from the pain and her way to cope. He had seen this look only twice in thirteen years: when her father had died, and when her good friend Karen's child had been stillborn.

"Please don't go away," Logan said, "Samantha needs you, and I need you. We can get through this together."

Claire shivered. Logan noticed a little more clarity in her eyes, but she still seemed distant when she spoke. "Sam came into the bathroom. I was... showering. She had her doll. She had decapitated it. Ripped its head clean off. She was bleeding. Not the doll. Sam. From the nose. Just a trickle. But still bleeding. She said Thelma was...oh no...she said..." Claire dropped to her knees then, unable to go on.

Logan quickly glanced at the stairs, praying that Samantha would stay in her room so she wouldn't have to see them like this. "What did she say?"

"She said Thelma is dead. She *knew* Logan. How could she know? Did she dream it? It did look like she was sleepwalking. This can't just be coincidence, can it?"

Ignoring the question, Logan said, "Is that all?"

"No. She said Scott, Carlson; they did this. And then she collapsed."

"Who the hell is Scott Carlson?"

"I think she meant two different names. Scott *and* Carlson. Probably from her dream. I don't know those names, do you?"

"Nope." Logan was biting his lip. "And it wasn't a heart attack that killed Thelma, at least I don't think so."

"What? I thought you just said it was." Claire looked confused.

"I didn't want to give you the details because I didn't want to worry you or freak you out. But in light of what you just told me, I think you need to know. Thelma just started bleeding from every orifice, as if she was being squeezed from the inside out. My coat and shirt are covered in her blood, and so were my arms and face. That's why I was in the bathroom. I was washing off her blood."

Claire was horrified. "How awful! What would cause something like that?"

"I don't know, I don't know," Logan said, shaking his head.

"God what a day this has been; this has, by far, been the worst day that I can remember."

"Well, since it's already the worst day of our lives, and we're probably already in shock, let me tell you the conversation I had with Thelma before ... well ... you know."

"There's more? It gets worse?"

Before Logan could reply, he heard a child's voice from behind him say, "Hi Logan, where are your clothes?"

Turning around, Logan saw Axle sitting on his haunches, grinning and wagging his tail. Samantha had her arms around the dog's neck and was hugging him fiercely, the way she used to hug her doll.

Now that the doll was destroyed, perhaps she would find the solace she required in the dog. At least Axle was a living, breathing animal instead of some inanimate object.

"Hi, sweetheart. Yes I'm home, and I took my shirt off because I was just going to change," Logan said. He tried his best to seem normal, like this was just another ordinary day but wasn't sure if he pulled it off.

"Honey, why don't you go upstairs and play a little more, okay? Logan and I need to talk about adult things. I'll be up in a little bit, all right sweetheart?" Claire said.

"Adult stuff ... yuck. Okay, I'll go up to my room and play. Come on dog," Sam said, pulling on Axle's collar.

Axle knew the little girl was okay now, not like before. Before, when the little girl woke from her nap, she had a sour scent, as if something was horribly wrong with her. But now she smelled of peaches and flowers, the way young humans – especially girl humans – were supposed to smell. Her voice was right again: loving, kind, full of mystery and excitement, not like the sharp, rage-filled tone Axle had heard earlier that day.

That girl was gone.

Axle happily turned and followed Samantha back up the stairs to her room; he would be stroked and petted, perhaps have his belly rubbed.

After Sam and Axle had gone back upstairs, Logan went in search of a shirt and Claire went in search of a drink. She knew that the implications of what happened to Thelma, and the experience with Samantha hadn't truly hit her yet. She was in shock. *But do people in shock know they're in shock?* she wondered.

In the kitchen, she poured a straight shot of whiskey and killed it in one quick swallow. It burned, but she hardly noticed. Then she poured another and killed that too. So what if she got drunk? On second thought, she better be careful. After the weirdness of today, who knew what might happen next. Better keep a clear head, at least for now.

Logan returned wearing a blue hooded sweatshirt with SEATTLE SEAHAWKS emblazoned across the front. After polishing off her third drink, Claire retreated to the living room and lay down on the sofa, waiting for the booze to calm her nerves. Logan joined her.

"Getting drunk?" he asked, smelling the whiskey on her breath. "Can't say I blame you, after all that's happened."

"Not drunk, just trying to take the edge off," she replied. "If we didn't have Samantha now, I'd get blasted." Her smile was weak and forced.

"Me too."

"Logan, what's happening? I mean really, this just seems out of the Twilight Zone or something. I … I'm not sure what to do, where to go from here. Any suggestions?"

He sighed and produced the business card Thelma had given him. Without a word, he handed it to her.

She took it and looked at it for a minute, turning it over in her hands. "Private detective? Why?"

Logan told her about Thelma's experience with the Ouija board after Claire had left. Logan took his wife's hands in his. "And now she's dead." For the first time in their marriage, Claire heard confusion in her husband's voice. Confusion mixed with fear.

"You don't think Thelma's death had anything to do with Sam, do you? How could it? Sam was here with me the whole time you were gone and I—"

"No, no, no … I don't think Sam is capable of such brutality. We do need to do something, though. We need to contact this Aaron guy and see what he can find out about Samantha's past. I don't think we have the whole story. I'm sure everything wasn't in those files. I also think we need to get her to a good psychiatrist. She's going to need more than love and a place to live, Claire." He squeezed his wife's hand and shook his head. This is turning out to be a lot more than what we signed up for, huh?"

"You can say that again."

"This is turning—"

Claire playfully clapped him on the shoulder. "I love you. I'm scared Logan."

"Me too," he nodded, "me too."

SEVENTEEN

Sylvia Tran shucked out of her robe and into a blue dress. She put on some makeup, combed her reddish hair to the side and applied a light film of lipstick.

She came out of the bathroom, switching off the light. Anna Day was propped up against the headboard of the king-size bed, reading the latest issue of People magazine. "You know that Brad Pitt feeds Coca-Cola to his little ones for breakfast to get them going? Nothing like drugging your children first thing in the morning, I always say," Anna said with a grin.

"What are you doing in here?"

"I'm not going to sit out there with a couple of corpses. And need I remind you that one of them is missing half his face? I think not, young Miss Tran, not today."

"I see your point. Did you call this mess into the office to have a cleaner sent?"

"I did," Anna said, popping her gum. "I'm a professional, remember, and I follow procedure to the T."

"Good. We need to leave before they get here, we don't want to be associated with any of this."

"Where are we going?" Anna asked.

"A little camping trip my dear," Sylvia said, "out into Mt. Baker National Forest."

Anna just looked at her and blew a big bubble, popping it all over her brightly painted lips.

Sylvia shook her head and went to the closet, retrieving a large, brown suitcase. She tossed it on the bed, at Anna's feet, and began packing the essentials: underwear, warm clothes, toiletries, and gloves.

"We need to stop by my place. I need to get some clothes too," Anna said.

"Okay, but you'll need to be fast."

"How long you think we'll be gone?"

"Not sure. A few weeks, a month, maybe longer."

"Great. Just great," Anna said, blowing another big bubble. This time, she was careful not to pop it on her face.

Sylvia reached under the mattress and pulled out a Smith & Wesson .38 Chiefs Special. She winked at Anna and tossed the weapon on top of the clothes in the open suitcase. Then she went to the closet and came back with a Smith & Wesson 9mm SW 1911. From the bottom bureau drawer, Sylvia grabbed the neatly folded pants and threw them on the floor. She removed the false bottom, revealing the M&P 15 VTAC II 5.56mm NATO Rifle.

Turning back to Anna, with the rifle in her hand, she smiled and said, "In this day a girl's just gotta be prepared for anything, ya know?"

"You planning on going to war?"

"Yes, in fact, I think the war has just begun."

Anna studied her friend for a moment. "You're serious, aren't you Sylvia. You really think there's going to be trouble, don't you?"

"Do those two bodies out in the living room look like trouble?" Before Anna could reply, Sylvia said, "Of course they do."

She placed the rest of the weapons in the suitcase, zipped it up. "Let's get going, lots to do."

Anna jumped off the end of the bed, chewing her gum like a six-year-old, and followed Sylvia out of the bedroom. They were careful not to step in the blood as they gathered what they required: cell phones, laptops, cameras and some beverages for the trip.

Sylvia had moved into this apartment six months ago; she knew that she would not return to this place. It was owned by her employer and had come to her completely furnished. She just took her personal items. In this line of work, you were always on the move. You got used to it.

Anna and Sylvia rode the elevator down to the covered parking garage, where Sylvia's car – a black 1999 Mercedes Benz C300 – was parked.

"What do we do about my car?" Anna asked as she climbed into the passenger side.

"The office knows that your car is here, they'll take care of it. No worries."

Sylvia pulled out of the garage and onto Eighth Street. It was almost six o' clock in the morning. The sun was just coming up over the horizon like a big yellowish-red balloon. There were a few wisps of clouds off to the east. Otherwise, the day was clear, the sky a hazy blue. Frost was on the windshield of the cars parked at the curb, and the sidewalks twinkled like the sun glittering off the ocean.

After they merged onto I-405 and headed north, Anna looked over at Sylvia. "Don't forget to stop by my place." At this time of day traffic was light, but in another hour it would be bumper-to-bumper with workday commuters. Sylvia hoped to be well out of town and headed to the mountains before that.

"We'll swing by your place, but you need to hurry, okay? Before traffic gets heavy. Can you get done in fifteen minutes with what you need to do?"

"Sure, if I have to."

"Good. And by the way Anna, you were great on the phone - keeping up the whole charade and all - that should keep them off our tail for a while."

"Thanks, Sylvia, but you should win an Oscar for your performance. Anyone listening in would have no idea that you weren't scared, that—"

"Oh, I was scared alright," Sylvia said.

"See what I mean? You're a great actress!"

"And I can't believe how good you are with a gun, how athletic you are … all that training has paid off."

"Thanks," Anna said, embarrassed.

At 6:45 am, Sylvia pulled the Mercedes into an empty stall in front of Anna's complex.

Anna jumped out and ran inside while Sylvia stayed in the car.

As soon as Anna disappeared into the building, Sylvia called Fred. He answered on the third ring.

"Sylvia, you on the move?" His voice was soothing, almost intoxicating. Fred looked great for a fifty-three-year-old - distinguished was the word that came to Sylvia's mind. He was the main reason she had been with the agency for the last nine years. Fred Richart was a man of integrity, honesty and a genuine love of humankind. He believed in his mission, in his agency. Although a man of few words, his passion was unequaled.

"Yes, we're on the move. I figure we should be there in a couple of hours. We had to make a quick stop so Anna could get her personal belongings and some warm clothes."

"Okay. I'll be at the cabin in less than an hour. I'm taking the chopper. I'll have more information for both you and Anna when you arrive."

"Okay, see you soon."

"Goodbye Sylvia," he said and hung up.

Sylvia sighed and switched on the radio. Reclining, she closed her eyes. Meatloaf's *Paradise by the Dashboard Light* came through the car's speakers and Sylvia thought of Fred. She was about to drift off when she heard a pounding on the driver's window. Sitting up with a start, she looked to her left, half-expecting to see a gun pointed at her face.

It was Anna. She was laughing.

Sylvia rolled down the window, furious. "What the hell! You scared me to death Anna! And what's so funny?"

"I-I'm sorry I ... I scared you," she said, trying to catch her breath. "But you should've seen the look on your face! Priceless! The car was locked, I tried the passenger side, even knocked, but you must not have been able to hear me over the music."

Anna was carrying a large suitcase and wearing a heavy overcoat. She was ready.

Anna had only been with the agency for two years, but when she came on board – and the agency was very picky about whom they took – Sylvia liked her instantly. She was vivacious, spunky, fearless (which could be a problem), and fun. Anna reminded her of a little kid when she giggled or popped her bubble gum that she loved so much, or when she laughed.

Sylvia pushed the unlock button on the Mercedes and Anna ran around to the passenger side. She opened the door and leaned in. "Would you pop the trunk please so I can get rid of this huge thing?" she said, nodding at the large suitcase hanging from her arm.

"Sure," Sylvia replied, pulling the lever under the dashboard. Anna ran around back, put her suitcase in the trunk, and rejoined Sylvia.

They headed back onto I-405 northbound. Traffic wasn't bad. Most of the commuters were headed south towards downtown Seattle. Sylvia looked at Anna and said, "Why don't you get some shuteye? I'll wake you when we get there."

"Okay, sounds good. I am a little tired, rough night you know." She smiled. "You're sure we're not being tracked, that there's not a transponder or some tracking device on the car?"

"The agency swept it already Anna, don't worry. They don't miss a trick. We're clean. Now get some rest."

Anna sighed. "I was afraid back there too Sylvia. I thought I might get killed, and I wondered, just for a moment, if it was all worth it."

"It's worth it, Anna, it really is. You'll see. Now get some rest."

"Okay." She made a makeshift pillow out of her jacket, leaned her head against the passenger window and closed her eyes.

From the 405, Sylvia merged onto I-5 northbound. The snow-capped Cascade Mountain Range was pristine, evoking a sense of peace and wonder. As a child, Sylvia had explored these mountains and forests, sometimes for days at a time, enjoying the solitude, the clean, crisp smell of the air, the sound of the running water and that feeling of being so alive that communion with nature always awakened in her.

Anna was snoring softly next to her.

They never made it to the cabin.

EIGHTEEN

Logan nervously punched in the numbers from the business card he was holding. It rang four times before he got voicemail: *You've reached Aaron Reynolds, private investigator. I'm sorry I'm not available right now, probably in a standoff or tied up somewhere. Please leave your name and number and I'll get back to you promptly.*

"Yes ... uh, hi, Mr. Reynolds. My name is Logan Keller, and I'm a ... was ... uh ... a friend of Thelma Grisham's; she told me to call you. I ... we ... that is – my wife and I need your help with something."

Logan stumbled through his message and then left his cell phone number. He hung up and looked at Claire, who was sitting on the sofa next to him, cradling and rocking Samantha in her arms.

"Sounds like our Mr. Reynolds is also a comedian," Logan said.

"What's a commodian?" Sam asked.

Logan smiled at the little girl. "Comedian, honey. That's somebody who makes jokes about things."

"Why?"

"Oh, I don't know. When you make fun of things, don't take life so seriously, it just, well, makes things easier," Logan said, tousling Samantha's hair.

She giggled.

Claire stood up, sitting Sam on the sofa and then squatting down to eye level. "Sam, do you remember anything about yesterday when you got up from your nap?"

"No."

"You don't remember coming into our bedroom, holding your doll Thelma, saying anything about a Scott or a Carlson?"

"No ... who are they?"

Claire sighed and said, "I don't know honey ... I don't know."

"Are you mad?"

"Of course not, sweetheart, why would you say that?" Claire asked.

Sam shrugged. "Can I go out and play with Axle?"

"Of course you can honey, but stay only in the backyard, inside the fence. Promise me you won't go out the gate," Logan said.

"I promise."

"Okay, good," Logan said.

Claire was smiling, but it was forced, like the painted-on smile of a clown.

Grabbing Samantha by the hand, Logan led her to the back door with Axle trotting along behind them. He was wagging his tail excitedly – he knew it was playtime. Before they reached the French doors that led onto the deck, Logan's cell phone rang.

"Logan."

"Mr. Keller?" The man's voice was unfamiliar.

"Yes. Who's this?"

"Aaron Reynolds, Mr. Keller. I'm returning your call. What can I do for you?"

"Oh ... Mr. Reynolds. Just a second please." Putting his hand over the mouthpiece he yelled, "Claire. Claire, please take Sam outside. I have Mr. Reynolds on the phone."

"Okay," Claire hollered back.

124

After Claire had taken Sam and Axle outside, Logan returned to his phone call. "Sorry about that, Mr. Reynolds, I had to take care of our little girl first, which is one of the reasons I called."

"Uh Mr. Keller, you mentioned on the voicemail you left that you were a friend of Thelma's. You didn't say you are; you said you were. Did you have a falling out or something? Thelma is a great lady, and I would do anything for her, anything."

"Mr. Reynolds, can we meet? Please? I don't want to talk about this over the phone and yes, it does concern Thelma."

Silence.

"Mr. Reynolds, are you still there?"

"There is a Panera Bread in Kent, off of Fourth, do you know the place?"

"Yes."

"Tomorrow at eleven, before the lunch rush. Gets crazy about eleven forty-five. See you then."

"Wait, wait, wait. How will I recognize you? I don't even know what you look like."

"I'll recognize you," Aaron said and hung up.

Logan stood there for a moment staring at the dead phone in his hand. *How will he recognize me? He's never met me.*

Disconcerted by the abrupt ending of the phone call, Logan went to the rear of the house to check on Claire and Sam. He watched them playing together, running around in the cold November air, Axle nipping at their heels and barking happily.

How did we ever get into this?

*

When Logan pulled into the Panera Bread parking lot, it was ten forty-five in the morning. The overcast sky threatened rain and the forecasters, in all their wisdom, were predicting showers. In

125

Seattle, that prediction was a safe bet – they were right more often than not.

He parked the Suburban in front and went inside. Since Logan didn't have a clue as to what this man looked like, he thought he would just order a coffee, have a seat, and wait to be approached.

Looking around the restaurant, he was relieved to see that it was nearly empty. At the counter, flirting with the young, good-looking clerk, was a man about six feet tall with short, dark brown hair.

Further down the counter, at order pick-up was another man. He was shorter than the man flirting with the clerk, perhaps five-six or five-seven. He had long hair, which was neatly pulled back into a ponytail. He sported a salt-and-pepper beard, neatly trimmed. He was patiently waiting for his order.

Running from floor to ceiling, in the middle of the restaurant, was a brick fireplace. Two women sat on the opposite side of the fireplace from where Logan now stood, talking and holding hands, as if they were having a secret rendezvous that their husbands were unaware of. The smells of fresh-baked bread, chicken, bacon, onions and spices filled Logan's nose. His stomach rumbled.

On second thought, why not order an Italian Combo on Ciabatta while he waited? It was, after all, almost lunchtime. He glanced at the clock on the back wall, above the counter, and noticed that it was ten fifty-five. Mr. Reynolds should be here shortly.

Logan ordered his sandwich and a medium fountain drink. He walked down to the far end of the counter to wait for his order. The man in the ponytail was gone. Logan stuffed his hands in the pockets of his jeans and surveyed the restaurant once more. As he was about to turn back to the counter, he spotted the man in the ponytail sitting at a table alone, looking at him. Then the man turned back to his sandwich, took a bite, and looked out the window.

Turning back to the counter, Logan smiled at the woman preparing his sandwich. "How are you today?"

"I'm fine, thanks. How 'bout yourself?"

"Good, good," Logan said, nodding his head.

The woman set a red basket on the counter containing his sandwich. "Is there anything else?" she asked.

"No, looks great, thank you."

"You're welcome, sir. Have a nice day."

Sir. He hated being called sir. It made him feel old.

He took his order, found a table in the far corner of the building, and sat down. As he was just about to take a bite, the man in the ponytail sat down across from him.

"Hi, Mr. Keller. I'm Aaron. Aaron Reynolds," the man said, extending his arm across the table. Logan hesitated, then took his hand and shook it.

"Pleased to meet you, Mr. Reynolds ... I must be honest, though. I didn't expect a man in a ponytail and a beard. And I thought you'd be taller." Logan clasped his hands, leaned forward and smiled. "You're just not how I pictured you that's all."

"I see. Let me guess, Mr. Keller. You thought I'd be six-six, two sixty, clean shaven with short hair cut above the ears wearing a three-piece, two-thousand dollar designer suit, right?"

"Well, all but the suit ... yes."

Now it was Aaron's turn to smile. "My appearance is extremely conducive to my work ... shall we say inconspicuous? Would you find me a threat, Mr. Keller?"

"No, not really."

"Exactly. Power is not physical Mr. Keller."

"Logan."

"Power is not physical, Logan. No, battles are won through wits and brains. And besides, I can still stop a three hundred pound man with a bullet." His smile widened.

Logan liked him instantly. He took a bite of his Italian sandwich, savoring the unique flavor and making a mental note to bring Claire - and their daughter - here for lunch.

"Mr. Reynolds—"

"If I'm going to address you by your first name, please show me the same respect."

"Of course, Aaron." Logan liked this man more and more. "How did you know what I would look like? You've never seen me before, have you? We've never met … at least I don't think so."

"No, we've never met. But remember my line of work Logan. I am a detective who spent twenty years in law enforcement, made a lot of friends in the department. I am fortunate to have access to records: DMV, National Crime Databases, things like that. I just pulled up your license so that I could recognize you by your photo. Then I checked out your background – criminal and otherwise."

"What do you mean, otherwise?" Logan asked.

"Oh, your line of work, have you been caught cheating on your taxes, have you ever been investigated, are you involved in your community, do you give to charity, what kind of family man are you. Things like that."

"You're kidding me…"

"No, I'm not."

"Why?"

"I always check the people involved when I might take a case and when you mentioned Thelma, well, it made it even more important to find out about you. Thelma has helped me in more ways than I can tell you."

"I-I don't know what … what to say. Frankly, I'm shocked, maybe even a little pissed – I feel like you violated my privacy."

"Don't take it so personal. The good news is you seem to be an upstanding citizen, an asset to your community, a loving husband, and a good businessman. Be proud, man," Aaron said, reaching across the table and clapping him on the shoulder.

At a loss for words, Logan took another bite of his sandwich.

"Now, please tell me about Thelma and why she sent you to me."

Logan looked at the man across from him, trying to figure out the best way to break the news of Thelma's death. Chewing thoughtfully, he hoped that Aaron would say something else, but the man just watched him eat, patiently waiting.

Logan finally took a long swallow of his Pepsi, and said, "She's dead. I'm so sorry, Aaron. Sorry for all of us. We loved her, too." Logan relayed yesterday's scene at Thelma's while watching Aaron carefully. He sat motionless and expressionless, listening intently as Logan described the circumstances surrounding her death. When Logan finished, Aaron sat back and sighed, rubbing his beard, tears welling up in his eyes.

After a few minutes of silence, Aaron wiped his eyes absently and said, "I will follow up with the coroner, see what they list for the official cause of death. She sure didn't die of natural causes, now did she?"

"No. No, she didn't."

Aaron studied Logan. "You don't believe much in anything that you can't taste, touch, feel or smell, do you?"

Logan didn't answer.

"One of the reasons that I loved Thelma so much was that she showed me another dimension to this world. She taught me to have an open mind and that things aren't always what they seem."

"Uh-huh."

"So why are you really here?"

"I don't really know … it's about my daughter – my adopted daughter – and some bizarre things that Thelma supposedly experienced."

"Like what?" Aaron asked.

Because Aaron believed in this stuff, Logan didn't feel so uncomfortable sharing Thelma's experience with the Ouija board and her words of warning. When he finished, Aaron said, "You want me to do background for you on Samantha, is that it? Didn't the adoption agency and courts give you all that information?"

"They gave us some files and background on the little girl, but that's all we know. Oh, and I did a little checking on the Internet."

"Anyone with a few bucks can put up a website, Logan," Aaron said. "Okay … here's the skinny: I'll take your case. I gotta eat, so it's five hundred per day, plus expenses."

"Wow! You must eat well."

"Sometimes," Aaron smiled and continued, "I will need all files, court papers and correspondence with the adoption agency, lawyers – everything you have and everything you know. How about if I come by tomorrow at around this time? Does that give you enough time to get everything together?"

"Yes."

"I would also like to meet your little girl and your wife. It is of great help to know the people personally in addition to what I find on paper. Gives them depth, makes them real and adds a much-needed dimension to the whole thing." He stood up, stuck his hand across the table and said, "Until tomorrow."

Logan stood up and took his hand. "Thank you … thank you, Aaron. We'll see you tomorrow."

Although he was a little man, Aaron carried himself with the strength and confidence of men twice his size. He walked with his shoulders back, and his head held high. Logan watched as he left the restaurant and climbed in behind the wheel of his battered Ford Taurus. On five hundred a day, you'd think he could afford a better vehicle, Logan thought. Or maybe he chooses to drive that piece of junk to fit his demeanor, to be inconspicuous.

Smiling and shaking his head, Logan left the restaurant and headed home.

NINETEEN

Ben Carlson was troubled by the visit from the man they called Richards. He wanted to kill the bastard. But he knew that he could never get to him, not with all that security and personal bodyguards. And if he could dispose of him, what would happen to his funding? What would happen to this project, this experiment?

He decided to take a walk around the underground facility known as New Life, mingle with the staff, clear his head and maybe pay Scott a visit.

He got up from his desk, where he had been going over the daily reports, and walked over to the security pad next to the door. He punched in his code, held his palm over the reader and then placed his left eye over the scanner. Instantly recognized by the system, he set his quarters to away mode, safeguarding his files and videos.

Most of the employees at New Life only had a nodding acquaintance with Dr. Carlson. They had immediate supervisors to whom they reported and were happily oblivious to the real workings of the facility.

Now, walking down the ten-foot wide hallways, listening to the echoes bouncing off the walls, Carlson thought about the little girl. He should never have agreed to let her out of the compound. They weren't ready yet. But Richards had commanded it, so he'd had no choice. The Keller family had been hand-picked.

Occasionally he nodded as staff went about their work: hurrying back and forth to the labs and computer rooms, delivering reports, fetching chemicals, and running tests.

Before Carlson reached Scott's room, he was cornered by Dr. Whiting, who was out of breath, as if he had been running.

"Jesus, Ben I've been looking all over for you!"

"Calm down," Carlson said. "What the hell is wrong now?"

"McFadden and Briggs. They're dead, they've been shot!"

"What? Who the hell shot them? What the fuck!" Ben was incredulous.

"I know you put surveillance on Sylvia Tran, had her watched because you didn't trust her. McFadden watched her carefully, and I think he had something on her. They were found dead in Sylvia's apartment."

"I'll kill the bitch myself. Do we know where she is?"

"No, not at the moment, but we'll find her."

"Correction. Scott will find her."

*

Near Bellingham, Sylvia turned east on Highway 542 towards Mount Baker. A light snow had begun to fall, and the driving conditions were becoming more treacherous. The car was not equipped for the road conditions - no studs or snow tires, no chains in the trunk - but they were close to their destination, and Sylvia was happy that traffic was light.

She glanced at her passenger, who was sleeping soundly with her head on her balled up coat. Sylvia had cranked up the Mercedes' heater to full blast. The closer they got to the cabin, the more excited Sylvia became. She could hardly wait to see Fred again, and the anticipation was both exciting and annoying.

About thirty minutes out of Bellingham, Sylvia noticed the green van behind them.

"Anna, wake up!" she said.

Anna mumbled something.

"Anna!"

"W-what ... what ... don't yell at me Mom," Anna said. After a few seconds, Anna realized where she was. "What? Did something happen?"

"Not yet," Sylvia said, eyeing the rearview mirror. "But I think we might have company."

"Who?" Anna asked, sitting up. "What are you talking about?"

"Don't turn around, but look in the side mirror. See that green van behind us?"

"Yup. So?"

"I think they're following us."

"It's a two-lane road. Of course, they're following us. They don't have anywhere else to go, you crazy woman."

"A few minutes ago, when the van was a little closer, I got a look at the driver. It wasn't a good look, but I could swear that it is one of Carlson's men."

"You're kidding, right?"

"No. No, Anna, I'm not. I wish I were."

"But I thought we took care of Carlson's strongmen back at the apartment."

"Come on Anna, do you think he only has a couple of guys?"

"Of course not, but I ... I didn't know that they could be after us so quick. How could they know where we are?"

"I don't know," Sylvia said, shaking her head.

Unlike Anna, Sylvia had spent the past two years of her life becoming a trusted staff member at New Life. At the direction and help of Fred Richert, whom she trusted implicitly, and believed in wholeheartedly, Sylvia had become enmeshed in the workings of the facility. Now she knew her cover, that she had worked so hard to build, was blown.

But after this morning and the showdown with McFadden and that freak Briggs, Sylvia knew that she could never return to New Life, nor did she want to. Fred would show her the next move; he would protect her. If she made it to Fred, that was.

The snow was coming down harder now. Switching on the radio, searching for an updated weather report, Sylvia kept glancing in the rearview mirror, straining to get a look at the driver of the green van. But the snow was making visibility worse, and the driver's face was obscured from view.

Returning her attention to the radio, Sylvia fumbled with the dial until she found an AM station that was reporting the current weather conditions.

Suddenly the Mercedes was hit from behind. The car lurched towards the right shoulder, sliding on the snow-covered highway.

"Shit!" Sylvia said, deftly maneuvering the vehicle into the direction of the slide. Nervously biting her lower lip, Sylvia looked over at Anna, who was now sitting completely erect, hands gripping the dashboard like an eagle clutching its dinner. She had paled as if the blood had drained out of her body.

Sylvia got the vehicle off the shoulder and back onto the main highway. Luckily for them, there wasn't any other traffic in sight, at least for the moment. Accelerating, she watched as the odometer climbed past fifty, too dangerous for road conditions, but it seemed to her that she had no other choice. Looking in the mirror again, she noticed the Ford had dropped back a few feet when she sped up.

Keeping one eye on the van and one eye on the road in front of her, Sylvia watched with a sinking feeling as the Ford sped up and began to gain on them.

"Go! Go! Go!" Anna screamed, still clutching the dashboard.

"Anna, calm down so you can help us here! Get your gun and try to shoot out their tires or something! Maybe they'll crash!"

Large evergreens hung over the roadway on both sides. To their right, the highway dropped off about ninety feet down an embankment. There was a river at the bottom of the ravine, running to God knows where.

Producing the Walther from her handbag, Anna unscrewed the attached silencer and rolled down the passenger window. "Less weight, better control," Anna said, noticing Sylvia's confused look.

Before Anna could lean out the window, their pursuers sped up, hitting them hard. Plastic shattered as the taillights broke. Metal screeched when the van's bumper crumpled the Mercedes trunk. This time, the car spun ninety degrees; they were now sliding sideways on the snow like some amusement park ride.

Anna screamed. And then she realized that, when they had spun around, it put the Ford van directly in her line of sight. She was staring at the two men barreling down on them. Without hesitation, she raised the Walther PK39, firing two shots. Sylvia was struggling with the wheel, trying to gain control; in her mind, she saw them going over the embankment and into the icy river below.

The first bullet hit the grille of the van, causing no damage; the second punched a neat, round hole in the windshield between the passenger and driver, missing them both.

Before she could get off the third shot, however, the Ford's passenger leaned out and shot Anna just above her left eye. Her head snapped back, shattering the side mirror. Anna's body went limp, hanging halfway in and halfway out of the vehicle like a life-sized doll.

"Anna! *Anna!*" Sylvia screamed. "No, no, no, no, *please God no.*"

But she knew her friend was dead.

Suddenly angered by all the death and violence she had witnessed in the last twelve hours, Sylvia vowed to kill these two in revenge. She knew that she was just adding to the violence, but she didn't care; she would avenge her friend's death.

Again she turned back into the direction of her slide, and although it was risky, she slowed the Mercedes to a more manageable speed, knowing that the Ford would be on her in seconds. Her mind raced through different scenarios, none of which came to an acceptable outcome.

Slowing the car did help in regaining control, and Sylvia managed to bring the front end around and get it pointed back in the right direction.

WUMP! As the van connected again, Sylvia was thrust forward.

WUMP! Harder this time, she fought to keep control. *I'm going to lose it!*

WUMP! WUMP!

Sylvia was really scared now. The Mercedes slid on the snow-packed road, rotating on the ice like a merry-go-round. As the car was spinning out of control, she saw the two men in the van laughing; then they were gone, then she saw them laughing again as she continued her dizzying spin. Hitting the shoulder at forty miles per hour, the Mercedes burst through the guardrail and over the embankment. Fortunately, it didn't roll but went over the edge nose first.

Halfway down the incline was a clump of thick-based trees. Sylvia turned the car at the last minute, narrowly missing the large evergreens, only to be greeted by the huge oak to her left. She slammed into the tree so hard that her chest hit the steering column at the same instant the airbag deployed. Pain shot through her face as the bag hit her already broken nose; she thought for a moment that she was going to pass out. Barely hanging onto consciousness, Sylvia looked back up the incline. Her hunters had pulled over and got out of their vehicle. Two men peered down at her.

The larger of the two put one hand on the still intact portion of guardrail, jumping over it like a gymnast doing a routine. His partner was not as graceful and almost tripped trying to follow.

They're coming down here. Where is the gun? She knew that it was back on the highway somewhere; the force of the bullet that pierced Anna's head had knocked the Walther from her grasp.

She watched as the men made their way down the incline. Right now she didn't care; she was too weak and too tired.

The men reached the wrecked vehicle: steam hissed from the mangled radiator, the windshield had imploded, tiny bits of sticky safety glass littered the interior and a battered and bruised woman sat dazed in the driver's seat. On its descent, the passenger had been thrown from the car and now lay in a crumpled heap a few yards from where the Mercedes had come to rest. The larger man yanked open the driver's door. It protested with a squeal.

Sylvia smiled up at the faces, which were becoming blurry and fading in and out of focus. Mustering all the energy she had left, she produced a wad of saliva and spat as hard as she could, hitting the smaller guy on the cheek.

Absently wiping the spittle from his face, the man curled his fingers into a fist as Sylvia watched, unable to move. His arm pulled back like a slingshot and then came forward as if it were spring-loaded. His fist connected with Sylvia's already broken nose, pushing it across her face, breaking two of her teeth and splitting open her upper lip. The pain was excruciating, but it only lasted for a second.

And then she passed out.

TWENTY

"Wow ... five hundred per day, plus expenses? And what kinda expenses you think we're looking at Logan?"

"Well ... the man did say he's gotta eat."

"Eat what? Steak and Lobster every night, maybe fly to France for lunch?"

"I know it's expensive, but I figure it shouldn't take him long to get some background information. We are talking about our little girl, Claire."

"Oh, I'm not opposed in the least if you're smitten with the guy. If he keeps you entertained and off my ass, the money's well spent," she said. "And you're right; it's our little girl were talking about here."

They were in bed, Axle lying at their feet. It was just after ten o' clock when they heard the scream.

"NO!" Sam yelled from the room across the hall. "No more needles, no more tests! You're just mean, Dr. Carlson!"

Throwing back the covers, Claire leaped from the bed and ran to Sam's room, Logan on her heels.

As Claire rushed to Sam's bedside, Logan gently grabbed his wife, stopping her. He put a finger to his lips. Logan quietly pulled her into the hallway and whispered, "Let's just listen. She might give us some clue as to what's going on or at least give us something we can share with our newfound hippy friend with the ponytail."

Claire nodded. Logan let go of her arm. Together they walked back to Sam's room and stood next to her bed, waiting for another outburst that might give some helpful information.

All they could hear was her breathing. She was quiet now and seemed to be resting peacefully. After a few minutes, they turned to leave.

As they reached the doorway, Sam yelled out: "Scott! Don't do that! You're hurting him!"

Logan and Claire looked at each other; they turned and walked back into the room.

And waited.

Nothing.

They stood beside Sam's bed for ten minutes, and then they went back to their room, their bed.

Back under the covers again, Claire turned on her side and propped her head up, facing Logan. "It's those names again, the same names she blurted out yesterday in the bathroom: Scott and Carlson. But did you hear what she called Carlson this time? She—"

"Yeah, I heard. She said *Doctor* Carlson. So we have a mean doctor on our hands, unless, of course, this is all just made up from some little girl's overactive imagination."

"I ... I don't think so," Claire said.

"Yeah ... for some reason I don't either."

"Logan ..."

"Yes?"

"I've made an appointment for Sam with a child psychologist - a hypnotherapist. She specializes in regression therapy."

"She?"

"Yes, she. Her name is Lynn Snellgrove, and she is one of the most respected in the field of hypnotherapy for children in the nation. People from all over bring their troubled kids to her."

"So are we on a two-year waiting list then?"

"Nope," Claire smiled. "I can be very persuasive when I need to be – appointment for tomorrow at ten."

"In the morning?"

"No, at night dummy. Of course in the morning."

Logan shook his head. Even after all these years, his wife still amazed him. "So how'd you do it?"

"Oh, I shared a few of the details with her, maybe embellished just a little." She held her thumb and index finger an eighth of an inch apart to emphasize her point and winked.

Sitting up, Logan said, "Remember we have Mr. Reynolds coming by tomorrow too, around noon I think."

"Call him and ask him to make it two o' clock. That will give us plenty of time. Dr. Snellgrove is only about thirty minutes away, in War-rington."

"Claire, don't you think this is going to be a lot for Sam? This might be hard on her. Maybe—"

"We'll tell her some friends of the family would like to meet her, that's all."

"And then stick her in an office with a strange lady who'll ask her all sorts of questions? Come on Claire."

"Dr. Snellgrove will make a game of it Logan, it'll be fun for her and she won't even know what's going on. Trust me."

Logan surrendered and threw his hands in the air. "Alright, fine. We'll go see this Dr. Snellgrove, but if Sam doesn't like her, or if she's uncomfortable in any way, we leave."

"Wow, talk about an overprotective father! And after only a few days! I love you," Claire said.

"I love you too, honey," Logan sighed. "What in the world have we done?"

*

Claire woke a little after five in the morning. It was dark and rainy. She lay in bed listening to the rain pummel the roof and tap at the windows like fingers of the dead. Logan snored softly next to her, mumbled something incoherent, and then rolled over on his side. Quietly slipping out of bed so as not to disturb her sleeping husband, she slid into her bathrobe and a pair of slippers.

As she was heading downstairs to brew a pot of coffee, a tiny voice stopped her.

"Claire? Don't leave me please; I'll be good, I promise."

She turned around and saw Samantha standing on the upper landing. Claire went back up and scooped the little girl into her arms.

"Honey, no one is going to leave you. Let's go downstairs and you can help me make some coffee, okay?"

"Okay. I don't like coffee, can I have chocolate?"

"You mean hot chocolate?"

"Yeah, yeah, yeah. Chocolate."

Axle watched them from Sam's doorway. "Did the dog sleep in your room last night?" Claire asked. Axle always slept with Claire and Logan. He was with them last night when Sam cried out, but when they went back to bed, Claire didn't remember Axle being with them. At some point, he must've gone into Samantha's room.

"Yes. He slept with me."

"Good boy Axle, good boy." His ears perked up; his tail began to wag fervently, and he appeared to be smiling. But then, he always appeared to be smiling.

The three of them went downstairs together, Claire carrying Sam and Axle following close behind.

Claire put on a fresh pot of coffee and heated milk for hot chocolate. "Samantha, why would you think we would leave you?"

"I've never had people stay in my life. And now I'm starting to remember things, things that are frightening," she replied.

From the corner of the kitchen, Axle whimpered. Claire stared at the little girl in amazement. Suddenly she didn't talk like a five-year-old, she didn't act like a five-year-old, and she didn't even look like a five-year-old. Her demeanor, the tone of her voice and the look in her eyes were that of a young adult. Chills went down Claire's spine. This is the person we'll see in twenty years, she thought. God, my imagination is getting the best of me. She's just a little girl!

"Sam, what kind of frightening things?" Claire asked, trying to keep her voice from cracking.

"W-what ... I, don't remember now...I...what?" she sighed, looking confused. As suddenly as that young woman had appeared, she was gone, and a five-year-old girl stood before her again.

It was just my imagination, Claire thought. She smiled and put a hand softly on Sam's cheek. "Oh nothing, honey. Nothing," Claire said, shaking her head. Let's have some of that cocoa!"

"Yaaaay!" Sam said, her confused look instantly replaced by one of joy.

"Shh," Claire said, putting a finger to her lips. "You'll wake Logan." She almost said you'll wake your father but caught herself.

"Oooh, sorry," she whispered. She looked so cute standing there in her Minnie Mouse pajamas, her bangs hanging straight down covering her forehead; the innocent expression of anticipation on her face as she waited patiently for her cocoa.

While waiting for Logan to wake, they enjoyed their coffee and cocoa together, Mother and daughter, at the little table in the nook. They talked about cartoons, dolls, makeup, and picnics, everything but the past and Sam's nightmares or visions or memories or whatever they were.

At ten past six, Logan appeared in gray sweatpants and a t-shirt. His hair was sticking up in all directions as if it couldn't figure out which way it wanted to go. He yawned and stretched his arms toward the ceiling as if he were worshipping some unseen god.

Walking over to the two most important women in his life, he kissed them each on the cheek and mumbled, "Good morning. Coffee."

"My name is not coffee and your breath stinks," Claire said, winking at Sam. She giggled.

Ignoring her, Logan reached down and rubbed Axle's head. The dog had jumped up at the sound of his voice, which usually meant food – people food. "I know what you want, you pig. I guess I should make us some breakfast, huh?"

"You gonna cook?" Claire asked.

"I might, yeah. What of it? Think I can't make a simple breakfast?" Logan put his hand on his hips and looked at them. "Are you questioning my culinary abilities, young lady?"

"Never," Claire replied. "Please, knock yourself out."

"If I knocked myself out, I wouldn't be conscious to cook, now would I? Boy, sometimes you just don't think things through Claire." Logan grinned. He felt good this morning and thought maybe it was because they were taking active steps to get some answers. And he was confident that this would all be behind them in a few days, and they could get on with life.

"What's culbinerry?" Sam asked, taking a sip of her cocoa.

Claire patted Sam's hand. "It's cooking, honey. It's just another adult word for cooking."

"Oh," she said, taking another sip of her drink. "Grownups are weird - why don't you just say cooking?"

"You're right; we should just call it cooking," Claire said. She looked at Logan. "So, hotshot, whatcha gonna make us for breakfast?"

"Eggs, blueberry pancakes, toast and sausage. And coffee, lots of coffee."

It all felt so right to Claire, sitting here at the table as a family, enjoying Logan's cooking together.

When they were finished, Axle gratefully cleaned up the leftovers, and they went upstairs to bathe and dress for their busy day. Claire gave Sam a bath and, because it wasn't very warm outside, dressed her in white cotton pants and a long-sleeved blue blouse. She put her shoulder length hair in pigtails, securing each side with a blue rubber band.

"Okay Sam, you can watch a show while Logan and I get ready to go."

"Dora, Dora, Dora, please Dora," Sam chanted.

"Okay fine."

Placing Sam on the couch in the upstairs family room, Claire switched on the TV and turned it to Dora the Explorer, then went into the master bath to join her husband, who had already showered and shaved.

"I'm getting a little nervous," Claire said, removing her bathrobe.

"About what?" Logan asked.

"Regressing Sam, I guess," she said hesitantly.

"If this psychologist lady, uh … what's her name?"

"Lynn Snellgrove."

"If this Snellgrove is as good as you say, then you have nothing to worry about. She'll know what's she doing, right?"

"I hope so, Logan. I really hope so."

TWENTY-ONE

The offices of Lynn Snellgrove were located twenty minutes south-east of downtown Seattle in Warrington, a bustling little community of small businesses and luxurious homes skirting the edges of Lake Washington. Some of the finest restaurants in the state, boasting the freshest seafood and best steaks, could be found in this small burg of seven hundred.

Even though it was drizzling and a little cold outside, Claire, Logan and Sam enjoyed the thirty-minute drive. They listened to the radio and enjoyed the scenery: huge evergreens loomed on both sides of the high-way, the Cedar River was full from swallowing the recent rains. And, at nine-thirty in the morning, traffic was light as most commuters were off the roads and in their offices taking care of business or flirting with co-workers.

Pulling into a freshly lined parking space in front of a small three-story brick building, Sam asked, "Who am I seeing?"

"Her name is Lynn honey," Claire replied.

"And we're gonna play games?"

Logan said, "Yeah…like a word game Sam. Remember I told you that Lynn is a psychologist?"

"Yeah … sigh … call … oh … just."

"Very good Sam," Claire said.

"And she will ask some questions, get to know a little about you. You'll have fun and make a new friend," Logan said.

Lynn Snellgrove's office was on the first floor, Suite 101, on the right. They entered through the double glass doors. A smiling reception-ist instantly greeted them. The waiting area was clean and neatly arranged with tasteful furniture; all kind of toys were in crates to the left and a bookcase, matching the décor of the room, was filled with every chil-dren's book imaginable.

After they had checked in, Logan and Sam headed to the toys. Claire watched them, a sinking feeling coming over her. *I wonder if we're doing the right thing.*

Claire approached the receptionist again and asked her if she could speak with Dr. Snellgrove in private before she met with Sam. The re-ceptionist assured her that Dr. Snellgrove always met with the parents first, to inform them about what was going to take place and to appease any fears the parents may have about the practice of regression therapy. *Yeah, but I bet she hasn't had a case like this.* She thanked the receptionist and retreated to the comfy couch.

As Claire was thumbing through the magazine selection and Logan and Sam were on the floor playing marbles, a woman in her mid-fifties appeared. "Miss Keller?" she inquired.

"Mrs. Keller, yes," Claire said, looking up at the woman.

"Sorry … Mrs. Keller, I'm Lynn Snellgrove." Her voice was pleas-ant and soothing. She held out a hand. Claire took it in hers.

After they had finished the introductions, Lynn told Samantha that she wanted to speak with Logan and Claire for a few moments in private. "Lindsay here," she said, nodding toward the receptionist, "will make sure you have plenty to play with. And we'll be right back. Is that okay with you?"

Samantha looked warily at Claire.

"It will be okay honey; we'll just be in the other room. We're not leaving the building," Claire said, giving her a hug.

"Okay," Sam muttered, "can I play some more?"

"Of course," Claire replied, standing up.

"Thank you, Samantha, we'll be back soon and then it'll be our turn to talk and play," Lynn said.

She turned to Logan and Claire. "Follow me please." They walked down a short hallway, turned right through the double doors and into Snellgrove's office.

"Please, have a seat," Lynn said, motioning to the couch. She sat down in the chair across from them. Claire looked around the office, noticing the walls were free of framed degrees from various high-end universities. Instead, there were children's drawings, finger paintings, poetry and other works, which added clarity and theme to Lynn Snellgrove's unpretentious office.

Lynn leaned forward, resting her forearms on her thighs, looking back and forth between them, as if she could read their thoughts by studying their faces. "First, Mr. and Mrs. Keller, I want to reassure you that what I do is not dangerous in any way, and if it ever gets to a point that is uncomfortable – either for myself or a patient – I terminate the session immediately. Your case, as you already know Mrs. Keller—"

"Claire."

"As you know, Claire, fascinates me because of the incident you witnessed in your bathroom with Samantha. The decapitation of her favorite doll, the sleepwalking and what she said all have a deeper meaning."

"And you're going to find that out?" Logan asked.

"Do you believe in God, Mr. Keller?"

Logan glanced quizzically at Claire, then back to Lynn.

"I believe in something larger or greater than me, yes … but I struggle with modern Christianity and some of its doctrines. And you can call me Logan. I'm not real comfortable with the formal stuff."

"What about Christianity do you struggle with Logan?" Lynn asked.

"What does this have to do with Sam and getting her help?" Claire asked.

Turning to Claire, Lynn said, "Finding out belief systems of parents has an enormous impact on my approach to a child and—"

"But we adopted her just a week ago. She is not a birth child and hasn't been exposed to our belief system. We're still getting to know each other. Her beliefs may not even be close to ours. Besides, is she even old enough to have developed religious beliefs?" Claire asked.

"You'd be surprised at what a five-year-old believes. But I don't ask you these questions to find out about the girl; I ask because I need to know what your take will be on what I do here." She paused, thought for a moment and then said, "Let's see if I can explain this better. Because of my work, I have come to believe in spirits or angels or whatever you choose to label them. Past lives are real. I've witnessed things through regression therapy that gives joy, wonder, and beauty to the world. And I've also seen the opposite – the darkness, the wickedness, frightening and terrible things."

Claire reached over and took Logan's hand.

Lynn continued, "I guess what I'm saying is, if you want to help your little girl, please be open-minded. I will be sharing with you whatever I find, and bias has no place in this field."

"So are you telling us that you might find something ugly?" Claire asked.

"Maybe. Or maybe it will be something beautiful, but we won't know until we start digging. I just want you to be prepared for whatever we find."

"You're making this sound like something out of the Twilight Zone," Logan said, visibly irritated.

"It can seem that way sometimes, even to me. Even after twenty-five years of doing this, I still get surprised, awed," Lynn said. She understood Logan's skepticism and took it good-naturedly.

Looking at Logan, Claire said, "We understand, Miss Snellgrove, don't we Logan?" She nudged him like he was a puppet and she was trying to get him to talk.

"Oh, I understand what you're saying; doesn't mean I have to like it, though."

"You still haven't answered my question, Mr. Keller," Lynn said.

"Oh? And what question is that?"

"What about Christianity do you struggle with?"

"Oh yeah … well … I don't believe that a baby is born into sin. I don't believe you have to go through a third party – such as Jesus - to get to God. I can't wrap my head around a vengeful, angry deity that would cause pain and suffering. Not my idea of God, not at all …" he trailed off, shaking his head.

Lynn smiled. "Great! I'm with you on those points, Logan. Just sit back and try not to be judgmental through this process, okay?"

Logan sighed. "I'll do my best."

"Logan, I think we should inform Miss Snellgrove here about our relationship with Thelma."

Lynn cocked her head to one side, eyebrows raised. "Who's Thelma?"

Logan became silent and wistful.

Looking down at her lap, Claire said, "She was a close friend and neighbor. She passed away two days ago."

"Oh, I'm so sorry," Lynn said.

While Logan sat silently on the sofa, Claire recounted their relationship with Thelma, how her husband had suddenly died and her turnabout to the spirit world. She left out the details of her death.

"You have some idea of what I'm speaking of then."

Logan perked up. "This isn't going to be like some psychic reading thing, is it?

"Remember, Logan, open-mindedness is key here. This is a radical approach were taking to the brain and repressed memories. Shunned by many, used successfully by others. When used successfully, however, the skeptics discount the results as being 'false' and 'coerced.' Do you believe in science, Logan?"

"Of course I do."

"Easier to believe in science than religion sometimes, isn't it?"

"Yes, it is."

"Recovered-memory therapy, in my mind, is a documented and proven means of getting to repressed memories. It is used in many different ways: helping amnesia victims, helping in severe cases of trauma and, well, the world you don't want to admit to Logan. The world of the unknown, which happens to bring out dimensions that we're not all that familiar with, the spirit side of things, if you will."

"Okay, so?" Logan said.

"So, do you still want to move forward with this?" Lynn asked, eyeing both of them carefully.

"Of course we do, Miss Snellgrove, of course we do," Claire said.

"Logan, what about you? I need you both supporting this and your daughter one-hundred percent," Lynn said.

"Yup … sure. Let's give it a try, see what happens."

"Okay, great. I will spend about an hour with Sam, so if the two of you want to go for a drive, run some errands or something—"

"Oh, no, no. We're staying right here with Samantha," Claire said. "We're not going to walk out on her now; this is when she needs us most."

"I understand your concern, but I can't have any distractions. Sam can't have any distractions. We need some time to get to know each other and build a little trust, and I can only do that one-on-one. Everything will be fine, don't worry. You're not abandoning her – she'll understand that. She'll know that."

"Come on Claire," Logan said, leading his wife toward the door. "Lynn's right; she needs to do her job with as little distractions as possible."

Claire mumbled something unintelligible and then let her husband lead her back into the lobby, where Sam was busy looking at The Lorax by Dr. Seuss. She was sprawled happily on the floor, a big smile on her face.

When she saw Claire and Logan, Sam jumped to her feet. She ran over to Claire, wrapped her arms around her legs, hugging them tight, almost causing her to fall. Claire reached down and brushed the bangs off her forehead. "Lynn would like to talk with you for a bit, Sam. While you do that, Logan and I will be out here in the lobby, waiting.

Her grip around Claire's legs loosened and she looked over at Logan.

Logan walked over to Samantha and bent down. "Honey, Miss Lynn wants to help you, wants to help all of us. Please believe me when I tell you that we will never leave you or do anything that would hurt you. We are only trying to help. So do this for us, and tell the nice lady what she needs to know, okay?" His voice was barely above a whisper, and there was a certain amount of resignation in his tone, which he hoped no one else heard.

"Okay," she said, smiling. "Anything for you."

He felt his throat tighten when she said that. Clenching his teeth hard, swallowing the big lump that had formed in his throat, Logan did his best to keep his emotions under control. Although it had only been a week, he had fallen in love with Samantha. No matter what befell them, she was his daughter now.

Logan looked at his wife. She smiled at him wanly and wiped her nose absently with the back of her hand.

"Come on honey, let's go talk a little, get to know each other," Lynn said.

Sam nodded and let the woman take her by the hand. As she was walking away, she looked back over her shoulder and smiled.

Back in her office, Lynn had Samantha choose whether she wanted to lie on the couch, lie on the floor or just sit. Sam decided to sit on the sofa.

They were facing each other, when Sam asked, "What's this about?"

Lynn was startled by the little girl's abruptness. "Well Sam, I just want to get to know you a little and maybe play a game."

"What kinda game?"

"Let's talk a little about you first; then we'll talk about the game we'll be playing." Lynn spoke in an assuaging tone, without talking down to the girl.

"Okay, what do you want to know?"

"Well ... what do you remember, what do you know about where you came from, your parents, what your life was like before you came to live with Claire and Logan?"

"Sylvia always took care of me. She's nice. I lived in a house with other kids. Sisters. Brothers."

"Where was this?"

"I don't know," Sam replied, shaking her head.

"Do you know what city or town you lived in Sam? Or for how long?"

"No, don't remember."

"What do you think of Claire and Logan?"

"They're great!"

"Okay, honey. How 'bout that game?"

"Sure," Sam said. "I love games!"

Producing a bright greenish-purple crystal from the left pocket of her sweater, Lynn held the object in her left hand, between her thumb, middle and index fingers. Holding the crystal ten inches from Sam's eyes,

154

above her forehead, causing the greatest possible strain on her eyes and eyelids, Lynn said, "It's beautiful, isn't it?"

"Yesss …"

"Keep your eyes on the glass, Sam, don't take your eyes from it. Focus only on the crystal: the color, the texture, the beauty of it. Your full attention must be focused on this exquisite piece of glass, do you understand?" Her voice was soft, mellifluous. Sam felt comfortable and safe.

"Yes, I understand." Sam's pupils dilated considerably and began to assume a wavy motion. Using the index and middle fingers of her right hand, which were extended and slightly separated, Lynn slowly moved her fingers from beside the crystal towards Sam's eyes. The girl's eyes fluttered and then involuntarily closed.

Satisfied, Lynn sat back in her chair. "Samantha, can you hear me?"

"Yes."

"Where are you right now?"

"In your office."

Lynn smiled. "Yes, you're in my office. And what town is my office located in?"

"Warrington … your office is in Warrington."

"And what is your name?"

"I don't know."

Sam no longer spoke as a child. She now spoke with the maturity, wisdom and confidence of an old soul. Lynn became hesitant in her line of questioning. She was not sure how this should progress. The little girl, who only moments ago had sat on the sofa across from her, was gone.

"I thought your name was Samantha Jennings."

The girl was silent.

"What is your—"

Lynn Snellgrove's head snapped forward and back in one quick motion as the bullet tore through the left side of her head, spraying blood on Sam's face and the wall behind her. Death was instantaneous. Lynn had not uttered a sound. The only report was the small *pop!* when the bullet pierced the plate-glass window at Lynn's back.

The splatter of blood snapped Samantha out of her trance, but she was unsure of what had just happened. She sat on the couch, dazed.

"Miss Snellgrove? Miss Snellgrove?" Sam asked quietly. She saw blood running down the left side of Lynn's face, and noticed the large exit wound that had destroyed half of her forehead. She saw the woman slumped back in her chair, arms dangling on both sides as if she was trying to scoop something from the floor. But Sam still didn't – or couldn't - register what had happened. When she turned to the wall behind her, noticing the blood splattered paint and a perfectly round bullet hole just above and to the left of where she had been sitting only moments before, it all became clear.

Someone had shot Lynn Snellgrove.

Before Sam could react, another round punctured the window, hitting Samantha in the chest, narrowly missing her heart. The force of the slug flung her backward, slamming her into the wall.

Clutching her chest, trying desperately to breathe, Samantha Jennings collapsed to the floor.

TWENTY-TWO

Mike peered once more through the high-powered scope secured to the Remington 700 and then looked over at his partner, Ralph, and smiled. They were on the third floor of The Tower, an office building that was home to a real estate company, a law firm, a document storage company, and a large construction company. The building was owned and operated by the Larenx Corporation. Suite Three-Fourteen, where Ralph and Mike were enjoying each other's company, was unoccupied. From their vantage point, they had a perfect view of the backside of Lynn Snellgrove's office and the high-powered scope made the subjects look as if they were standing two feet away.

"It's over," Mike said.

"The girl's dead too?" Ralph asked.

Mike nodded.

"Let's get outa here then," Ralph said, "this place makes me nervous. Cops will be here soon."

"Probably not. We didn't make any noise, and unless they screamed, which I don't think they had a chance to do, nobody will know anything is wrong until they don't come out from their session." He looked at his watch. "Still have about twenty-five minutes or so."

"Yeah, maybe ... but we should still move our ass," Ralph said, licking his lips. "Somebody could have seen us sitting up here and tie us into the killings."

Mike's cell phone rang. "Hello?" Ralph watched as Mike wrinkled his face in disapproval. Holding the phone away from his ear, he flipped whoever was on the other end the bird. Ralph nudged him and nodded to the video camera mounted in the corner.

Shit, Mike mouthed, his back to the camera. Then he grinned and shrugged his shoulders as if to say nothing I can do about it now.

"But- ... yeah, okay," Mike said into the phone. He flipped it shut and looked grimly at Ralph. "We kill the man and the woman too when they come out. Or, if I can get a shot, when they enter the shrink's office."

"Oh damn," Ralph said. "I knew I shoulda went to college. Coulda been a banker or lawyer or—"

"Ditch digger."

"Fuck you. Shouldn't have done got messed up with this crap. Jail and I don't go good together Mike; I don't wanna be nobody's bitch boy if you know what I mean."

"Calm down Ralph. Nobody even knows we're here. We haven't been seen – and we won't be seen – nobody's going to jail. Relax my friend, calm down."

"Yeah ... well, let's just get this suck job done and over with and get the hell outa here quick, alright?"

"Sure, this will be over soon."

Ralph sighed and sat down on the carpeted floor. It was disconcerting being in an office without any furniture. Every time he spoke, his words seemed to bounce back to him, amplified and echoing.

They sat on the floor and talked for ten minutes, Mike looking out the window now and then, watching for any activity from Lynn's office.

While he was chatting with Ralph, Mike noticed movement and turned back to the window. He watched as Logan stepped outside, into the parking lot, looking bewildered and frazzled as if he didn't know what to do next, and then, amazingly, he saw the little girl.

How could that be?

On the heels of the little girl was the woman.

Mike quickly re-secured the scope, pointed the Remington through the open window and set his sights on the little bitch. The instant he squeezed off a shot, Samantha moved to her left, and the bullet ricocheted off the brick façade with a zzzing! narrowly missing her. Small chips of brick flew in the air; the trajectory of the bullet caused it to bounce off the pavement and fall harmlessly to the ground fifty feet away.

Reacting quickly to the gunshot, Logan screamed, "Get in! Christ Claire, get Sam and move! Hurry!"

Then the passenger window of the Chevy imploded in a spray of safety glass. Logan felt the air move a few inches from his face as the bullet barely missed him.

"Claire!" Logan screamed, jumping in the driver's seat and slamming the door. His hands were trembling, and he fumbled the keys, but he didn't drop them. "Shit! Shit!" Logan mumbled, as he finally got the keys in the ignition. The Suburban started on the first turn of the key. "Oh, thank God," he whispered. Although it was chilly outside, he was sweating and breathing hard.

Through the passenger window, he saw Claire running with Sam clutched tightly to her chest. Come on! Come on! She was a few feet from the Suburban when another shot rang out, this one hitting its mark. Logan watched in horror as his wife slammed into the side of the Suburban, propelled by the force of the bullet. He briefly saw her face through the window, twisted with pain. And then, still holding Sam, she dropped to her knees, her body a protective shield around the child.

"NO!" He bolted from the vehicle and ran to his wife. Lifting Claire, he helped her and Sam into the vehicle as a fourth shot rang out. He barely heard it as the slug met steel. He would find out later, upon closer examination, that the bullet had barely missed them, penetrating the passenger door and embedding itself in the passenger seat.

Samantha was crying and burying her face deeper into Claire's chest as Logan loaded them into the vehicle. Adrenaline ran through his veins like gas through a pump.

His hand came away wet and slick with blood. Can't think about that now or we're all dead. He somehow managed to get around the vehicle and behind the wheel without getting hit.

Slamming the Chevy into reverse, Logan tramped on the accelerator, tires smoking and squealing. "Stay down!" he screamed, as he put the gearshift in drive and sped towards the freeway. He was shaking violently; his chest pounding as if someone was rapidly hitting him with a hammer. He looked over at his wounded wife and daughter, slumped in the passenger seat, and began to cry.

Across the street, in the empty suite, Mike said, "Shit! They're getting away! I hit the woman, though. I think she's hurt pretty bad."

"I thought you said the kid was dead, Mike," Ralph said, stepping back nervously as Mike swung around with the Remington still in his hands. The barrel was pointed directly at Ralph. "Put that thing away; they're gone." He unconsciously backed up two more steps.

"She was dead!" Mike said, "I saw it with my own eyes!"

"Shhh Mike, you'll be having the other tenants wonderin' what's up."

Glaring at Ralph, Mike flipped open his cell. He pressed two, waited a few seconds and then said: "We have a problem here. They're getting away, all of them except the shrink, that is. Heading towards I-5 in a green late-model Suburban, didn't get—"

There was a pause as Mike listened to the person on the other end. "Whaddaya mean, you know all about the vehicle and where they're going?" Another pause. "Right, okay." Looking annoyed, he flipped the cell closed. "They have a tracking device on the vehicle," Mike said, more to himself than to Ralph. "Well of course they do. Of course."

Logan drove too fast for conditions, but he couldn't see where he had any other choice. His hands were slick with sweat. He continually blotted them on his jeans, worried that they might slip on the wheel of the SUV when he was trying to turn at a crucial moment.

"Logan," Claire whispered, coughing. "Logan, I … I … we need to … to … get Sam … Sam somewhere safe … not home."

Taking a deep breath, Logan tried to sound strong. "I need to call the police, we need—"

"Call Aaron first. I-I think we … should follow … his directions." Claire was gasping for air now. Samantha, who had been clinging to Claire with a grip that almost hurt, sat up and looked at Logan solemnly, her head cocked to one side, and then turned back to Claire without a word. Sam slowly began to unbutton Claire's blouse.

"What the hell are you doing?" Logan asked.

Sam glanced at him and then turned her attention back to Claire.

"L-let … let her … do what … she's doing," Claire gasped, intuitively trusting the child.

Logan turned his attention to the speedometer. He was doing over sixty in a thirty-five and almost laughed insanely when he thought: better slow down before I get a ticket.

"We need to get you to a hospital, Claire!" Logan was racking his brain trying to remember the location of the nearest medical facility. If he headed north on the freeway, he was bound to see the blue sign of a hospital. This was a populated area, after all, there would be medical help close by.

"Call Aaron, do … do what he says."

Samantha had completely unbuttoned Claire's blood-soaked blouse. She pulled it open, revealing a tan bra. Just above the left cup, a few inches above the heart was a rough-edged hole about the size of a dime, where the bullet had made its exit. The skin surrounding the wound had turned purple-black as if bruised or infected. Blood continued to flow briskly from the opening. Worried that the bullet had nicked the pulmonary artery, or worse, the aorta, Logan looked at Claire, slumped in the passenger seat with eyes closed and a concerned little girl sitting in her lap. He whispered again, "We need to get you help … and fast."

Taking her right hand, Samantha spread her fingers and then bent them into a claw shape, like she was going to scratch someone's eyes out. She took her left hand and rested it softly on Claire's cheek.

Placing the makeshift claw over the open wound, her other hand still cupping Claire's face, Sam turned to Logan and smiled for the first time since leaving Lynn Snellgrove's office. Logan stared in silent fascination as the little girl's fingers closed slowly around the wound and as if watching some illusionist at a Vegas show, the rough, bruised skin slowly filled the opening left by the bullet, as if knitted together by unseen hands. Sam's eyes rolled up into her head, hiding the iris and pupil, revealing only the dense white membrane. She reminded Logan of something out of a horror movie, like the Exorcist or The Omen.

The blood slowed to a trickle, then stopped altogether as the skin melded together as if it was never damaged at all.

As the hole in Claire's skin evaporated, purifying blood flowed freely into the bruised skin and, as Logan sat speechless, the epidermis turned from an angry purplish-black to a healthy light-brown, like the top of a freshly baked biscuit.

Samantha removed her hands from Claire and slumped against her chest, her eyes closed. Within seconds, she was fast asleep, as if the exertion of the act had sucked out all the energy in her tiny body. Claire's eyes were still closed, too.

It was all so surreal. Logan was sure he would wake up at any moment in his bed, Axle at his feet and Claire snoring softly next to him.

Although it seemed like forever, only ten minutes had elapsed since the incident back at Dr. Snellgrove's office.

Claire opened her eyes. "Logan? Is she okay?" Claire whispered, nodding at Samantha, who was snoring softly against her bosom.

In shock, Logan looked disbelievingly at his wife. "Did you see what she did Claire? *She healed you.* My God, how can this be, I … I don't understand at all … I don't know …" He shook his head. "How do you feel, honey, do you have any pain? Trouble breathing?"

"Physically, I feel great but mentally I'm a basket case. Should start making them right now, I think." She smiled weakly. "That way I'll be one step ahead when they admit me to the psycho bin."

"W-what do we do now, Claire, huh? If I keep driving like this, someone is going to call 911 and tell them there's a maniac on the road and then we'll have the cops on our tail, which would probably be a good thing. But how are we going to explain what happened? Do you think anyone would believe us? I don't. I have this uneasy feeling that we need to stay on the move because if I stop, I'm afraid bullets will start flying again."

"Call Aaron, like I said. At least he'll give us some direction, tell us what to do from here. I'm with you on the not stopping, but I think you need to slow down, not draw so much attention to us until we figure out what to do. In fact, let me do it since you're driving." Claire shifted Sam in her lap, being careful not to wake her as she reached for her purse.

"Wait, honey, use my phone. I programmed Aaron's number yesterday," Logan said, handing Claire the Samsung. "Speed dial four."

Claire dialed and waited as it rang Aaron's number. After the fourth ring, voicemail picked up with Aaron's cheery voice coming through. Sighing deeply, Claire said in a shaky voice, "Mr. Reynolds, this is Claire Keller, you met with my husband, Logan, yesterday regarding our little girl. Thelma Grisham recommended you … anyway, we need help and fast; someone is trying to kill us! We're afraid if we go to the police, that our story is so bizarre they won't believe us, but worse, we think if we stop right now that we will be under attack again. Please, please call us back right away!"

"What do we do now?" Logan asked.

"I-I don't know, keep driving I guess."

TWENTY-THREE

The air smelled delicious. The trees were sublime. The gurgle of the
river as it flowed downstream was inspiring. Scott Riley took all this
in. Up until now, the only stimuli his senses had received were that of
the cold, hard man-made underground complex. He was awed by the
wonder of it all. In the seven short years of his life, Scott had never set
foot on land or been exposed to nature's beauty: fresh air, clouds, sky,
trees, fresh-flowing water, flowers, and shrubs. Marvelous!

Dr. Carlson stood by his side. Five hours earlier, they had been
standing in the arid Utah desert, waiting to board the Bell Chopper,
which would take them to Washington State and Samantha Jennings.
The excitement had become almost unbearable as they sat on the tarmac
waiting to depart. Scott knew, however, that if he were going to accomplish what he wanted, he would have to keep control over his emotions.
In truth, he wanted to rip the pilot's head off for making them wait and
fly the thing himself.

After almost three hours in the air, they landed on a private estate
just outside of Mount Vernon, which was owned and operated by the
Larenx Corporation. From there, they took the company Escalade and
drove for another hour to the Mount Baker National Forest.

According to Scott, this was where they needed to be. There was something about this area that he was drawn to. Although he wasn't sure exactly why and what was going to happen here, Scott was confident that within a fifty-mile radius of this place was the birth of the future, his future, and the eradication of their opposition.

His soul longed for the wonders of the physical flesh, the excitement of adventure in this newly found world. Mostly, though, he hungered for control and power, which was his driving force, even at the tender age of seven.

Looking over at his incompetent, fat companion, Scott smiled. "Wow, Dr. Carlson, the air smells so good, not like the dense, thick air at New Life."

"Yes, yes it does, especially up here. This is fresh air: untouched by car exhaust, factory pollution, and individuals releasing their toxins into the atmosphere. That kind of crap you find in the city, not here."

They had parked the Escalade in a scenic turnout off the highway to stretch their legs and take in the view before they continued their journey to the company-owned cabin in the mountains. It wasn't a cabin really; it was a rendezvous point for operatives of The Corporation, an information gathering facility where the best minds compared notes and planned their next course of action.

"You brought me out here to test me, didn't you?" Scott asked Carlson, not taking his eyes off the spectacular view of the snow-capped mountains.

He knows what I'm thinking, probably knows everything.

"Well, yes … yes, Scott, I did. I thought it better - and safer - to bring you up to the mountains without a bunch of people around for your first attempts at greatness outside the controlled environment of a laboratory." His use of the word "greatness" was Carlson's vain attempt at humoring the boy, but he didn't know what else to do. If he did know his thoughts, then it was all over anyway. But the boy needed him – he needed him to help find the girl, needed him for food and shelter … didn't he?

Scott shuddered slightly as Carlson placed a meaty arm around his shoulders. Pointing to a boulder the size of a small car, Carlson said, "Can you move that?"

"Of course. But you think it's a good idea to do something like that standing here on the side of the road? What if a car comes along to enjoy the view and pulls in here right in the middle of the vanishing stone trick? Do you want that kind of publicity?"

"No … no, we don't."

"Didn't think so. Why don't we continue to this cabin you spoke of, and then figure out what the next step is, huh? And if it's as secluded as you say, I can practice further up in the mountains without the threat of being exposed."

Ben was shocked listening to the boy. It seemed that he was maturing at a rapid pace. His thought processes, the way he carried himself, were those of a man leading a country, or the world. Scott's self-confidence, fortitude, and determination aroused fear in Carlson, fear of this seven-year-old, laboratory derived human being taking over and quite possibly destroying the project in the process. Little beads of sweat popped out on Carlson's brow; he wiped them away with his handkerchief. He removed his arm from Scott's shoulders.

"Sounds like a great idea, let's head out," Ben said, turning and walking towards the Caddy. With his back to the boy, Ben casually felt inside his sports coat pocket and smiled when his fingers touched upon the packet Dr. Whiting had given him before their departure. "Once ingested, the drug will put him in a coma and then you can decide what to do with him," Whiting had said. "It can be mixed with liquid as it dissolves quickly and has no taste or smell. When you are ready, put it in his drink." Whiting had smiled then. Ben knew that Whiting wanted the boy destroyed. He didn't trust Scott and never grew to like him, or even accept him. Not like the girl. For some reason that escaped Ben, Whiting had adored Samantha.

Although Ben now shared some of Whiting's fear of the boy, he wasn't going to let a little paranoia stop him from using Scott to gain the control and power he deeply craved. If, however, things went awry, he had his alternate plan – it rested inside his coat pocket, waiting to be used. He could always begin again. His father always told him: if you fall off the horse, you just get right back on.

Never quit.

Never.

TWENTY-FOUR

When she first woke, she thought she was blind. Panic set in. Then she realized that she wasn't blind, she just couldn't open her eyes; cotton balls had been taped securely over each eyelid and then covered with a blindfold, which provided no infiltration of light. Her hands were behind her back, secured to the chair in which she sat, the wrists bleeding from the bailing wire that cut into her skin. Her face was no longer a face, but a mound of excruciating pain, with a broken nose and two broken teeth. Her upper lip was twice its normal size; her left eye was black, and her cheek was caked with dried blood. It looked as if she had been in a terrible auto accident in which her face came to an abrupt meeting with the windshield.

Sylvia Tran couldn't understand why she was here, why she was alive. She was certain that death was imminent. Her only conclusion was that these bastards wanted information - information she would not give no matter what the outcome.

Sylvia sat quietly on the hard, unpadded folding chair, listening. The only sound was her own breathing. She held her breath.

Nothing.

She suddenly realized that she wasn't gagged, which in her mind could only mean one thing: she was in a place where no one could hear her scream.

And then she did scream. Something scampered over her shoeless and sockless feet. They had taken her shoes. Tiny claws scratched her flesh; she felt something hairy brushing her ankles. And then there were more of them: scampering, running, clawing and, finally, biting. With a sickness in the pit of her stomach, Sylvia realized what these little creatures were: rats. She had rats running over her feet, biting and clawing her!

She could hear them now. They were squeaking and squealing as they ran back and forth over her bare feet, searching for the food that had been left on the floor next to her by the men who had beaten her and left her handcuffed to a chair, blind. She fought the urge to throw up. She swallowed hard. She bit off another scream and tried to pull her feet up off the floor. They were bound to the legs of the chair.

The heavy sound of metal wheels rolling in their tracks had her temporarily forgetting the horror at her feet. She cocked her head, listening as the large warehouse doors were rolled open, emptying sunlight into the dark warehouse; sunlight she, unfortunately, could not see. She heard men laughing and then footsteps echoing off the cold concrete walls of the empty storehouse, coming closer.

"I always wondered what an Asian would be like," one of them said.

"You've never had an Asian before?" the other man said incredulously.

"No, I never have, I've pretty much stuck with my own kind. I'm not like you. You'd do anything that moves, wouldn't you, you sick pervert."

She could smell them now. Mixed with the body odor and sweat, was the pungent tang of Brut, as if dowsing themselves with after-shave could replace showering. She heard the rats scurrying away as the men approached and although she was scared, she felt relief too. She didn't know which was worse: being beaten and raped by two men who smelled of sweat and Brut or slowly being eaten by rats.

Now, as one of them leaned in, she could smell the stink of halitosis. In her mind's eye, she saw a mouthful of discolored, rotting teeth and abscessed lips. Sylvia shuddered.

"And how are you today, Miss Tran?" a voice whispered in her ear. "Scared the rats away for you, we don't want to frighten you now do we? I'm Pete, and my friend here is Bradley."

"Hi pretty lady," Bradley said, "you sure is pretty for a China woman!" She could hear the drool. *Drool from the fool*, her crazed mind screamed. *Am I going nuts?*

"I-I'm not from China, you dimwit, I'm Vietnamese," Sylvia said through the pain of her busted up mouth.

"Yeah? I've heard about you Vietnamese girls—"

"That's enough Bradley, leave her alone. Nobody is doing any of that today, so just take it easy. We have other business to take care of." Sylvia heard a scraping sound on the concrete as Pete pulled up a seat in front of her, turned it around backward and sat down facing her, his arms folded across the backrest, chin resting on his hands. "Now let's just get you a little more comfortable," Pete said, removing the blindfold. He slowly and carefully removed the tape, like a surgeon removing bandages after an operation, and discarded the cotton balls covering her closed eyes.

The infusion of light hurt like hell. It felt like a thousand sharp needles jabbed in her eyes all at once. Tears were running down her cheeks. She slowly opened each eye a fraction of an inch, waiting for them to get acclimated to the brightness. How long had she been in the dark? Hours? Days? The last thing she remembered was going over an embankment and slamming into a tree.

After a couple of minutes, she could see faces in front of her. Looking around at the huge abandoned warehouse, Sylvia thought it miraculous that the roof hadn't fallen in on her. Wooden support columns were rotting through as if infested with termites; the concrete walls were cracked and water fatigued. There was the stench of black mold, urine, and feces. The homeless had, at one time, made this warehouse their private dumping ground.

"Please put those back on my eyes so I don't have to look at the both of you," Sylvia snarled.

Pete looked over his shoulder at Bradley and grinned. "Spunky isn't she? Even after being beaten up, thrown from a car, tied up with bailing wire, having rats run over her feet, she still has her spunk." He shook his head in disbelief.

"Betcha she has that spunk when she does the dirty deed too, I just betcha! Let me have just one whack at her, Pete, just one!"

"Go whack yourself," Sylvia said.

"Okay simmer down, the both of you. We have business to discuss, don't we Miss Tran?" Pete said, turning his attention back to her.

"I don't know what you're talking about, I-I really don't," Sylvia said, nervously licking her bruised and swollen lip.

"Of course you do Sylvia, of course you do. Now where are your headquarters?"

"Headquarters of what?" Sylvia asked.

Pete got right in her face like he was going to kiss her. Staring her right in the eyes, pursing his lips in anger, he said, "Knock off the shit!" He sighed and sat back. "Let's just make this simple … easy, okay?"

"Okay. I don't know what you're talking about. Simple enough?"

"Let me make this real easy for you - I'll give you a choice. If you don't tell us what we need to know, I'll put you in total blackness again. I will keep you in the middle of this empty shell of a building with no food or water, making sure you're bound to the chair, and then I will place rat food all over your feet, the floor around your feet, on your body, in your hair, everywhere. And then me and my pal here will walk out of this place, closing those big steel doors behind us. Then the rats will begin their feasting, first on rat food and then on human flesh. Or, you can talk to me now. The choice is yours. Simple."

She would never betray Fred or the organization that she believed in. She would lay down her life, even a torturous end like this, for the cause.

"I don't know what you're talking about," she muttered, looking down at her bare feet in resignation.

Pete stood up abruptly, knocking over his chair. He paced back and forth, his chest heaving up and down as he took deep breaths to calm himself. He stopped and glared at her. He stood there for a few moments and then started pacing again. After he had calmed himself, Pete said, "Okay Sylvia, you win. You're one tough woman. I'll give you that. However, I did save the best for last, just in case you decided not to cooperate." He winked at Bradley, who just smiled.

From his pocket, Pete withdrew a small vial filled with a clear liquid. Bradley produced a syringe, still sealed in its protective plastic wrap and handed it to his partner.

Sylvia's eyes grew wide as she watched. "W-What ... what ... are you going to do?"

"Well ... Sylvia Tran, from Vietnam, I'm going to have a heart-to-heart with you about anything I damn well please. But first, I need to give you something to help you relax. Ever hear of Scopolamine?"

Sylvia shook her head.

"No? Of course not, but that is what this pretty clear liquid is," he said, holding it close to her face. He stood up, unwrapped the needle from its package, poking it through the top of the vial. Pulling back the plunger, he extracted the liquid. Holding the needle up in the air, in the light, he flicked it a couple of times with his middle finger and looked at her sadly. "Don't want you to die from an air embolism before we get what we need."

Sylvia squirmed in her chair; the bailing wire cut deeper into her wrists.

Pete nodded, and Bradley walked behind the chair in which Sylvia sat. From his back pocket, he pulled out a pair of wire cutters. Grabbing a clump of Sylvia's hair in one gloved hand, he jerked her head back, putting his nose up against her now exposed neckline. He sucked air in through his nose, getting a whiff of her scent like some animal, going up and down her neck and then burying his nose in her hair. Still holding her firmly, Bradley cut the bailing wire from the chair, freeing Sylvia's hands. The moment her hands were free, Sylvia lashed out behind her, trying to claw his face, or at least grab something she could hurt.

Moving away from her flailing arms, Bradley stepped back and yanked on the handful of hair in his hand, whipping Sylvia's head toward the ceiling. Moving with the speed and grace of an Olympic athlete, he produced a razor-sharp knife from his belt, thrusting the cold blade against her throat. "Move bitch, and you're dead!" he gasped.

Pete stepped in and grabbed Sylvia's left arm, turning it palm up. "Don't move, don't struggle or it will just make me miss. And if I miss, and you struggle, Bradley here will probably slip with that knife of his."

Sylvia closed her eyes as she felt the needle puncture her skin and the tip enter her vein.

TWENTY-FIVE

Every species of flower, every color, size, and shape bloomed in the grassy, sun-filled meadow: azalea, begonia, dahlia, daffodil, geranium, impatiens, jasmine, lilac, marigold, orchid, petunia, roses (both white and red), tulips, tiger lilies and many more.

The smell was so sweet, and so thick it overwhelmed the senses, drowning out all else. Yet it was exquisite. Strange, though, as these flowers normally would not mix, for they grew in separate climates in different conditions; yet here they were sharing the same space, the same ground and the same air.

The area in which she stood was barren, though. A six-foot wide circumference of dead space surrounded her. No blooming sun-worshiping flowers, no luscious green grass at her feet. The ground below was covered in a red, sticky liquid. Fascinated, she watched as the soil turned from blood red to a healthy brown-black of fertile soil.

As if watching time-lapse photography, grass began to sprout on the outer edges of the circle, moving its way inward, filling the gap. Flowers followed the grass. As the greenness filled the void, azaleas, roses and impatiens bloomed on the fringes of the circle. They also moved inward, as if closing a wound.

Off in the distance, perhaps a hundred yards away, was a dog, a Labrador or a German Shepherd. It seemed to be chasing something. Every few minutes it would jump in the air, snapping at something unseen, its ears flopping lazily. And then it noticed her standing waist deep in the midst of the flowery field. With a yelp of excitement, the dog bounded through the foliage towards her, destroying flowers along the way; it disappeared for a second, then reappeared, disappeared again, and then reappeared as it leaped in and out of the tall flowers. Up and down. Up and down. Its tongue flopped out of its mouth comically.

She knew this animal; there was no fear. His name was Axle, wasn't it? They were best friends. He was almost upon her now. He disappeared once more down among the flowers, and when he reappeared, he was on top of her. The momentum of Axle's flight knocked her down onto the soft ground, the dog's paws on her chest like a wrestler pinning his opponent. She could've sworn he was smiling down at her.

Her head began to ring when she hit the ground.

Suddenly she was sitting in a car, on Claire's lap, a cell phone ringing on the floorboard beneath them.

"Oh crap," Claire said, "I dropped the phone." She smiled at Sam as she leaned down to retrieve it. "Hi honey," she said, as she answered the call.

"This is Claire."

"Mrs. Keller, Aaron here ... what's happening? In the voicemail you left, you said people were trying to kill you. Why would anyone want to kill you? And where are you right now?" His voice carried a trace of alarm.

"We're on the freeway heading north towards Everett right now. Just driving to nowhere, afraid to stop, afraid to go home, we don't know what to do. We need some direction here. We're scared, Mr. Reynolds," Claire said, looking at Logan with tears in her eyes. She held out the phone. He took it. Sam looked up at Claire with concern in her young eyes and then laid her head against Claire's breast, snuggling close. Claire stroked the girl's hair and kissed the top of her head.

"Hi Aaron, it's Logan. You won't believe what has happened, and I don't have time to go into it right now. Is there somewhere we can go … somewhere safe where we can meet?" He was afraid he sounded desperate, out of control, but he couldn't help it – he was scared. Logan's eyes kept flitting to the rearview mirror; at any moment, he expected to see a vehicle bearing down on them with men hanging out the windows, guns drawn like in some Hollywood action movie. Only he didn't feel like an action star. He felt like he was in a nightmare from which he could not wake.

"Exactly where are you?" Aaron asked.

Logan looked at the next road sign, which read: SW 128th STREET, EXIT 169, with a large white arrow pointing to the next exit.

"We're at exit 169 in South Everett, 128th Street, know the place?"

"Yeah … take the exit if you still can. There's a motel off 128th, by the Denny's if I remember correctly. Make sure you're not followed. If it looks clear, then get a room and call me back with the room number. Park around back, out of sight, I'll be there in about forty-five minutes or so. Okay?"

"Okay."

"What have you guys gotten into?" Aaron asked.

"I was hoping you could tell me. I'll call you back shortly," Logan replied, flipping the cell phone closed. He exited towards the Denny's and, just as Aaron had said, there was a rundown motel hidden directly behind the restaurant.

Mentally and emotionally drained, he just wanted to sleep. He was exhausted. Although he desperately needed rest, he was afraid to sleep; he needed to stay alert to protect his wife and child.

They drove up the street, made a legal U-turn at the light, and headed back to the motel and the promise of help. Except for the few words of encouragement Sam had spoken to Claire, the girl had been uncannily subdued. Claire was also quiet.

He pulled the Suburban around back, shoved it in park and shut off the engine. Turning to Claire and Samantha, he said, "I'm going up front to get a room. Lock all the doors and wait. You should be safe back here. You can't be seen from the road or the restaurant."

As he started to get out of the vehicle, Claire grabbed his arm. "Logan, don't you think we should go with you? I mean ... shouldn't we stay together? I-I guess I don't ..." she trailed off, not knowing how to finish her thoughts.

"I won't be gone but a few minutes, honey, and I think it's better that just one of us goes up front. Why don't—"

"I'll go then. Stay with Sam."

"But Claire—"

"No, stay with Sam, please. I think she'd be safer with you and if anything happens, just drive away as fast as you can."

Logan couldn't believe what he was hearing. "I would never, never leave you by yourself, Claire. Not after today, no fu—" He stopped in mid-sentence, glanced at Sam, who was watching him with those big, brown eyes. His face reddened. "No way," he whispered, "no way."

"Alright then, but we can't just sit here having a conversation while those people – whoever they are – look for us. I'll be right back." She jumped out of the Chevy, shut the door and disappeared around the side of the one-story motel.

Logan sighed and leaned back against the driver's door, facing Samantha. He pulled his knees up to his chest, locked his arms around his legs and rested his chin on the tops of his bony knees. "Scared?"

She nodded.

"Do you know why people are after us Sam, did we do something to upset somebody?"

She just shrugged.

Sam crawled over the middle console, and Logan sat up, dropping his legs to the floor. She crawled into his lap and curled up. Logan rocked her, stroking her hair. "How did you heal yourself and Claire honey? How did you do that?"

"Don't know," she whispered.

"It was a miracle, a real miracle. We'll get through this together, figure it all out, I promise you."

Claire entered the motel office. On the counter were a computer screen and a wire display rack displaying various pamphlets of not only local interests but also tourist attractions in Canada. To her right was an empty newspaper stand and next to that was a blue sofa that appeared to be a gift from the local Goodwill. The air had a thick, musty smell, as if the proprietor of this fancy establishment had smoked in here for the past twenty years.

The place was empty. On the left end of the counter sat a bell with a note that read: RING FOR SERVICE.

Ding! Ding!

After a few moments, a large woman wearing an oversized dress that looked more like a sack appeared from a doorway in the back. Her hair couldn't decide which direction it wanted to go and looked as if it hadn't been friends with a brush for a long time. Because the woman had left the door ajar, Claire could hear the television in the background. Pat Sajak was asking a contestant to pick a letter.

"Hi. Can I help you?" the woman asked. She seemed annoyed, as if a paying customer wasn't worth missing Pat Sajak and the excitement of the spinning *Wheel of Fortune*.

"Yes … yes, I believe you can," Claire said. "I would like a room with two beds, please. My husband and little girl are with me. They're out in the car." Claire forced a smile.

The woman looked at her silently, sighed and grabbed a form from a cubbyhole behind the counter. She tossed it in front of Claire and barked, "Fill this out."

Greg Meritt

"Do you have a pen?"

More annoyed than ever, the woman grunted and pulled a pen from the pocket of her baggy dress, and, without a word, tossed it on the counter next to the form. Claire noticed the woman's fingers and teeth were stained yellow-brown from years of nicotine addiction.

Claire picked up the pen and started to fill out the form. She stopped suddenly, wondering if she should put down their real names. She intuitively knew she should pay cash. But if she put down fake names, what if the woman asked for identification?

Claire bent over the piece of paper and wrote: Daniel and Mary Stern. She grinned and then put down a fictitious address where Daniel and Mary resided. She made up a license plate number and wrote it in the space provided, hoping the woman wouldn't walk around back later and check.

She hasn't walked that far in years. Probably hasn't walked further than this counter to her TV, Claire thought.

After finishing the check-in paperwork, Claire looked up at the woman. "How much?"

"Fifty-nine plus tax, comes to sixty-four dollars and seventy-eight cents. For the deluxe room and all, ya know; it's got HBO so you can watch movies, two queen beds, plenty of comforts, that room. Shoulda called this place Comfort Inn, but that's been taken." She laughed at her own attempt at humor, and then held out her hand, waiting for her money.

Pulling her purse off her shoulder, Claire retrieved her wallet, dug out four twenties and handed them to the woman. The proprietor took the money and walked over to a locked drawer. From her pocket, she produced a ring of keys and slipped one into the lock. She stuffed the twenties into the drawer and counted out change. "Room 137, around back," the woman said, handing Claire a key with a green plastic diamond-shaped tag with 1 3 7 stamped on it. Claire wanted to say, "Can't

180

afford to change the locks over to key cards, move into the twentieth century?" But she thought better of it and kept silent.

Claire thanked the woman and left the office, relieved that the inefficient proprietor hadn't asked for ID. Probably rents to drug addicts and prostitutes all the time, Claire thought as she walked to the back of the motel.

Upon seeing the Suburban, she let out a long, deep sigh. Claire wasn't aware until that moment that she had been holding her breath.

Logan, his back still against the driver's door, jumped when Claire rapped on the window; he smiled at her and opened the door. "Did you get a room?"

"Yes."

"I hope you paid cash."

"Who do you think you married, some ditzy girl that doesn't know how to handle herself in dangerous situations? Huh? Of course I paid cash," she said, like she faced people shooting at her on a daily basis.

Logan gave her a wan smile.

"And I didn't even use our real names, Daniel."

"Daniel – you couldn't think of a better name for me than Daniel? Why not Pierce or Jeanne-Claude?"

"Are you kidding me? Have you looked around lately? Do you really think a Pierce or Jeanne-Claude would be caught dead around these parts? I think not," Claire said, shaking her head and walking to room 137, the key dangling from her hand.

Carrying Sam, Logan followed his wife into the motel. The room wasn't as bad as Claire feared; it was clean, smelled of disinfectant, the sheets had been changed, and the coverlets on the two queen beds weren't stained and didn't sport cigarette burns. There was cheap artwork on the walls and next to each bed was an end table with a plain-looking lamp. Against the wall at the foot of the beds was an old – almost antique – dresser on which sat a thirty-two inch Sony television. On top of the TV was a channel guide.

Squealing delightedly, Samantha jumped on the bed nearest the door and began jumping up and down. And then she plopped down on her back, stared up at the water-stained ceiling, and folded her hands across her small chest.

"I need to call Aaron," Logan said, "before anything else happens." He pulled his cell from the right front pocket of his jeans, flipped it open and dialed. Aaron answered before on the second ring.

"Logan?"

"Yes."

"What room?"

"One-thirty seven, around back," Logan replied.

"On my way, don't use the phone anymore, I'll explain when I get there, ten minutes tops. Bye." The line went dead.

Logan stared at Claire, rubbing his chin. "That was weird. He said not to use the phone anymore, that he would explain everything when he gets here in ten minutes. He must be close."

His heart leaped in his throat when he heard a car pull up close to their room as soon as he hung up the phone. Samantha was jumping and giggling again. Logan turned to her. "Samantha! Quiet please, I need to hear, there's somebody outside.

Pulling back the edge of the curtain slightly, Logan peered through the tiny crack. Claire was at his back; he could feel her breath on his neck. Then he felt her slip her arms around his waist.

An older model green Ford Escape pulled in next to the Suburban and parked. Claire felt Logan's muscles tense as the driver's door slowly opened. A tall, skinny man wearing a cowboy hat got out, went around to the back of the Escape and retrieved two suitcases. While the man was getting the luggage, a little girl around eight years old jumped out of the backseat. A woman got out of the passenger side.

Relieved, Logan let go of the curtain and turned around to face his wife. He kissed her, lightly at first and then deeper and harder, as if it might be the last time they shared an intimate moment. Sam giggled and clapped her hands as she watched them.

Letting go of his wife, Logan went over to the bed Sam occupied and bent down. "Sam, we don't know what's going on right now, but we might have to move fast, so I need you to do Claire and me a favor."

"Okay."

"Please just do whatever we ask, even if it seems silly or dumb and don't ask why. We'll figure all that out later. We don't have time for a lot of questions right now, understand sweetheart?"

"Unnerstand.

"Thank you, honey." Logan stood up and went to the window. He peeked out through the slit in the curtain and then walked across the small room. He turned around and walked back. He sat on the bed. A second later he got up and paced the room and then he sat back down. He turned on the TV and began flipping through the channels.

Finally, Claire grabbed the remote from Logan's hand. "Stop it! You're driving me nuts! Nothing we can do now but wait. Aaron will be here soon, so why don't you just find one show to watch, something to take your mind off things for a few minutes, okay?"

"Yeah," Sam snickered.

Logan couldn't help but chuckle. "Okay, okay, you girls are right. Let's find something to watch," he said, taking the remote from Claire.

Then there was a knock at the door.

TWENTY-SIX

They got back in the Caddy, buckled up and headed north towards the cabin on the twisting blacktop that led further into the mountains. Carlson was behind the wheel; his considerable belly barely fit behind the steering column. Although the seat was back as far as it would go, every time he made a turn, Carlson had to suck in his gut a little.

"How much longer?" Scott asked.

"About an hour, maybe less. Why? Are you getting bored with the drive?"

"Not so much bored with the drive as bored with the company," Scott said, giving Carlson a deplorable look.

Ben was silent. He wasn't sure how to respond. Was he just kidding around, or did the boy despise him like he despised everyone else?

After a couple of miles in which neither spoke, Scott finally said, "Once we get to this meeting place, what are we going to do? What are your plans?"

"Not my plans, but the plans of the projects creator. First, we will work on control of your power so you can use it at will and the outcome will be exactly as planned. No mistakes. And what better place to work on and perfect your gift than Mother Nature herself? Up here there aren't the distractions - or obstacles - we would encounter in the city or other populated areas. Up here we only have to contend with the few people on the staff of the Corporation and any wildlife that might happen to wander across our path. Casualties will be few, if any. Once we are ready, we will find the girl, and you can do what you need to do, but you must kill her when you're finished."

"Of course."

"And then, well … it is up to the director. My goal, since you've asked, is to prove to the Federal Government and the general public that we are capable of eradicating disease and ending war. And for that, my dear boy, they will have to pay."

"So you're in this for the money? You're in—"

"Now wait just a minute. I know that you have powers beyond even what I can comprehend but remember one thing: I created you. Without the Larenx Corporation - and me - you wouldn't even exist. And just because you can move inanimate objects without use of your physical body, read someone's thoughts, and even kill, you need to know something. Other people on this planet, gifted people, can read minds too. They can move objects. And any of us can kill or be killed. You read about that every day in the newspaper or hear it on the news. None of that makes you unique. What makes you – us – special, Scott, is that we are going to do things that haven't been done, or even attempted, ever before."

"Wow, you make it all sound so exciting, I can hardly wait," Scott said sarcastically, rubbing his hands together excitedly in mock anticipation.

Ben wanted to slap the boy. He clenched his jaws hard and sucked in a deep breath, trying to contain his anger. "You don't like me very much, do you?"

"Now what makes you think that?" Scott asked, smiling.

"Why don't we just work together, huh? You get what you want, I can help you with that, and you can help me get what I want. I scratch your back, and you scratch mine."

"What?"

"Never mind ... let's just work together, okay?" Carlson kept his voice under control, but in his mind's eye, he was drugging the kid. He watched with bemused satisfaction as Scott slipped into unconsciousness, and then Ben proceeded to wrap his pudgy hands around the child's throat, slowly squeezing the life out of him.

I hope he doesn't try to read my mind now, Carlson thought nervously. After some effort, he finally shook the mental image from his head.

"Yes, let's work together so we both get what we want. But after this is all over, we go our separate ways, and you leave me alone, and I leave you alone, got it?" Scott said.

"Got it," Ben replied, although he knew that would never come to pass.

The trees seemed more daunting the further they ascended into the mountain range. Tall Evergreens reached across both sides of the roadway as if they were trying to shake hands, blotting out the sun and most of the sky, leaving only a small crack of light above. After another mile, they turned off the paved highway and onto a dirt road, which barely fit the width of the Black Caddy.

They bounced through the storm-created ruts and swerved around jagged stones while Carlson shouted and cursed. After the arduous half-hour journey, they crested a hill and started down the other side. Scott took in a deep breath and Ben grinned as they marveled at what was before them: a pristine meadow with an icy river running in the middle; to the east, the sprawling compound of the Larenx Corporation. Even from this distance, Scott noticed that this wasn't a conventional structure; it was more of a mansion you would perhaps find in super expensive areas of the country. The dwelling stretched over three acres;

there were four different buildings, which were connected by covered walkways.

Off to the west, directly opposite the Corporation's mountain headquarters, was a fabricated concrete helipad. A Bell Huey II currently occupied the pad. All of the roadways and the landing pad were cleared of snow.

"Why didn't we just fly in?" Scott asked, looking at the helicopter as they descended the hill and drove towards the buildings.

"Only room for one up here, and that's for Richards," Ben replied, nodding at the helicopter. "That's his baby. It's only for his bodyguard, his family, and his closest advisors."

"Not for you then," Scott said matter-of-factly.

"Yes, not for me."

They pulled up to the front of the main building, parked and stepped out of the Caddy, breathing deeply of the fresh air. Scott tilted his head to the sky and raised his arms above his head as if he were a sun worshiper. Carlson watched silently for a moment, and then he grabbed Scott by the arm. "Let's go," he said, "not a good idea to keep them waiting."

Scott angrily pulled himself from Carlson's grasp and headed up the steps to the large porch, which ran the length of the building. Carlson hurried after him. He didn't want the boy out of his sight where he could get into trouble. He still fooled himself into thinking he had some modicum of control, however slight.

Before they could ring the bell, the door opened. There stood a man, about six foot five, wearing a dark blue suit, sunglasses and a face that looked as if it had never smiled.

"Looks like the Secret Service," Carlson whispered to Scott.

"Who?"

"Nothing, never mind."

The big man gestured for them to enter. Scott bounded into the big foyer, marveling at the size and architecture of the room: a huge antique chandelier hung from the center ceiling, expensive marble lay at his feet; the wainscoting surrounding the room was hand-carved. Two spiral staircases, one on Scott's left and one on his right, joined together on the second floor forming the long expansive hallway.

"Follow me," the man in the sunglasses said.

They followed him down a long hallway. Expensive artwork decorated the walls. At the end of the hall, they turned right and entered what looked to be a front room. French Doors opened to an expanse of greenery that would rival the best golf course. Two men sat on the L-shaped leather sofa. One was drinking a Diet Pepsi; the other was enjoying a sandwich.

"Have a seat, Richards will be out in a minute," said the man in the sunglasses, pointing to the empty section of the leather couch.

Scott sat down. "Wow, would you look at all these electronics!" he said, referring to the HD Video displays, which showed every area of the property and every room in the building. A bank of sophisticated computers controlled everything from the climate to the shades to the communications system.

Carlson sat next to the boy. The two men glanced at them without a word, nodded, and then went back to watching the football game on the seventy-inch wall-mounted screen.

Ten minutes later, Richards entered the room and the two men respectfully stood up, as if the guy were royalty. Waving a hand at them, Richards said in a husky voice, "Go away, leave us alone now." The two men did as directed, disappearing from the room in a hurry.

"Well, well ... Dr. Ben Carlson, so nice to see you again. And who do we have here?" Richards asked, nodding at Scott.

"The projects first real success, sir," Carlson replied. "This is Scott Riley, the seven-year-old prodigy."

"Prodigy of what?"

"Everything and anything," Ben smiled. "Anything you want."

Richards grunted. "We'll see 'bout that!"

"I want to go home," Scott whined. "I want my trucks and my special Lego set." When he spoke, he sounded completely unlike the crazy power ridden man-boy that Carlson knew. Now he was just a seven-year-old who wanted to play.

"Is this some kind of joke?" Richards asked, his face turning purple-red with rage.

"I-I don't know what ..." Carlson trailed off and turned to Scott. "What's got into you, Scott? Show Mr. Richards here your special talents and how you can manipulate solid matter. Talk with him about the work you've done back in Utah at the lab – the cracking of code; the solving of complex puzzles in minutes instead of months and years.

"What?" Scott asked, looking genuinely perplexed.

"I ... I don't know what to say, sir." Now it was Carlson who turned red, not out of anger, but out of embarrassment.

Scott began to laugh.

"What's so funny?" Carlson asked.

"You are ... you shoulda seen ... the look ... on your ...face!" Scott said, trying to catch his breath.

Richards stared at them in disbelief. "Just what is going on here?"

"Aww, nothing, just playing around," Scott said. "I can do whatever you need me to do, sir, help you get everything you want, under one condition."

"And what might that be?"

"Get rid of him," Scott said, nodding at Carlson.

Now it was Richards turn to laugh.

TWENTY-SEVEN

"Quiet," Logan whispered. "Go hide in the bathroom or something."

"What good is that gonna do? If it's trouble, we're screwed, we don't have anything to fight with, and there's no way out," Claire said. "We'll just stay right here with you."

Logan knew she was right. Once more he pulled back the curtain of room 137 and peered out. His knees buckled with relief when he saw Aaron Reynolds standing at the door. Logan removed the safety chain and opened the door. Aaron immediately stepped inside, closing the door and replacing the chain. He was carrying a black duffel bag, which he placed on the floor at his feet.

He smiled and extended a hand towards Claire, who was sitting on the edge of the bed. "You must be Claire ... I'm Aaron, as you are probably well aware, and the beautiful young lady sitting next to you must be Samantha."

Smiling back, Claire took his hand in hers. "Yes, I'm Claire. Your powers of deduction amaze even me. No wonder you have been so successful in your career as an officer of the law and then in your own private practice."

His smile broadened. "Logan, you forgot to inform me that the woman you married was not only good-looking but smart as well."

"Yeah … I'm so used to it now that I forget to warn people."

"Please to meet you, Mrs. Keller and Miss Samantha," Aaron said. Samantha giggled. Claire smiled and said, "Pleased to meet you too, Mr. Reynolds. Somehow I thought you'd be taller."

"I believe your husband mentioned the same thing. Sorry to disappoint," he said good-naturedly. But we need to hurry and get serious real quick."

Claire instantly liked this soft-spoken good-hearted short man with the ponytail sticking out of the back of his Mariner's baseball cap. For some reason she couldn't put her finger on, she felt safer with him around.

"What do we do now?" Logan asked.

"First, we need to dump your vehicle and—"

"Dump the Suburban? But why?" Claire asked.

"I'm sure – no, I'm positive – that you'll find a transponder planted on it somewhere. Whoever is after you knows where you are right now. We will need to be very careful. I have a car outside, of course, but we'll dump that later after we're sure that we're not being followed."

"You just said that they know where we are right now, so if that's true, why don't they just come in here, snatch the girl and kill us?" Logan asked.

"At this point, I believe they aren't worried about losing you. They are watching and waiting for the best time to make their move. You're in a public place, which is why I directed you here – lots of traffic. Too risky for them, especially if they know they can track you wherever you go. They're just biding their time."

"Why is all this happening? ... I mean it doesn't even seem real, and it doesn't make any sense. We've never done anything to anyone, we're decent members of our community, and we try and help others. We lead a good life." Claire sighed deeply. "I just don't get it. This is like something in a movie; it doesn't happen to real people."

"But it does," Aaron said. "Unfortunately, it does. You wouldn't believe what I've seen in my years of law enforcement, Claire, it sometimes sickens me."

"Then why do you do it?"

"To help people like you ... I believe in what I do and still believe that most people are good. As long as I feel that way, I will continue the fight."

Throughout the conversation, Samantha had sat on the edge of the bed, silently watching. Now she said, "It's me they want...I'm sorry." She hung her head for a moment and then looked up at Aaron. "Will you help us?"

Aaron bent down, cupped Samantha's face in both hands and looked her directly in the eyes. "Yes, sweetheart, I'll help all I can. This isn't your fault at all, don't ever think that it is, because that would not be the truth."

"Okay."

Standing up, Aaron picked up the black duffel bag and dropped it on the bed. He unzipped it and reached inside, pulling out a Smith and Wesson .45 Colt revolver. He handed it to Logan, who hesitated and then took it reluctantly.

Aaron pulled out another one exactly like the one he'd given Logan, as if he had a bottomless armory in the black duffel bag. He handed it to Claire.

"Oh great ... what do I do with this? I can't even hit anything at the arcade shooting gallery," Claire said, turning the gun over in her hands. "And those targets aren't shooting back."

"When you're in need, instinct will take over, trust me," Aaron said. "And what about you Logan, ever fire a gun?"

"Well, yes … a few times when I was younger, a lot younger, many years ago and then only in the woods with my father. I don't own a gun, never have and actually despise them. You read all the time about some kid getting shot because they found a gun in the house, or an innocent person killed by the very gun they bought for their protection! No thanks." He handed the gun back to Aaron.

"I understand that you don't like firearms, a lot of people don't, but this is a unique situation. We're dealing with some dangerous people here and I—"

"Wait a second, how do you know what we're dealing with? I just met with you yesterday and—"

"And I did a bunch of digging last night and this morning. I'll fill you both in after we get moving, okay?"

Claire said, "Take the gun, Logan … it would be unfortunate if you needed it and didn't have it."

"Fine," Logan said, taking the gun back from Aaron's outstretched hand.

Aaron nodded and turned his attention back to the black bag. He tossed Logan a disposable cell phone.

"Where's mine?" Claire whined, winking at Sam. She was doing her best to stay upbeat not only for Samantha but for all of them.

"I have about fourteen in the bag, so you can certainly have your own," Aaron said, tossing one to Claire.

"Why so many cell phones?" Logan asked.

"When you use one, make the call fast and to the point. Then toss the phone. Each phone is for one call – we won't give them time to trace. From now on, do not use your personal cell phones at all. We will be leaving them in the vehicle when we ditch it and switch cars. That way, our friendly pursuers will think we're still with the vehicle. And, of course, they'll know where the vehicle is by way of the transponder."

"They're tracking our cell phones?" Logan asked.

"Yes."

Claire sucked in a deep breath. "This is like some James Bond shi - er, stuff or something."

"Who's James Rond?" Sam asked.

Claire laughed nervously.

"We need to move," Aaron said, unbolting the chain from the door. "I'll be driving the Green Ford Taurus, and I want you to follow me. If we get separated, use the disposable cell to call me – I have already programmed in the number for you. We'll all be riding together shortly if all goes to plan. Any questions?"

Claire and Logan both shook their heads.

"Samantha?" Aaron said, "Do you understand what we're doing?" She nodded.

Aaron slowly pulled the door open a crack, peering out to the parking lot beyond. Claire held her breath. She watched helplessly as Aaron's back blew apart as the gunfire tore through his body. She closed her eyes and shook her head. When she opened them, Aaron was still standing in the doorway, still peering out, his back still intact.

"Okay, move!" he said, walking rapidly to his Ford while Sam, Claire, and Logan headed to the Suburban. Claire's heart pounded in her chest.

They left the motel parking lot without incident, Logan following the Ford Taurus onto I-5. After two miles, Aaron took the exit ramp. Logan followed. They drove through residential streets, turning right, then left, right again, as if in a maze. "What's he doing?" Claire asked.

"I don't know … maybe he's making sure that no one is following us," Logan said.

Finally, Aaron pulled to the curb, in front of a nondescript house, and shut off the car. Ahead a few yards, Logan found a space and parked the Suburban. "Okay guys, grab what you need, and let's go," Logan said.

"Give me your cell, honey, remember what Aaron said. I'll put it in the glove box."

He handed her his cell, grabbed the disposable, pocketed his keys and joined Aaron on the sidewalk. Seconds later, Claire and Samantha were standing next to him. Thunder rumbled off in the distance. It was only two-fifteen in the afternoon, but the dark, chilly November day made it feel much later.

"Any minute now," Aaron said.

"Any minute now what?" Claire said.

"Aha! There she is now, right on schedule. The best assistant a man ever had!" They stood on the sidewalk watching as a blue late model Ford Explorer turned towards them and then stopped in the middle of the street, not bothering to pull to the curb.

With the engine still running, an older woman of perhaps sixty or so stepped out of the Ford and approached them, almost at a run. She was slightly taller than Aaron and about ten years older. Wrapping her long arms around him, the gray-haired woman gave him a big hug. "Promise me you'll be careful Aaron!"

Looking embarrassed, Aaron said, "Of course I will, aren't I always?"

"No, no you're not. Sometimes I think that you believe you're invincible like you're being watched over by angels or something."

"Maybe I am, maybe—"

"You're still human, and the human body still dies Aaron, so be careful, darn it!" She turned toward the others and smiled.

"And you must be the hunted … er, sorry, the victims. No, no, no, that's not right. The pursued … yeah, that's better … the pursued. My name's Connie, friend of this guy-" she jerked her thumb at Aaron – "who thinks he can save the world. I keep telling him that-"

The loud honk of a horn startled them. "Move your goddamn car!" a man screamed from the street. The Explorer was still idling in the middle of the road.

"Just go around, we'll be done in a minute. Go around," the woman yelled back, waving at the man like some flagger on a road crew.

"I can't! The driver's door is wide open, blocking the street! There's not enough room! Who the hell stops in the middle of the street? Move this piece of shit now!"

"Calm down young man, you do not need to curse," Connie said, walking towards the Ford. "Didn't your mother teach you any manners? You do not talk to elders that way; it's disrespectful!" Watching the woman in amazement, Logan turned to Claire and shrugged. Claire held out her hands, palms up, and shrugged too. In a vague way, this woman – Connie - reminded her of Thelma. Claire felt the hot sting of tears and the emptiness in her heart.

Upon reaching the vehicle, Connie didn't climb behind the wheel but instead she slammed the driver's side door and stepped out of the way. Then she motioned for the man to go around. Really pissed now, the man swung around while lying on his horn and giving Connie a close-up view of his middle finger as he drove past.

Connie came back to the group, leaving the Ford in the middle of the street, still running. "I packed some food and some extra blankets, flashlights, water, and a few other items you might need." Aaron, looking more embarrassed than ever now, said, "Thanks, but we need to get going...you shouldn't have gone to the trouble—"

"Aaron," she said, shaking a finger in his face, "don't you start with me. Just get your rear end outta here before they find you." She gave his short-cropped beard a tug, lightly pinched his cheek and then started walking back the way she had come.

"She's a good angel," Sam said, nodding.

"What honey?" Claire asked.

"Huh? Oh ... that lady is a good angel, very good."

"Yes, she was very nice." Claire glanced at Logan, who was watching Connie thoughtfully as she disappeared around the corner. Maybe she reminded him of Thelma too.

"Is that your mom?" Samantha asked Aaron. Logan and Claire both began to laugh, and a few seconds later, Aaron joined in.

"No, sweetheart, that lovely woman isn't my mother, although sometimes she thinks she is. Connie and I go way back, and I'll tell you about her, but right now we need to get out of here and stay on the move. Come on, let's go."

Because they were leaving their vehicles in some unknown neighborhood, Logan had the uneasy feeling he might never see his Suburban again and even if he did, he was afraid it might be devoid of tires and wheels. They clambered into the Ford: Aaron behind the wheel, Logan in the passenger seat, Claire and Sam in the back.

"Where are we going?" Logan asked as they moved out of the residential area and back onto the freeway.

"A place a couple of hours from here where we have some help waiting … it's hard to explain. Better just to show you. And that gives me plenty of time."

"Plenty of time for what?"

"To tell you what I found out about your newly adopted daughter," Aaron said, staring grimly at the wet road ahead.

"What did you find out?"

"You're not going to believe this."

"Try me."

Aaron glanced at Logan, looked over his shoulder at Sam - who was starting to drift off – and smiled at Claire.

Clearing his throat, Aaron began to share what he had learned since yesterday.

TWENTY-EIGHT

She waited for the slight burn that normally accompanied injections, but none came. Instead, she heard a dull thud as Bradley, the man who held the knife to her throat, dropped to the concrete floor on her right. At the same instant, the guy who called himself Pete relaxed his grip on the needle's plunger as he turned to see what had happened. When he did, his face met a fast-moving sledgehammer that thoroughly smashed his skull, impregnating bone fragments into his brain, killing him instantly. He never knew what happened.

Sylvia cracked open one eye and what she saw made her happy - very happy indeed. Holding the bloody sledgehammer - and whistling - was Matt, her very good friend and co-worker for the past seven years. Behind her, working on the bailing wire that bound her hands, was a young blonde, Lisa, another operative who was one of the best Sylvia had ever known. Good thing these people were on her side.

"Blimey sweet'art looks like somebody tried to disfigure ya, make ya unrecognizable. You look like hell! What'd they do, bash your head against the wall?" Matt asked. His Australian accent always sounded so sexy to her.

"You might be cute and have a great body, but I think you might want to look up the word "tact" and try to put the concept into action there, Matt. I don't believe you're helping our girl much by telling her how banged up she is … I think she's well aware, aren't you honey?" Lisa said as she finished cutting away the baling wire from Sylvia's bleeding wrists.

Sylvia tried to smile but instead she began to cry. "Oh, it hurts so much," she gasped, sniffling. "I-I really … really thought I … thought I was dead." She hung her head, closed her eyes and wept. All she wanted to do was sleep; she was so tired. And weak. She didn't think she could walk.

Matt looked sullenly at Lisa and then at Sylvia. "I'll carry ya to the van. Lisa, you'll need to give her some medical attention an' clean them wounds." Putting his left arm under her knees and his right arm around her shoulders, Matt lifted Sylvia from the folding chair as if she were a pile of laundry and carried her out of the dark, empty warehouse to the waiting van. Lisa ran ahead and opened the sliding door.

The inside of the van was equipped like an ambulance: shelves of medical gauze, crèmes, tourniquets, syringes, and bandages; removable gurney, oxygen tanks, diagnostic equipment, and defibrillators occupied every available space.

Matt set her gently on the cot. "Get 'er patched up best you can, and I'll drive careful, trying me best to skirt any ruts an' potholes in the road," he said as he climbed behind the wheel.

"Okay," Lisa replied, jumping in the back next to her friend. She gently took Sylvia's hand in hers, being careful not to hurt the battered woman and brushed the hair off her forehead. Sylvia murmured but did not open her eyes. Leaning down next to Sylvia's ear, Lisa whispered, "I'm going to give you a shot of morphine for the pain, honey. After it begins to work, I will clean you up and get some bandages on those cuts and scrapes, set your nose, okay?"

Sylvia nodded slowly and opened her eyes about halfway before closing them again. Lisa gave her the morphine and then went to work laying out salves, creams, and bandages to patch up her friend.

Matt did the best he could not to jar and bounce the van, but the road was in such disrepair that even the most skilled driver would not have been able to avoid every furrow.

"Do you think they know about us?" Lisa said from behind him.

"Does who know 'bout us?" Matt replied.

"The people who did this to Sylvia. Do you think they know about the rest of us?"

"No. No way. Mr. Rickart wouldn't let anyone find out 'bout us. Never."

"So how do you think they found out about Sylvia?"

He shrugged. "Prob'ly caught 'er sayin something bad 'bout Carlson or the Larenx Corp, but Sylvia never would say nothin' 'bout us ... she's too smart for that."

"Yeah ... maybe, but it still greatly concerns me that they found out about Sylvia. I mean look at her Matt ... look at what they've done!"

"Yes, it's awful."

Lisa sighed. She opened a package of alcohol wipes and gently cleaned Sylvia's wounds, bracing for her to cry out. But she never did. Lisa was relieved to see Sylvia's chest rise and fall with each breath. She had entertained the idea of putting Sylvia on oxygen, but if a patient could breathe without aid, that was a sure sign of strength and recovery.

In her twenty-eight years, Lisa Eshleman had witnessed more atrocities than most people were ever exposed to in an entire lifetime. Her tenure as a military nurse overseas brought not only strength and perseverance but also a quality hard to find: a reverence for life and the appreciation of human kindness. Thrown into the midst of war and death, most became hardened and unappreciative. The effect on Lisa had been the opposite. She became more caring and more loving, not less. Men were attracted to her aura of love and goodness, but she also was physically striking. Her one hundred seventeen pounds sat proportionately on her five-foot-six-inch frame; her complexion, which was once a landscape of teenage hormone-induced pimples, now boasted a smoothness that most dermatologists envied.

After cleaning and bandaging Sylvia's wounds, setting her nose and checking her vitals, Lisa kissed her friend on the forehead and joined Matt up front.

"How's she doing?"

"Sleeping. She's pretty banged up, but amazingly her only broken body part is her nose. Her wrists are cut fairly deep from the bailing wire they tied her up with, and she's going to have some big purple-green bruises, but she'll live. She'll hurt for a while, but she'll definitely live."

"Why don't you get some rest? I'll wake you when we get there, okay?"

"Thanks, Matt - that sounds good – I'm exhausted. Wake me if Sylvia needs me for anything - anything at all."

"Course."

Lisa curled up best she could in the passenger seat and closed her eyes.

And dreamed of a world without violence.

TWENTY-NINE

"I like this boy, I really do," said Richards, still chuckling and look-ing at Carlson. "And if he can do the things you've suggested, Doctor, I will be one happy man and all these years and all the money spent will have been worthwhile." He stopped pacing and squeezed his three-hundred-plus frame into the black overstuffed chair, his cigar sticking out of the right corner of his mouth like a torpedo. "Now let's talk about these so called "powers" that—"

"We refer to them as talents," Carlson said, "don't we Scott?" As soon as he'd spoken, Ben knew he'd made a mistake. Carlson could feel the large man's eyes burning into his psyche, like some laser burning away a malignant tumor.

"Don't you ever interrupt me," Richards said in a tone that made the hair rise on the nape of Ben's neck.

"S-Sorry...I-I don't know what I was thinking. It won't ever happen again; I assure you." Oh how he hated this arrogant, egotistical son-of-a-bitch, but he knew that he needed to use this man's money and power, at least for a little while longer. And then, well, let's watch his brain fry like an egg on high heat, Ben thought.

Scott kept the snickering to himself. Both these men were fools, great fools who didn't have any idea of what was coming down the pike.

"Better not," Richards remarked, glaring at Ben. "Now, let's discuss what talents - as you call them - this young man here possesses. Fill me in."

"Scott here can manipulate solid matter through the power of his mind, which I – and the team at New Life – have found out with the help of modern equipment and technology. He speeds up his thought process to vibrations – or speed, if you prefer – to unheard of levels, which is something that we didn't have the capability to track until recently. Now, what exactly happens after the energy—"

"Carlson, Carlson, I don't care about all this scientific mumbo jumbo horseshit. Just summarize what the boy can do, what you've created after all these years and then let's see some examples."

"Certainly. Scott can move objects, but not while you're watching."

"What do you mean, not while I'm watching?"

"You've heard of teleportation, right?"

"Yeah, so?"

"That's not what this is. This is not getting an object to move across the room like a poltergeist or something. This is about dematerializing matter, speeding up the atoms and molecules of an object to such a rapid frequency that it just disappears from sight. Then the matter – or energy – is projected to a different location and rematerialized, which means the molecules and atoms are slowed back down and reformed into the original particle, but in a different location." Carlson became excited just talking about it, but Richards sat there with his cigar poking out of his face, unimpressed.

"Yeah ... what else?"

Carlson looked over at Scott, who seemed to be in a faraway place. He was staring out the French doors, watching the security men. They had gone outside when Richards asked them to leave the room. Scott had a strange look in his eyes. He was oblivious, or so it seemed, to the two men who were talking about him.

"Scott can read people's thoughts. Now we believe, with some patience and practice, that our young man here will be able actually to get a subject to do whatever we want through the power of mind control – actually replacing the subject's thoughts and actions with our own.

Richards was leaning forward in his chair, captivated. "Fascinating, just the power to read thoughts has unending possibilities, doesn't it? To get inside the minds of great leaders and know what their plans are before they happen, just think what we can do! Knowing when great military minds are going to attack; better yet, knowing their strategy! And if we can actually control their minds, why, there's nothing I won't be able to do!"

"Well … yeah … but there are still a few things to work out," Ben said quietly.

"Oh?" Richards replied, raising his eyebrows and plucking the half-chewed cigar from his mouth. "And just what do you need to work out?"

"The few times that Scott has entered someone's head, there have been repercussions. The first mishap was one of our colleagues at New Life, Dr. Hammond, a brilliant neurologist. Dr. Hammond's brain is oatmeal, sir, and he lies in a coma with no chance of recovery. The only reason he is still breathing is so the staff at New Life can study and learn from this unfortunate case. As Scott would tell it, he was—"

"I was testing the waters when the good doctor tried to shut me out," Scott said, looking away from the back forty; he was looking directly at Richards now, ignoring Carlson. "He fought it, and I freaked – I admit that – but this was before I knew what was happening; before I had any semblance of control. It was and is a terrible accident, just an accident."

"No doubt in my mind, boy, no doubt at all," Richards said. "Are you ready to show me what you're capable of?"

"Of course."

"Okay, let's start with moving an object. See that golf ball out there on the putting green?" Richards asked, pointing to the white dimpled ball lying about one-hundred-fifty feet from the back doors just past the security men.

"Yes."

"Can you drop it in my lap?"

"Yes."

Only a few seconds after the word passed his lips, a small, white golf ball appeared in the fold of the man's crotch. Scott laughed as Richards jumped out of his seat with a squeal, and although he would never say it out loud, the man sounded like a little girl.

"Wow! Holy Shit!"

Carlson smiled. "That was nothing."

"Yeah? It was sure something to me. This is great! How about something a little bigger Scott?"

"Sure, like what?"

"Oh … I don't know. Have you ever tried something heavy or really large?"

"Such as?"

"A piece of furniture? An appliance? An automobile?"

Carlson said, "Now wait a minute, let's be careful here and not hurt the boy in the process. The biggest thing he's teleported has been a laptop computer and—"

"The concept's the same. It doesn't change from a golf ball to a computer to a car to a house," Scott said.

"Maybe…" Carlson said, rubbing his chin. "But you must have to exert more energy to manipulate larger matter. We just haven't had the chance to build up to larger—"

"The best way to test something is just to do it; that's what I always say," Richards said, looking at Scott.

"I couldn't agree more, sir. How 'bout we move this couch – while the doctor is sitting on it – to the back porch?" Scott stood up just as the sofa and Carlson disappeared, but they didn't suddenly reappear.

Richards looked at Scott. "What happened?" he asked worriedly. "Did you lose control over your power?"

"Oh no, not at all. Just leaving them out in limbo for a bit, their molecules and atoms spread out in the universe. Of course, the couch won't know or care, but Carlson will." Scott grinned like a little kid going on his first carnival ride; he was having so much fun!

Richards watched him for a moment, chewing thoughtfully on his cigar. He suddenly had a vivid and very concerned feeling about this boy. The world was Scott's playground and everything in it was his toy. "Scott, bring them back now. I would like to see what else you're capable of. I think—"

The leather couch appeared on the porch on the other side of the French doors. Carlson was sitting on it clutching his chest.

"Good God! I think he's having a heart attack!" Richards said, getting out of his chair. Before he made it to the door, however, his security men were helping Carlson off the sofa. He appeared to be okay. He was no longer clutching his chest, although he looked extremely pale. Opening the doors, Carlson stumbled back into the living room. He glared at the kid. Scott smiled back and shrugged.

"Just what did you think you were doing?" Carlson yelled. He was no longer pale. Color flooded his face.

"Calm down man, calm down," Richards said.

"I'm not gonna calm down!" Carlson said, still looking at Scott. Spittle was flying everywhere; now he looked like his ticker was going to blow. "We ... you ... have never dematerialized a human before, only inanimate things! You could have killed me, or worse! I could have been left with my matter spread all over the place and ... and ..." He sat down on the floor, hard. Carlson buried his face in his hands and rocked back and forth. The two security men brought the sofa back into the home the old-fashioned way: they carried it. Careful not to step on the man sitting on the floor, they quickly and quietly set the piece of furniture back into its original position and then left the room.

"Carlson," Richards said, "let's chalk this up as another success. This must be the first time in history that a human has actually transported! It's like something straight out of Star Trek." He chewed on his cigar and said, "But it's not time travel, is it? I mean the little boy here didn't send you into the future and back in the past – can you do that young man?"

"Probably ... don't know ... never tried. And I'm not a little boy!"

"Okay, okay, didn't mean anything by it."

Carlson shakily stood up, grabbing the edge of the couch for support. "I-I'm fine now, but that scared the hell out of me!"

"What was it like? How did it feel? Were you aware or was it like when you sleep - were you conscious?" He had a million questions, but what ran through his head were the potential possibilities once this power was harnessed. He didn't trust the boy, though. There was something off about the kid; that meant he needed Dr. Carlson and his staff to corral and channel this fascinating scientific breakthrough.

"I don't remember anything. I was here one second and the next thing I know I was on the back porch. I did feel drained, like I had just run a marathon or something and it felt like my chest was about to explode. That must be a side effect of the molecules and atoms being rearranged and then slammed back together. What a ride! Don't ever do that to me again!" Carlson said.

Scott shrugged and held up his hands.

"Okay, okay, it's over, let's move on, shall we?" Richards said. "Now, what about this mind-reading thing? So you can tell what people are thinking?"

"Sometimes."

"Sometimes?"

"When I want I guess," Scott said.

Ben Carlson sat on the couch. "We have done many controlled studies at the lab in Utah, and it is evident that our young genius can read minds at will. However, because what we know is based on a set of particular circumstances in a controlled environment, we cannot tell what may happen when you bring other factors into play."

"Other factors? Such as?"

"Each person is unique and that includes brain function and brain development. So it is impossible to test every subject from the lowest IQ to the highest, all at different ages and at different stages … most of this is done by trial and error. Suffice it to say that Scott can read minds; however, he did destroy an intelligent man in the process. Because this was done without authorization and the victim was completely unaware of what was happening – which was not true in the lab tests – the outcome was terrible and horrific. But I believe with the proper guidance and practice that Scott can pull back before the onset of irreparable damage to the subject."

Richards shook his head. "I told you before, *I don't care* about all this scientific mumbo jumbo – can he read minds, tell what someone else is thinking?"

"Yes, of course."

"Let's see a demonstration then." He took the cigar out of his mouth, looked disgusted at the wet, chewed up end and threw it into the fireplace. He turned back to Scott. "See the skinny one?" He nodded to the tall, thin security guy on the veranda.

"Yes."

"I like him, so read the other one's mind." Richards laughed at his own wit.

Scott closed his eyes.

"He's thinking about how good a half-pound burger with everything on it would taste right now."

"Yeah … of course he is. What else?"

"He's excited about going to town and applying for the opening at the Police Department. Always wanted to be a cop. He thinks this job sucks, hates it."

"Oh?" Richard's eyebrows went to the top of his head.

"And he thinks you're a power hunger prick."

"Enough, Scott," Carlson said.

"No, no. I want to hear more," Richards said, fascinated now. "What else does he think about me?"

"We don't have any proof that any of this is true, we need to find a subject with whom we can verify the information," Carlson said.

"We know the part about the burger is true, just look at that guy's stomach – why it's almost as big as mine!" Richards roared.

As they were watching, the big man standing on the back porch wiped the back of his hand across his upper lip. It came away slick with warm blood.

His nose had suddenly started to bleed.

THIRTY

"Children's World does not exist, at least not in the State of Washington. I did—"

"Wait, what did you just say?" Claire asked from the backseat of the Explorer. Trying to get comfortable, she slumped against the window. Sam's tiny frame was stretched out across the rest of the seat, her head resting lightly on Claire's lap. Trying not to disturb Sam, Claire sat up and leaned closer to the men in the front.

Glancing over his shoulder, Aaron said, "Claire ... Logan, there is no such place as Children's World in Washington State, not that I could find anyway. No such company is registered with any state or governmental authority nor listed with any non-profit organization."

"How can that be? We went and met with them, went to their office, checked their website, read the company history," Logan replied, shocked.

"Anyone can build a website ... can't believe everything you read on the Internet. In fact, there is so much fraud and theft on the World Wide Web that special task forces have been assigned to target only that venue. Not like it was when we were growing up, it's a different world now," Aaron said with a sigh, longing for time to be turned back to the world of his childhood.

"When I couldn't find any record of Children's World, I decided to pay a visit to their office. This morning while you guys were out having fun, I went to the address on the business card Logan gave me. You know what I found? Nothing. Nothing except for the law offices of Waltham, Mather, and Tate; I checked the address again, making sure I had the right suite, which I did."

"So there aren't any offices for Children's World and the place Logan and I went to last week is a lawyer's office? How can that be, Aaron? I don't get it," Claire said.

"Is the lawyer's office a front for something?" Logan asked.

"No … I don't think so," Aaron said, biting his lip. He looked like a construction worker going to a job site: battered jeans, T-shirt stained with paint, and a Mariner's baseball cap with his gray ponytail poking out the back like a horse's tail. Nobody would mistake him for a private detective.

"So what is it then?" Claire asked.

"When I arrived at the building the first thing I noticed was the names on the directory. The plaque for suite five-twelve, which is the one listed on the business card you gave me, looked as if it were newer than the others; it looked like it had been put there in the last few days. I went up to the fifth floor, noticing the same thing on all the signage in the building, like somebody had just moved in recently and when I went in and asked the receptionist at the front desk she informed me that they had occupied this space for the past seven years!"

"It wasn't a mirage we walked into; the offices were real, and Sylvia was real. Maybe you were in the wrong building Aaron," Claire said.

"Yeah … there has to be—"

"Logan … Claire, please. Let me finish."

"Okay," Logan said. "Go ahead, sorry to interrupt."

"So I asked the cute young woman behind the desk if she was at work every day for the past month. First, she told me it was none of my business until I told her I was investigating a crime and she could be in a lot of trouble if she withheld information. After a little persuasion, she told me she wasn't at work every day. The company had sponsored a weeklong getaway for all the hardworking employees and their families of Waltham, Mather, and Tate and – get this – the time the company was shut down for this extracurricular activity coincides with the time that you two came to visit Children's World. Weird huh? Coincidence? Nope, don't think so."

Sam, who was sleeping in the backseat, moaned and turned over on her side without waking.

"So this was all planned out?" Logan asked.

"Looks that way," Aaron said. "Then I requested to see one of the lawyers. After flashing my credentials and reminding the young lady about obstruction of justice, she rang one of the partners, a Mrs. Tate. I sat in the outer office for over twenty minutes waiting for this person to talk with me and was about ready to give up when she came out. She was stunning, about forty or so. She had her hair pulled up in a bun. She looked very smart, very professional. Mrs. Tate shook my hand and asked me what my visit was about. I told her. She explained to me in a curt way that it is customary to make an appointment and that her time was valuable. I told her I under—"

"Aaron, just get to the point, would you please?" Claire said. "My goodness, we don't need a blow by blow."

"Sorry. We went to her office to talk, and I asked her who had arranged for the company to spend all that money to send their employees away for a week, not to mention shutting down their business entirely. I mean, who does that? Nobody, that's who. She told me we were done and if I wanted or needed anything else, to get a lawyer. And then she laughed - she sure thought that was funny!"

They had been on the road for about an hour when it started to drizzle. Aaron turned the Ford's wipers on delay. "Hope it doesn't turn into snow as we get further into the mountains," he said. "Somebody paid those lawyers off, sent everyone away, cleaned out the building, and then proceeded to set up an office."

"That still doesn't make any sense to me. Why this building, why go to all the trouble to vacate and then set up shop – why not just rent some vacant office space?" Claire said, shaking her head. "I don't get it."

"Sure is weird," Logan agreed.

"Look, guys, I have a theory: I think the reason that this particular firm was targeted instead of just leasing some vacant office space and setting up shop, which would be the normal way to do things, is because this law firm is involved somehow. How I do not know. But I'm sure they are. Maybe the firm represents the people or company that is after your little girl. That would make sense. They use the lawyers' office to set up a 'dummy' office because there wouldn't be records, there would-n't be a paper trail."

"What about the employees, wouldn't they get suspicious?" Logan asked.

"If you were given a week off from work with pay and sent on a fun-filled, all-expense paid vacation, how much would you question? I mean really Logan, if it were handled correctly by the law firm, it would just seem like a huge perk, and that's all."

"Yeah … I guess so."

In the back seat, Sam stirred and murmured softly. Suddenly she sat bolt upright and, with her eyes still closed, shouted: "NO! Don't do it Scott! Don't do it!" And then she collapsed back down on the seat, still asleep. Claire scooted close and gently lifted Sam's head, placing it once again in her lap. She looked helplessly at her husband.

"We'll find out what's going on and put an end to all this Claire, I promise. Somehow, I swear, we'll get to the bottom of all this and help Sam. And then we can live a normal life," Logan said.

"I don't think our life will ever be normal again," Claire said, stroking Samantha's hair. "I believe it's too late for that."

THIRTY-ONE

Just past milepost 41, Matt Hemming turned left off the two-lane black-top and onto the obscured dirt road. He was as careful on this rugged terrain as he had been on the pothole-filled road back at the abandoned warehouse they'd left a few hours earlier.

Sylvia was awake now, the morphine slowly wearing off. She sat up groggily and looked around, trying to get her bearings. Man she hurt! Lisa was curled up in the passenger seat, sleeping. Matt was driving. In spite of everything that had happened, Sylvia broke into a grin. "We're almost to Omega aren't we?"

"Yes, we're almost there," Matt replied. "Great to see you hon. We was worried 'bout you."

"We sure were … still are," Lisa said, yawning and sitting up. She stretched and smiled at her friend. "Are you in pain?"

"Yes," Sylvia replied, tears in her eyes.

Lisa nodded. "Only time is going to heal those bumps and bruises, and that busted up nose. But you will have to do something to help you heal."

"Yeah, what's that?"

"Stay away from the people that keep beating you up."

"Yeah, okay," she laughed, "I would love to, believe me. How much longer?"

"About ten minutes, isn't that right Matt?"

Matt shook his head. "Give er take a few minutes."

"Fred knows exactly where you are at all times ... you know you're his favorite. How do you think we found you way out there in the middle of nowhere in that broken down excuse for a warehouse? Fred, that's how."

Sylvia mumbled something incoherent and then lay back down on the gurney. She crossed her arms over her chest in an X, each hand palm down on opposite shoulders, as if she were being laid to rest. All that was needed to complete the picture was a single rose placed between her breasts and underneath her crossed arms.

Matt continued staring at the road ahead, doing his best to avoid jarring and bouncing. Lisa, who was fully awake now and staring as intently as Matt at the path before them, was getting more stressed the closer they got to Omega, their term for the underground off-the-radar entity of which the three of them belonged. When the Chevy rounded a curve, the road magically turned from a rut-filled, wet, muddy trail into a road that was as smooth as unblemished skin. It stretched upward, cutting its path through the trees. A hundred feet from the transition of dirt to pavement stood a gate, blocking access to anyone who should happen upon this stretch of land. Matt pulled the van up to the large gated doors, which were attached to a twenty-foot high stone wall. To dissuade intruders from scaling the structure, electrically charged barbed wire ran the length of the compound. It reminded Matt of a prison camp. All that was needed to make it complete was a couple of guard towers with marksmen pacing back and forth, ready to shoot any intruder.

Matt climbed out of the van and walked over to the wall left of the gate. He counted three down and four across and then removed the light stone façade that covered the entry control panel. He punched in four digits and placed his palm on the reader. A computerized female voice spoke to him, granting him access. He went back to the van, waited a few seconds for the large gate to swing inward and drove on. Matt watched in the rearview mirror as the gate locked back into place. Three minutes later they pulled up to the large, five-thousand-square-foot cabin. Omega headquarters.

Matt parked the vehicle next to a nondescript Ford sedan. Before he reached the other side of the van, Lisa was preparing Sylvia for traveling the short distance into the building. She strapped her down on the gurney like a patient on her way to the operating table. "Can I help?" Matt asked.

"Yes ... yes, you can. Go around to the back and open the rear doors."

"Okay."

As Lisa was securing her friend, Sylvia opened her eyes again. "W-what are ... are you doing?"

"We're here honey," Lisa said, brushing the hair from Sylvia's forehead. "I'm just strapping you to the stretcher so you don't accidentally fall off when we're taking you into the house, it's just a precaution. As soon as we're inside, I'll get you into a nice warm bed, probably hook you up with an IV to get you nourished again. You're pretty banged up."

"Oh?" She tried to sit up, but it hurt, so she lay back down. "Okay."

The back doors of the Chevy now stood wide open. Lisa pushed the gurney towards Matt. Before they got her out, they heard the drone of an engine off in the distance. Coming down the smooth paved road, about half a mile from where they stood, was a Ford Explorer that neither Matt nor Lisa recognized.

"Quickly, get her inside!" Matt said.

Lisa swung the gurney around, helped Matt with the front, and then snatched the rear near Sylvia's feet, laying it gently on the walk. Snapping the side rails into place, as if she'd done this a thousand times, Lisa wheeled her friend up the wheelchair ramp and into the cabin, closing the door behind her. The entry and living area were empty; a fire burned in the fireplace on the north wall. Lisa heard movement and voices upstairs above her. She jumped when she heard a door slam. Turning, she saw that it was Matt, coming in from the back of the cabin.

"Matt!" Lisa said, clutching her chest. "You scared me half to death!"

"Sorry."

Sylvia tried to sit up again but quickly thought better of it. Now they could hear footfalls becoming louder as people made their way downstairs. A man dressed in a black turtleneck sweater, blue jeans, and a light beige sports coat was the first one to reach the bottom landing. His hair was dark black without any hint of gray. His clean-shaven countenance exuded compassion and knowledge. Following on his heels were two other men; both appeared to be middle-aged, but in relatively good shape.

The man in the black turtleneck smiled good-naturedly and nodded. "Lisa, Matt." His smile waned as he walked over to the gurney. Leaning down, he lightly kissed Sylvia's forehead and whispered something in her ear. She mumbled something back and tried on a small smile, but her face hurt so that she couldn't sustain it. The man whispered something else and Sylvia lay still.

"Fred, we need to move fast … I don't know how, but when Matt and I were bringing Sylvia inside, another car was coming down the road! I don't know how they got through the gate—"

"Lisa, it's okay," Fred Richart said. His voice was calm, soothing. Lisa had been working with Fred for the past six years and she never once heard him raise his voice to anyone, even when he was deeply frustrated. The man had an air about him like a great yoga master or monk or perhaps a priest. She didn't know anything about Fred Richart's personal life, but she was certain that he had found a sense of peace that most people cannot even fathom. "They're friends."

Lisa raised her eyebrows. "Friends? Who are they, Fred?"

"They will be in here in a minute so you can speak with them yourself. But right now let's get Sylvia in the back room, I have a bed all prepared for her." He was talking slowly, without any sense of urgency. Most of the time it was assuaging, but sometimes it became annoying. This was one of those annoying times. Lisa took in a deep breath, trying to follow Fred's suggestion and calm herself.

When Lisa and Matt began to wheel Sylvia to the back room, there was a knock on the cabin door.

"I've got her," Fred said, stepping in and gently nudging Lisa away. "I would like you two to meet our company and get to know them. They are going to be a big, big help to our cause. Please let them in while I take our girl here ... thanks." He took Sylvia out of the room.

Lisa looked at Matt. He shrugged and then looked over at the two men who had come downstairs with Fred. "You guys know who's at the door?"

It was the younger of the two who spoke. "Yup, sure do." He stepped off the landing and opened the door. A huge grin broke on his face. "Aaron! Come on inside! Bring your friends!" The young man stepped aside, holding the door. His partner, who until now had watched the exchange from the landing, joined them in the entryway. He was smiling too.

Matt looked back at Lisa, perplexed.

"John, you know these people?" Lisa asked the younger man.

"I know Aaron ... and I know of these other three here, but this is the first time we've met. Hi, I'm John, and this is Lucas." He gestured to his companion and then stepped forward, extending a hand to Logan.

"Hi, John. Hi, Lucas. I'm Logan, and this is my wife, Claire, and our daughter Samantha. Pleasure ... and you are?" Logan asked looking at Matt and Lisa.

"That would be old Matt and Lisa. Excellent agents ... the best—"

"Hey! Now wait just a minute Aaron," Lucas chimed in. "They're good, yes ... but what about us? What are we? Chopped liver?"

"No, no, of course not Lucas, of course not," Aaron said, shaking his head and smiling. "It's just that … well … you know, you still have a lot to learn. I mean what are you … like twelve?"

"Aren't you funny," Lucas said good-naturedly. He wrapped his arms around Aaron, who only came up to his chest, and gave him a squeeze. "It's so good to see you again, seems like it's been awhile."

"Yeah. Too long Lucas, too long."

Samantha had been holding Claire's hand, but now she pulled away and approached Lisa. "Hi. I'm Sam."

Lisa squatted on her haunches. "Pleased to meet you, Sam, my name is Lisa—"

"And I'm Matt."

"Didn't your momma tell you not to interrupt? That's rudy."

"Rude, honey," Lisa said laughing. "Rude is the word, and that describes Mr. Matt perfectly."

Like Samantha, Claire was drawn more to Lisa than the others. It wasn't something she was cognizant of, but she knew in her heart that this was a person she could trust. She didn't know how she knew this. Perhaps she was beginning to follow Sam's lead, to trust that her daughter could read people better than most adults. Didn't they say that animals instinctively knew whether people were inherently bad or not? Especially dogs? So why not little girls?

Matt looked at them and smiled. "Hey, I'm not rude, am I? Sorry to interrupt."

"Yeah, yeah whatever," Lisa said, turning back to Sam. "How old are you Sam?"

"I'm five," Sam said, holding up five fingers. "Almost six."

"Wow, that's getting up there. Pretty soon you're gonna have a boyfriend … or do you already?"

Sam giggled and scrunched up her shoulders, swaying from side to side. "Not yet."

Standing up, Lisa put out a hand. "Hi, Claire."

"Hi. What's this all about? I don't even know what we're doing here or why anyone is after our daughter. I'm lost."

The room suddenly became silent. Claire turned around and noticed a man leaning against the wall, his arms folded across his chest, legs crossed. His demeanor was one of friendliness and amusement. His face was kind, compassionate.

Claire glanced at her husband and then around the room at these strangers. She felt at home, though, and she knew that Logan and Sam felt it too: safety.

The man who was leaning on the wall unfolded his arms, stood up straight and nodded to the back of the building. "Would you be so kind as to follow me?" he asked as he turned and walked away.

Claire grabbed Sam's hand and followed the man in the black turtleneck, glancing over her shoulder to make sure Logan was following them. He was. Aaron, however, just nodded and turned back to his friends, as if he knew exactly what was going on.

They followed a short hallway to a set of double doors, which opened into a large room that at one time may have been a den or a living area, but was now a makeshift medical facility.

What she saw made Claire gasp and squeeze Sam's hand a little too tightly.

"Ow!"

"Oh, sorry honey," Claire said absentmindedly.

Lying in a large bed was Sylvia Tran. The bed's metal railings were fully engaged on both sides, an IV bag filled with a clear liquid solution hung from the hook attached to a four-legged pole next to the bed. Clear plastic tubes were stuffed in each nostril.

"It's Sylvia!" Sam said.

"What the hell is going on here?" Logan asked.

Sam let go of Claire's hand and looked over at the man in the black turtleneck, who still had not identified himself, and then she turned her attention to the battered woman in the bed. She walked closer and rested her tiny hand on the cold steel safety railing, looking at Sylvia, who seemed to be asleep.

"Hi, Sylvia it's Sammy. We'll get who hurt you, won't we Logan?"

"Sure honey, yeah … sure."

Sylvia moaned. Her swollen, bruised eyes slowly opened about half-way and her lips, which were twice their normal size, broke into a painful – yet happy – small grin. As she tried to sit up, the man in the turtleneck hurried to her side. He gently pushed her down while whispering to her to rest and take it easy.

"Hey mister, you mind filling us in on just what the hell is happening here? I don't get it … I thought Sylvia was an adoption specialist and—"

"Logan, I will tell you everything shortly. My name is Fred Richart and we – the men out front, Sylvia – belong to a group known as Omega. Let me get Sylvia comfortable and then we can go upstairs where I will tell you everything. I brought you back here for one simple reason: to see Sylvia's condition and what these people are capable of doing to an-other human - what we're up against. But also to show you what our people are willing to endure for you and your wife and daughter."

"But why—"

Claire put a hand on her husband's shoulder and squeezed gently. This was Claire's way of telling him to relax, to not press it right now. He turned to her and nodded: *okay*.

Samantha was still by Sylvia's bedside, watching her. "I'm sorry those bad people did this Sylvia … it's my fault …"

Sam's head suddenly jerked back; her hand dropped limply from the metal railing and her eyes rolled skyward, burying her pupils somewhere deep in her head, only the whites now visible.

Claire rushed to her daughter's side and got to her as she started convulsing. Sam was flopping in Claire's arms like a freshly caught fish.

"Quickly, get her on the floor!" Fred said, "and be careful, so she doesn't hit her head!"

"What's going on?" Claire screamed.

As Claire laid her daughter gently on the carpeted floor, Fred reached into Sam's mouth, making sure she didn't swallow her tongue. Pulling out his wallet, Fred somehow got it into Sam's mouth, protecting her from biting her tongue.

"Jesus help us!" Claire whispered. Logan knelt down next to them and watched helplessly.

She jerked.

She flopped.

Blood, dripping from her nose now.

"Claire, you're going to need more than Jesus to help you with what we're dealing with," Fred said, holding Sam down as best he could and wiping the blood from her upper lip.

"What the hell are we dealing with?" Claire yelled, visibly shaken.

"Something bigger than all of us," Fred replied, holding Sam down.

THIRTY-TWO

Hearing the commotion coming from the back room, Aaron, Lucas and John stopped talking and immediately went running to see what had happened. Although he was the shortest, Aaron was the quickest and reached the door before his friends. He opened the door and stood there in shock. "Oh … My God."

Samantha was thrashing on the floor with something black and bulky inside her mouth. Her cheeks were flushed, and her nose was bleeding. Fred was on his knees holding Sam by her shoulders, trying to keep her from hurting herself. Claire was next to him, looking distraught and frightened. And Logan was standing a few feet away, his hands stuffed in his pockets, looking ashen. Sylvia was in her hospital bed. She had given up trying to sit up. Now she lay there, her eyes closed with quiet tears running down her face.

With the strength of two grown men, Samantha sat up abruptly, pushing Fred's hands aside and screamed, "NO! NO!"

Claire scrambled backward and almost fell. Logan didn't know what to do. The three men stood in the doorway, gaping as if this was some nightmare from which they would soon wake.

Samantha's convulsions ended as suddenly as they had started. Her eyes were not just sclera now; the beautiful blue of her irises had returned. She wiped the blood from her face. She shook her head rapidly as if to clear it of some unconscionable thought and then she surveyed her surroundings, getting her bearings.

"Enough!" she said. Sam's voice had taken on the timbre of someone much older than five. It carried with it the force and heat of undeniable determination.

Her shoulders slumped forward as she looked around the room. Her voice became quieter again, that of a little girl. "Enough, Scott," she whispered.

Logan picked Sam up and hugged her tightly, burying his face in her neck. "What's happening honey? I know you know something – maybe not consciously ... but I'm so lost and confused." He was on the verge of tears.

"Okay everyone, let's go upstairs to the meeting room, please. We'll talk about what's next and fill in the Kellers about the events that have led up to this point in time. I'll make sure Sylvia is comfortable and join you shortly. John ... Lucas, please take everyone upstairs except the little girl; I'd like to talk with her and Sylvia for a moment."

"If you think for one minute that I'm going to let her out of my sight, you've got another thing coming! I don't even know who the hell you are and—" Logan began.

"It's okay...really...it...it's okay." Logan looked into Sam's eyes, and he saw something that startled him. Inside that small child's body was something much, much older and wiser than any five-year-old. It was like this little girl had wanted him to see into the depths of a world far greater, far more mysterious, than anything Logan had, up until this point, ever imagined existed. As she continued to stare, Logan went not only physically numb but mentally as well. His mind went blank. No one in the room noticed what transpired over that two or three second period between the man and the little girl.

Lucas took Logan by the arm. "Logan, let's go upstairs and I'll get you something to eat."

"Not hungry," he mumbled, stumbling backward.

"Okay, something to drink then."

"Hmm … okay," Logan replied, looking like he'd just come out of a deep sleep. He put Sam down, kissed her on the cheek and then silently left with Lucas. Claire, who still looked frazzled and bewildered, started after them, but then stopped and turned to Fred. "She's gonna be okay, right?"

"She's got a busted nose and—"

"Sam … I mean Samantha – I know Sylvia will be okay."

"Yeah, she'll be fine Claire, she'll be fine." His voice sounded strong and convincing, but he wasn't so sure if his words were true. "Now please go with the others."

Claire sighed, stood her ground for a moment more, then turned and walked out of the room, blowing Sam a kiss as she did.

After everyone had gone, Fred quietly shut the double doors and went to Sylvia's bedside. Her eyes were open now, staring at the ceiling. Fred motioned for Sam to join them. She walked over and climbed on the chair Fred had placed next to him. He smiled at her and said, "You know we have to end this, don't you Samantha?"

"Yes."

"And soon, before anything irreversible happens."

Sam nodded.

Fred realized then that Sam was scared. It had not occurred to him that the little girl might be up against something more powerful than she. God, he hoped that wasn't true.

"Y-you're mu … much stronger … stronger than they … are," Sylvia managed, half-sitting now. She grasped the metal railings and pulled herself up further so she could face Fred and Sam directly. This time, Fred didn't try to stop her. "You're stronger Sam … because … well, because you're *pure* … in heart and soul."

Smiling furtively, Sylvia looked at Fred. "And you … it's so good to see you … so great to be back here, Fred. You know I have to be a part of this. I'll … I'll be okay … just give me a couple of days … you won't be doing anything for a few days right? D-don't do this … without me. After losing Anna—"

At the thought of her friend, Sylvia became silent. Her chin dropped to her chest in sorrow. Fred held her hand but said nothing. After a few moments, Sylvia continued. "I just have to be … have to be a part of this. The conclusion I mean … no matter what the … outcome."

"Okay Sylvia, okay. We'll wait until you're strong enough to venture out and since you don't have any broken bones, except that lovely nose, I don't see where it will take you too long to regain your strength. Perhaps you're right, maybe only a few days. And besides, that will give us time to get acquainted with our newfound friends, do some bonding, which could give us an edge."

Sylvia lay back down, out of breath and exhausted. Fred squeezed her hand and then let her go, turning his attention to the little girl sitting next to him. Samantha looked like a million other five-year-olds: cherubic face, brown hair pulled into pigtails, innocent looking eyes, small lips, trusting smile.

"Honey … Sam, remember when Sylvia and I first came to you?"

"Yes."

"And remember us talking about how things might get … well … kinda crazy? Kinda weird?"

"Yes."

"Well, the time has come to use those powers you've been gifted with honey, the powers—"

"I know."

"Good Sam, I'm glad you're ready, but I need you to know that it is not just Scott we're talking about here."

"Carlson."

Sylvia moaned.

"Yes honey," Fred said, "Carlson too, but others. There are others, and they are very, very dangerous."

"Okay. What do you want me to do?" Sam asked, although she already knew what she was going to have to do. She had dreamt about the others many times over the past month. But she was not going to worry these extraordinary people about what was to come, about what horror lay before them. Maybe the end would turn out differently than in her dreams.

"I'm going to join the others so we can discuss what the next step should be. Will you do me a big favor honey, and keep an eye on Sylvia, let me know if she needs anything?"

Samantha nodded.

Fred stood up, leaned over the metal railing and kissed Sylvia lightly on the lips. "I'll be back to check on you soon," he whispered.

Fred took Sam by the hand. "There are some books and puzzles in the other room if you get bored and want something to do."

"Okay, thanks."

"How are you doing, sweetheart?"

"I'm scared."

"Me too, honey. Me too."

THIRTY-THREE

Scott Riley was laughing with Richards and playing games with his staff. He had inched his way into the mind of the fat guy – the one they called Scooter – who now stood on the covered veranda wiping his bloody nose with the back of his hand. Scooter then produced a neatly folded handkerchief from inside his coat pocket and wiped away what little blood remained. He looked perplexed and confused as he stared at the red blotch on his previously white hanky.

Bored, Scott closed his eyes, sending out the spiral of thought, which searched the universe for the one who was named Samantha. Everyone had a unique mental signature, and the invisible filament Scott released could scan millions of molecules and cells within seconds. He could locate a subject anywhere on the planet and, he supposed, anywhere in the infinite universe. As his talents increased and his skill level grew, he became increasingly confident.

Cocky.

Strong.

Within perhaps five minutes after leaving Scooter to his bloodied nose, Scott located Samantha. Although he still lacked the capacity to pinpoint a subject's exact location, he intuitively knew that she was close.

How close he wasn't sure. Distance didn't matter when he wanted to get inside your brain.

With Samantha, he wasn't going to inch his way in because she would instantly become aware. No, the only way to do this was a full quick attack, infiltrating her mind before she could react. His goal was to gain control, but he didn't want to kill her – not yet.

Slamming his way into Sam's head felt like diving into an icy river after roasting in the desert sun. The shock to the system was surprising at first and then it was refreshing, almost comforting, as if this was where he belonged.

When Samantha screamed, however, the comfortable, warm feeling disappeared. The shattering scream was inside her head; she hadn't vocalized it to the people around her, she only went limp and began to shake violently.

He needed to gain control and quick before Sam locked him out. And something else suddenly occurred to him. Could she turn the tables on him? Was he giving her direct access to his mind? Startled by those thoughts and wishing they would have come to him before entering Samantha's head, Scott started to pull back but changed his mind. Since he was already in her head, he wanted to see what he could find. Perhaps she would, unknowingly, give him their location or even something more: their plan.

He was nervous now, though. Samantha knew he was inside her, of course, and she was blocking him out with everything she had. He wasn't in her head long when his musing was interrupted by a sharp and sudden force, like a giant hand slapping his whole being.

His mind was being squeezed, crushed in this giant fist and the sound inside his head was so loud he thought his eardrums would soon explode. He could make out the words: NO! NO! followed by the shrill, high-pitched sound of sirens or bells or whistles; he wasn't sure exactly, except for one thing: these sounds were at such high intensity and frequency that they wouldn't even register on a decibel chart. And they would kill a mere mortal, of that he was certain. Before gathering any useful information, Scott had no choice but to pull out. It never occurred to him that he might not be able to do so and as he let go, as he tried to pull out, the imaginary fist gripped him tighter still as if he were the one now trapped.

With a mental pull that was more forceful than any he had ever attempted, Scott was able to free himself of the invisible grasp, but not without some damage. He heard something tear in his head, like the ripping of a sheet of paper. And then his nose began to bleed. Thankfully, it was just a small amount of blood, and his ears were clear, which told him the damage was nil. He had retreated from Samantha before she could hurt him. He wasn't inside her head long enough to get information or to kill the girl, but he knew that he'd instilled more fear into her.

"Did Scooter do that to you?" Richards asked. He was leery of the boy now. If a mere bodyguard, who had never displayed any kind of mental powers, could hurt this young boy, then the kid wasn't as powerful as Dr. Carlson tried to get him to believe.

"Of course Scooter didn't do this!" Carlson nearly screamed. "Some fat ass good-for-nothing security guard would never be able to do anything to this young man! Never! It was that damn girl, wasn't it? You pulled out of Scooter's head and went into the girl, didn't you Scott?"

"Yeah ... so?"

"Yeah, so? Is that all you can say is yeah ... so? This is a problem! You're not to go into her head – or anywhere else, for that matter - without me knowing about it, understood? She could kill you or damage you or ... or anything." Carlson ran a shaking hand over his half-bald head. "We need to talk about a plan of action before you go off doing shit on your own! You—"

"Calm down," Richards said, grabbing Carlson's arm. Without any thought and with a quick jerk, Ben yanked his arm away. He was panting now, trying to catch his breath.

"I-I'm sorry...I didn't mean to go off like that—"

The French doors opened and in walked Scooter. He looked pale. There was a small patch of dried blood under his nose, and Ben noticed a trickle coming from his left ear. *Even without any effort or force, even without meaning too, he can slowly kill,* Ben thought.

"I don't feel so good, Boss. I need … need to take the rest of the day off, w-would that be okay?" Scooter asked, placing a shaking hand on the armrest of the sofa, steadying himself. Finally giving up, he plopped down on the couch with a deep sigh, like he had just finished a long day of physical labor instead of standing out on the porch talking.

"Sure, sure take the rest of the week off if you need to. Spend some time with your family." Richards smiled.

Scooter smiled back. "Thank you, thank you, I'll make it up to you, I promise I will."

Richards dismissed him with a wave of his hand.

Scooter got up, and before he made it halfway across the room, he collapsed. When his head hit the floor, blood poured from his ears and nose.

Jumping to his feet, trying not to get blood spatter on his good shoes, Richards said, "What the hell? Thomas! *Thomas!*"

Expressionless, Scott looked at Carlson and then at Richards. He wanted to smile; he wanted to laugh out loud, but once he saw the look on their faces, he thought better of it. Now was not the time. They didn't find this turn of events funny at all.

A man burst into the room. "What … what happened to Scooter?" Thomas asked, immediately kneeling beside the man. "My God, he's bleeding everywhere!"

"Get him to the helipad and fly him into St. Mary's right away. Page Doctor Childress and have him meet you there, got it?"

"Yes, boss, got it. Don't just stand there with your mouth hanging open, help me with him!" Thomas said to Scooter's skinny partner, who was staring down at the floor, twisting his hands.

"Okay," he mumbled quietly, bending down and grabbing Scooter's legs while Thomas lifted the man under his arms. They carried him out of the room.

After the men had left, Richards turned to Scott. "I want you to assure me that you will never try to get inside my head, for if you do, you will be eradicated from this planet so fast you won't know what hit you. Don't think I haven't taken every precaution necessary to deal with someone like you. Even though you are only seven, you have powers unseen – as far as I know – in this world to date. Sure, there have been people who can read minds, but manipulate? Extract information? Kill? Not that I'm aware of. However, if anything ever happens to me, my staff - which number in the thousands - have been given direction to kill you immediately, understood?"

"Of course."

Carlson watched this with amusement. Richards still was clueless as to what he was dealing with. Ben had already resigned himself to an early grave and knew in his heart it would be at the hands of this boy. But he did have an agenda to fulfill and, of course, he did hope that he was wrong about the early grave. Perhaps he could get what he needed with the boy's help and without dying himself.

Richards continued: "I work for one of the wealthiest men on the West Coast. This man has always been fascinated with the power of the human mind, and he is responsible for your abilities, young man. He is the genius behind New Life."

"Which means he created the girl, too?"

"Yes, unfortunately, this is true." Richards paused, pouring himself a drink from the well-stocked bar. "Ben, would you like something?"

Carlson shook his head.

"What about me?" Scott asked.

"And what about you ... would you like some juice, maybe a Capri Sun?"

"Funny. I'm seven physically, but I'm much old—"

"Exactly. The effects of alcohol on a body your size could be very damaging. Besides, we need you to be sharp, and ingesting booze at your young physical age could be very detrimental to our plans."

"Carlson let me drink - quite a few times, in fact."

Richards shot a glance at Ben and then shrugged. "Perhaps he did, but it was not good judgment on his – or your – part. And now I think it's time we draw up some plans on taking care of the opposition so we can move forward with our primary objective."

"And just what is our objective?" Scott asked.

"Why, to control the world, of course," Richards replied, "to control the world."

THIRTY-FOUR

The large, glass-topped conference table was fashioned from two mammoth tree trunks that had been petrified and coated with layers of lacquer, making it look slick and shiny - it matched the interior of the room. One wall boasted a fireplace with a cemented river rock chimney running the height of the structure. A red and black throw rug partially covered the wooden floor.

Claire sat back in her chair with her arms folded across her chest, irritated. She had questions – *lots of questions* - and as she watched the people around the table laugh and joke, she became more than irritated – she became angry. Just as she was about to speak, Fred walked into the room.

The chatter quickly subsided, and all eyes turned to him. Claire silently watched as Fred took his chair at the head of the table. He smiled and sat down, placed his folded hands on the glass tabletop and quietly surveyed his team.

"I believe we owe Mr. and Mrs. Keller an explanation of why Aaron brought them here - along with their daughter – and what they can expect going forward. So, with that in mind, I will start by going around the table and introducing everyone. To my left is Lisa Eshleman. Lisa has been with Omega—"

"What's Omega?" Logan interjected.

"In Greek mythology, Omega - or Kratos - is the personification of strength and power. We believe there is strength in numbers, but even more power in knowledge. We will give you more history of our organization and why and how we came about soon, Mr. Keller. But for now, we need to get on with the task before us." Nodding at Lisa, Fred continued, "You've been with us six years, I believe?"

Lisa nodded.

"Lisa has extensive medical knowledge. She served in the Gulf War as a medic. Stateside, Lisa has worked in trauma units and emergency rooms, has been in many life-and-death situations and her medical expertise is invaluable to our operation."

"Hi. It's a pleasure meeting you," Lisa said smiling at Claire. "And nice meeting you, Mr. Keller."

Logan smiled thinly.

Nodding to the man sitting on Lisa's right, Fred said, "And then we have Matthew Hemming." Fred sighed and shook his head. "What can I say about Matt? He can be a loose cannon, but he would die for his friends and the causes he believes in. His expertise is in hand-to-hand combat. You don't want to tangle with Matt – you'll lose."

Matt nodded and smiled.

"Across the table, we have John Belk and Lucas Crosby. These two men are former Secret Service agents who were personally in charge of protecting the President of the United States. They joined our forces four years ago when they left the Service for what they tell me is a much more fulfilling job, a job they can really believe in."

Logan looked at Claire, mouthed the word "wow" and then shrugged.

"As for myself, before starting Omega, I was head of the Special Activities Division, part of the United States Central Intelligence

Agency's National Clandestine Service, responsible for covert operations related to psychological warfare." Fred paused for a moment, and then continued, nodding at Aaron.

"And you know Aaron, former Police Officer Extraordinaire, turned private detective. Aaron became a private detective mainly to help our organization and fly under the radar, isn't that right Aaron?"

"Yes, that's right," Aaron said.

"And Aaron came to learn of our organization through your good friend and neighbor – God rest her soul – Thelma Grisham. Thelma lent her unique talents to our cause on many, many occasions and became an indispensable part of our little family. Unfortunately, we have lost two – almost three – good people in our fight against power and corruption."

Sitting up straighter, Claire asked, "Who ... who have you lost?"

"Thelma, of course. And a young woman named Anna, who was a close friend of Sylvia's – and almost Sylvia herself."

"So what is this with Sylvia anyway, Mr. Rich—"

"Fred."

"Fred. When Claire and I first met her, she seemed like a sweet person who only wanted to help children in need. And now she is like some gun-toting, crazy woman who isn't anything like the person she portrayed herself to be when we were introduced to Sam," Logan said.

"Mr. Keller," Fred sighed, rubbing his face, "Sylvia is not at all the way you just described her. In fact, she is exactly the person you met at Children's World; she was just undercover. She did – and still does – have Sam's best interest at heart - and yours. Just look at the state she's in right now. She has gone through these beatings and come close to death all because of this little girl and what she represents."

"I-I still don't ... I don't understand," Claire said. Mentally and physically tired, she longed for home and bed and for this nightmare to be over.

"No ... no, I realize you don't Claire. Sam is special ... incredibly unique. And a threat."

"You're joking," she said, exasperated. "A threat to who?"

"I really don't know how to explain this other than just to start at the beginning."

"So then start at the beginning. It's not like we've got anywhere to go. I don't even know where I am," said Logan.

Fred Richart spent the next two hours detailing the operations of the underground facility in the Utah desert that went by the name of New Life. This place, Fred told them, was where Samantha Jennings came from, where the little girl was born through science and bred for destruction.

As Fred continued, Claire and Logan became increasingly agitated and shaken.

"But we have in our midst something very, very special," said Fred. "You see, the experiment didn't go as planned. The universe had other ideas for this little girl. It seems that Nature always tends to right our wrongs, to produce the yin to our yang, the good to our bad. And Samantha, through some Divine Intervention, is pure love, but with the same power as the seven-year-old-boy who was born two years earlier."

"My God," Claire exclaimed.

"So what you're telling us is, our adopted daughter is a monster! Some Freak of Nature that was mixed in a test tube in an underground lab in the middle of fucking nowhere!" Logan was standing now, his heart pounding in his chest. He felt like he was going to pass out. With a shaking hand, he grabbed the back of his chair to steady himself as Claire looked on in disbelief.

"Logan, you don't understand, you have it all wrong," came a tired voice from behind him. He turned around. Sylvia Tran was standing there in a hospital robe, bruised and beaten, eyes black, nose broken. Although she was exhausted, there was something Logan noticed that amazed him: her brush with death had not deterred her in the least; in fact, the woman was more determined than ever to extirpate her adversaries. He could see it in her eyes.

"Sylvia, what … you shouldn't be … where's Sam?" Lisa stuttered.

"Sam's downstairs playing, she's fine."

"Sylvia you should be resting, you should…" Fred started.

"I'm alright Fred, just a little winded. I told you, I need to be a part of this … I've spent too many years of my life involved with these cretins, and I'm not stopping now – not until it's finished." In bare feet, Sylvia shuffled over to Fred and wrapped an arm around his waist. "I'm okay; I'll take it easy. Promise." She kissed him lightly on the cheek and then sat down at the table with the rest of them.

Looking at Logan, she continued: "I was there through it all. I have been with Sam since she came into this world, and I'm here to tell you that this young girl is as human as you are Logan. She has a soul. Just because she was born artificially in a test tube doesn't change that fact. She was born of sperm and egg, incubated and nurtured just like any other human being - it is the same as artificial insemination that doctors perform all the time. The only difference was her incubator. Instead of the wet warmth of a human female womb, Sam was nourished in a man-made, environmentally controlled machine."

"Okay, so you're saying she's just like any other five-year-old girl?"

"In many ways, yes … yes, she is. But the unique thing about Sam is that something in her system, and we don't know what exactly, fought off the drugs these madmen injected her with - drugs used for control, manipulation, brainwashing," Sylvia said.

"And not only that, but Sam knew they were trying to control her … and she played right into it. Her intelligence is off the charts, and her psychic abilities are like nothing we've ever encountered. She followed orders and did what she was told. It was about survival. Sam used her powers only when required and when no one would be hurt. However, as they asked more and more of her and had her trying some things that could quite possibly hurt others, Sam withdrew her abilities from these men. She pretended that she couldn't do what they asked of her, that she was losing her unique talents," Fred added.

"So Carlson approached me … and told me to figure out what to do with her. That's when I … when I worked out the whole adoption angle. We set up shop and brought you guys on board. This was no random thing, Logan … Claire. This was well calculated, well-planned," said Sylvia. The words came out in short bursts. When she spoke, Sylvia felt like a giant hand was squeezing her. Her ribs, which were bruised but not broken, hurt something terrible and it was hard to catch her breath.

Visibly upset, Claire said, "You purposely brought us into this? But why?"

"Because of Thelma, Claire. She knew that you and your husband were the right couple to take care of this girl and, more importantly, would be able to handle this awful situation. It was at Thelma's insistence that we got Sam into your care. It's sad, though, that she's not here with us," Fred said quietly.

Logan's eyes flitted around the table. "You all knew Thelma?"

"Uh huh."

"Yup."

"Sure did."

"Wow, this is just so much to take in."

"Yes, Logan, it is, and that's why we need to get some rest and resume this in the morning. Tomorrow we will have a quiet day of rest and go over our plans in detail. This will give Sylvia more healing time and give us the opportunity to become more acquainted." Fred smiled and stood up, nodded at the group around the table and left the room.

Two hours later, Claire and Logan were lying in a Queen bed covered with a hand-made quilt. The bed itself was fashioned, like so much of the other furniture in the cabin, from oak and cedar. Sam was asleep in an adjacent room. His hands behind his head, Logan stared at the ceiling. Claire was trying to read a book she had found in the room but was unable to concentrate. She found herself reading the same paragraph over and over again. Finally giving up, she put the book aside with a sigh.

"I find it really weird," she said.

"The book?"

"No, no, silly, not the book."

"Then what?"

"That we find ourselves up in the mountains, snow imminent, our adoptive daughter asleep in the other room, madmen possibly after us and I'm super horny!"

"You're what?" Logan said.

"Horny. Terribly."

In spite of the predicament they were in, Logan smiled. "Sorry, but I don't think I can help you at the moment. Stress, you know, makes it -" he glanced down at his quilt-covered crotch – "not work too well. And I – we have a lot of stress right now. Besides, what if one of these kind strangers walked in on us?"

"I'm not asking you to jump on me Logan; I just said I find it weird. You're such a guy. You take everything so literally." Claire was propped up on her elbow. "Logan, how did all this happen? What did we do in our life to deserve this kind of fate? I always thought we were good, caring people who deserved a decent life filled with joy and love."

"Man, you're such a girl!" Logan said. "And just a little naïve Claire, don't you think? I mean come on, do you really believe that just because somebody leads an honest, compassionate life that nothing bad will ever come to them? Do you—"

"No, of course not. I'm not stupid, it's … well, it's just that I only wanted a simple life with you, a child, a nice home, and some good friends. Not too much to ask." *This must be how an innocent person in prison feels*, Claire thought.

"Claire, in my mind we only have two options: trust in these people and see this through or abandon that young girl and go home. But if we did the latter, I don't think I could live with myself. And they would probably come after us anyway."

"Yeah, they would. Come after us and kill us. We stay and fight Logan; we stay and fight. And hope we don't die in the process."

She kissed him on the cheek and rolled over, switching off the bed-side lamp.

THIRTY-FIVE

They woke to the exquisite smells and sounds of bacon crackling, coffee brewing, eggs frying and syrup warming on the stove. The aroma reminded Claire of her childhood when her mother would wake her and her father on Saturday mornings with these same smells permeating the house. Besides Logan, Claire didn't have anyone to cook for and weekend breakfasts at the Keller residence had turned into instant coffee, breakfast bars and the occasional bowl of cereal. If we get out of this alive, I am going to start cooking, Claire thought as she stumbled sleepily out of bed, yawning. She noticed that the bed was empty; Logan and Sam were already up and out of the room, probably already enjoying the freshly made breakfast.

Throwing on the bathrobe that hung on the back of the door and sliding her bare feet into a warm pair of slippers, Claire stepped out of the bedroom without bothering to comb her hair. She figured these people were family now, and she had a lot more to worry about than her looks anyway.

Finding her way to the kitchen, Claire found Fred and Aaron working together like a couple of master chefs, playing off each other as if they had cooked together all their lives. Past the kitchen, at the far end of the cabin, was a large picnic-style table, which could hold at least ten people, maybe more. Logan and Sam sat next to each other; Lisa, Matt, John and Lucas sat directly across from them, chatting about who knows what. Sylvia was nowhere to be found; Claire figured she was in the back room licking her wounds.

"Good morning gorgeous," Aaron said when he saw Claire. "Beautiful hair." Grinning, he turned his attention back to his frying eggs.

Putting her hands on her hips, Claire said, "And what's that supposed to mean, short stuff?"

"Hey now … I pay you a compliment about your beautiful head of hair, and you attack my height? Now that's just not very nice, now is it, Mrs. Keller? And where did you learn manners anyway?" he asked sarcastically.

Fred watched all this with mild amusement as he continued filling up a large serving platter with eggs, bacon and pancakes. He nodded at Claire. As he headed toward the gang, he glanced back over his shoulder. "Claire, won't you join us?"

"Uh … yeah. Sounds great, but Fred, what about my hair?"

He laughed. "Well, it does look like you were just electrocuted, but we're all friends, don't worry about it." He winked and continued. Claire followed.

"Hi sweetheart, we were just talking about you!" Logan said when Claire arrived at the table. "Wow, nice hair!"

"What is it with my hair, anyway?"

"Take a look," Lisa said handing Claire her compact.

Looking into the mirror, Claire couldn't help but smile. On the left, her long black hair was squished and flattened; on the right, it was sticking straight out; on top, it was just a tangled rat's nest. "I didn't know that hair could go in so many directions … wow. Talk about a bad hair day!"

Looking out the large window, Claire marveled at the beauty of the day and the mountain land. The sky was dark blue with a few puffs of white off in the distance; the evergreens bowed slightly under the weight of the previous evenings light snowfall; birds flitted from branch to branch as they exercised their wings and searched for the perfect nest-building location.

Under other circumstances, this would be the perfect vacation, Claire thought as she sat next to her husband.

Fred placed the platter of food in the center of the table. "Logan and his daughter, Samantha, have some news that they would like to share with all of us, but they wanted to wait for Claire to arrive. And now that we're graced with her presence, we can eat and listen to what they have to say. Logan, the floor is yours." Fred sat at the end of the table.

Clearing his throat, Logan said, "Last night, before going to sleep, Sam unwittingly heard our opponents' plans through thought waves or some type of supernatural means that are completely lost on me. But I believe everything this young girl tells me. I believe … I *know* … that Sam is incapable of telling a lie. I realize that she is just a five—"

"Almost six—" Claire said.

"Yes, almost six. Anyway, I understand that this is like something out of a science fiction movie, but after the past week, even I'm beginning to believe in things I never thought possible. I mean, why not mind control, telekinesis, teleportation? Look how far mankind has come since the advent of the computer chip. And what about the advances in medicine? Look at all the new things we're discovering every day. Things that a few years ago we said were impossible. I—"

"Logan … Logan, okay, we get your point. We believe too. In Omega's short existence, we have witnessed things that are so foreign it's astounding. So we have learned to keep an open mind. Let's move forward, okay?" Fred said.

"Yes, please. What does Sam know?" came a voice from behind them. While Logan recounted the previous night's events, Sylvia Tran had entered the room quietly. She looked better this morning: the bruises weren't as angry-looking, the swelling of her lips and nose had gone down, and she seemed rested.

"Sylvia!" Sam yelled, running to her side.

"Hi honey, what can you tell us?"

Sam's eyes took on a distant look, as if she had left her body and traveled to a different place far away. She seemed to be looking at something no one else could see. Claire was reminded of the incident in their bathroom last week when Sam had collapsed on the floor with her mutilated doll. The look was the same.

"At one o'clock on Wednesday, they will infiltrate an important meeting at the Naval base. Scott Riley is going to send a Navy Jet, an F/A-18 Hornet, into oblivion in front of hundreds of people, many of them very influential. They will use this event to get the attention of the President."

Listening to Samantha sent shivers up Claire's spine. This was not the little girl she knew. Someone or something had taken over Samantha's body, using it to communicate.

Logan licked his lips nervously. He looked helplessly at Claire.

"Why do they want to do that?" Lisa asked.

"Don't know," Sam said, shaking her head. To Claire's relief, Sam sounded like herself again.

"My guess would be if you could get the attention of the most powerful man in the nation, then you would have access not only to the military but other world leaders as well. It's all about control and power," Fred said.

"Why wouldn't you just jump in the President's head and get what you wanted?" Claire asked.

"It doesn't work like that Claire. To use this power, the subject has to be within a certain distance," Sylvia said.

"You mean like cell towers or radio frequencies?"

"Exactly."

"But that would mean they're close by," Claire said.

"The data from the lab tests revealed that after about forty or fifty miles, the power becomes extremely weak, almost non-existent," Sylvia replied. "So yes, they are close."

"Best guess is within a fifty-mile radius," Fred said, standing up. "Matt, how are we for transportation?"

"We 'ave the copter, which seats four, and six vehicles."

"John, Lucas, you guys gather up all the firearms and ammo we have, pack them for transport. We'll be going by ground, not by air. I want to get close to the situation in case it turns out to be more than just a magician making a jet disappear. For some reason, I don't think this is just going to be a David Copperfield show."

"Okay," John said. Chewing a mouthful of eggs, Lucas nodded agreement.

"No hurry though guys ... the drive is only four hours, and we still have a day and a half. Enjoy the breakfast, the sunshine and each other's company."

Because this might be the last time you have the chance, he thought but did not say.

THIRTY-SIX

S cott spent Tuesday hanging out with Charlie, Richards's bodyguard, and Thomas, the caretaker. Charlie and Thomas watched in awe and fascination (and with a little fear) as Scott solved college-level problems that many highly regarded and highly intelligent men and women found difficult. They understood, after sitting in a briefing with Richards, the unique talents of the boy. They were aware of the danger inherent in a creature such as this; they didn't see Scott as a human being, but as an abomination that encompassed everything wrong in the world. They humored the young man, all the while realizing that the boy might, at any moment, know that these two grown men feared him. Perhaps he could smell it on them like an animal smells fear, or maybe Scott would just quickly peek inside their thoughts, thus knowing that their friendliness was strictly a survival mechanism and not indicative of genuine interest in the boy.

After spending a couple of hours together, however, Charlie found out that Scott loved sports, especially football. So Charlie popped in a DVD of ESPN's greatest moments of the NFL and settled back to watch some of the hardest-hitting players perform some of the most incredible feats ever recorded in the history of the National Football League.

After Thomas had left the room to take care of some maintenance issues, Charlie gathered up all his nerve to ask Scott the one question that had been burning in his gut for the past day and a half: "Scott, why is it that you want that little girl – what's her name?"

"Samantha. Samantha Jennings."

"Yeah … Samantha, right. So why's it so important for you to have her to yourself when we could just snuff her out at any time? Is there something special you need her for?" Charlie shifted nervously on the couch knowing that he might be playing with fire. He didn't want to piss the kid off. But his curiosity couldn't be quashed.

Smiling, Scott said, "I want to find out every power she is in possession of, what I can learn from her to integrate into myself. The girl is capable of way more than any of you know - I sense it. And I also know that I can meld her genius into mine and become even more powerful. In many ways, she is stronger than I am, but she is weaker too. She is weaker because of her age. We will kill her, but only after I have milked every last part of her psyche."

Before Charlie could reply, Richards entered the room.

"Where's Dr. Carlson?" Charlie asked him.

"Ah, he's out strolling the mountain hills. Getting prepared for tomorrow, feeling a little sorry for himself, I suppose. Dr. Carlson seems a tad upset that we are going directly after power and money and not chasing down the Nobel Peace Prize." Richards let out a belly laugh that sounded like St. Nick himself.

He plopped his meaty frame into the nearest chair and pulled a fresh cigar from the inside pocket of his suit coat. He unwrapped it and stuck it in his mouth. As he chewed thoughtfully on the end of his unlit cigar, he said, "Charlie, I want you to fetch Thomas and Freeman and Dr. Carlson. I want to talk about tomorrow's expectations and the purpose of our little show; I want to make sure everyone understands what is supposed to happen."

"Okay," Charlie said, getting up. "Be back in a bit."

*

A t Fred's direction, Claire, Logan, and Sam – along with the others – were packing up their minuscule belongings for the trip back into town. It seemed such a waste to Claire – to come up into these pristine mountains and spend an enjoyable few days with great people, only to head back out to what felt like certain death.

"What do you think is going to happen?" Claire asked Logan as they were gathering up underwear and toothbrushes.

"Happen?"

"Yeah … when we get back into town, at the Naval Station, what do you think is going to happen?"

"Well, I would venture to say, Claire, that what Samantha said will happen, will happen. That young boy what's-his-name will make a jet disappear, and everyone watching will freak out; they will call their superiors, and then I'd bet they quarantine the kid and run all sorts of tests on him. Why do you ask?"

"Don't think it will happen that way," Sam said.

"Oh?" Logan replied, raising his eyebrows in surprise. "And just what do you think will happen?"

"Leave her be, Logan. Do you want to try to guess how all this is going to turn out? Do you think that Samantha – or any of us – really has control of what will take place, of what will happen? I don't think anyone in the universe can predict how things will turn out. I don't want to know anyway."

"Okay, okay. We'll put our trust and faith—"

"Hi, guys!" Sylvia said, poking her head into the room, looking more like her old self. "I was wondering if we could chat for a few minutes."

Greg Meritt

"Of course." Claire had finished packing the few items they had brought with them; she zipped the suitcase closed.

Sylvia walked over to Sam and knelt down in front of her. "I have this excellent game in my room that you can play, Sam, while I talk to Claire and Logan. Would that be okay with you?"

"Sure. But why don't you want me here?"

"It's grown-up stuff. I know that you're much more intelligent than a five-year-old, but this is still stuff I don't want you to hear. I'm sorry, really I am, but we're just looking out for you. Okay?"

"Okay."

"Alright then, I'll come get you when we're done here."

After Sam had left the room, Sylvia closed the door.

"Wow, you sure look better. It's amazing what a couple of days can do," Claire said.

"Yeah, a few days and a lotta love. I don't know what I'd do without these people Claire; I really don't. They've been my life for the past seven years, and I can't imagine being without them."

"You're a lucky woman, Sylvia. To have people like this in your life is a gift from … well, from God, if you don't mind me saying," said Claire.

"What did you want to talk to us about?" Logan asked.

Sylvia sighed and sat on the edge of the rumpled bed. "I've run this through my head at least a dozen times, trying to figure out the best way to say this. And I haven't found an easy way to say what I've come here to say."

"What? Why all the mystery?" Claire asked. She walked over to the young Asian woman, whom she had grown to love over the past few days. She cupped Sylvia's face in her hands, tilted her head up and looked into her eyes. "I don't think there is anything you can tell us that will shock us now, not after everything we've been through, after everything we've seen, so just say it."

"If we don't come out of this alive – I'm talking about Fred, Lisa, Matt and myself – and you guys manage to escape, you will need to know the truth. And that is why, after much discussion, we have agreed to reveal the identity of the woman who is responsible for the creation of our little group."

Claire let go of Sylvia's face and took a step back, her hands on her hips. "What do you mean the truth? Have you been lying to us all this time? And who is this woman?" Claire asked.

Logan watched the two woman in silence.

"Oh no, we haven't been lying, not at all. There's just more to this, that's all. More information that you don't need, information you don't want to know – at least not right now. As for the woman, I can't tell you who she is, but you'll understand when this is all over. Please, please trust me, it will all become very, very clear."

Claire glanced at her husband and shook her head. Her face was expressionless, but her eyes told a different story. After all their years together, Logan knew his wife's body language like he knew his own heartbeat. Claire thought the withholding of information at this point to be unfair and unjust; she was irritated, but what choice did they have?

"Okay, so we trust you Sylvia, and then you all die, what then? Oh that sounds morbid, doesn't it?" Claire had calmed some and tried to smile, but it didn't come off well.

Between her thumb and forefinger, Sylvia held up a small round object, which looked no bigger than a grain of rice. It was barely discernable to the naked eye. "On this computer chip, Sylvia explained, "is the contact information for a man who has the key to a safety deposit box at a bank known only to him – even we don't know the whereabouts of this bank. Contained inside this safety deposit box is information that will direct you to the woman I mentioned, the woman who will explain and show you everything you need to know. All you need to do is follow the instructions."

"This man, what does he know about us?" Logan asked.

"Absolutely nothing. And he prefers it that way. He is well-compensated and well-trusted to do only as he's told. We've used him and the United States government has employed him for top-level work. He carries out his mission and then moves on to the next assignment, never asking why or for what reason."

"And just how are we going to keep from losing something as small as that chip you have in your hand?" Claire asked.

"Oh, that part is easy."

"Really."

"Yes, really," Sylvia said. From her handbag, she produced what looked like a stun gun. "This is a micro-implanter, and it is used to inject these computer chips just under the skin. The process is virtually pain-free and after a few hours leaves no discernable marks on the skin, no trace of anything abnormal."

"And just what do you propose to do with that?" Logan asked, referring to the gun.

Sylvia grinned. "Computer chips can undertake a variety of functions: helping to identify individuals, used as tracking devices, monitoring medical information. How do you think Fred and the gang here knew where to find me, knew exactly where I was?"

"You … you have a chip implanted?" asked Claire.

Sylvia nodded. "Yup," she said, rolling up the sleeve of her blouse, exposing the smooth skin of her forearm. "I have a chip implanted right here," she said, pointing to just below the crook of her elbow. "A tracking chip so Fred knew where I was at all times."

"Wow … technology – isn't it wonderful. You're not going to shoot me with that thing, though," said Logan, referring to the micro-implanter hanging at Sylvia's side.

"Don't worry about it, you big baby. She can implant that little micro-chippee thingee in me; I don't mind. Then I can have something else besides my husband under my skin," Claire said with a wink.

"What about skin infection or poisoning?" Logan asked, ignoring his wife.

"Safe and tested. Do you really think I would do something like this if it weren't safe? Come on Logan, give me a little credit, would you?"

"Okay, so you implant this chip in my wife's body and then – and I really don't want to say this – you all die, then what?"

"Then you go to a doctor and have the chip surgically removed. It can be done with a local anesthetic right in the doctor's office; it's a simple process. After you have retrieved the chip, extract the information, contact your man and follow directions."

Logan was silent. Claire held out her left arm. "How about the same place where you have yours?"

"Certainly," Sylvia said loading the implanter with the small chip. Gently holding Claire's arm, Sylvia pressed the nozzle of the gun to her skin and pulled the trigger. Claire winced. There was a faint *pphhh*! as the chip buried itself just under the epidermis. A small welt formed at the point of entry.

"Don't worry, that will disappear in a couple of hours and, without the proper equipment, you won't be able to even tell where it is, so you'd better remember which arm we've impregnated." Sylvia laughed.

"We'd better get Sam; she's probably beginning to wonder what's happened to us." Logan looked at his watch. "And, according to Fred, were scheduled to head back down the mountain in less than thirty minutes."

As they grabbed their belongings and headed out of the room, Claire turned to Sylvia. "So what happens if we all come out of this alive? We won't need the information on the chip in my arm?"

"Nope. If we all come out alive, and I believe we will, then I personally will share with you the complete history of Omega, the woman I mentioned, and anything else you may want to know. We – Fred and I – will answer all your questions. Because, you see, once this is over we won't have to worry about all the history – the truth – getting in the wrong hands."

"Wrong hands, what do you mean, wrong hands? Are you saying that Claire and I can't – or shouldn't – be trusted?"

"No Logan, of course not, that's not what I'm saying at all." Sylvia looked hurt. "Only a few of us know this vital information for one simple reason—"

"And what might that be?" asked Claire indignantly.

"If only a couple of us know the whole story, then there is less risk. The odds of the boy tooling around in everyone's brain are slim, and besides, it would probably be taxing on the kid if he were to overdo it. If he were going to do any mind jumping, it would be Samantha or one of you two. So we feel it's best – for your protection and ours – to keep you guys as innocent as possible. The less you know, the better."

When they arrived at Sylvia's room, they found Sam on the floor playing games on a Sony laptop. She looked up and excitedly exclaimed, "Look what I found! Cool! S-Sorry Sylvia, I got tired of the other game, and then I found this. That okay?"

"Yes, it's okay Sam. We need to get going honey; it's time to head on outta here," Sylvia said.

Sam mumbled something inaudible.

"What did you say, Sam?" Claire asked.

"I don't want to go."

"Neither do I, honey; neither do I."

THIRTY-SEVEN

Scott Riley, Ben Carlson, and Richards tossed a few personal belongings in the back of the black Mercedes ML320 as if they were going on a casual fishing trip. Freeman and Thomas packed the jeep with an arsenal of weapons large enough to start World War Three. Ben didn't see the point; if they had to resort to gunfire and explosives, then the whole purpose of their mission had been thwarted.

Roman, the copter pilot, would be chauffeuring the gang in the Mercedes, while Freeman and Thomas followed in the jeep. They would leave in the morning, after an evening of drinking, gluttony, and entertainment.

At eight-fifteen that evening, while the men watched in fascination, Scott closed his eyes, concentrating. After ten seconds, the nine-hundred-pound Browning gun safe and all its contents disappeared from the room, as if it had never existed at all. Scott opened his eyes. He felt slightly sick. His head hurt.

Although he had witnessed the boy performing similar phenomena earlier in the day, Richards was electrified. "How long can you keep an object suspended? Does it hurt?" He was leaning forward on the couch rubbing his hands together like a child anticipating a present.

"How the hell would I know how long I can keep something suspended?" Scott said with an air of contempt. "As long as I have so far, huh? And the next time I suspend an object longer than the previous time, well … then that will be how long … and so on."

Richards stared quietly at the boy. He chomped thoughtfully on his cigar.

A violent scream and loud crash came from next door, as if a plane had hit the building. "What the hell was that?" Freeman yelled, jumping out of his seat and running for the door. The other three men followed.

Reaching the sleeping quarters ahead of the other men, Freeman opened the door. Protruding out of the floor was the steel safe. Freeman and the others looked up at the stars through the hole in the roof. The safe had been dropped from the heavens by a giant hand and had come crashing through the building. Its progress had slowed some as it crushed the man lying in bed. Both bed and man had been slammed through the floor to the hard-packed earth a few feet below.

Freeman turned to the others, who had stopped without uttering a sound. They were staring at the unbelievable scene before them. Thomas walked tentatively to where the safe had landed; he knew that Roman must be dead, but he had to be sure. Leaning over the hole in the ground, Thomas looked into the man's dead, vacant eyes. A few feet from Roman's torso lay a severed leg. Although he tried to swallow the bile back, Thomas was quickly relieved of his dinner.

"That scream was Roman - he must've been lying in bed and saw that safe come through the roof and screamed right before it landed on him. Poor fellow, what a mess. Why in the world would Scott do this?"

And that was when they noticed Scott had not followed them here. "He must still be over at the other building," Carlson said.

Thomas and Freeman bolted from the room, running back to the other building. They wanted to make sure that Scott wasn't up to any more tricks.

They found Scott in the middle of the room, lying on the floor and moaning, holding his stomach. A small trickle of blood ran out of his left ear canal. A few seconds after the men entered, Scott staggered to his feet. He looked at Freeman and Thomas and whispered, "The girl – it's the girl."

"So this is Samantha's doing? She plucked that gun-safe outa the universe, from wherever you sent it and dropped it on us like some weapon?" Richards asked.

Scott nodded his head.

"And how do you know for sure?"

"I know," he whispered.

Worriedly, Richards approached the boy. He produced a hanky from his pocket and cleaned the trickle of blood, which had run down Scott's neck. The care Richards took with him reminded Freeman of a father taking care of his son after crashing a bike or falling off a skateboard.

After he had cleaned up the blood, Scott pushed Richards away. Although he was irritated, Richards noticed something more than anger now, something else. Was it fear?

"Okay, alright … the show's over for now. We need to get our rest, get some sleep—" Richards started.

"Our sleeping quarters have a big hole in the ceiling now; it will get colder than hell in there. Besides, I don't feel all that comfortable sleeping with a corpse," Thomas said.

"Yeah, I'm not sleeping over there either," Freeman said.

"We need to do something with the body, give him some respect with a proper burial and all," Richards said. "Shit, I can't believe this is happening. And how are we going to get a thousand pound safe off the man?" He unwrapped another cigar, bit off the end and lit it up.

Incredulous, Carlson stared at Richards, wondering how he could be so smart as to run a company, and yet be so dumb. "Just have Scott move the safe back to its original resting place."

"Oh, yeah … I guess that'd work," he replied, taking a long puff off his cigar.

"Scott, how do you feel?" Carlson asked the boy. "And just what did that little bitch do … did she get inside your head?"

"It was like a tug-of-war … I … I was going to bring the safe back when I felt a sharp pain in my head - it was quick, real quick, and then I was on the floor, and the safe was out of my control. I saw it all in my head as if she were giving me a blow by blow of what was happening. It was like she was mocking me."

"Richards, I think we need to kill that little girl soon, or we all could be in some real trouble," Carlson said quietly.

"We will; we will. Don't worry, they will show up, so we don't have to go after them. They will come to us and when they do …" Richards trailed off, blowing the sweet smelling smoke from his cigar into the air.

"What … what are we going to do?" Freeman asked.

"Destroy them all - not just the girl, but every last one of them."

Freeman looked at Thomas.

He just shrugged and smiled.

THIRTY-EIGHT

Tuesday night was a restless one for Claire. Worry and stress about their future – the future of her family and her little girl – weighed heavily on her. The more she tried to sleep, the harder sleep came.

The evening had been filled with fun and laughter. Everyone had gathered in the formal living area to swap stories, tell jokes, have drinks and get acquainted with their newfound friends. Fred knew they would all be in a better frame of mind and perform sharper if they could dispel some of the mounting tension through laughter and friendship. He also knew that the closer they became, the more they would trust each other and, under duress, would instinctually do the right thing without hesitation or forethought.

In front of the roaring fire, Sam sat on Claire's lap while Logan, drink in hand, rested his back against the cabin wall a few feet away. They were listening to Fred describe the beginnings of Omega, how it came to be and why.

"Working for the US Government for so many years, seeing the limits placed on us by politicians who are virtually unaware of the real problems of the world, problems that are hidden from the masses ...

well, there had to be a better way of approaching these issues without interference. We needed more freedom, but we also needed funding for the tools to fight the evils that face us without the red tape that would ruin us; thus came Omega." Fred opened his arms as if he were unveiling a well-kept secret. He reminded Claire of the tent revival preachers of her childhood. She tried not to laugh.

Sylvia sat next to Aaron on the couch. She leaned over and whispered, "I've heard this speech so many times I could recite it word for word. He's doing this for your benefit and theirs, not ours." She nodded to Claire, who nodded back and smiled. "I haven't heard him talk this much in years!"

Off in the far corner, John and Lucas were enjoying drinks and their own quiet conversation. Like Sylvia, they had heard this before. Logan, however, found it fascinating. He felt as if he had been thrust into a new world – a world that he never knew existed. In the past few weeks, his whole reality and perception on life had changed. He had climbed over the fence of normalcy into the pasture of possibilities; he could never go back.

After Fred's dissertation, the gang resorted to charades, more drinking and plenty of stories, all the while being mindful of tomorrow.

About an hour after the gathering, Fred and Sylvia wandered off to be alone. Samantha had fallen asleep in front of the fire, and when Logan bent to pick her up, Claire put a hand on his arm. "Let her sleep right here for a bit; she's exhausted."

"I was going to put her to bed," whispered Logan.

"Later, honey."

"Sure."

Samantha suddenly moaned in her sleep: "We ... you ... need to ... stop! ... here is ... your safe!" She shook violently for a moment and then she grinned. "One ... one less ... to worry ... about! ... you ... and ... and the ... doctor are next!"

Claire, Logan, and Aaron exchanged concerned looks. Nobody said a word as they waited to see if more would be forthcoming, but it appeared Samantha was done ranting. She was sleeping peacefully again, her breathing deep and steady. There wasn't any blood this time, and Claire was thankful for that.

"I wonder what that was about," Aaron said, shifting uncomfortably on the couch and staring at the fire.

Logan sat next to him. "I'm kinda getting used to it—"

"Well, I'm not!" Claire said.

Raising an eyebrow, Logan turned toward his wife. He started to speak, then thought better of it. He turned back to Aaron and said, "My guess is she had a dream about the good doctor and the boy. Sam seems to dream of them often. When this is all over, I'm sure the dreams will go away. At least I hope they will."

He stretched an arm around the back of the couch and tugged on Aaron's ponytail. "Tell me a little bit about your friendship with Thelma – that is if you don't mind."

At the mention of Thelma, Claire perked up.

"Don't mind at all; in fact, it's an honor for me to talk about Thelma. She was one of a kind."

Leaving Samantha sleeping on the throw in front of the warm fire, Claire joined the two men on the couch, intrigued.

Logan wrapped an arm around his wife. She snuggled against him, resting her head on his shoulder. What a perfect evening, she thought. If only we were here under different circumstances.

"I first met Thelma," Aaron said, "through the captain of the Southwest Precinct, Trevor Martin, when I was still with the SPD. This was about nine months ago, I believe. Trevor had worked with Thelma on a cold case file, which at the time was over fifteen years old."

"How did Thelma get involved with the Department and the Captain in the first place?" Logan asked.

"I'm not sure; she never did tell me. But I learned from Trevor that this lady was something else. She was charming and funny, but what impressed him the most, I think, was that she reminded him of his mother. She had that way about her, you know."

"Oh yes, we know," Claire said. She felt the sting at the corner of her eyes.

"Anyway, Trevor supplied Thelma with a few articles from the archives of the case: a pair of earrings, and the victim's underpants."

"Underpants?"

"Yeah … the victim was raped, tortured, and then left to die in the woods. They found her nude - nothing but a pair of earrings. A search of the area turned up the underpants, but nothing else. Weird, huh?"

"Yeah, weird," Claire said. Logan tightened his arm around his wife.

"No fingerprints – the killer wore gloves. No murder weapon. So Thelma took those items into a small room, where she sat for almost an hour. When she came out, she gave Trevor the name of a man, a man who would have been just a boy of seventeen at the time of the murder. This man was a respected member of the community with a wife and three children."

"You've got to be kidding me!" Logan said excitedly. "It wasn't …"

"What?" Claire asked. "What are you talking about? And keep it down, honey, you'll wake Sam!"

"Yes, it was," said Aaron nodding. "The name Thelma revealed to Trevor, the one she said murdered that poor girl over fifteen years ago was none other than the Governor of the State of Washington!"

"I remember that! Oh my God! Thelma was involved in that?" Claire could hardly believe what she was hearing. "Why didn't she tell us?"

"Because she was instructed to keep quiet about all dealings with the police and with any cold case files. She was just following protocol, Claire." Aaron sighed. "I left the department about a month later to start my own private investigation firm, but I had become good friends with

Thelma by then. Over the next six months, she helped me locate a few missing persons, reunite a couple of families, we did nothing but good for the community …" Aaron trailed off.

Logan clapped him on the back. "We loved her very much too Aaron."

"I know. She spoke of you guys all the time. You were like the kids she and Harold never had."

Claire stood up. "We should probably pack it in guys; we need to get our rest. Honey, would you please carry Sam?"

"Of course. And then can I come back and carry you?"

Aaron shook his head and smiled.

"No, you may not mister. We don't need to be falling down and breaking anything, especially now."

"So what are you saying Claire? – I'm not strong enough to carry you or that you're just getting fatter?" Logan smiled at Aaron and winked.

"Goodnight guys," Aaron said with a laugh.

"Goodnight Aaron," Claire replied. Logan gently picked up Samantha, being careful not to wake her. He nodded at Aaron.

Logan followed Claire to Sam's temporary bedroom. Reaching the bed ahead of her husband, Claire pulled back the coverlet for her sleeping daughter, and Logan laid Sam gently on the bed.

Silently he took his wife's hand, switched off the light and walked out of the room, his thoughts turning morosely to tomorrow.

THIRTY-NINE

Wednesday morning, Scott Riley was more excited than he'd been in his seven short years. His excitement stemmed from thoughts of absolute power - power and talent he would squeeze from the girl as he watched her die. He knew they were close – very close – and was confident their paths would cross today. Scott had come to think of these people - their adversaries - as contamination, a blister on the heel of his foot that needed attention, needed to be squeezed until it popped, letting the infection run out and down the cracks of humanity into oblivion.

"Morning Scott!" Richards said, smacking him on the back. The force of the clap brought Scott irritatingly back to the moment and away from his much-loved fantasy.

"Morning," Scott said.

Refreshed from a good night's sleep, Dr. Ben Carlson entered the room, ready for the day. A few minutes later, Thomas and Freeman joined them.

I wonder if they're gay, Ben thought. Gotta be, they're inseparable.

"Since Roman, God rest his soul, isn't here to cook and I have absolutely no culinary talent—"

Scott nudged Carlson and whispered, "Sure looks like he's never had a problem getting food."

"—I thought we would eat once we get into town. Because it's a three-hour drive, we won't be eating anytime soon. Everyone okay with that?" Richards asked.

They nodded.

"Okay then. Let's get moving."

They bundled up against the cold mountain air. The morning had dawned bright and clear and cold, the mercury dipping to just below freezing. The sun had not yet risen above the treetops.

Thankfully it hadn't snowed for the past few days, so the roads were clear. Richards climbed behind the wheel of the Mercedes. Carlson sat next to him in the passenger seat, and Scott was in the back, playing a computer game on Richards' laptop. Thomas and Freeman were close behind in the jeep.

The trip into town was uneventful. After about an hour, Scott fell asleep. Richards didn't talk much, which was okay with Ben, although the silence was a little uncomfortable.

They finally got off the mountain road and onto the main highway. Traffic up here was light, especially on a weekday, so they made good time. Richards pushed the Mercedes well past the speed limit. He knew the chances of being pulled over for speeding way out here was very slim.

At eight forty-five in the morning, the gray Mercedes ML350 pulled into the Roadside Diner's gravel parking lot, which sat barren and empty at the foot of the mountain, like a lonely widow, just off Route 3. By this time, Richards' stomach was screaming. He salivated at the thought of fluffy pancakes covered in butter and soaked in blueberry syrup. Seconds later, the green Jeep Cherokee pulled in and parked next to the Mercedes.

Richards stepped out of the vehicle and walked up to the diner's single glass door, followed by Ben and the boy. The clanging of a bell affixed to the top of the door announced their arrival. The smell of freshly brewed coffee, toast, and frying bacon once more ignited Richards's palate.

Fifties-style swiveling red barstools lined the front counter; the rips in the seats half-heartedly repaired with duct tape. Placed frivolously on the countertop were partially filled plastic ketchup and mustard containers, napkin dispensers and food-splotched menus. The faded linoleum floor was grease-stained and peeling - it looked to be as old as the mountains themselves. A broken jukebox sat darkly in one corner; the P on the red neon OPEN sign was burned out and was now flashing: *O EN. O EN. O EN.*

An elderly man, with three days' worth of gray stubble, appeared from the back room. He looked as if he hadn't slept in a fortnight.

"It looks like I got my first customers of the day," he said, wiping his hands on his dirty apron. Because of his missing teeth, it came out as *fist cus'omers*. The old man looked them over as if he was figuring out whether or not to fire up the griddle. The bell clanged again. Thomas and Freeman joined the others, who were standing in the dusty lobby, staring back at the old man.

"'Ave a seat, folks, don't jes stand there! I'll whip you up a breakfast like nothing you've seen before!"

"I'll bet," said Thomas, "and we'll probably be lucky to survive it too."

From behind him, Freeman chuckled.

"Nonsense. I'd wager my reputation that the food here is better than most places, isn't that right Pops?" Richards said.

"Yup. The best for miles 'n miles. Why don't you have a seat in one of them booths while I getcha some menus," he said, pointing to the dark seating area by the dead and outdated jukebox.

"Will do," Richards said. "Come on gentlemen, let's have a seat, take a load off. We can partake of Pop's gourmet cooking and discuss our expectations of this afternoon – and the future."

Scott watched in amusement as Richards sucked in his enormous belly so he could slide his massive frame behind the table. Carlson sat across from Richards.

Freeman and Thomas secured the booth directly behind the two men.

"Join us, Scott, would you please?" Richards said. Scott hesitated. He realized that he hated both these men, but perhaps he despised Richards more.

Scott slid in the booth next to Ben. For a fleeting moment, he wondered why he didn't just kill them both. It would be over in a few seconds, and then he would be free. But he needed these men to get what he wanted. Once that was accomplished, then he could dispose of them.

"Here ya go," said the old man, handing out menus that looked like they hadn't been wiped down since the day they were printed.

"Don't you have a waitress or any other help? It's not just you now, is it?" Freeman asked the old man. "I mean, don't you have somebody to clean up the place a little? Wipe down the tables, clean off these dirty menus, sweep and mop the floor. I can't imagine what the toilet might look like." He half-expected to see an army of cockroaches start marching across the table at any moment.

"Toilets not too bad. Yup, not too bad at all," the old man mumbled to himself, shaking his head. "Now, what can I gets ya gentleman?" he said, ignoring Freeman.

The air in the diner suddenly went cold, dropping twenty degrees in a matter of seconds. Scott shuddered as his eyes rolled back into his head. The old man gasped and grabbed his chest, stumbling backward into a table, spilling the condiments onto the floor.

Freeman jumped out of the booth and went to the old guy, who was still on his feet. Gently grabbing him, Freeman guided the man down to the floor next to the spilled ketchup, being careful not to lay him in it.

"Scott, stop this right now!" Richards demanded. "Stop hurting this man who has done nothing to you!"

Scott's eyes were still turned upward as if he were trying to look at his own thoughts. "I-I'm … not doing … not doing … anything!" he barely managed.

The old man on the floor clutched at Freeman's shirt with a bony hand, pulling him close so he could hear. "Asthma attack!" the man whispered, "need inhaler … under register … front counter …"

Prying the old man's hand from his shirtsleeve, Freeman rushed to the front of the diner, around the counter and to the cash register. Sitting in the cubby directly underneath the register was the inhaler. Freeman snatched it and raced back to the old man, who was wheezing loudly now. Slipping his left arm under the man's head, he lifted his mouth to the inhaler's tube and pressed down, filling the man's lungs with Salbutamol.

Richards, Carlson, and Thomas watched as Freeman administered first aid to the strange old man on the floor.

Scott shouted something incomprehensible. His eyes returned to their normal state, and the temperature in the room began to warm.

"What did you say, Scott?" Carlson asked.

"They're here."

FORTY

Logan pushed open the door and peered into the room. According to the digital alarm clock on the nightstand, it was five o'clock in the morning. Samantha was asleep on the full-size bed. He approached her quietly, being careful not to wake her. For five minutes, Logan just stood there looking down at his daughter, relishing the moment. He prayed that nothing would happen to this beautiful little girl; he would gladly give his life to save hers. He had a sinking feeling in the pit of his stomach, however, that today was a day of death.

She stirred, rolled over, mumbled and opened her eyes. At the sight of Logan, Samantha's mouth turned up into a huge smile.

"Hi, sweetie." He sat down on the edge of the bed, next to the girl, placing a hand lightly on her cheek. "I'm so lucky, Sam, so lucky you came into my life, you know that? I love you very, very much. I just wanted to tell you that before we join the others. Before we head out of here and into whatever future awaits us."

She looked at him quizzically for a moment; her head cocked to one side as if she were trying to figure him out. After a few minutes, she broke into a grin. "Oh, Logan, it'll be fine!"

It occurred to him that this was no ordinary girl. Although that thought had come to him before, now he was certain there was something different, something special about Samantha Jennings. Not just a precocious child but also an undeniable – and indefinable – quality that few people possessed. "We'd better get going, honey. The sun will be coming up soon, and Fred said that we're leaving at sunup!"

"Where's Claire?"

"She's taking a shower or putting on makeup or doing whatever it is women do to look pretty."

"Claire's always pretty."

"Yes, of course she is Sam, of course she is." He smiled at her as she threw back the covers and stretched. Logan bent down and wrapped his arms around the child. She reciprocated, wrapping her arms tightly around his neck and squeezing hard. He didn't want to let her go; he wished he could just hug her forever.

Sam kissed his neck and whispered, "Better put me down now, we need to leave."

Her voice had changed once again; it was the grown-up voice. He set her down. "Better get dressed now, baby."

"Okay."

"Come get us when you're ready."

"I will."

Logan left the small room in search of his wife. He found her in the shower, and, desiring some normalcy, thought about stripping down and joining her. However, now was not the time to be amorous.

Sam got dressed. Claire finished showering and put on makeup, while Logan sat quietly on the floor in the middle of the room, meditating.

As the rest of the group gathered their belongings, Fred Richart was in his room with his head bowed and hands folded in front of his personal shrine, praying to the God of his understanding. And the God of his understanding was a God he didn't understand at all. This did not change the fact, though, that he did indeed believe in a Higher Power, an intelligence that ran the universe. There was irrefutable evidence of a higher intelligence running through Nature and The Universe, an order to it all. Fred also knew that evil was man-made, not the wrath of some jealous, envious deity.

Truth was love and love was truth. The two were inseparable and interchangeable, but undeniable. Whatever happened, Fred was on the winning team and no amount of arguing or persuasion could or would ever change his mind.

It was six-thirty when they gathered in the large eating area to have one last breakfast together. Looking out the large window, Claire marveled at the view of the mountainside: evergreen trees swayed under the weight of snow-covered branches; the expansive white fluffy meadow cut through the middle of the forest like a winding backcountry road; the river flowed effortlessly to its destination, and the animals that frolicked fearlessly on the mountainside were untouched by human hands. She sighed, wishing she could stay here forever, knowing she could not.

The chatter at the table steered clear of the day's upcoming activities - they talked about everyday things: sports, weather, the state of the economy, anything, to keep their minds off their fears and demons.

When they had nearly finished eating, the talk, out of necessity, turned to who was riding together. They agreed that Sam, Claire, Logan and Sylvia would take the white Chevy Panel Van - which Fred would drive - while Aaron, Matt, Lisa, John, and Lucas would enjoy each other's company in Aaron's Bronco. Aaron would be driving – it was his Bronco, after all.

The group silently cleared their dishes, gathered up their personal belongings and walked out to the waiting vehicles.

When Sylvia stepped out of the cabin, Claire noticed the woman had more life in her step and more enthusiasm than she had exhibited in the last few days. Of course, the poor girl had taken a beating that would have most people bedridden for weeks, if not months, but Sylvia was not an ordinary person. None of these people could be classified as ordinary.

Fred was the last one out. He stood on the cabin's porch for a moment, took in a deep breath of the clear mountain air, and then turned and locked up. Climbing behind the wheel of the van, he turned to his passengers in the back. "You guys ready?"

"For what?" Logan joked nervously.

"For the guided scenic tour performed by yours truly," Fred replied, smiling.

Claire sighed. "Ready as we'll ever be … I guess."

Sam, nestled in the crook of Claire's arm, looked up and said, "I'm scared."

From the passenger seat, Sylvia smiled nervously and shook her head. "I think we're all a little scared, and that's pretty normal. If we weren't scared, I'd be worried."

Fred started the van. He looked over at Sylvia. "Here we go." Although he tried desperately to hide it, his voice had a faint but noticeable touch of fear hidden under the mellifluous baritone.

He turned the Chevy around and headed down the specially paved narrow mountain road, towards the gate. Aaron followed in the Bronco, where the mood was a bit lighter. Perhaps it was the fact that the testosterone outweighed the estrogen four to one. But whatever the reason, the guys seemed ready for a fight. They bantered, ribbed and joked about what they were going to do to Richards and his people if they didn't act reasonably and see things their way.

"So you guys are going to walk up to this man and say what? 'Please stop this nonsense and come with us?' And you expect him just to respond with 'I don't know what I was thinking, sorry 'bout that guys?' and then he'll just follow you off into the sunset with his men and the boy, where you'll all become the best of friends? Yeah, good luck …" Lisa smirked.

"I guess you're right Liz," Matt said in that down-under drawl. "We'll just pump 'em full of holes and feed 'em to the fish!"

Chuckling, Aaron said, "The way I see it, we have enough firepower and explosives to blow through half the city of Seattle, let alone a couple of guys."

"Um ... aren't you guys – and gals – forgetting something?" Lucas said.

"And what's that, my good man? Whatever could we be forgetting?" Matt asked.

"Well, for one thing friends and neighbors, this isn't an ordinary situation we're dealing with here. We're up against something we've never seen before; we're facing a power that might make our guns, rifles and explosives obsolete." Lucas looked serious. "I mean ... what if they don't work?"

"Huh? What do you mean not work? Of course they'll work," Aaron said, looking suddenly uneasy as if the thought never occurred to him until now. "Why wouldn't they work?" he whispered to himself, biting his lower lip.

They had been on the road for about an hour when Samantha, lying in the back seat of the van next to Claire and Logan, sat up with a jerk. Her eyes were glazed and distant. She looked out the Chevy's windshield not at the scenery, but at something the other inhabitants of the vehicle could not see, something that was only visible to the little girl.

"Uh-oh," Sylvia said from the passenger seat. "I've seen that look before."

"The diner ... they're at the diner with ... with him." Sam was expressionless as she spewed those words as if she were so far away as to be untouched by enemy hands. She showed no signs of fear, or anger, or sorrow.

"W-What is she talking about?" Claire asked Sylvia.

"And why would you think I know what she's talking about Claire?"

"Because you've known her the longest and you just said you'd seen this all before," Claire said. "I just thought—"

"I don't know any more than you do. I'm as frustrated and confused as you are. I can only guess that she sees them – Scott and Dr. Carlson and whoever else is with them – in some diner. And the only diner I am aware of that is even close is—"

"The Roadside Diner," said Sam, who was no longer expressionless. It seemed she had come back to them and back to the possibility of real pain and suffering. She wasn't concerned with physical pain; her threshold for that was relatively high and besides, she could stop the hurting, heal any wounds.

Yes, she could heal the physical wounds but not the emotional ones; her deepest fear, her real panic was the possibility of loss of some - or perhaps even all - of the beautiful souls she was fortunate enough to be with and to have as caretakers and friends, even at such a young age. They were family - her family and they were all she had. She was scared for them, not for herself.

"Yes, the Roadside Diner. Who all did you see in the diner and what are they doing?" Sylvia asked.

"Carlson and Scott and another fat guy … he's trouble … two other guys. One's skin is dark."

"You mean his skin is black?" asked Sylvia.

"Yes, black. They are going to have breakfast."

Sylvia looked at Fred, who glanced at her out of the corner of his eye. He turned his attention back to the road and said, "Call the guys and tell them what Sam just told us. Tell them we will be stopping for breakfast at the Roadside Diner. We will be there in about twenty minutes."

"Are you sure we should just go stomping in there without any kind of plan or idea of what we're going to do? Are we just going to start shooting up the place like some scene out of a Hollywood movie? Good way to get us all killed if you ask me," Logan said, putting an arm around Claire.

Sylvia said, "I think Fred's right. We need to try and stop this before they make it to their destination. Maybe it's a blessing that they stopped for breakfast so we can put an end to this right now. And we're not going to waltz in there and start shootin' up the place; that's just crazy! No, we'll be more discreet than that, won't we Fred?"

"When you call the guys, tell them to drive on past the diner and once we're clear, I'll pull over. There's an old logging road about a mile or so past the diner. We'll turn off there and drive far enough so as not to be seen from the main road. Then we can put our heads together and plan the best course of action."

Taking the cell phone from her purse, Sylvia called Lisa. She informed her of Fred's plans; they chatted for a few minutes and then Sylvia hung up.

As they approached the diner, their moods became darker and more somber. It was almost nine o'clock when they passed the old-fashioned restaurant. The large neon sign screamed the location of the eatery; it reached into the sky like a giant arm. A thin layer of snow blanketed the graveled parking lot. If it didn't snow in the next couple of days, the parking lot, like the roads, would become clear and barren. Sitting there now were three vehicles: a beat-up, rusty seventies Ford station wagon, a black Mercedes M350, and a green Jeep Cherokee.

About a mile past the diner Fred turned right onto a rarely used logging road. Aaron followed. Once he was confident they wouldn't be seen from the main highway, Fred stopped the van and got out. The rest of the group soon joined him. Although the sun was out in full force, it was hindered by the tall evergreens. It would be a few hours yet before the big orange ball reached over the treetops and down on civilization, warming the air.

Claire spoke first: "Call me slow, call me ignorant, but I still don't understand why we have to do this now. I mean, why can't we just see what happens over the next couple of weeks and—"

"Because a lot can occur in a few short weeks, Claire. We don't think they're going to wait to go after what they want and we need to stop them right now before there is irreversible damage. We'd better figure out what we're going to do before those guys back there finish their breakfast," Sylvia said.

"Yes. Okay, here is what I think," Aaron said. "These guys don't know me, have never seen me before, right?"

"Right," they all said.

"So I'll go in like any other guy looking for a meal and a cup a Joe, scope the place and see if I can get any information that will help us."

"Okay, say you get some information, then what?" Logan asked.

"Then he tells us what he learned and we decide what to do then, right pal?" Lucas said, putting an arm around Aaron and giving him a squeeze.

"Right," Aaron replied.

"We need to stop talking about it and do something," Matt said.

"Aaron, you go on back to the diner. We'll wait here. If I don't hear from you in thirty minutes, we're coming in," Fred said.

"Okay," Aaron replied as he climbed into the Bronco, his ponytail sticking out through his cap like a limp piece of linguini.

They all watched as Aaron drove off. Logan pulled his wife as close as he could. Claire was holding Sam's hand and Sylvia was leaning heavily on Fred. The mood was heavy, yet hopeful.

While driving back to the diner, Aaron retrieved the high-performance Glock 31 .357 from his waistband. The long-range, high-performance pistol was lightweight and easy to maneuver and small enough to conceal underneath clothing. From under the driver's seat, Aaron got a box of ammunition and loaded the empty pistol. He tucked the loaded gun in the back of his pants.

He was nervous when he pulled into the diner's graveled parking lot. His mind raced through different scenarios and outcomes. He had to keep his thoughts in the present, constantly reminding himself that working from adrenaline and instinct was more effective than thinking through his next move. He was a man of action and gut-level superiority, not an analyzer.

He got out of the Jeep, took a deep breath of the morning mountain air and deliberately walked to the front of the diner with his head up and shoulders back. Though he was only five-seven, Aaron found out long ago that walking tall instilled a confidence that helped him face tough situations. Besides, it put his adversaries on the defensive, for dealing with a man who was sure of himself was always harder than dealing with a man who was scared.

Upon entering the Roadside Diner, Aaron knew immediately that this had been a mistake. To his left sat his killers. They were eating a coronary producing breakfast of greasy sausage, pancakes soaked in syrup, bacon fried in its own fat and orange juice. Orange juice, Aaron thought. Well good for them, having something healthy with the rest of that killer meal.

He started toward the counter when a voice from behind him said, "Mr. Reynolds, won't you join us?"

Aaron stopped and turned. He was waiting for his head to explode or his body to be punctured with fast-moving lead, but nothing happened.

Instead, when he turned around, he was faced with a group of smiling, joking men enjoying their breakfast. If he didn't know better, he would've thought this was a group of guys going on a camping and fishing trip to get away from their wives for the weekend.

"How do you know my name?" Aaron asked as he coolly approached the table. "Do I know you?" I might get out of this alive if I keep them talking long enough for the rest of the gang to get here.

From the booth to his left, a black man said, "Don't play with us Mr. Reynolds, please. We know all about you, Samantha Jennings and her adoptive parents. We also know all about the Omega group."

285

Richards grunted between mouthfuls of flapjacks. Syrup ran down his double chin like molasses. Wiping his fat face with a napkin, Richards waved him over. "C'mon son, come sit with me, let's have a little breakfast."

Although the man repulsed Aaron, he slid in the booth next to him. He was conscious of the Glock tucked into his backside and silently prayed it wouldn't tumble out of his belt and fall to the floor. Aaron tensed as the man's pudgy, sticky fingers wrapped around his shoulder.

Before he could speak, however, an old man wearing a grease-smeared apron and a dirty T-shirt walked up to them and smiled a half-toothless grin. "What can I getcha young man?"

"Uhm … just coffee, black," Aaron replied nervously.

"Ya sure ya don't want somepin' to eat?" the old man asked.

"No … no thanks, I'm fine."

Without another word, the old man walked away, shaking his head. Aaron glanced furtively at his watch. He had been in the diner for only ten minutes, which meant the cavalry wasn't due for at least another twenty minutes. It seemed like he had been here for at least an hour.

"You should have ordered something," Richards said. "You know, like a last meal." He laughed.

"Excuse my friend here," said the man across the table. "I'm Dr. Ben Carlson and the boy …" he cleared his throat, embarrassed. "Of course, you know who the boy is, that's why you're here now, isn't it?"

"I just came in for a cup of coffee, going up on a little fishing expedition with a couple of buddies. I … I don't know what you're talking about."

"Cut the shit, Aaron," the boy said, looking at him with a smirk.

Aaron was shocked to hear the boy speak not because of what he said but how he said it. The tone of Scott's voice was one of authority, power, and wisdom. This wasn't a seven-year-old he was sitting across from; Aaron's blood ran cold. He shivered.

Aaron said, "Okay … you're right. I'm not here just for the coffee, although that sounds good right now."

As if on cue, the proprietor of the diner returned with a pot of freshly brewed coffee, which he set in the middle of the table without a word. Then he left.

Pouring himself a cup of the steaming java, Aaron said, "I came to meet the boy here, see what all the fuss is about."

"What fuss are we talking about?" Richards asked. "And how do you know of young Scott here? How did you know we'd be at this diner? Today? At this exact time?"

Aaron calmly slipped his hand in the left pocket of his coat. "I'm a private detective, Mr. Richards, and I've been following people for years. When you do it for a living, you become somewhat good at it." Aaron felt the phone in his pocket. He ran his fingers over the keypad until he was certain his thumb was on the number three. Earlier, Aaron had programmed Claire's number into his cell, setting it to speed dial. He pushed it now, praying that Claire wouldn't make any noise when she answered. If she did, it was over. It was probably over anyway.

"What about the others?" Richards asked between mouthfuls.

"Others? I don't know—"

"Right. They're just down the road waiting for Aaron to bring back information on us. Aren't they Aaron?" Scott said with an irritating smugness.

On an old logging road in the middle of nowhere standing next to strangers she had just met, Claire Keller's cell phone rang. She pulled it out of her purse and her breath caught in her throat when she saw who was calling. "Shhhh!" The group abruptly stopped chattering and looked quizzically at Claire. "It's Aaron … why would he call?"

"Everyone quiet when Claire answers," Fred said. "Claire, don't say anything, just listen, we don't want to give ourselves away in case they can hear us."

Greg Meritt

She nodded. Holding her breath, Claire accepted the call. From the other end came muffled voices. It was difficult to discern what was said and who was saying it.

And then Aaron's voice muffled but intelligible: "No, they're not just down the road, as you put it. Whatever gave you that idea? And who are you talking about anyway?"

More muffled voices, and then someone screamed.

FORTY-ONE

Dropping her phone as if it were on fire, Claire frantically blurted, "What do we do, what do we do?"

"Was that Aaron screaming? What the hell is going on in there?" Lisa asked.

"Didn't sound like Aaron, but 'ard to tell," Matt said, heading to the van. "We need to get down there."

"Hold on, just hold it a minute, let's think this through," Fred said.

"We don't have time to think this through, Fred. Someone is in serious trouble in that eatery, and it could be – probably is – Aaron. Waiting might mean his death. We need to move," John Belk said, running his hand over his bald head.

"Yeah Fred, John's right," Lucas said.

"Breathe guys, be calm," Fred said quietly. "If it's Aaron we're too late anyway. He purposefully called to warn us, I believe. We should think this through, at least for a moment."

"So what do you want to do?" Logan asked.

All eyes were on Fred. He stood quietly, searching their faces. Before he could reply, Sam said, "Aaron didn't scream … it was someone else."

"You sure, honey?" Lisa asked.

"Yes."

"Let's move then," Fred said suddenly, heading around the front of the van to the driver's side. He climbed behind the wheel and started the engine as the rest of the group, without a word, hurriedly joined him.

A few minutes later, they were in the parking lot of the Roadside Diner. Fred pulled up beside the Cadillac, parked, shut off the engine and stared at the large, plate glass windows. He knew they were being watched, but because the windows were tinted to keep the sun out, he couldn't see in. It made him nervous. In his mind's eye, he saw men on the other side of the windows with their weapons drawn, waiting for him to step out of the vehicle so they could unload the magazines in a spray of gunfire.

"Everyone wait here," Fred said, cautiously opening the driver's side door. "Don't do anything, make any move, until I give you the go ahead. If something happens to me, get out of here. Sylvia, you know what to do."

Because of the angle of the van to the restaurant, he was partially protected by the vehicle. Once he stepped out of the protection of the van, he was completely vulnerable to gunfire and blind to his enemies.

Steeling himself, Fred walked around the van and headed directly to the front of the diner. His gait was brisk. Although it was cold outside, beads of sweat popped out on his forehead; he absently wiped the droplets off with the back of his hand. He made it to the front door without a single shot fired.

Sylvia sat in the passenger seat. She watched, heart racing, as Fred walked across the parking lot and into the diner. Like Fred, Sylvia expected gunfire to erupt at any moment and the man she loved to be riddled with lead, tearing him away from her forever. But Fred made it to the door and went inside unharmed. Because the others couldn't see anything from their windowless position in the back, Sylvia kept them informed of Fred's progress. "He's made it to the front safely," she reported, "and now he's going inside. Well, that's it then, I can't see anything else - not a goddamn thing. We'll just have to wait and see what happens."

"What did Fred mean when he said 'Sylvia you know what to do'?" Claire asked.

"Nothing really. Tell you later."

"No, tell us now," Logan said. "We don't have anything better to do, now do we? Might as well fill us in as we wait to see what's going to become of us."

"Leave her alone, please," Sam muttered.

"It's okay, Sam," Sylvia said, turning to face Logan. "As I told you guys back at the cabin, this goes deeper than you know and when Fred made that comment, he meant for me to contact … well, I'll just say a higher up."

"You mean the woman who started this group, don't you?" Claire said.

"Yes. If something happens to Fred and Aaron in there, if they don't come back to us, then she'll know what to do."

When Fred entered the diner, it took a few seconds for his eyes to adjust to the gloom. To his left were two booths, both occupied. Sitting in the booth farthest from the door was the man they called Richards. Aaron sat by his side.

At the sight of Fred, Richards' somber face broke into a grin. "Bastard here stuck a knife in my leg, can you believe it?" he said, nodding at Aaron. The wound wasn't too deep and hadn't punctured any major arteries. The old man had brought Richards some towels from the kitchen, which he had wrapped around the superficial wound, tying them off like a tourniquet.

Aaron shrugged. "He deserved it the way he talked about killing Sam and you and the rest of us. Figured I'm dead anyway, might as well cause a little pain on my way out."

"So you were the one who screamed," Fred said to Richards.

"Yup ... hurt like hell."

Without acknowledging them, Fred walked past Thomas and Freeman and sat next to the boy, directly across from Aaron. "Thought we might be able to talk things over, come to some sort of agreement, help each other," Fred said, looking at Richards.

"That's not what you think at all," Scott said from beside him. "You're here to put an end to me and the rest of us. You and your people have no intention of reaching any agreement with us, and you know it. Too risky."

The man sitting on the other side of the boy craned his neck, trying to get a look at Fred. "I'm real sorry about all this, Mr. Richart, really I am. Unfortunately, these men would prefer to see you and your friends dead and out of the way. They see you as a nuisance," Carlson said. "And what of the girl? Is she with you? Is she—"

"She's here too," Scott said, staring out the window. "Out there." He nodded at the van parked next to the Caddy. "Out there with the rest of them."

"Yes, yes, Dr. Carlson's a tad upset with us for the violent way we're handling things. You see, Fred - you don't mind me calling you Fred, do you?"

"No."

"You see, Fred, the good doctor would prefer to win the Nobel Peace Prize and take the credit for the development of a drug called Triclomamine. This drug greatly enhances the mind's natural ability to see the future, control inanimate objects and read others thoughts! Think of the possibilities!"

"You're playing God then," Fred said.

"Maybe … maybe," Richards said, pushing his empty plate away. From the inside pocket of his blue blazer, he pulled out a cigar, unwrapped it and bit off the end, rolling it around in his mouth before spitting it into the leftover syrup on his empty plate. He stuck the cigar in his mouth, unlit.

He leaned over the table and said, "Dr. Carlson envisioned us showcasing young Scott in a much different fashion than I had in mind. You see, through this young lad, we can control the world. Just think, Fred, we will know the thoughts of Presidents, the next move of Generals; we will have in our hands the world's best weapon."

"You're insane! So you would turn the world's governments into dictatorships, into totalitarian governments? It can't … it won't … work! The world will end up in chaos and eventually collapse, can't you see that?" Aaron said.

"You won't need to worry about that, now will you?" Richards replied.

"Fred, we can't let them do this … can't let these crazy bastards run things—"

The temperature in the diner suddenly began to rise. The old man, who had been standing behind the counter watching in fascination, went over to the thermostat on the wall thinking it had malfunctioned. Before he could ascertain the problem, he heard a scream, the second one that morning. First, the Fat Man had screamed, now it was the short guy with the ponytail. He should have called the cops ten minutes ago, but he hadn't seen this much action since the war; he was fascinated. And scared.

When he turned around, it was his turn to scream, but nothing came out except a tiny croak. The man with the ponytail was gouging at his eyes as if he were trying to tear them out of his head. Blood had splattered the white plates and the table covering, turning it a dark maroon color. Blood dripped from his ears, running down his neck and pouring from his mouth as if he were being turned inside out.

Before the old man could look away, Richards reached down behind Aaron, grabbing the Glock from his waistband. As he raised it up to table height, Fred saw what was happening. But he was too late. The bullet caught him just below his left nostril, obliterating that side of his face. His head whipped backward hard enough to snap his neck.

Carlson scrambled frantically over the top of the booth, joining Thomas and Freeman in the middle of the small diner. They looked on in horror as Richards cackled crazily and the man beside him succeeded in removing his eyes from their sockets.

It was getting hot. Scott threw his head back and stared at the ceiling, shaking violently.

In the diner's parking lot, Samantha Jennings slammed into the wall of the van. She thrashed and kicked for a moment, and then sat down calmly. She looked at Sylvia sadly. "Fred and Aaron are both gone; we need to finish this now before more people die."

"W-what ... what do you mean Fred's dead?" Sylvia shrieked, shaking Sam by the shoulders. "He can't be dead goddammit! He can't be!" She jumped out of the van and ran towards the diner.

"Sylvia NO!" Logan yelled, running after her. "Sylvia, don't go in there!"

Claire turned to Sam. "Stay here honey, promise me you'll stay here!" Sam's demeanor was strangely different. There was a sense of calmness about her that Claire had not witnessed before; it was unnerving. "Sam, are ... are you okay?"

"Yes, I'm okay ..."

Claire ran after her husband, shouting his name as he disappeared into the blackness of the restaurant. Without any thought for their own safety, Lisa, Matt, Lucas and John exited the vehicle like some Special Forces tactical unit.

But after only a few steps, Lucas stopped and turned to Sam, who was still sitting on the floor of the van. "I'll stay with you sweetheart, in case we need to make a run for it." He looked after his friends, who were almost to the front door. "Hey Liz," he yelled, "I'm gonna stay with Sam, make sure she's safe!"

"Okay," Lisa hollered back over her shoulder.

And then she disappeared into the abyss.

FORTY-TWO

When Claire entered the restaurant, the cold metal of the Glock's barrel was already pressing hard against Logan's forehead. Richards smiled at her, an unlit cigar poking out of the corner of his mouth like an extra finger.

And then she noticed Aaron slumped over the table in the far booth. Blood everywhere. Across from him, looking up at the ceiling with expressionless eyes, sat Fred.

He was dead, half his face gone.

Claire turned and lost the last bit of food that remained in her stomach. She continued with the dry heaves until her stomach muscles cramped and hurt; after a few minutes, the dry heaves finally subsided.

With the back of her hand, she absently wiped away the long string of spittle that was hanging from the corner of her mouth.

She didn't hear the rest of the group come in, or Richards' laughing. When she straightened up, she noticed the boy standing next to a good-looking black man of about twenty-five or so. Next to him was another man, whose pockmarked face and rough features reminded her, for reasons she didn't understand, of a drug addict. Sitting at a table away from the crowd was another man who had his back to them as if he didn't want to associate with this group.

Claire observed all this in a matter of seconds. Sylvia had grabbed her arm when Claire straightened up and was holding onto her for support. Claire could feel the woman shaking with fear and grief. But she thought some of the shaking might be out of rage and hatred too.

The door to the diner opened, and Samantha Jennings walked in with Lucas. "I-I couldn't stop her, I—" he stopped in mid-sentence and looked around the room, assessing the situation quickly.

"Oh no, Samantha!" Claire said when she saw her daughter enter the diner.

"See, what did I tell you? They will come to us," Richards said, smiling. "And now that we're all here in this cozy little place, let's get this over with, shall we?"

"We know all about your plans for Scott and Dr. Carlson, Mr. Richards. By the way, which one of you is Ben Carlson?" Matt asked. "I'm guessing here, but I'd put my money on the man sitting by himself at that table across the room."

"Yup, that'd be him. Why your interest anyway?" Freeman wondered.

"No reason, just curious," Matt replied, walking toward the man sitting alone.

"Would you please lower that pistol?" Logan asked Richards as politely as he could. "My forehead hurts, you don't have to press so hard."

"Oh, pardon me, my good man," Richards said with a chuckle. He lowered the gun to his side, keeping it at the ready.

"Pops! Hey, Pops!" Richards yelled. "Come out here!"

Shuffling out of the kitchen, the old man walked like he had urinated in his drawers. Claire felt sorry for him. Talk about being in the wrong place at the wrong time, she thought.

"We need you to lock this place down now. Turn off that open sign and lock up the doors. Put a closed until further notice sign on the door and—"

"People driving by are going to see the vehicles in the parking lot and think the diner's open for business," Thomas said. "Pops, you have somewhere we can hide the cars?"

"Round back behind the building, you can park 'em there," he said nervously. "Watchya gonna do? I'm just an old man who wants to sell the place and retire … I didn't … I … I … don't know …" he trailed off, shaking his head.

"Don't worry none, Pops," Richards said, clapping him on the back hard enough to make the old man stumble. "My beef ain't with you and if you do as I ask, nothing will happen to you okay? The sooner you move your ass, the sooner this will all be over."

The old guy just stood in the middle of the diner, as if he were a statue instead of a living, breathing man.

"Move your ass!" Richards yelled.

His paralysis broken, the old man went in search of his keys and a piece of cardboard to make a sign for the front door. Lucas and Carlson sat at a table across the restaurant, their backs to the crowd; they appeared to be in deep conversation. Everyone else was silent, waiting for direction.

"Keys, I want all the keys to the vehicles," Richards demanded. "Now!"

"You'll have to dig through those two dead men's pockets if you want the keys to our vehicles," Logan said, nodding to the lifeless bodies slumped in the booth.

"No problem. Thomas, would you please get the keys from these gentlemen? I'm sure they won't give you any trouble," he said sarcastically, chomping on the unlit cigar and grinning as if he were having the best time of his life.

"Yes sir," Thomas replied, heading off toward the dead men.

The mountain sunlight filtered through the tinted glass of the large storefront windows, illuminating the dust particles, which floated lazily in the air, causing the diner to become gloomier. It was so surreal; Claire half expected to wake up at any moment to find her husband beside her, snoring softly in their bed, wearing nothing but a pair of boxers and a smile.

She had to sit down before she fell. Grabbing the back of the chair nearest to her, Claire steadied herself for a second before she sat. Logan took the chair next to her and motioned for Sam to join them at the small table. Expressionless, Sam walked over, her eyes flitting around the room, watching.

Although he couldn't see his face and, from this distance, couldn't hear what he was saying, Freeman kept a watchful eye on Carlson and Lucas. He never did trust the guy.

Still gripping the Glock, Richards sat at the table with Claire and her family.

"Your plan will never work," Logan said.

"That a fact?"

"Yes, that's a fact, you fat prick," Logan replied. Claire put a hand on Logan's arm and shook her head. He covered her hand in his and then looked at Sam. "Honey, why don't you go and see what Sylvia and Lisa are doing? I don't want you to hear what I have to say to this man."

"Okay." Sam stood up and surveyed her surroundings. Two dead men in one booth, Carlson and Lucas sitting at a table across the way. Lisa, Sylvia, John and Matt stood in a dark corner having a quiet conversation about something – retaliation perhaps – and the boy intently watching her, as if he were waiting for the exact moment to pounce.

The old man came out of the back storage room holding a big piece of cardboard on which was scrawled: CLOSED UNTIL FURTHER NOTICE, a roll of duct tape tucked under his left arm.

He walked over to the flashing neon sign and unplugged it. Then he went to the front door, opened it and peered out. Thomas had moved all the cars around back, out of sight of the main road. Tearing off a long piece of duct tape, he fastened the makeshift sign to the glass of the single entry door. When he finished with that, he stepped back inside, turning down all the blinds, making the place even darker.

A few minutes later, Thomas entered. "All the vehicles are out of sight Boss," he said.

"Perfect. Pops, please lock up now that we're all here and cozy and accounted for," Richards said.

I wish he'd light that damn cigar, Logan thought. I'd pluck it from his mouth, stick the ember in his eyes and blind the man.

"Never got any business this early on a weekday mornin' anyways," he mumbled as he locked the door.

Logan looked up and noticed that Sam hadn't joined the group in the corner, but was sitting with Dr. Carlson and Lucas. They were discussing something. Sylvia noticed, too. She started heading that way.

Turning back to Richards, Logan said, "So you have this need to control everybody and everything, like you control these men here huh?" Spittle was flying from his mouth.

"Logan, Logan, calm down," Claire said.

"I'm not going to calm down Claire. This man is an abomination, and he needs to be stopped."

"And who's going to stop me? You?" Richards laughed. "Please."

Shaking with a rage he didn't know he was capable of, Logan wanted to kill the man. This primal urge was more about his own – and his family's – survival than about revenge or retaliation. Catching himself before he did something stupid, Logan took a deep breath and sat back in his chair, never taking his eyes off the lunatic.

"Why are you doing this … why do you want to destroy the world as we know it? - and what's with the young boy?" Claire asked. She really did want to understand, wanted to know his motive. It never occurred to her rational mind that there might not be an answer to that question.

Maybe he didn't know why, perhaps he didn't care, perhaps there wasn't a reason.

From the corner of her eye, she saw movement. Ben Carlson was coming towards them. Lucas was on his heels. Sam, however, was still sitting at the table with her back to them, deep in thought.

Richards was smiling at Claire, his tongue flicking the saliva-soaked cigar around in his mouth. When Carlson was almost to the table, he lifted a handgun from behind his back. Before anyone could react, he shot Richards in the heart at close range.

As soon as she saw the gun, Claire pushed back from the table, toppling the chair with her in it. Logan yelled something incoherent as he reached for his wife.

He missed.

Claire's head bounced off the dirty linoleum; her world went black.

Scott screamed, "NO! ... NO!" The temperature began to rise again as his eyes rolled skyward; a thin, almost transparent film of what looked to be mucus covered his eyes like a second cornea. Carlson began to shake.

I'm not going to let him get me," Carlson thought.

With great effort, he forced the handgun to his temple and pulled the trigger, splattering blood and brain tissue on Lucas and the jukebox behind him.

Logan watched numbly. He was sitting on the floor with Claire's head resting in his lap. He unknowingly stroked her hair as the chaos continued around him.

As soon as they heard the shot, Freeman and Thomas were on the move to try and protect their boss, but they were too late. They watched helplessly as Richards died from the fatal gunshot wound to his heart and Dr. Ben Carlson took his own life.

From a dark corner of the restaurant, Lisa nudged Matt and, grabbing John's arm, quietly nodded to Sam and Sylvia's table.

Samantha was now sitting on the floor next to the table in a lotus position, eyes closed and hands resting lightly on her knees, palms up, like a monk in deep meditation.

Her elbows on the table and her chin resting in her hands, Sylvia watched the girl with fascination.

Scott was in a fugue and, for the moment, was gone from this world.

Sam knew this was the time to strike, the moment Scott was most vulnerable. She concentrated, hard. In her mind, Sam increased the vibratory frequency of the energy field until it was at such a velocity she could hardly contain it. Focusing everything she had, Sam directed the energy at the boy and held it there, waiting for the perfect moment.

No one in the diner moved or barely took a breath. The lights began to flicker. Electric currents swirled in the air like tiny fingers. The atmosphere began to get heavy; it felt as if a giant hand was pushing down on them and it was getting harder and harder to catch their breath. The temperature continued to climb. The thermometer's mercury pushed past the ninety-degree mark.

Claire moaned and, wiping sweat from her forehead, sat up next to her husband. The air smelled different, thick somehow, and Claire could almost taste the thickness on her tongue. Logan was relieved to see his wife was not seriously hurt.

Scott was still in a trance, but now he was shaking violently. Claire and Logan scrambled across the floor, away from the boy, running on nothing now but adrenaline.

Before Samantha could unleash her fireball of power, Lucas was lifted off his feet and thrown violently across the restaurant. He hit the wall with such force it broke his back; he immediately burst into flames.

The old man, the proprietor of the Roadside Diner, peered over the edge of the empty counter, exposing only enough of himself to catch a glimpse of the horror. The old guy's eyes widened as he watched a man being lifted off his feet and flung across the room by some unseen force.

As he retreated to the kitchen, he expected to be grabbed from behind and killed like the others. But the old man made it through the kitchen doors without harm. He immediately went to the storage closet and shut himself inside.

Freeman, who had reached his boss a few seconds too late, suddenly grabbed his own throat, as if he were choking. He stumbled backward, almost tripping over Claire, who tried to get out of his way. His mouth opened and closed, as he tried to fill his lungs with life-giving oxygen, but he could not breathe. His lungs have collapsed, Claire thought.

Freeman's neck began to swell as he continued to open and close his mouth. He looked like a freshly caught fish just pulled from the water. He fell next to a booth, his back resting against the seat. His legs began to thrash. His eyes began to bulge.

Sylvia looked at Freeman, then at Sam and back to Freeman. "Stop it, Samantha, stop it right now!"

Sylvia's words had no effect. Sam sat quietly, eyes closed, hands gently resting on her thighs. She looked to be in the most serene state of mind, like she had found Nirvana.

Wanting to help his friend, Thomas rushed to Freeman's side. Freeman was shaking, thrashing and gasping for air so violently that Thomas couldn't get close to his friend without being kicked or hit. It was like going into a corral with a wild horse.

Without warning, Freeman sat up, grabbed Thomas's arm and looked at him beseechingly with those grotesque, bulging eyes. Then he fell back against the seat.

Dead.

As he got to his feet, Thomas snatched the Heckler and Koch from the shoulder holster underneath his winter coat. He pointed it at Samantha, who was still sitting on the floor with her eyes closed, and fired twice. The instant Thomas squeezed the trigger Sam's eyes flew open.

And then the world slowed down, way down. The two bullets were rotating rapidly, but they seemed to have stopped any forward momentum as they hung on the air, as if they had reached an invisible bulletproof wall they could not penetrate. Thomas's jaw dropped. He quickly squeezed off another shot. The gun backfired and the bullet caught him in the throat, as if he had turned the gun on himself. The two shots that hung in the air dropped harmlessly to the floor.

Scott was coming back to the present - his eyes began to focus once again on his surroundings, and he no longer shook like a palsied old man.

Screaming, Matt was lifted off his feet. At the same time, his head was crushed by an invisible weight. The fragments of his skull pierced the soft matter of his brain like a knife. He dropped lifelessly to the ground.

Lisa screamed and headed toward the kitchen.

Claire was on her feet now. She wanted desperately to run but she could not; she had a little girl now, and she would never leave without her. Logan stood up and grabbed his wife, gently leading her away from the chaos to a darker corner of the diner.

There isn't a safe place from this, he thought. This thing, this power which crosses all dimensions of time and distance.

"Now Sam! Now!" Sylvia screamed.

With a great sense of relief and a vague sense of sadness, Sam unleashed the ball of rapid vibratory energy.

Scott got up and walked in Sam's direction, a hideous and grotesque grin on his lips. The young man's gait was jerky, stilted. He looked like a toddler just learning to walk. His head lolled back and forth on his neck as if it were spring-loaded.

Halfway across the room, Scott fell forward, landing on the greasy floor. He tried to stand, wobbled, and fell to the ground again, resigned. He looked up at Samantha, who looked back at him not with hatred or anger, but with sorrow and compassion.

"I'm sorry."

The diner's windows imploded, spraying tinted glass everywhere. From the darkness of the closet, the old man heard yells of surprise as people dodged shrapnel-sharp pieces of flying glass. They dove to the floor and under tables, trying desperately to get out of the way.

Scott made an unsettling mewling sound, like an injured animal; he twitched and jerked. After a few moments, his movements ceased. And then he shrieked like some strange, exotic bird; a dark blue-black color seeped out from the boy's skin like steam rising off a pond. At first, it was thin and transparent. Then it began to thicken and grow, slowly infiltrating the diner, blotting out the light. The brume climbed to the ceiling and shadows of what looked to be sharp-clawed creatures played on the walls, mouths revealing sharp fangs.

An unpleasant odor overtook the restaurant then: a mixture of sulfur, burnt flesh, coffee, and human putrefaction permeated the place.

Sylvia looked at Samantha – this five-year-old girl – with complete and unblemished wonder and fascination.

Had this little girl been stripped of the joys of childhood? Or did the knowledge and peace Sam was given by some unseen celestial being outweigh and outshine the wonder of early childhood? Since she did not have access to Sam's thoughts or feelings, Sylvia knew she would never know the answers to these questions.

Once more Claire doubled over as her stomach protested the information her senses inflicted upon her.

After a few minutes, the mountain breeze came in through the glassless windows and gently carried away the putrefying odor, replacing it with a freshness that was invigorating, even under these circumstances. The misty shadows followed and slipped silently out the windows in the wake of the smell, as if chasing a part of itself.

An eerie stillness invaded the diner then. Timidly, cautiously, people slowly emerged from underneath the tables, carefully maneuvering around the broken glass. They stood up, brushing the dirt and dust off their clothes.

Logan looked around the diner, which was now bright with sunlight coming in through the shattered windows.

Turning to his wife, he said, "I think it's over now."

FORTY-THREE

The Roadside Diner looked like a war zone: blood, food, glass and dead bodies littered the floor.

Claire joined her husband. "Oh Logan, I-I … can't believe this … w-what … is this real?"

Not waiting for an answer, shaking her head in disbelief, Claire walked towards Sylvia, her husband at her side. She put an arm around Logan's waist, pulling him tight. *Was the killing over? Please, God, let it be over.*

When they reached Sylvia, Claire said, "I-I'm so confused, this is all … I don't know …" she sighed and laid her head on her husband's shoulder.

"Claire … Logan, I'm not sure what just happened here, but I think the evil that was Scott is gone now," Sylvia said, shaking her head. "I … this is just too much."

Her voice was soft, almost inaudible. She seemed to be walking the edge of sanity and looked like she had aged twenty years in the past twenty-four hours. Without another word, Sylvia walked across the diner to the booth where Fred stared silently at the ceiling and Aaron's eyeless corpse slumped over the tabletop. Blood congealed on the table and seats; the bright redness had turned to a dark blackness.

"We need to go, we need to get out of here before anyone shows up, before the cops come," Sylvia said, holding Fred's limp, dead hand in hers. She patted it, kissed him on the forehead and softly said, "I'll see you on the other side, my love, I promise you that." Her voice cracked, and one of her tears dropped on Fred's cheek and rolled down his face.

Sylvia felt a hand gently tugging her arm. "Yes, Sylvia, we do need to go – come on, we need to hurry," Logan said.

Letting go of Fred's hand, Sylvia turned and fell against Logan, weeping. Wrapping an arm around her shoulders, Logan led her to the front of the diner. Stepping over the broken glass and the bodies, Claire and Samantha followed.

Halfway to the front door, Claire stopped suddenly and said, "Lisa! What happened to Lisa?"

"I'm here … I-I'm okay," came a voice from the back of the diner. Stepping out from behind the counter, Lisa joined them. "During all the commotion, I just went and hid in the corner by the cash register, hoping that freak would forget about me," she said. "M-Matt … Fred … John … Luc—" she burst into tears.

Claire went to the woman's side and held her close. She whispered, "It'll be okay; it's alright … it's over now." To her own ears, however, she sounded pompous and stale, unemotional.

"We have to go now," Logan said hurriedly, "before somebody comes driving by and decides to stop for a bite to eat. We've been lucky so far."

Following Samantha, Claire led Lisa towards the front door. Logan, with his arm around Sylvia, brought up the rear.

Once outside, they all took deep breaths of the fresh mountain air. Anything was better than the putrid, rancid atmosphere of the diner.

They went around back and found the vehicles parked behind the restaurant, out of view of the main road. Logan fished the keys to the van, which he had found in Thomas's pocket, out of his pants.

After everyone climbed into the van and Logan was behind the wheel, Lisa said, "What about the old man? He's still alive, isn't he? Where'd he go?"

"Shit," Logan said, "In all the confusion, I forgot all about him."

"He's in the kitchen somewhere," Sam said.

"Okay, everyone stay here, I'll go back and talk to the old guy and see if he wants to come with us. If—"

"Logan, we can't take him with us," Sylvia said.

"Why not?" Logan asked.

"We can't expose him to the project, to New Life, to the organization. He can't—"

"Are you kidding me? After what the poor guy just witnessed in his restaurant? It was a massacre for Christ sake – a massacre that destroyed that man's diner! And just what do you think he's going to do when the cops show up? He's going to identify you and the rest of us Sylvia. And then what'll we do?" said Logan.

"The organization will hide us, and they will take care of dealing with the local authorities, Logan. We won't have to worry about it – about him," Sylvia replied, nodding at the diner. "We have some very powerful people on our side – this never happened."

"But it did happen, Sylvia and that man in there … well, we're responsible for him," Claire said. "Logan's right, we need to help him."

Sylvia sighed. "Fine. Do what you feel you need to do but hurry up about it, will you?"

And then they heard the unmistakable sound of vehicle tires crunching over the graveled parking lot at the front of the restaurant. *Someone was here.* From the back, they couldn't see anything, so they didn't know if it was the police or just some hungry hiker looking for breakfast. And what did it matter? If it were just a hungry person in search of food, as soon as they saw the devastation, the murders, the place would be swarming with police and the media.

As the occupants of the van were holding their breath, waiting and wondering what to do next, Samantha closed her eyes and quietly folded her hands in her lap. She looked like a tiny Buddha in the middle of extreme concentration, as if she were conversing with the gods.

And then they heard the sound again: tires on gravel. This time, however, the noise gradually became fainter, as if the person or persons decided to leave without investigating the diner's menu. Maybe the hungry hiker changed his mind and decided to find something closer to town.

Logan got out of the van. "Be right back," he said, as he disappeared around the corner of the building. Within seconds he poked his head back around the corner and gave everyone the "thumbs up" sign. "Going to talk to the old man," he yelled and disappeared once more.

Logan stopped at the entrance to the Roadside Diner and took a deep breath. In his mind's eye, he saw himself walking through the door only to be greeted by the smiling Richards, a cigar poking grotesquely out of the corner of his mouth, and blood oozing from the hole in his shirt.

Taking another deep breath, he grabbed the handle of the door and stepped inside. Without looking at them, Logan made his way past the bodies as quickly as possible and went directly to the kitchen.

"Hey! Old Man! It's all over! I promise! You can come out now!"

Logan stood in the middle of the kitchen with his arms folded across his chest, surveying his surroundings. To his left was an institutional steel gray dishwasher piled with dirty dishes. In front of him, along the back wall about thirty feet away, was a long prep table with stainless steel double sinks. Lettuce, mushrooms, tomatoes and green peppers were strewn about on the table, waiting to be chopped and sliced. Next to the prep table was a large stainless steel door that looked to Logan like a vault - the entry to the cooler. On his right and about fifteen feet away was the pantry door, now closed.

"He's either freezing his ass off in the cooler or he's hunkered down with the can goods in the pantry," Logan mumbled to himself.

He wandered over to the door and opened it. And there he was, the proprietor of the Roadside Diner, lying against a hundred pound sack of russet potatoes, curled up like a baby.

When Logan had opened the pantry door, it had startled the old guy. Logan thought the old man was going to have a heart attack or stroke and was going to die right on the spot.

But he didn't. He just lay there and looked at Logan helplessly.

"What's your name? We never did ask you your name," Logan said, extending his arm. His tone was one of grave concern.

Reaching up and grabbing Logan's outstretched hand, the old man replied, "Prock Robertson."

"What?" Logan asked as he lifted the man to his feet.

"Prock is my name, yours?"

"Logan."

"Nice to meet you, Logan." It came out as 'nithe to meeth you, Logan.' "I don't want to go out there; I don't want to see what happened – I could hear what happened, and that was enough, believe you me."

The old guy was frightened and disoriented, and Logan wondered if he could convince Prock to leave his restaurant and join them.

"You can't stay back here forever, Prock, although you would have plenty to eat," Logan said smiling. "There are others outside – survivors - waiting on us. Isn't there a back way out?"

"Uh … oh … yeah, of course there is, what is wrong with me?" Prock said. "Just go back to the cooler," he said, pointing to the door at the back of the restaurant, "and take a right down that back hall. The door at the end of the hall leads out to the dumpster."

"Come on then," Logan said, walking toward the back. Once he realized Prock wasn't following, Logan stopped and turned around.

"Let's go, Prock, we need to get out of here. I know that this place, this diner, is probably home and your life's work, but I don't think it's safe right now. We'll figure all this out and, if you want, you can come back here later after the mess is cleaned up, okay?" Logan walked back to the old guy and put an arm around his shoulders, trying his best to comfort him. He started walking, gently pulling Prock with him and, thankfully, the old guy didn't resist.

Once outside, Prock took in a deep breath; Logan could feel some of the tension leave the old man's body as he began to relax. Getting out of the building and away from the smell of death and destruction was a relief in itself.

Logan helped Prock into the van and introduced him to everyone. They mumbled hellos and nodded their acknowledgment, but smiles were in short supply.

Turning to Sylvia, Logan said, "Where to?"

"Head back towards town and I'll give you directions as we go," Sylvia said. She was exhausted, and all she wanted to do was sleep for the next month or two, but she had to stay awake and get these people to safety. With Fred gone, it was now her responsibility to make sure that there was an end to all the pain and horror.

She knew, however, that they would never be the same again.

FORTY-FOUR

They drove west on Highway 2 in silence, each person quietly reflecting in their own way on the events that had just transpired, and what - if anything - it all might mean.

Ten minutes later, Logan turned to Sylvia and said, "Where am I going anyway?"

"Just keep driving," Sylvia replied, checking her watch as if she were late for an appointment.

"What do you think will happen when the police show up at the diner? Don't you think they'll find us?" Logan asked.

"As I said before, Logan, the agency will take care of that, don't worry. Right now we'll just stay one step ahead of them."

Looking in the rearview mirror, Logan felt overwhelmed with pride as he watched Samantha resting quietly in his wife's arms. Lisa sat next to Claire, her head leaning back on the seat, eyes closed. The young nurse looked like some college kid, not an agent fighting some crazy war.

The old man sat behind Lisa and Claire. He seemed to be in a state of shock. Logan feared for the man's sanity. Even though it looked as if this were over, Logan couldn't imagine any of them having a normal life. Not now. How could they after everything that had happened?

Fifteen minutes later they pulled into the small town of Granger - home to a gas station, a small country store, a restaurant and a ranger station.

"Pull into the ranger station please," Sylvia said.

"Why?"

"Please, just pull over, I can't do this anymore."

"W-what? Can't do what anymore?" Claire asked from behind them. "Sylvia, I don't understand – what are you talking about?"

"Just pull over and I'll tell you everything, I promise." She slumped back in the passenger seat, not looking at Logan, but looking out the window at something they couldn't see - a past of trouble perhaps or maybe a future with no hope.

Logan turned the van into the ranger station parking lot. At eleven o'clock on a Thursday morning in the middle of winter, the place wasn't busy. Only one other car was in the lot, and Logan figured it probably belonged to the Park Ranger.

After he shoved the gearshift in park and shut off the engine, Logan turned curiously to Sylvia, wondering what this was all about.

"Lisa, would you please take Samantha and our newfound friend on a little hike or maybe visit the inside of the ranger station if it's too cold out? I would like to have a private discussion with Logan and Claire if you don't mind," Sylvia said.

Lisa tilted her head slightly and scrunched her forehead, perplexed. She stared silently at her friend, this person she had known for the past seven years, the woman she had come to not only love but to admire and respect. And because of that respect and admiration, she didn't question her.

"Let's go, guys, you heard the lady," Lisa said, taking Samantha by the hand. "Let's go and talk with Mr. Ranger and see if he can educate us on the wildlife around these parts." Trying to keep up everyone's spirits, Lisa winked at Logan and Claire as she stumbled out of the van. "Don't let her talk you into anything dangerous." she shouted over her shoulder as she walked with Sam in the direction of the station. With his head down, Prock silently walked by their side.

When they had climbed the steps and disappeared into the log building, Claire leaned forward and poked her head into the front of the vehicle between Sylvia and Logan.

"What's this all about Sylvia?" Logan asked.

"Yeah Sylvia, what's going on in that head of yours?" Claire said, softly tapping her on the head.

"I really don't know how to say this; I don't know where to start so—"

"The beginning is usually a good place to start. Why don't you just blurt it out right from the beginning, get whatever it is off your chest; we're not going to think less of you—"

"Oh, but you might … yes, you might think a lot less of me," she said. In the short time they had known Sylvia, they had not seen her like this, so distraught and worried - it was unnerving.

Logan and Claire looked at each other, bemused. After what they had just been through, after all they had witnessed, what could this woman tell them that would possibly shock or upset them more than they had already been shocked? What other news could top what they had found out about life and the universe? They had, after all, had their world turned upside down and inside out, what appeared to be real might be fiction and what appeared to be false, might be the truth. Imagine that.

Sylvia sucked in a deep breath and held it, as if she were trying to break some world record, then she let it out in one long exhalation. Claire was reminded of the deep breathing exercises she learned in her Yoga class; the exercises meant to calm and reduce stress. Sylvia turned sideways in her seat, facing Logan.

317

Claire had scooted forward with her hand on the back of the seat and her face inches from Sylvia's. When her hand began to hurt, and her knuckles started to turn white, Claire realized she was clutching the seat hard enough to leave indentations in the pliable blue vinyl. She relaxed her grip.

"Okay, here goes." Sylvia took another deep breath and then blurted: "Samantha is my biological daughter." As soon as the words came out, she turned away from them, ashamed, and looked out the window, waiting for their reaction.

Incredulous, Claire said, "She's your d-daughter? What? Fucking look at me, Sylvia! What the hell—"

"Wait a minute Claire, wait … just wait a minute," Logan said, pulling his wife towards him and away from Sylvia. "Before we do or say anything we might regret later, let's get the whole story, okay? Let her finish—"

To Logan's surprise, Claire violently yanked her arm from his grip and turned back to Sylvia. "She's my … uh … she's *our* daughter Sylvia; we adopted her! She's not even Asian, doesn't look like you at all … what do you mean she's your daughter? Huh? Answer me goddammit!"

Logan realized then that this was the stress and anxiety of all they'd been through, that this explosion was not his wife, but the culmination of the past few weeks tumultuous turn of events.

Sylvia turned from the window and looked at Claire. She spoke quietly, her eyes never leaving Claire's: "Seven years ago I was approached by the organization and given an opportunity that I just couldn't turn down. You see, I always wanted to have a child, but I was unable to conceive … I was infertile. The proposition was simple: they would take my egg and inseminate it artificially, in a test tube in a lab."

"Okay. So?"

Sylvia broke eye contact and looked down at the van's floor. "Well … the lab they had in mind was located inside New Life; they wanted to get another operative in, someone they felt could befriend the staff and become one of them. The best way to shut them down was to get closer to what they were doing, to be a mole."

"Another operative? Are you saying you guys already had someone else inside?" Logan asked.

"Yes."

"Who?" Claire asked. Her heart had softened now, for she could relate to Sylvia's struggle with infertility and the pain of wanting a child and the inferior feeling of being somehow inadequate or incomplete as a woman.

"Dr. Tom Whiting. Tom was a member of Omega who, because of his credentials and acquaintances, got on the staff at New Life and became, over time, a respected member of their team. In fact, his sperm was used to fertilize my egg. That's why Sam doesn't look like me. Her father is Caucasian, and the New Life scientists manipulated my genes so Samantha *wouldn't* look Asian."

"Sylvia, what were you thinking? I mean, didn't you worry about your child being shot full of experimental drugs that could damage her for life or worse, kill her?"

"Of course I did, Claire. Tom and I both were constantly worried about Samantha. We took turns during the testing phases to make sure that she wasn't getting the injections of Triclomamine. Tom Whiting was a doctor and—"

"Was?" Logan interrupted.

"They killed him, the boy – *that freak* - killed him," Sylvia said, obviously shaken.

"Oh God," was all Claire could say.

"Tom's expertise was in the field of pharmacology, and he would change Sam's injections to something non-harmful, like a vitamin shot or something. I'm not sure exactly – I trusted him, though. She was his daughter too, after all."

Out of the corner of his eye, Logan noticed Lisa standing on the covered front porch of the Ranger Station. Next to her stood Samantha bundled in a thick down coat, a colorful scarf wrapped around her neck and a matching stocking cap pulled down over her head, which completely covered her blondish-brown hair. The old man from the diner was not with them. He was probably still inside talking it up with the Ranger on duty. Or maybe he'd slipped out a back door and was even now running away from them as fast as an old man of seventy could move.

Logan made a silent gesture informing Lisa they needed more time. She nodded, took Sam by the hand and led her down the stairs. At the bottom of the stairs, they turned left and headed down a well-marked trail; a few seconds later, they disappeared around a bend.

While he was watching the girls trek hand-in-hand down the man-made hiking trail, Logan heard Claire say: "Why didn't you do in vitro with a regular clinic? They do this all the time. You didn't have to risk everything by—"

"Look, Claire, I know what you're going to say ... at least I think I know what you're going to say. I took them up on their offer for two reasons - no, that's not true - three reasons. First, I didn't have the money to do the in vitro route – you know how much that costs?"

"A lot, I suppose," Logan said.

"Yes, an awful lot, way more money than I had at that time. And the odds of being successful the first time around are not good."

"Okay, so it was cost-prohibitive at the time. You could have waited awhile, you know, see what the future held," Claire said in a tone of disappointment. "What if—"

"What Claire? What if what? You weren't there. You don't know what it's..." Sylvia trailed off as the realization struck her that Claire knew exactly what it was like. "Sorry," she mumbled, shaking her head. "Oh, I'm so sorry, I don't know what I'm saying!"

Unmoved, Claire said, "Okay, so it was too expensive - what were the other reasons?

"Fred."

"Fred?"

"Yeah ... Fred. I loved him, but he didn't want marriage or a family - he was strictly a career man - and I thought ... well, I believed that if ... I've never told anyone this before, ever. Now it sounds crazy even to me," Sylvia said. A tear slowly ran down her cheek, hung for a few seconds on her chin like a dewdrop, and then fell to the floor.

"What Sylvia?" Claire asked. Her patience was wearing thin, and her compassion for this woman was quickly waning.

"I thought if I could take my egg and his sperm—"

"Wait a minute," Logan said, "his sperm? You just said he didn't want a family so why would he give you his sperm?"

Sylvia silently stared out the window at the trees.

"You were going to take it without his knowledge, weren't you?" Claire said, angry now.

Sylvia nodded.

"What?" Logan couldn't believe what he was hearing. "How do you do that without someone's knowledge?"

Quietly Claire said, "There are ways honey, it's fairly simple."

"Okay, okay. So you somehow took Fred's sperm, then what happened?" asked Logan.

"New Life wouldn't accept sperm from the outside; it had to be from their donors, staff personnel that were screened and hand-picked. I found this out after I received a sperm sample from Fred. But at least it was fun getting it," Sylvia said sans smile. "Looking back, I realized that if I were able to use Fred's sperm, I wouldn't be able to tell him the child that emerged from our union was his anyway."

"And why not?" Logan asked.

"He would never forgive me for being so deceitful; he would never trust me again," Sylvia replied. "And I would never be able to live with that. I-I don't know what I was thinking back then, but I'm not that person anymore. Please, please don't judge me ..."

"What's the third reason?" Claire asked, aware that she was once more clutching the seat in a death-grip.

"What?"

Claire sighed. "You said there were three reasons."

"Oh yeah. Well, I was young and enthusiastic, and I had this passion for justice. I wanted to be a part of something, make my mark in the world and help make this country a better place. So, when I was approached about using my eggs to infiltrate New Life and the organization would take care of my identity, my credentials, my residence – my whole life, how could I say no?"

Claire and Logan were silent.

"Look, I was helping, goddamn it! And I was going to have the child I always wanted—"

"You mean the child that you can't – and don't - even take care of? And what about that little girl? Did you ever stop to think about Sam and her feelings? What kind of life she might—"

"Of course I thought about her, that's why you and Logan are involved, Claire. Don't you see? After Sam was born and a few years had passed, I realized that I had to make a choice."

"A choice about what?" Logan asked.

"Either give up the hope that I would be able to raise Samantha as my daughter and throw myself into the organization completely or quit Omega and lose Fred but gain Samantha forever."

"So you chose a career over being a parent? Wow, Sylvia, this wasn't like you were making a choice of getting pregnant or not, you already had a child! You were making the decision to abandon Samantha!" Claire was so angry she was shaking. Logan stared incredulously at Sylvia, unable to wrap his mind around what she was saying.

"No, no, no you have it all wrong," Sylvia said.

"What?" Claire said. "What do I have all wrong? Samantha is—"

"Claire! Stop, please! Let me finish!" Sylvia blurted.

Taking a deep breath, turning away from the woman sitting in the passenger seat, Claire was silent.

"I had no other choice," Sylvia said quietly.

"Yes ... yes, you did," Logan said.

"No Logan, I didn't. You see, they told me that I could never leave the organization without losing Samantha too. The only way I could watch her grow up – and that would be from a distance - was to stay with Omega."

"I d-don't get it," Claire said. She met Sylvia's eyes, and Claire realized then that this woman was living with the weight of a burden so great it would eventually crush her.

"I was informed that if I tried to leave Omega, I would never know that I even had a daughter."

"What do you mean, you would never know you had a daughter? How do you figure that? Nobody ... nobody can forget they have a child, even if they gave that child away," Logan said, shaking his head. "Nobody."

"Well Logan, one can certainly forget if they help you forget."

"Huh?"

"If I left ... or tried to leave, they would find me. And when they did, when they tracked us down, they would eradicate my memory."

Logan just looked at her, speechless.

"And I would never know that Samantha ever existed."

FORTY-FIVE

As Logan opened his mouth to speak, Samantha came bounding down the hiking trail holding Lisa's hand. Silently, Logan opened the door to the van, and Samantha jumped up on his lap, smothering him playfully with kisses.

Lisa climbed in back next to Claire. "Where's the old man?"

"You don't know?" Claire asked.

"He was inside talking with the Ranger when Sam and I left to go on our little hike, which was beautiful by the way. You really should check out these mountains, what a gorgeous place."

"Yeah, yeah, we will Lisa, but right now we have more serious issues that need our attention, wouldn't you agree?" Logan said from the front seat. Samantha was sitting up on his lap now, surveying the gloomy occupants of the van.

Lisa felt her cheeks get warm. Of course they had more important issues, but when she went around the bend of the trail with the little girl she felt her fear and worries melt away, as if all that had happened were the remnants of some distant dream, that it wasn't real. Lisa was certain now that the little girl had everything to do with how she had felt as they ventured further away down the hiking trail. The girl could make things – emotions, feelings – change somehow.

"Yes, of course we have more important things Logan, that's not what I meant," she replied quietly.

"Things are better now," Samantha said. "We should get grand-daddy and go."

"Granddaddy?" Claire repeated.

"You know, the old man from the food place."

"Prock. Right," Logan replied, holding Sam around the shoulders, pressing his forehead to hers. "Honey, why don't you get in the back with your mom and Lisa while I go and get Granddaddy okay?"

"Okay."

Sam didn't question Claire being referred to as her mother. She took it as a matter of fact. *I wonder if she knows Sylvia is her biological mom*, Logan thought.

"Be right back," Logan said as he departed the van. They silently watched as he disappeared inside the Ranger Station.

Lisa noticed that the mood in the van was more depressing (if that was even possible) than when she had left to go into the Ranger's Station. "Did something else happen while we were gone?" Lisa asked.

"Did something else happen while we were gone?" Claire mimicked in a sarcastic, biting tone. "Now what would make you ask that? Shit … uh, sorry Sam …"

"It's okay."

"We watched people die, people that we loved and you have the nerve to ask if something happened!" Claire said, bursting into tears.

Lisa leaned closer to Claire and put an arm around her. "I didn't mean anything by it, Claire, really I didn't. What I meant was we're alive, and we have the chance to have a future, a future—"

"A future of what?" Claire replied pushing away from her. She sud-denly realized Lisa didn't know that Samantha was Sylvia's daughter - or did she? Maybe they were in on it together. Perhaps everyone in the organization knew. Claire's head was spinning, and she felt like, once again, she was going to vomit.

As if reading her mind, Samantha climbed over the center console and onto Claire's lap. Softly cupping Claire's face in both her hands, Sam pressed her nose to Claire's, looked directly into her eyes and said: "I love you."

Turning away from the passenger window she had been staring silently out of for the past ten minutes, Sylvia said, "We need to continue on our little journey as soon as Logan returns. She's going to wonder why it's taking us so long."

"Who's going to wonder?" Claire asked. "Is it the woman you spoke of earlier, the woman who runs your organization – Omega, as you call it?"

"Yes Claire, it is."

"When did you last talk with her?"

"About an hour ago, right before we went into the Roadside Diner."

"She knew you were going in to face those maniacs, and she didn't stop you?" Claire couldn't believe it. Although she hadn't met the woman who ran Omega, Claire already disliked her. It was unfathomable, in her mind, to let beautiful people walk into death and destruction without at least trying to stop them.

Through the driver's side window, Sylvia watched Logan come out of the Ranger station with the old man. She sighed, thankful that the old guy hadn't split out some back door to spread the grisly details of the Roadside Diner massacre to the media and splash their names all over the local news.

Turning to Claire, Sylvia said, "She tried to stop us from going into the diner Claire, but Fred wouldn't listen. He probably knew that he was signing his death warrant, but he also knew that this had to end before the boy – Scott - got any stronger. Too many lives – the world, really – was at stake here and Fred knew it, we all knew it." Sylvia spoke softly,

327

barely above a whisper. She was saying this more to herself than to Claire, Lisa or Sam.

In her own way, Sylvia was paying homage to Fred, trying to make sense of the senseless. If she could convince herself that Fred and the rest of the gang died for the greater good, that it was a supreme act of selflessness few could ever commit to, it would give Sylvia a reason to go on - not to avenge their death, but to honor it.

"I-I don't ... don't know w-what to say ...," Claire stuttered.

Before Sylvia could reply, the driver's door opened and there Logan stood with Prock by his side.

"Climb in the back old man," Logan said.

"Who ya calling old, ya wimp," Prock said showing his gums.

"You, that's who, now get in."

Prock slid next to Lisa; Logan got in the driver's seat.

"Welcome back. Did you have a nice chat with the Ranger?" Lisa asked.

"Sure did good-looking. Damn, I wish I was forty years younger ... I was a looker in my day, yessirree!"

"I'm sure you were, Pops," Lisa said with a mixture of amusement and repulsion.

"Claire, are you okay?" Logan asked. His wife, who was sitting in the back with her head down and arms folded across her chest, was despondent. He could tell she'd been crying again.

Please God, help her – help all of us - recover from this.

"Yeah ... I'm okay."

"We need to get moving," Sylvia said.

"Why? Is there someone else after us?" Logan asked. "Because if there is I think I'm done ... I'm already tired of running. Guess I wouldn't make a very good fugitive."

"No, there isn't anyone else chasing us, at least not that I'm aware of, but we have someone to see, and we shouldn't make her wait. Plus the police will probably be combing the area soon, so we should stay on the move."

Sylvia turned away from Logan and stared out the window at the snow-covered evergreens that dominated the mountainside. At any other time, it would strike her as beautiful, but right now she didn't see much beauty in the world.

"What's her name?" Logan asked.

"Barbara. She is the founder of Omega and is one of the brightest women I have ever met. She will fill you in on everything, so let's just get moving, okay?"

"There's more to all this, isn't there Sylvia? More that we don't know yet, things you've been waiting to reveal, things still to show us," Claire said, "I can sense it. I'm right, aren't I?"

Sylvia fidgeted in her seat but said nothing.

The distant wail of sirens was growing louder, closer. Logan reached over and placed a gentle hand on Sylvia's shoulder in an attempt to let her know he wasn't angry. No, he wasn't angry; he was more hurt and disappointed that they weren't trusted enough to be debriefed on the situation. And, like his wife, he knew there was something more, something they still weren't telling them.

Quietly he said, "Sylvia, please look at me."

She slowly turned and faced him. The sirens were getting closer. As they grew louder, Logan became more and more nervous.

"Talk to me … there's more isn't there?"

Sylvia remained quiet, yet she didn't turn her back on him.

From behind him, Lisa said: "Leave her alone, Logan."

The sirens were so close now that he expected to be surrounded any second by a bunch of uniformed cops, guns drawn and a bullhorn-enhanced voice yelling: "Come out with your hands up!"

He watched this movie unfold in his head for a few moments before he noticed the sirens beginning to fade. They had passed the turnoff to the Ranger Station and were continuing to the site of the Roadside

Diner, where the department's best detectives would be met with the challenge of dissecting and piecing together the events that had left nine people dead.

Shaking now, his heart in his throat, Logan looked over his shoulder at Lisa. "Okay Lisa, what the hell do you suggest? The police will be after—"

"No, Logan, the organization has this all wrapped up. You need to have some faith, please trust us … the police are being handled, stop worrying."

"Are you kidding me? Stop worrying! Do you even hear yourself? I can't—"

And then Sam started to cry. It wasn't a soft sobbing sound, but more of a wail that pierced the interior of the vehicle like a knife. It seemed that everyone had forgotten there was a child among them: a gifted child, true, but she still harbored the emotions of any five-year-old, didn't she?

Claire was quick to come out of herself and focus on Sam. She pulled the girl onto her lap and rocked her while stroking her brownish-blonde hair. Claire whispered, "We'll take care of you, sweetheart. We'll get through this, I promise." She lightly kissed Sam's forehead.

Logan turned back to Sylvia. "Okay, where to?"

"Back to the highway, follow it for about an hour, I'll let you know when we get close."

"What city does this woman live in?"

"She's in Gourd, a small town in the middle of nowhere," Sylvia said trying to smile.

The old man was asleep in the farthest seat. Samantha was huddled contentedly next to Claire. Lisa and Sylvia exchanged pained expressions, and Logan longed to wake up from this nightmare.

He pulled the Chevy back onto the main highway, heading for Gourd.

And, hopefully, the truth.

FORTY-SIX

Coming down out of the mountain on Highway 2, Logan's ears protested the change in elevation by greeting him with a slight *pop!* that made the world sound clearer. He wasn't sure, though, if he really wanted to hear clearly. It seemed that everything he saw, felt or heard this past week pushed his tired mind to the edge of reality. It was a sharp edge, and he was afraid if he took the leap he would be cut to ribbons. But there was no turning back now.

For the past hour, everyone had either been sleeping or resting quietly, even the old man. Logan looked at his watch. It was almost two in the afternoon and the rain had slowed to a slight drizzle that barely warranted the use of the wipers; they scraped annoyingly against the partially wet windshield.

To his right, Sylvia moaned and shifted in her seat. She mumbled: "Please let me keep her, please. She is mine after all. I don't want to … don't want to do this anymore." Her eyes remained closed and her breathing heavy.

Logan reached over and gently shook her.

"What? Is it time to go to school already?" Sylvia said in a young girl's voice, her head rolling slightly with the motion of the van. "Five more minutes mama, please … just five more minutes."

And then she sat up in the passenger seat, eyes wide. The look of loss and sorrow on her face was painful for Logan to see.

Trying to help her shift her thoughts away from whatever was barreling through her head, Logan said, "About five minutes ago we passed a sign that said Gourd was fifteen miles up the road. Does Highway 2 run straight through this little burg, or do we have to turn off on some side road?"

"There's a turnoff a few miles up," Sylvia said, wiping the sleep from her eyes. "You'll see the sign; it's hard to miss. I'm awake now anyway. Um … Logan … did I say anything weird in my sleep?"

"Like what?"

"Oh, like anything about the organization or Barbara?"

"No, why?"

"Oh nothing," she sighed.

"Sylvia," he whispered, not wanting to wake the others, "how did you get involved in all this? And why?"

"Did you ever care about something so deeply that you would do anything, including giving up your life, to protect it, to make sure of its survival?"

Logan was quiet for a moment. He looked out the window at the expanse of flat land that stretched for miles. Cows grazed on the grassy fenced-in fields, oblivious to the rest of the world. The pristine land housed a few old barns and some old silos. Twenty miles up the highway civilization began to take hold again.

Logan turned back to Sylvia. "If you would have asked me that a few years ago, I would have told you no. My life - *our* life," he said, "was mundane at best. It was the same old same old: go to work, come home, watch TV, do some stuff around the house, make love once in a while, go to work … well, you get the idea. But once Samantha came into our lives, everything changed, at least for me. And I'm not talking about the bizarre and crazy things that have happened in the past few weeks; I'm talking about what you just asked me."

"You love her so much, you would die for her, right?"

"Right," Logan said nodding his head, "I have never felt this much love in my entire life."

"And there you have the answer to your question. Why am I part of this organization? I believe in the principles of what Omega stands fo—"

"And what are those principals?" asked a tired voice. Startled, Sylvia looked over her shoulder. Claire was awake now, doing neck rolls and trying to loosen up the kinks she got from sleeping in such an awkward position.

"How long have you been awake?" Logan asked.

"Just woke up. Why? Are you guys trying to keep secrets from me? God knows, Sylvia, you've kept enough secrets and—"

"There's the sign Logan, right turn ahead," Sylvia said. "Sorry, Claire, didn't mean to interrupt … and no more secrets, we're done with that, promise."

Claire sighed and said, "I sure hope so."

Logan turned off the main highway and onto the narrow two-lane blacktop, heading east towards Gourd. That feeling of impending doom, that uncomfortable anxiety-ridden feeling of something-is-about-to-happen-and-it-isn't-good was back with a vengeance. It sweated his palms and clenched his throat, as if invisible hands were wrapped around his neck working to cut off his air supply.

He struggled to take a breath.

"Honey, are you alright?" Claire asked. She was concerned for her husband; he looked a little too pale, and the recent stress had put ten years on his handsome face.

"I'm … I'm okay … it's just that I … could hardly catch my breath, but I'm alright. Really I am."

Sylvia guided them the rest of the way. They went through the small town of Gourd - population 79 - and five minutes after that, they turned left onto a long, graveled, single-lane gated roadway. Logan slowed as the gate swung inward without provocation. He noticed the cameras mounted on the columns marking the entrance to the compound.

"Everything here is automated ... everything. She has been waiting for us," Sylvia said.

They continued in silence for another half-mile. When they rounded a bend in the road, the mansion came into view. Claire's breath caught in her throat. It was magnificent, more fantastic than anything she had seen in her lifetime. This was equivalent to the Queen's palace.

"Wow," Claire murmured. She was craning her neck to get a better look, but the place was so massive she couldn't see all of it from this angle.

Logan parked in the large, cobblestone circular drive feeling awestruck and out-of-place. Lisa stretched, yawned and rubbed her eyes. "Ah, we have arrived!" she exclaimed with a smile.

Samantha sat up straighter, smiled and poked Claire. "Wow, this is cool."

The old man was still snoring.

As they departed the vehicle a man who looked to be in his mid-fifties opened one of the massive oak double doors and watched them from the entryway, expressionless. Logan expected staff for a place like this to be wearing tuxedos or at the very least, shirt and tie. But the man who stood in the doorway was dressed in blue jeans, white tennis shoes, and a blue sweatshirt. His brown hair was marked with streaks of gray. He was average height and average weight.

"Better wake the old man," Sylvia said to Logan.

"Sure." Logan disappeared into the van.

Holding Sam's hand, Sylvia climbed the marble steps leading to the main entrance. The man in the sweatshirt continued to watch them, his arms now folded across his chest. Sylvia waved at Claire and Lisa, beckoning them to follow.

"Hi Adam, you're looking happy as usual," Sylvia said.

The man grunted. "She's in the library waiting for you and your friends." He looked at her for a moment and then stepped out of the doorway.

"Okay, thanks," Sylvia replied, entering the huge house with Sam at her side. Lisa and Claire followed.

Claire looked up, marveling at the exquisite glass chandelier, the focal point of the entryway. In the large sitting room to her right, a fire burned brightly, bringing warmth to the house. The staircase leading to the second floor lay ahead; the steps were marble and the brass handrails were polished to such a shine you could see your reflection clearly.

The staircase entrances beckoned on both sides of the large room; they came together on the second-floor landing like long lost friends.

The long hallway ran underneath the stairwells. Once out of the massive entryway, the hallway narrowed. Expensive artwork adorned the walls on both sides. Claire noticed many closed doors and could only guess what lay behind them: bedrooms, ballrooms, sitting rooms, living rooms, game rooms, libraries; the kind of places one would find in a mansion. She hoped, however, that behind one of the mystery doors was an old-fashioned bathroom. She really needed to go.

Grabbed from behind, Claire almost screamed.

"A little jumpy, aren't we?" Logan whispered in her ear, wrapping his arms around her waist.

"You scared me!" she said. "And I have to pee!"

"The second door on your right is a bathroom, Claire," Lisa said, pointing to a door. Lisa had been so quiet that Claire almost forgot she was there. Being a member of the Omega group, Lisa knew this house well, although she still wasn't allowed in certain parts of the building.

"Thanks," Claire said, disappearing into the bathroom.

"What a cool place! Sure beats the ole' shack I call home," Prock said. "What the hell is goin' on anyways?"

"Let you know when I know Pops," Logan said, putting an arm around the old man and giving him a squeeze.

Adam, the laconic doorman in the blue sweatshirt, brought up the rear. He followed them silently.

And then Sylvia stopped. They were now facing a set of large double doors, which had been hand-carved with the depiction of famous authors: Hemingway, Hawthorne, Dostoevsky, Dickens and more. She squeezed Samantha's hand lightly. "Here we are, folks ... the library where Barbara awaits."

Sylvia raised her hand to knock—

"Wait!" Adam said, startling her. She lowered her fisted hand and looked at him with a puzzled expression. "Let me go in first, make sure she's ready," Adam said.

"Ready for what?"

Pushing Sylvia out of the way, Adam opened the door just wide enough to slip through, and then closed it.

"Hey!" Sylvia yelled, pounding on the door. "What was that about?" She tried the door, but it was locked. "Son-of-a-bitch!"

Claire came out of the bathroom. "What's going on? Why are you standing there yelling?"

Logan said, "Sylvia is a little frustrated with the doorman or whoever that guy is."

"You mean the gentleman that greeted us at the front door? The man who looked like his face would crack if he smiled? That guy?"

"Yeah, that guy," Logan replied.

After a few moments, the door opened, and Adam appeared. "The old man and the girl need to come with me. Barbara will see the rest of you now."

He bent down on his haunches, putting his hands on Sam's shoulders, looking her in the eyes. "Wait until you see the game room honey, it has a miniature dollhouse with everything you could imagine, everything you could ever want." His voice was authoritative yet calm.

"Neat," Sam said apprehensively. She looked up at Claire, who was watching them.

"I think she needs to stay with us right now," Claire told the man in the blue sweatshirt.

"I'm sorry, but that's not possible. Don't worry. She's safe. Nothing will happen to her."

"Claire, it's alright, let her go. He's right; she's safe here," Sylvia said.

Claire raised an eyebrow. "Really Sylvia? And that's supposed to comfort me somehow? Didn't I just come out of the bathroom to see you yelling hysterically at this man? And you have admitted lying to us. Now you just expect us to trust..." she trailed off.

In the open doorway of the library sat an old woman in a wheelchair, silently watching them.

Claire's eyes grew wide; she clamped a hand over her mouth. Logan turned to see what Claire was staring at; his knees suddenly buckled.

Thelma Grisham was sitting in a wheelchair, watching them from the doorway.

FORTY-SEVEN

T helma!" Claire gasped. "My God! We thought you were dead ... w-
what happened?"

"I was there for God's sake! You died in my—" Logan started.

"Shhh, calm down for a second, please. I know this is a shock to
you, but I can explain," the woman said.

"You ... you don't sound like Thelma," Claire said.

"Because I'm not. My name is Barbara, and Thelma is ... *was* my
twin sister."

"Twin sister?" Claire was astounded.

"Yes, sister."

Before Claire had a chance to respond to this news, Barbara said,
"Sylvia, Adam, please take the little girl and this older gentleman" – she
nodded at Prock – "to the game room and have Susan bring them some
refreshments and keep them entertained while I speak with our guests."

"Certainly," Adam said.

Sylvia started to protest, then thought better of it. "Of course," she
said quietly.

Sam stood her ground as if she wore lead boots. She looked at Claire
and Logan for approval.

"Go on, sweetheart, go with Sylvia and gramps. Don't worry about
us; we're going to talk with the nice lady for a while and see if we can
figure things out, okay?" Logan said.

"Okay." Sam smiled and turned to Lisa. "You coming?"

"No honey, I'm going to stay with the nice lady, too," Lisa said, tousling Sam's hair. She leaned down and kissed her cheek. "You go and have fun!"

Sylvia took Sam's hand and walked back down the hallway; Prock and Adam followed.

Claire watched them for a moment and then turned back to Barbara. But she wasn't there. She had gone back inside the library with Lisa.

Claire reached out to her husband, grabbing his hand. It felt good to hold him, to touch him, even if it was just his hand. The warmth was comforting, like the sun hitting her face on a cold winter day.

They walked into the library together, hand-in-hand. Every inch of available wall space was lined with books: mysteries, horror stories, classic literary novels, biographies and history books from big-name authors to less well-known wannabes.

At the far end of the room, next to the fireplace, were two high-backed sitting chairs and matching sofa. The beautifully detailed rug upon which they sat looked like it cost more than Claire's first house.

Claire imagined curling up in this room, next to a blazing fire, and enjoying the vast buffet of reading material for hours, even days at a time.

Sitting between the two chairs, in her wheelchair, was Barbara. Lisa sat on her right.

"Please, have a seat so we may get acquainted," Barbara said, nodding at the sofa.

Without a word, Logan and Claire sat.

"I just can't get over how much you look like Thelma," Logan finally said. It was unnerving looking at this woman; he felt like he was talking to the dead.

"That's why they call them twins, Logan my dear," Barbara said with a smile.

"I don't understand why Thelma never told us she had a sister. She said she was an only child and that her parents had died in a horrific accident when she was seven, and she went to live with her aunt, who raised her until she was old enough to go out on her own. That's the story she told us anyway. I don't know what to believe anymore," Claire said sadly.

"It's not so terrible Claire, once you understand. These are good people, really good people that are looking out for not only your best interests, but the worlds," Lisa said. "They had to cover up a few things, tell a few white lies for your protection."

"Well isn't that fucking noble," Logan said with contempt in his voice.

"Let's get to the heart of the matter then," Barbara said, her smile fading to a grimace. "And you will not talk like that in this house, young man!" Barbara said, her voice firm and unwavering.

"Young man? I'm forty-seven years old for Christ's sake! We have witnessed bizarre, terrible things in the past few weeks and you expect us to sit here and listen to more lies, to—"

"Stop it!" Claire yelled. "Please, just stop it!" Her hands were balled up into fists, which she pressed to her temples as if she were trying to squeeze out the terrible pictures in her mind.

"Come on guys, let's start over, okay? We're all tired and stressed and, as Logan already pointed out, been through more than most people ever will in their lifetime. Let's just hear Barbara out before we go making judgments and coming to erroneous conclusions." Lisa looked imploringly at the couple sitting across from her.

Logan leaned forward and stared mockingly at the old woman. He knew that he was behaving like a child, but couldn't help himself.

Claire just sighed, slumping back on the sofa. She could sleep for the next two weeks without a problem.

"Okay," Logan said, "let's hear it."

"Ten years ago I started this group to stop people like Carlson and Richards. People like Richards think they're above the law. By greasing the palms of politicians and corrupt law enforcement personnel, they can do whatever they please, by any means, without consequence. It's because they have money and with money comes power. Power makes some people do strange, weird and bizarre things. Things you and I could never fathom or dream about doing."

She stopped to catch her breath.

Claire couldn't shake the feeling that she was sitting here with her good friend Thelma, although the woman didn't sound like Thelma. Barbara's voice was deeper, huskier, like a smoker.

Winded now, the woman looked older than her seventy-something years. If she is indeed Thelma's twin, that will make her seventy-three.

She looks ninety-three, Claire thought.

Barbara's liver-spotted hands shook. In places where her hair was exceptionally thin, you could see her scalp. The skin on her cheeks sagged with the years and the skin on her neck hung loosely like a rooster's wattles.

"The organization is small, and we like it that way. You don't need a lot of people to be effective; in fact, we've found we're more efficient with less."

Logan looked over at Claire with raised eyebrows. She shrugged.

"The only effective means to stop something," Barbara continued, "is to hit it at its source: the head honcho, the big cheese, the mastermind, whatever name you'd like to give it. Eradicate that, and the structure tumbles and falls apart unless the man - or woman - behind it all is replaced with someone of equal power and intelligence. And that must be done quickly before the infrastructure begins to collapse."

"O-okay ... and?" Logan looked perplexed.

"So I recruited one of the best CIA operatives I've ever known, Fred Richart, explained what I wanted to do, and gave him a choice."

"I'm kinda lost here Barbara … may I call you Barbara?" Logan asked, hoping to start over on better terms.

"Of course."

"Running an organization such as Omega, even if it were small, would take plenty of capital. So is this government money with military backing?"

"No, Logan, not at all. This is and has been an entirely private venture, no government involvement. We fly below the radar and cannot be bought off like some politicians and the people we employ are of the utmost moral capacity and—"

"But you can never be sure," Logan broke in.

"What?"

"You can never be sure if one of your people might turn on you, though, can you?"

"There is nothing that is one-hundred percent certain in life; you know that. But the operatives we employ are checked out more thoroughly than the Secret Service or any high-security positions on the planet. I assure you."

She started to wheeze then. Lisa took Barbara's hand, patted it and said: "Take long, deep breaths. I think you've talked enough. I can finish telling Logan and Claire what they need to know."

Still holding Barbara's hand, Lisa turned to face Logan and Claire.

"I'm going to get right to the point."

"Please do," Claire said curtly.

"Of course. The capital you spoke of comes only from this lovely woman. Barbara is the second wealthiest woman on the planet, and she could never spend the money she has in fifty lifetimes. And, since she's childless, the only heir she had was her sister, Thelma."

"Wait, wait. Where did she get all this wealth? And how much are we talking about?" Logan inquired.

Lisa turned to Barbara with questioning eyes. Barbara managed a weak smile and nodded.

"Twenty-seven billion dollars."

"Billion? With a B?" Logan was incredulous.

"Yes."

Claire gasped. "Wow. But you still haven't answered the other half of the question. Where did she get it?"

"Ever hear of Fathom Holdings Inc.?"

"Of course, who hasn't? They're into just about everything, aren't they?" Logan asked.

"Fathom Holdings has many subsidiaries reaching into all aspects of our lives: mining, transportation, pharmaceuticals, clothing, you name it, and Fathom probably has its hand in it."

"Okay?" Claire said.

"Barbara was married to the Founder and CEO of Fathom for twenty-seven years; when he died twelve years ago, she inherited everything and became the second wealthiest woman in the world."

"What's this got to do wi—"

"About ten years ago, Barbara was approached about helping to finance an underground experimental facility that would perform pharmaceutical research for the enhancement of what we call the "sixth sense": clairvoyance, telekinesis, precognition, well … you get the picture," Lisa said.

"I had had some dealings with this man when I sold some commercial properties in the downtown area. Although he was an uncanny businessman, I never liked him personally. He was fascinated with the field of parapsychology and, I must admit, his argument was intriguing," Barbara said. "However, the man is … *was* … a snake and I didn't trust him - never would. So, I refused because I believed - *I knew* - he would use whatever findings for his own purposes and not for the good of the world."

"Was? Did something happen to him?" Claire asked.

"Yes," Barbara replied with a slight smile. "Two days ago, we had him terminated."

"You mean murdered," Logan said.

Barbara shook her head. "No, no. Logan, this man was the mastermind behind New Life. He was responsible for putting that freak Richards in charge and—"

"And you murdered him," Logan repeated.

The old woman began gasping for air.

FORTY-EIGHT

Lisa got up and hurried to the other end of the room. She returned lugging a large, green canister. It was an oxygen tank. Grabbing the clear plastic mask connected to the cylinder, Lisa gently placed it over Barbara's mouth and nose, securing it with the elastic straps, fitting it snuggly over Barbara's head.

Logan watched, fascinated, as the mask fogged up and then cleared as Barbara exhaled and inhaled. It was hypnotic and strangely comforting watching the rhythmic breathing of this elderly woman.

Now, sitting down again in the high-backed chair, Lisa said, "We don't murder people Logan. We do what has to be done and sometimes it's not pleasant. Barbara started the Omega group to keep people like this from using their power to hurt others. These people think they're above the law and can do whatever they want."

"So Omega is a modern-day vigilante group," Logan said.

"If you want to call it that, but there is much more to us, Logan, and I think you know that. So Barbara recruited Fred, and he assembled the team you guys met in the mountains and … and …" Lisa trailed off, put her head in her hands and quietly wept.

Claire gave her husband a sad look, got up, and walked over to Lisa, putting an arm around her. "Take all the time you need," Claire said, which just made Lisa cry harder. For the next few minutes, no one spoke.

The only sound was the eerie *ooooob ... abbbbb ... ooooob ... abbbbb* of the old woman sucking oxygen out of the tank that stood next to her wheelchair.

Lisa finally looked up. "Sorry," she mumbled.

"It's okay honey," Claire said, joining her husband on the sofa.

"Okay, I need just to get through this, as hard as it is," she said, producing a Kleenex from her sweater pocket and blowing her nose. "Sylvia is no longer going to be a part of our organization."

"What?" Claire said. She couldn't believe what she just heard.

"But she told us if she ever tried to leave, her memory would be erased and—" Logan's eyes grew wide. "You don't mean?"

"Yes, but it was her choice. We tried to talk her out of it, to show her how valuable she is to our cause and to us, didn't we?" Lisa said, turning to Barbara.

The old woman nodded through her mask.

Claire looked at Lisa and tried to recall how it felt to be so young. Her twenties seemed ages ago, but she did remember the excitement she had for the future and how she felt so alive. And if she was honest with herself, she had to admit that the past few weeks had given her back that spark, an enthusiasm for life she hadn't felt for some time. The sense of adventure ignited within her had been intoxicating. And frightening.

"So are you telling us that Sylvia asked you to erase her memory? How could she do that, she has a little girl! And is that really possible? And what will happen to her, who will she become?" Claire asked.

Removing the mask from her face, Barbara said, "Honey, don't worry about Sylvia, we truly love her, and we will make sure she is well taken care of. She will have a fulfilling life and will work, love and laugh like any normal person. But she will never know we existed, or you, or Samantha."

"Or Fred and the gang," Lisa broke in. "She will be free from the pain of loss, of remembering what was, which can be more debilitating than any physical ailment. Who she will become, well …"

"Well what?" Logan said, leaning forward, intrigued.

"It will have to be somebody who passed away at her age. With the same height and build—"

"And she will assume their identity."

"Yes, she will assume their identity."

"This seems like something out of a Hollywood movie," Claire said. "Not real life."

"Oh, it's real alright. Look what you've seen with your own eyes. There is so much more to the world than we can even imagine, more for us to learn and discover," Lisa said. From behind the oxygen mask, Barbara grinned.

Like a couple of giddy girls, Logan thought.

"Maybe we can talk Sylvia out of this, talk her into staying with us and helping to raise Sam, like an aunt or something," Claire said to Logan.

"Not possible," Lisa said.

"And why not?"

"The old man from the diner and Sylvia are gone. They have been taken to another facility and will be implanted with specific memories of—"

"Somebody else's life!" Logan said. He was saddened that this was so abrupt, they didn't even get to say goodbye and now, if they even got to see her again, she wouldn't know who they were. They would be strangers to her.

After a few minutes, Claire asked, "Why the old guy?"

"We have to clean up the mess from the diner, and tie up loose ends and the old man is a big loose end. Because he doesn't have a history with us, and since he is so old, we will employ him here at the house to help keep up the grounds, do light maintenance and cleaning."

349

Barbara removed the oxygen mask and set it on the floor beside her. She folded her hands neatly in her lap and stared at the couple across from her with a look of endearment that made Claire's heart leap in her chest. Claire was suddenly back at Thelma's, sitting at her tiny kitchen table, holding the old woman's hands. Thelma had the same look of endearment on the day Claire discussed the adoption with her, as Barbara had now. It was unnerving and uncanny.

"You are not here by mistake, no, not at all," Barbara said, shaking her head. "Claire, Logan, you were destined to be a part of all this, don't you see?"

"What do you mean?" Claire asked.

"Once I knew of the facility in Utah and what this man was planning, it all became very clear."

"What became clear?" Logan asked.

"Your neighbor and good friend was my twin sister. She was like a second mother to you, wasn't she?"

"Yes, she was," Claire replied.

"You were childless, couldn't have children, so you made the decision to adopt. And, according to my sister, you were kind-hearted, ethical people that respected others and believed in doing what's right, no matter what the cost. You couldn't be bought for any price, at least that's what Thelma said." Barbara laughed. The laugh quickly turned into a coughing fit.

Lisa bent down, picked up the oxygen mask from the floor, and placed it over Barbara's mouth and nose. After a few minutes, the coughing subsided. After a few more minutes, Barbara took the mask off and continued.

"You see, it all fits. We needed to find a home for Sam, a home where we could keep an eye on her, so a home close to Thelma made sense."

"Thelma was a part of this the whole time?" Claire asked.

"Yes."

"Why didn't she just tell us?"

"Tell you what Claire?" Lisa said. "That you needed to adopt this little girl that had abilities – powers – beyond anyone's imagination so you could fight evil? You would never have believed any of it; besides, you wouldn't have wanted anything to do with Samantha or us. You probably would have thought we were insane. We couldn't risk it; we needed you."

"Needed us for what? To be Samantha's parents?" Logan asked warily, watching them. "But that's not all, is it?"

Lisa sighed and turned to Barbara. "Do you want me—"

"No," Barbara said, shaking her head. "I'll ask them."

"Ask us what?" Claire said.

"We want you both to run the organization, take over from Barbara, reassemble a team. Which means giving up everything: your home, your business, your friends, everything."

"I-I … um … well … *Jesus*," Logan ran a hand through his hair and looked at his wife. He felt a tingle of excitement at the thought of a strange and adventurous future, mixed with the fear of leaving everything he knew, of leaving the comfort of the familiar.

Claire looked back at him with a twinkle in her eye.

Lisa said, "And you will raise Samantha as an operative, who someday will take over when the two of you are no longer capable."

"And what about you, Lisa, why don't you run Omega?" Logan asked.

"I'm one of those people who are better following orders than giving them," she said.

"You will have everything you need, I'll make sure of that," Barbara said. "A comfortable place to live, money at your disposal, and all the resources you need to help us in our fight."

"And what exactly is our fight, Barbara?"

"To stop the corruption, especially in governmental agencies and private corporations who abuse their power; to help make a better world for our children, Logan. For Samantha."

"What about our friends, my employees at the firm, Claire's clients … won't they file reports, try to find us when we don't come home?"

"I believe I heard something about a lunatic coming into a diner and wiping out all the patrons who were enjoying breakfast. And I also read that the Keller family just happened to stop at that very diner while on their way home from a camping trip - how very, very sad." She smiled. "Your funeral, closed-casket because of the mutilation, will put an end to your past, but it will be the start of your future."

"Take some time and talk about it, think it over," Lisa said.

"Oh, I don't think that's necessary," Logan said, smiling at Claire.

Claire smiled back at her husband, winked, and said, "You look pretty good for a dead man!"

Barbara grinned.

Lisa jumped out of her chair and hurried over to Claire. She hugged her and kissed her cheek. And then she hugged Logan.

"I'm so happy!" Lisa said.

"There is one small thing though before we moved forward," said Logan.

"And what's that?" Barbara looked worried.

"We need our dog, Axel. I refuse to give up our dog, under any condition.

Barbara's laugh turned into a wheeze. She sucked more oxygen from the tank beside her, turned back to Logan and said, "Of course, my dear."

Lisa crossed the room, stopping at the antique bureau, which rested against the north wall. She bent down, opened the bottom drawer and removed the false bottom, revealing an array of handguns. After a moment, she returned with a .45 ACP semi-automatic. She held it out to Logan.

"What's this?"

"It's called a gun," Lisa said, smiling.

"Aren't you funny."

"Now that you're going to be a part of our little family, there's one more thing you must do before anything else," Barbara said. "Call it your initiation if you like."

"What's that?" Logan asked.

Lisa told him.

Logan's eyes grew wide in disbelief.

He sat back on the couch, speechless.

He suddenly needed to throw up.

FORTY-NINE

The house was dark; the green digital readout from the radio next to the bed revealed that it was one-forty in the morning.

She sat quietly, patiently.

And then she heard the front door open downstairs. The footfalls on the hardwood sounded heavy and hard, like a man's. Listening intently, she heard the refrigerator open followed by some grunting and mumbling, as if the man was disappointed in what he found inside.

A few minutes later, she heard the click, click, click of footsteps on the staircase.

She quieted her breathing, taking short, shallow breaths through her nose. Her hands were now slick with nervous perspiration, and her mouth was dry. God, she wanted a drink, and not just water to quench her thirst, but something stronger to quiet her nerves. But she had to stay sharp, on her toes.

He was near the bedroom now. She held her breath.

The light came on.

He gasped in shock when he noticed the woman sitting in the rocker, the .45 resting on her lap like a sleeping puppy.

She looked up at him from the chair, and a smile crossed her lips.

"My God! What are you doing here?" the man said. He didn't bother to keep his voice down, didn't seem to be concerned about the neighbors.

"Nice to see you too," the woman said standing up, walking towards him.

The man took two steps back, then stopped. "What's goin' on here anyway? I don't get it, where's your husband?"

"Oh, he's around," she said, slowly threading the Evolution 45 sound and flash suppressor onto the end of the pistol.

He took another step back. "Claire, what the hell are you doing here in the middle of the night? And what's with the gun?" he said nervously. "And where's Amanda?"

"Oh, you mean the whore you've been sleeping with? That Amanda? And who was it last month Peter? Celeste? And before that? Ever think about your wife or your children?"

"I-I … well … where is Amanda, you fuck!" he screamed.

"Peter, there is no reason to shout obscenities. I thought your mother taught you … oh, never mind. I forget that you're a product of that bastard Greg Ellison and, if I remember correctly, your mother divorced your father years ago, before I'd had the pleasure of your acquaintance; seems she couldn't stand the bastard either."

Peter Ellison took one step toward Claire but abruptly stopped when she raised the gun, directing the muzzle at the spot between his eyes.

"Please Claire," he whined, "what's this all about? Can't we talk about this?" Now, with a gun pointed at his head, he seemed like a frightened little child.

But Claire knew better. Peter was an actor and a great manipulator. To him, this was all a game.

Look what he's done to his family, Claire thought, and he's about to take over New Life. We can't let that happen.

"Don't worry about your girlfriend. I sent her away; it's just the two of us now."

"How'd you know I'd be here?"

"Oh, we know a lot more than you think we do Peter. We – Logan and I – know that you and your father were experimenting with cloning, psychotropic drugs, and brain manipulation. You were trying to play God with no thought of the human life you were destroying."

"Claire, listen to me..."

"And we are going to put a stop to this craziness. The agency already took care of your father and now we are going to take care of you."

"Claire, you don't understand," Peter said. His eyes got wide, and he looked shocked. His left hand clamped over his open mouth, stifling a scream, as he pointed over Claire's shoulder.

"Look out Claire!"

When she turned to look, Peter moved as swiftly as an Olympic athlete. He was on her before she knew what was happening; he knocked her off her feet. Upon impact with the carpeted floor, the gun flew from her hand and under the bed.

She was on her back now with Peter straddling her. Claire thrashed and squirmed, but he was too strong and within seconds had her arms pinned.

And then he hit her in the face as hard as he could.

Claire screamed.

Through blurry, watery eyes, Claire watched helplessly as Peter pulled his arm back to hit her again.

And then his forehead exploded in a warm spray of blood; he fell on top of Claire like an exhausted lover.

Logan stood in the bedroom doorway, shaking. He held a gun in his hands.

Claire struggled and thrashed, finally managing to roll the dead man off.

Greg Meritt

She got up, went over to her husband, threw her arms around him and began to cry.

He unwittingly put his arm around his wife and tucked the gun into his inside jacket pocket. He stood there for a few moments, his arm around his wife, staring at the dead body of his business partner and one-time college friend.

And then he turned to Claire. He tried to smile, but it didn't come off very well.

Sniffling and wiping her eyes, Claire said, "I think we've passed the initiation, don't you?"

Once more, Logan looked past Claire to the still body lying on the bedroom floor. He sighed.

"Yes, I believe we have. Let's go get our daughter."

ABOUT THE AUTHOR

Greg Meritt was born and raised in Western Washington, not far from Seattle, where he continues to reside with his wife and three adopted children and a crazy dog.

Aside from writing fiction, his hobbies include reading, watching movies and hanging out with his family.

The Adoption is his debut novel. He is currently hard at work on the sequel.

I NEED YOUR HELP

Thank you for taking the time to read *The Adoption*. If you enjoyed the story, please consider sharing with your friends and leaving a review on Amazon. Reviews might not matter much to the big-name authors, but they can really help the small guys grow their readership. And it doesn't need to be long, just a sentence or two that lets people know what you liked about the story.

For more information, please visit:

Website: gregmeritt.com
Facebook: facebook.com/gregmerittauthor
Twitter: twitter.com/greg_meritt

Made in the USA
Columbia, SC
05 March 2018